A Cowboy's Forgiveness

by

Sophia Ryan

A Cowboy's Forgiveness

Contact Information: info@thewildrosepress.com

Cover Art by *Diana Carlile*

The Wild Rose Press, Inc.
PO Box 708
Adams Basin, NY 14410-0708

Visit us at www.thewildrosepress.com

Publishing History
First Yellow Rose Edition, 2017
Print ISBN 978-1-5092-1820-2
Digital ISBN 978-1-5092-1821-9

Published in the United States of America

**Love brought them together,
but only forgiveness can keep them there.**

Josh strode forward in a slow measure that allowed her time to appreciate his hard form, his full lips that tasted like sin, his desire pulsing toward her. She wanted it all. Was ready to take it all.

Stopping a foot from her, he pulled her wedding ring from his pocket and took her left hand. His eyes never leaving hers, he slid the ring into place.

Before she could voice the disappointed "Why?" clanging in her heart, he explained. "You're safer with it on."

"Maybe I don't want safe."

"What *do* you want, Charleigh?"

His need-you gaze was locked so tight on hers, she swore she could feel him inside her mind, strolling through every naughty, delicious want blooming there, each one more colorful and intoxicating than the one before. He knew her well enough to know exactly what she wanted—their bodies locked into each other, giving pleasure as only they could.

But they weren't alone. Ruby and Derrick were in the house. And she had never been a quiet lover, at least not with Josh. And the more sensible part of her knew the move would be a disaster. Tonight, she'd go with safe.

"I'd settle for another kiss," she said.

"Settle? That doesn't sound like the Charleigh Cooper I know."

He wanted to kiss her again. She knew it. Knew his signs. What she didn't know was why he wasn't taking the step that would give them what they both wanted. Maybe he needed a little push. She took her cue from the song on the radio.

"Are you gonna kiss me or not, Flores?"

Dedication

To my mom for planting the seeds of this love story,
and my dad for nurturing them to life.

Chapter One

"No!" Charleigh Cooper glared at the white plastic stick in her hand. "You can't be blue. I can't be preg—" Panic clamped down on her lungs, and she couldn't even force herself to finish the word. "Obviously you're a defective piece of shit."

She threw the obviously defective POS into the trash and grabbed the second stick she'd peed on minutes earlier.

At the sight of the pink plus sign, beads of sweat popped out across her forehead. "Oh, come on! We skipped the condom once. Once! What about all the times we were ridiculously responsible? Don't they count for anything?"

Reasoning with the stick didn't convince it to change the plus to a minus, so she slammed it into the trash, too.

She swallowed back the nausea and turned worried eyes toward stick number three lying patiently on the counter. "Help me out, and I promise never to be reckless again."

Taking a deep breath, she snatched it up, held it before her eyes. There, in a no-nonsense all-caps font, was the same damning conclusion. Well, shit. Three for three.

Leaning against the bathroom wall, she slid down to the faded linoleum floor, brought her knees up to her chest, and hugged them, trying to control her runaway thoughts and sinking heart as she stared her new reality in its cold, hard face.

She was an eighteen-year-old waitress with no husband, no family, no money, and a high school diploma with the ink still wet on it. She could barely take care of herself much less a baby. And her baby-daddy had ambitious plans for the future that didn't include being saddled with a wife and child. Although she'd assumed she'd be part of his future, she'd never heard those words come from his lips.

She banged her head back against the wall. "How am I going to tell him?"

The stick had already given her all the answers it could. She tossed it into the trash alongside the other two harbingers of doom and pulled herself to her feet to get ready for work.

A wave of vertigo swept over her, and she grabbed the edge of the sink to keep from collapsing into blackness. The book she'd leafed through at the library mentioned dizziness as one of several signs she could look forward to. At least she hadn't been hit with vomiting yet.

Drawing in several large breaths, she fought through the feeling and kept her footing. When it had ebbed, she eased upright, and with a shaky hand wiped the fog from the mirror above the sink.

The girl in the reflection, with scared amber eyes, a pale face, and wild blonde hair didn't look like no momma she'd ever seen. But that didn't change the fact that in about seven months she would be. Her gaze dropped to her abdomen that as yet showed no sign of the tiny spark of life the damned sticks said was growing within. Her hand rose and moved across the still-flat surface as she tried to picture her future... Belly full and round in pregnancy. Baby nursing at her breast. Toddler calling her mom.

To make the terrifying images more bearable, she put Josh in them... Him rubbing her belly and whispering to his unborn child. Holding their baby in his arms, a proud, loving smile on his face. Bouncing the toddler on his knee as they played *ride a little pony into town.*

It was a lovely little fairy tale. But in her experience, fairy tales only came true in kids' books and romance novels. Josh loved her, or so he said. But did he love her enough?

****

Josh Flores pulled off his cap and stuffed it into his backpack before combing his fingers across his skull to reverse any hat hair that had settled in after the two-hour drive from his university to Chismes Point. Charleigh liked his hat off, so he'd do it now to make her happy.

"Drop me at the café," he told the pickup's driver, his long-time friend Will Simms, when they rolled into the outskirts of town.

"You're not going home first? Clean up?" Will said as he headed on into town instead of taking the right that would take them to the Flores ranch. "You reek, dude."

Josh lifted his arm and sniffed. Musky, but nothing a quick shower couldn't fix. He'd come home from his workout to find Will ready to go and unwilling to wait the ten minutes it would take him to shower. Then acted like he was doing him a favor giving him five to pack.

"Charleigh and I'll clean up together." Josh grinned, thinking about climbing into the shower with her, their hands washing each other.

"It's not right, man. What you're doing to her."

Will's comment pulled Josh from his shower fantasy. "What is it you think I'm doing?"

"She deserves more than you showing up every weekend with a box of condoms in one hand and a shitty little doodad in the other."

"And in your *expert* opinion, what does *my* girlfriend deserve that I'm not already giving her?"

"A home. Stability. Security. You know how important those things are to her."

He knew. She'd lost her parents a month before she turned sixteen and had been shuffled off to the ass crack of New Mexico—Chismes Point as the locals called it—to live with her only relative, an aunt who never let her forget she was unwanted and a burden. The tightly knit ranching community that was never overly friendly with outsiders hadn't been much more welcoming.

She had no one but him. But he was enough. More than that, he was her everything—her words, not his. And that suited him just fine because, truth was, he needed her as much as she needed him, maybe more. She was his only bright spot in an otherwise shit life.

His supply of family was as shallow as hers. He'd lost his baby sister when he was five, his grandmother when he was eight, his mother when he was ten, and his granddad less than a year after that.

It had left him on his own against his father, who eased his grieving demons by drowning them with whiskey and then beating the holy hell out of his son. At least until Josh had gotten big enough to hit back.

Then daddy-dear used his words instead of his fists, which, oddly enough, struck deeper.

"Do you love her?"

Will's question yanked Josh's thoughts back into the present. "You change majors to marriage counseling or something, asshat? Not that it's any of your fucking business, but yeah, I do. Doesn't mean I'm ready for something serious."

He downed the remainder of his water and tossed the bottle into the backseat where it joined at least a case of empty soda and beer cans, water bottles, and a couple dozen or so paper bags from fast food joints. The mess irritated him, especially at this moment, but it wasn't his pickup, so whatever.

If he had a ride this nice, he'd keep it spotless, take care of it so it would last forever. But as his granddad had always said, *the things that come easy are often less valued than the things worked hard for.* And Will Simms had never worked hard for anything in his life. Good fortune seemed to just fall into his lap, like manna from heaven. He hadn't been as lucky getting Charleigh, though, who was worth more than all the treasure in the world. In Josh's eyes anyway.

"Is she?" Will asked.

"Is she what?"

"Ready for serious," Will clarified on a huff.

This conversation was beginning to feel like a thousand devil's claws gripping his gut. Josh flipped down the visor to check his teeth in the mirror, and the guilt in his eyes pissed him off. He loved her. He'd do almost anything to make her happy. That's all he could offer now. It had to be enough. He prayed it was enough.

He breathed into his palm to test his breath. "She never said." Which was the truth. He and Charleigh had never talked about marriage, or kids, or even the distant future. They'd both taken it for gospel that they'd be together.

Will scoffed. "She is."

Josh grabbed the tin of mints Will kept in the glove box and popped a couple into his mouth, chewed them to bits. "What makes you so sure?"

He ran his tongue across his teeth. Hell, he really should go home first, clean up. But dammit, he couldn't wait to see her.

"She's a woman," Will said. "Women are always thinking about marriage and babies. Even if they don't say it."

Marriage. Babies. The words lodged like barbs under his skin. "We're not ready, neither one of us. Maybe after college we'll…" A half shrug finished his half sentence. 'After college' was too far away to talk about or even try to envision. He had his undergrad work to finish and vet school on top of that.

School was their ticket to a better life, a life away from this soul-sucking place. For both of them. He wouldn't do anything to risk it. Besides, things were great between them as they were. If she wasn't pushing for a change, why change? As his granddad always said, *if it ain't broke, don't fix it.*

"You're not worried some guy'll put a ring on it while you're deciding whether you're ready?"

"No." His voice was as firm as his conviction that Charleigh had no interest in any other guys, that she loved only him. That he knew. With a hundred percent certainty. And he loved her, too, wasn't interested in any other girls.

But marriage? Babies? The very thought made his stomach pitch. He couldn't take care of a wife and a baby. Hell, he wasn't even sure he wanted kids, but he damned sure didn't want any before he was in a position to take care of them.

"You should be," Will said.

Should be what? Worried? His gaze cut to Will. "Why? What have you heard?"

Will shrugged. "Nothing. It's just a no-brainer."

"What is?"

"Dude, she's the hottest girl in town. That ringless finger of hers is an open-season sign. The first decent guy who offers her a big rock and a way out of town might change her mind about waiting for *some day* with you. You know how much she hates this place."

Josh's remaining threads of tolerance and good humor snapped at the thought of Charleigh with another guy. "She's not like that."

"All women are like that. They've got this one gene whose sole purpose is to drive them to cull the best stud in the herd, hack off his balls—after popping out a couple of kids, of course—then hogtie him for life. Or at least until the money runs out. Take it from me. I know."

Josh knew that part of Will's relationship bitterness was fueled by the fact that Kelly, his long-time girlfriend, dumped him when he refused to buy her an engagement ring before he left for college, and he'd just been dumped by a sorority princess for his lack of interest in what he called spending wads of his dad's cash on her, or as she called it, commitment. He understood his friend's bitterness but wasn't in the mood to cut him some slack.

"Man, you don't know shit. Charleigh and I don't need to slap a label on our relationship to know it's solid. It just is."

"Okay, don't say I didn't warn you." Will tapped his fingers on the steering wheel to the beat of some rock song blaring on the radio—one Josh had heard Charleigh singing to last weekend.

Will's warning made it clear that he needed to be reminded that Charleigh was in a committed relationship. And damned if Josh wasn't ready to remind him with his fist.

"And now I'm warning you. Charleigh's mine, not yours. I know what she needs and wants, and I'm taking care of it. So shut your damn mouth."

Will's damn mouth kept shut for the remaining minutes it took to get to the café, but it twisted at his own internal irritation and his fingers stopped tapping to the music only long enough to crank it up.

They pulled up in front of the café, and Josh reached into the back to grab his backpack. Picturing the gift inside had him sharply wishing he'd brought her something other than the university-branded T-shirt and fresh box of condoms.

Will was right about one thing. She deserved more than a weekend of sex four times a month and shitty little doodads from the university bookstore. Especially since he'd be asking her to wait years to have anything more substantial. Maybe he'd dip into his meager savings and buy her a cell phone so she wouldn't have to go to the payphone at the gas station at night to talk to him. An action like that would help keep them connected, prove he was committed.

"Pick me up here Sunday morning, usual time," he said and got out.

"Hey…" Will ejected the CD he'd been listening to and held it out to Josh. "I burned a CD of the Sewernuts' latest for Charleigh. They're her favorite band, you know."

Charleigh had never mentioned the band much less said it was her favorite. And how did Will know? Had the two of them been talking behind his back?

He wasn't entirely sure of the meaning behind the undertone in his friend's words today, but he knew he didn't like it. The only thing stopping him from diving back into the pickup and punching Will in the nose was the overriding need to get to Charleigh.

Ignoring the outstretched CD, he slammed the door and was at the café entrance as the pickup raced off toward the Bar S, the million dollar ranch Will was set to inherit. What the rich bastard couldn't seem to get through his thick skull was that Charleigh loved him, only him, and wouldn't dump him just because he wasn't ready to "put a ring on it" as Will said.

He drew in a few deep breaths to cool his anger. He didn't want to bring this mood into his weekend with her. Their time was short and precious, and he wanted it to be memorable for only good things.

A glance at his watch told him she had just under an hour left on her shift. God, he needed her. Now. It had been almost a week, and his body was buzzing with wanting and a strong need to cement his claim on her.

The smell of grilling meat, onions, and grease assaulted him as he pulled open the door. His eyes zeroed in on Charleigh delivering food to a booth where the Barton brothers sat. Unbidden jealousy raged through Josh that the two, whose family owned a peanut farm outside town, always seemed to be at the cafe when he came home.

He'd kicked Randy's ass a few times in high school for coming on to Charleigh. Lance was all right, but a bit full of himself. He was in his last year of vet school and had come back to town for the semester to do an internship with the local vet.

Josh approached the booth, not liking what he was seeing and hearing.

"When you gonna marry me, sweetness?" Randy said as Charleigh topped off his coffee.

"Never, peanut butter brain." The sass in her voice had the other customers laughing.

"Yeah, peanut butter brain," Lance said and threw a balled up paper napkin at his brother. "She's marrying me."

"Better flash me a big-ass ring when you say that, *Doctor* Barton." She filled his cup.

"Just you watch, darlin'," Lance said. "One day I'll come in here, drop to one knee, and slide a big-ass diamond ring onto that pretty little finger of yours."

"You do, and I'll shove that ring up your ass, Barton," Josh said, stopping a few feet from the booth.

Charleigh spun around, and the smile she gave him lit up his heart and sweetened his sour mood. So did seeing the silver heart-shaped locket dangling around her neck—the necklace that symbolized their love. He'd given it to her the day they'd made love for the first time. From that moment on, she'd worn it and never taken it off. She'd said she always wanted his heart next to hers.

Setting the coffee pot on the table, she rushed to

him and jumped into his arms. Legs around his waist, arms around his neck, a hand clutched in his hair, she pulled his mouth to hers and kissed him. Whistles and randy expressions filled the café, but with Charleigh in his arms, her tongue in his mouth, her body wrapped around his, none of it mattered.

"I missed you, Flores," she whispered against his mouth. She didn't mention his sweat, his pungency, his scruff. She just showed him her love.

"Missed you, too, Cooper," he whispered, his pulse pounding like a drum through his body. This was what kept him going. The feel of her. The scent of her. The taste of her. In her arms, he felt balanced and right, like all the pieces of him that had been scrambled throughout the week without her were settling back into place. She did that. Her smile. Her touch. Her love. "Can you take a break?"

A bell dinged at the kitchen window, followed by Molly hollering, "Orders up!"

Charleigh glanced at her boss before sending her attention back to him. "I'll be done soon. Then you can have me all to yourself." She kissed him again, her tongue making promises it would later keep. With a low moan and a whispered "I love you," she left his arms.

He settled into a booth to wait, and she dropped him off a glass of water.

"You hungry?" she asked.

He took her hand and kissed her palm. "Just for you."

She gave him another sweet kiss, then delivered the two orders. Three more came up. Then another. And she brought him a cheeseburger and fries. In between, the customers asked for more coffee or iced tea or water or soda or napkins or silverware, keeping her hopping, keeping her away from him, making him wait, making him wrestle with his thoughts.

He knew she wasn't serious about accepting any man's ring, but it sent his thoughts back to his conversation with Will. *The first decent guy who offers her a big rock and a way out of town might change her mind about waiting for you.* Damn the bastard for putting doubts in his head. He shifted uncomfortably on the cracked vinyl seat, antsy to get her the hell out of here and reclaim what was his. Only his.

Less than forty-five minutes later, Charleigh had cleared everyone out. It took her another fifteen to help clean up and prepare for the following day. But then, finally, leaving Molly to lock up, Charleigh grabbed his hand and the two of them raced upstairs.

After a too-short kiss, she pushed out of his arms. "Let's move this to the shower. I want to wash off the diner stink."

She pulled him into the bathroom and turned on the shower. Wasting no time, he stripped off his clothes, she hers, and they climbed in. Her hands immediately went to his hardness, but he caught her hand and linked their fingers.

"No, baby, if you touch me, this'll be over. Just let me touch you. Get you ready for me."

"I've been ready for you since the second you left me last Sunday," she said.

He kissed her, running his hands down her back, over her butt, and squeezed her close to him. She did the same to him, both of them doing a half-assed job of washing each other but a stellar job of accelerating their desire.

She lifted her leg and wrapped it around his hips, opening herself to him and encouraging his exploration. Keeping one arm around her, he slid a hand between her thighs and cupped her, squeezed her, parting her flesh with his fingers and burying a digit into her wetness. She gasped and arched against his hand, her thrusting movements and low moans letting him know she was as ready as she had claimed.

Her breathing was tight, and her breasts were falling and rising like she was out of air and grasping for even the tiniest breath. Her head dropped back against the shower wall, but she kept her pleasure-hazed eyes glued to his, so he could see how much she wanted him.

"I'm so ready for you, Josh."

He was ready for her, too, and couldn't wait any longer. If they didn't have to use condoms, he'd love her now, here in the shower. But safety trumped desire.

Shutting off the water, he grabbed a towel and hurriedly dried them off, then pulled her to bed. He ripped open the new box of condoms in his backpack and grabbed one.

She took it and rolled it on him, then reached out for him, pulling him down beside her. She clasped him to her and kissed him hard and hungry, rolling her tongue around his, sucking it, sucking his lips, tasting the inside of his mouth.

He matched her, kiss for kiss, suck for suck, taste for taste.

Keeping her mouth on his, she shifted up and straddled his hips, opening herself to him, and he glided into her heat.

The connection ripped his breath away, like it

always did, and for a moment he couldn't move, only feel. Forget pearly gates and harp music. This right here was heaven. Being connected to Charleigh as one body, one soul, one heartbeat. It was his reward for anything he'd ever done in his life that God considered righteous. And the reason he'd sell his soul to the devil to keep her.

She squirmed on him, telling him she needed him to move. Wanting to give her what she needed, he gripped her hips with both hands, fingers digging into her flesh to hold her in place, and arched his hips up to drive deeper, to give her his all.

Leaning over him, she gripped his shoulders so she could take more, give more. His hand cupped one breast and fed it to his mouth, first one, then the other, devouring her, greedily satisfying the hunger that had plagued him all week.

Her low, deep moans urging him on, he increased the pace, his sole mission to satisfy the hunger that twisted and burned inside her, to give her the pleasure she deserved, the release she needed. The sounds and smells of their bodies joining, the feel of being so deep and tight inside her body, was sending his brain to black, and he fought to hold on until she had found her pleasure.

Seconds later, she groaned his name as she threw her head back, crying out in loud, nonsensical noises at the release he was pulling from her.

She had never been a quiet lover, and he had no complaints about it. It made him feel good that he could make her feel this good. It fed his desire and accelerated his rhythm, making it urgent, hard, fast, and steady, and sending his fingers digging into her flesh to hold her tight on him for the coming explosion.

"I love you, Josh," she moaned, her words the amen to his prayer.

Growling her name, growling his pleasure, he released everything that was him into her body, let his world go black. Heart racing, lungs fighting to catch a breath, he collapsed against the bed as she melted down over his chest.

The release had stripped his stores of energy, but he used the last remaining drops to wrap his arms around her and hold her close. He inhaled deeply, pulling her scent into his lungs, absorbing it. He never wanted to let her go. She kissed him, her hands raking his hair, holding him tight, too, as if she didn't want to let go either.

"CC," he whispered, and she let her sleepy eyes tangle with his. The love in her honey eyes filled him with joy. He brushed back the wet storm of tangled hair from her face with his knuckles and cupped her neck, drawing her closer. He kissed her forehead, her eyes, her flushed cheeks, whispering, "Baby, I love you."

She kissed his mouth, deep and sweet, the actions as good as the words.

He needed to withdraw soon, but he didn't want to yet. They had precious little time together, and he wanted to enjoy every second of this moment connected to her. But then she shifted off him and lay beside him. He sat up to remove the condom and drop it into the trash basket at the side of the bed, then lay back down beside her.

With a satiated and satisfied sigh, she settled into his arms, her head against his chest, her arm draped across his hips. "I missed you so much."

He brushed his hand down her hair, crown to tips, tugging the end of one curl to stretch it, then releasing it. "Me too," he kissed into her forehead.

"If we lived together, I swear we'd make love six, seven times a day." She trailed her fingers across his chest in a soft caress. "Even then, I'm not sure it would be enough."

He'd heard stories from friends about their girlfriends who used sex to manipulate them into doing what they wanted. Charleigh wasn't like that. If she was horny, she'd tell him. If she was happy, she'd tell him. If she was mad, she'd tell him and tell him why. If she wanted anything from him, she came right out and asked. He loved that about her. Her honesty, her directness. He loved her. Everything about her.

He caught her hand and brought it to his mouth, kissed it, then sank into the peace and happiness of her arms. *I'll never let you go, Charleigh. Never.*

"How'd you do on that chem test you were worried about?" she asked.

"Aced it."

"Ha! Didn't I tell you?"

He could feel her grin on his chest, and it brought one to his mouth. "Yep, you told me. Not sure I could've done it without your help studying."

"Maybe I should move in with you so I can help you study for all your tests. Except math, of course."

His soft chuckle at her statement belied the alarm it had triggered inside him. It was her second reference to them living together. They needed to get off that track, and fast.

"Except math," he echoed and eased out of her arms. "I brought you something." He leaned over and

16

grabbed his backpack.

"Baby, you don't need to bring me things. Having you here's all I want."

"I know. But I want to. Close your eyes."

When she had, he pulled out the T-shirt, unrolled it, and held it up so she could see it. It was green—her favorite color. "Okay, open them."

Her face lit up, and she jumped up, took the shirt, and held it against her. It was too big, but then he had planned it that way. He hoped she'd wear it to bed and think of him.

She clutched the T-shirt to her chest. "I love it!" She wrapped an arm around his neck and kissed him. "I'll wear it to bed every night so it'll feel like you're here with me."

It's like she could read his mind. Just one more way they were perfect for each other. He lay back and pulled her with him, and she snuggled up against his side, the shirt between them.

"How are things here?" he asked.

She gave a little shrug. "Same as always."

Her flat voice reminded him how much she hated being in this town, working at the diner, living in this one-room studio, having few choices for a different life. He'd get her out of here, just as soon as he finished school. He'd make sure she never wanted for anything again.

"The café was packed tonight," he said.

"Yeah, business has really picked up over the past couple months."

Since he'd left for college. Coincidence? "Hope that's translating to good tips."

"Really good considering I'm a lousy waitress,"

she said with a chuckle. "Molly says the only reason she doesn't fire me is because the customers like the way I fill out the uniform. I swear some of those hayseeds come in just to see whether my boobs are going to pop out of that pink nightmare."

He thought back to how that uniform had seemed tighter than usual tonight, really straining the button across her breasts. He lodged one hand behind his head, also remembering how all the guys in there had noticed it, too.

"Do those guys always flirt with you like that?"

"Like what?"

"Asking for kisses, asking you to marry them, flirting with you, making you laugh."

"Yeah, but they don't mean anything."

"Do you?"

"What are you asking me?"

"I'm asking if you're interested in taking any of them up on their offers."

She laughed. "Course not. Besides, they're just yanking your chain. They all know you're the one I'm going to marry."

Marry. The word tightened his chest. That was three. As his granddad had said, *three trees is a forest*, meaning take note of things that come in threes because they're trying to tell you something important. "You know we can't," he said, a little too quickly, a little too forcefully. He tempered it with, "School's my priority. I can't take care of a wife now."

"First of all, I know school's your priority," she said, her response as quick as his. "You've made it really clear. Second, I don't expect you to take care of me. I'd work, like I do now."

"You're not really suggesting we get married now? At eighteen."

She shrugged. "Get married, or at least live together so we can be together all the time, not just weekends."

The thought of them moving in together had crossed his mind, but he'd nixed it. He had to give school his full attention—for himself, for Charleigh—so they could have a good life together one day. A live-in girlfriend and everything that relationship required might derail his plans. His grades in high school had suffered some because in the choice between her and homework, he had usually chosen her. If that happened in college, he'd lose his scholarship.

"I like the way things are now," he said.

Her angry gaze pinning him to the bed told him his firm tone hadn't settled this as cleanly as he'd hoped it would. Her words confirmed it.

"You mean you coming here on the weekends for sex, then going back to your real life."

There was so much bite in her statement he could feel the teeth. "You never had a problem with it before."

She sat up. "Well, maybe I have a problem with it now. Maybe I want more from you than a few days of sex over the next decade."

Her words were so like the ones Will had used. Had the two of them been talking about this behind his back? "More? Like what? A big-ass diamond ring?" His tone dripped with sarcasm.

Her eyebrows furrowed. "You know I don't care about that. I just want you."

"You have me."

"I want a life with you, Josh. Not a part-time fuckmate. I want to marry you. I want to…" She licked her lips and wrapped her arms around herself. "I want to have your babies."

Marriage. Babies. How in the hell had they gotten on this demonic topic? The whole conversation was squeezing his throat and his gut with ever-tightening fists. He held up his hand, palm toward her, to halt her thoughts in their tracks. "I'm not ready for all that shit."

"I am."

His anger and anxiety responded for him before his brain could stop it. "Well, it won't be with me. Hell, I don't even want kids."

Her eyes went from rounded surprise to narrowed fury in a split second. "So, I'm supposed to live in this shitty little room, work at that shitty little café, have my whole life revolve around you coming here on the weekends for sex? Wait years until you're *maybe* ready to think about having a life with me? Is that what you're saying?"

The way she said it made him sound like an unreasonable, selfish prick. But what was completely unreasonable was the corner she had backed him into. Like a trapped animal, his only choice was to bite and claw his way to freedom or die.

"Wait or don't wait," he said. "That's your call, not mine."

The shock and sadness filling her eyes at his statement made him want to take it back and reach out to comfort her, but he couldn't. He couldn't back down now, or he'd give in and jump heart first into a situation that would be disastrous for both of them.

"Ask me to." Each word was wrapped in a thick

layer of pain.

"What?" he asked, more to stall than for clarification.

"Ask me to wait for you, and tell me you'll marry me when you graduate."

He wanted to ask her to, wanted to agree to anything she wanted, but with his back up against the wall, he was too strangled by the thought to do it. To ask her to wait was to promise there'd be a payoff—marriage—at the end of it. His granddad had taught him that a man's word was his bond. If he wasn't one hundred percent sure he could keep that promise to her, he wasn't going to make it. Last he checked, ninety-eight percent wasn't one hundred percent. And six years was a long time. Anything could happen.

When he couldn't get out a breath much less a response to her request, she added, "I need some token of commitment from you, Josh. Tonight. Something that says all my waiting, all my love, all my commitment to you will pay off, in marriage, when you finish school."

Here in his tight, airless little corner, his brain had shut down, and he couldn't think of a thing to show his commitment that didn't include giving in to her demands. Goddammit! Why wasn't she trusting him, trusting that things would work out for them? He'd shown her and told her he loved her often enough over the past two years for her to have no trouble believing it.

The silence stretching between them was so sharp he felt it piercing his lungs, but he managed to choke out a response. "What if I can't give you that?"

The tip of her nose twitched and turned red, the

way it did when she was about to cry. But she wasn't crying. Her tongue snaked between her parted lips, smoothing the way for the coming words, words he knew would be life-changing. "Then leave. And don't come back."

Pain ripped through his body. Not in a million years had he expected that response.

"You don't mean that," he said, wanting to make sure.

She swallowed hard. "I do mean it."

He stared into her eyes. Waited for her to tell him she didn't mean it. But she didn't.

She looked at him like she was waiting for him to cave. But he wouldn't.

Well. Shit. Will was right. All women were alike. Even Charleigh.

His body feeling sore and abused, he got out of bed. He dressed and pulled his cap on, down close to his burning eyes to hide his shattering emotions. He grabbed the just-opened box of condoms with the intent to shove it into his backpack but, in a surge of anger, hurled it across the room along with a loud "Fuck." The box hit the wall, condoms exploding from it and scattering across the scarred floor alongside the shredded chunks of his heart.

Arms tight around herself, Charleigh stared at him from the middle of the bed, eyes big and round and wet, lush lips trembling, breasts fuller and firmer than he'd ever seen them. She looked lost and alone and fragile. But that was her fault, dammit.

He swallowed, his throat tight, his chest tight, his skin tight like it was about to split open and peel off him from the emotions throbbing inside him. One of them needed to say something to undo this mistake, this gigantic fucking mistake. But the silence stretched on.

He zipped his backpack, slung it over his shoulder, and forced his feet to take him to the door. Hand on the knob, he looked back at her one last time, just to be sure. That look told him all he needed to know. She wasn't changing her mind. This was the end.

Jerking open the door, he went through, slamming it behind him. He stopped on the other side of that thin barrier, waiting, listening, hoping to hear her call out his name and beg him to come back, or to see her yank open the door and pull him back inside, begging him to forget what she'd said so he could then beg her to wait for him. But those saving graces never came.

Feeling empty, dead, he slogged down the steps and stood at the bottom, his world in ashes on the ground. His mind was fuzzy, and everything inside him hurt.

Turning back, he stared up at her door. He put his hand on the rail, his foot on the first step. What he wanted to do was rush back up those stairs, yank her into his arms, and tell her that if he had her, he had everything he needed, and that if she wanted to marry him, she needed to do it now. Tonight. So they could cement their life, blow this town, and never be apart again.

The thought set his heart to pounding against his ribs so hard his lungs burned. If he did that, their life would never amount to anything more than what it was at right this minute. They'd get married, and she'd get pregnant. They'd need money for all kinds of shit, and he'd end up quitting school to get a meaningless, low-paying, full-time job to take care of them.

Or worse, go back to ranching with his dad. Living with his dad again? With Charleigh? And kids? Hell, no! They'd live on the streets before he put her through that hell. He squeezed his eyes shut, drew his hands into fists, and swallowed hard. Dread cinching his chest, he did the hardest thing he'd ever done. He left her.

Needing a way home, he headed to the bar down the road. His dad was there, in his usual spot, in his usual condition. Josh helped him to the pickup and drove them home. On the way, when his dad berated him for being a stupid, disloyal, no-good piece of shit, Josh silently agreed.

****

He left.

Oh, God, he really left.

Charleigh jumped out of bed and rushed to the door, held her breath, waited for Josh to come back through, apologize, tell her she was his everything and he couldn't live without her. She gripped the knob, wanting to turn it and pull open the door, wanting to rush down the steps and beg him to forget everything she'd said. But she didn't do any of it.

If he didn't want her after all they'd meant to each other, he wouldn't want their baby. She wouldn't insist that he be in their lives. It had to be his choice to come back, to commit, or it would never work. They'd all suffer.

Long seconds ticked by before she accepted he wasn't coming back. The air squeezing around her was dead quiet, icy cold, painfully somber, as if the life source that had kept it warm and bright and nourishing had been slain. Pressing her hands against the door, forehead to the backs of her hands, she sobbed hot tears that blurred her vision and stole her breath.

Her heart shattered, her body aching, she stumbled to their bed, grabbed the T-shirt he'd brought her. It was green. Her favorite color. She put it on, pretending it was a hug from him. She gripped the heart locket dangling at her heart. It had always made her feel like his heart was next to hers, and had comforted her. But now it was as frozen and lifeless as her own heart.

Her eyes rose to the photo on her nightstand. Arms around each other, smiling faces touching, happiness radiated from them like golden rays from the summer sun. They had just made love for the first time—the first time for both of them—and Josh had given her the necklace he'd said represented his love for her. He'd captured the aftermath of that life-changing moment with his phone camera. Since she didn't have a phone, he had printed and framed a copy of the photo for her.

The T-shirt. The necklace. The photo. All the little gifts he'd given her, from the wooden box with the Flores brand emblazoned on it to her favorite crystal snowflake ornament. And, oh, the lingering scent of him on the shirt, on the pillow, in the sheets, on her skin. These were her last connections to the man who held her world in his hands.

The threads of her life had been interlaced with his for over two years, and now he was gone, leaving nothing but a hole where a raging monster was slowly clawing her soul to pieces.

"Oh, God. What have I done?" She hugged his pillow to her body, curled around it, and cried herself into an uneasy sleep.

Automatic pilot took over to get her through the minutes, the hours, the days without Josh until she felt like an observer in her own life, a bystander watching her pretend to be alive. Her one accomplishment was that she had made it through a week without Josh and hadn't died.

Friday evening, at the same time Josh usually arrived, Will came into the cafe. Her gaze swept past him, hoping to see Josh sitting in the pickup, or standing by it, or about to walk in. But no such luck.

"Hey, Charleigh." Will slid into the booth where Josh usually sat.

"Hey." She wanted to ask him to sit anywhere but there, but Molly would have her hide. So she just sucked it up and did her job. "Are you eating here?"

"Yeah, I thought I would for a change."

She grabbed a laminated menu and a glass of ice water and set them in front of him.

"It's pretty dead in here tonight," he said.

"The Halloween party is tonight."

"You mean, the fall dance and carnival," he teased.

"Yeah." Halloween was a four-letter word in these parts.

"How're you doing?" he asked.

"Fine, thanks." Flat and emotionless made for poor customer service—and lousy tips—but she couldn't summon anything better. All her energy was going to remembering to breathe. "Tonight's specials are—"

"Josh told me you guys broke up."

The tears his words triggered were immediate and sharp. But she caught them in her throat and swallowed them down. All she could do was nod in response.

As if he could see she was on the edge of losing it, he took her hand, eased her down into the booth beside him, and she was powerless to stop it, even though waitresses weren't allowed to sit with customers.

"Have you heard from him?" he asked.

She shook her head. She hadn't called him either, but every night after work she had walked to the gas station, to the payphone, where they used to talk after her shift. Without feeding coins into the slot, she'd press in his number and pour out her heart. *I made a mistake, Josh. I love you, and I'll do whatever it takes to hold on to our love. I miss you. Please come home to me. I'm pregnant with your baby, and we need you.*

In the long hours following their breakup, she had come to see that she shouldn't have backed him into the corner the way she had and slapped him with an ultimatum but simply told him about the baby so they could face their situation head on.

She also had come to see that she really did need to tell him. He might feel differently about being together if he had all the facts. Or, he still might not want them. But she had to tell him. It was his child, too. However, she couldn't tell him until he came home. This was not a conversation to have over the phone, and she didn't have a way to get to his school.

"Is there anything I can do to help?" Will asked, bringing her attention back to him.

His thumb brushed over the back of her hand. Sympathy warmed his dark eyes to a pool of rich chocolate. A kind smile lifted his lips. He wanted to help. And he could.

"Yes."

"Name it. Anything."

"Would you give me a ride to the university so I can talk to Josh?"

The light in his eyes and the warmth in his smile

27

faded at her request. He released her hand.

"If that's what you want." Grabbing his glass of water, he took a long swallow.

She was surprised at the disappointment in his voice. He was Josh's best friend. Surely, Will would want to help him fix the relationship that had meant so much. Unless Josh no longer wanted it, and Will knew and just didn't want to add to her pain by telling her.

But it didn't change what she had to do. "It is. I have to talk to him. Before it's too late."

"I'll pick you up Sunday morning at nine."

The first spark of joy she'd felt since losing Josh lifted her mouth into a genuine smile. She hugged him. "Thanks, Will. You're a life saver."

"Yeah, that's me," he said with a sarcastic chuckle and rubbed her back.

"Order up," Molly snapped.

She left his embrace, took his order, and continued her shift with renewed hope. Two more days until her life changed. She felt it.

****

"This is going to be your ranch someday, William, and by-God, you need to show a greater interest in it."

Will's dad had started in on him at breakfast Saturday morning, making Ruby's prize-winning biscuits taste like chalk in his mouth. Not that he was surprised. His dad had been pushing him to quit college since he'd started and come home to take the reins of the ranch his grandfather had built.

No way in hell would he live this life. It wasn't going to happen. The sooner the old man came to terms with it, the better. "I'm not taking over the ranch, Dad."

His old man reared back like he'd been slapped.

"What kind of fool talk is that?"

"It's not fool talk. I mean it. After I graduate, I'm not coming back here."

The flushing of his dad's already ruddy face was the first warning that this conversation was going to go badly.

"I've slaved and sacrificed my entire life to build an empire worthy of the Simms name. Something future generations could be proud of. A legacy you could hand down to your own sons. And you have the gall to spit on it? You ungrateful little shit."

Will dropped his napkin onto the table, rose from his chair, and walked away on the insult toward his room to grab his still-packed bag and head back to school.

His dad caught his arm and pulled him around to face him. "We're not finished talking about this."

Will yanked his arm away. "Oh, we are so finished. I'm leaving."

Wyatt stabbed one stubby finger at him, and Will noticed it shook. "You leave, and I won't pay for school, your pickup, your credit cards, your phone…nothing." A hard cutting swipe of his hand fortified his words. "You hear me? You ready to test your mettle out on your own without the Simms money?"

Will hadn't meant *leaving for good* when he'd spoken of leaving. But now that the idea was out, its scent and taste filling the air, he suddenly realized it was the answer he'd been dancing around for years. He didn't want the ranch, and he'd never have Charleigh. There was nothing in this town for him. It was time to go, find a new place, start a life of his own making. The cinch around his chest loosened and for the first time, he took a deep, cleansing breath.

"I'll get by." Hope bursting inside him, he rushed down the hall to his room, grabbed his bag, added a few items to it, and headed to the door, urgent to get away.

Wyatt followed behind him. "If you leave, don't come back. You won't be welcome here again. The ranch will—"

"Fuck this ranch, old man. It's the only thing you ever loved."

Wyatt's fist swung toward him in a lightning quick arc, striking Will solidly in the jaw.

Will rocked backward at the force of the blow, his bag dropping to the floor. He recovered his wits quickly, fists at the ready to strike back. But then he realized he didn't care enough to use them. It would only delay his departure. That punch was the nail in the coffin on his old life. Wiping the blood from his grinning mouth, he grabbed his bag and headed outside, Wyatt behind him.

"I'll disown you, William." His voice was shaky, as if the blow had rocked him, too. "I mean it."

"Do whatever you want. That's exactly what I'm going to do." He jumped into the pickup, which had been a graduation gift and, therefore, rightly his. Cranking the engine, he sped off down the washboard road.

He had better plans in mind than pissing away four years in school and endless fights with his father. It was *his* life, *his* future. And he was going to live it *his* way.

When he hit the blacktop, he gunned it toward school to pack up there. Feeling free for the first time in his life, he hit the call button on the console and instructed it to "Call Zack."

After graduation, Zack Romero had left Chismes Point, moved to a little town in California, and opened a tattoo shop. He'd been trying for months to get him to come up and work with him.

"Dude, how's it hanging?" Zack's sleepy voice came through the phone.

"Hey, man," Will said. "Just wondering if that job offer's still good."

"Oh, hell yeah."

"I'm done with things here. I can be there in a couple days."

"Awesome! Call me when you get here, and I'll hook you up."

"Thanks, man. I appreciate it."

Several miles down the road, he remembered his promise to Charleigh. If it were anyone else, he'd have kept going. But it was her. The girl he'd loved since the day he saw her. He turned around and headed to town. It would be his last gift to her.

****

Charleigh hurriedly counted the wad of singles, folded it in half, and stuffed it back into her apron pocket, smiling. The tips hadn't come easy. Demanding customers had kept her and Leanne hopping since six-thirty that morning. Saturday always was the café's busiest day, especially mornings when farmers and ranchers in the area came into town to shop and gossip. It was when she made her best tips.

But today it felt like half the county had come in to sample Molly's greasy fare. It was just past nine, and she'd amassed well over two hundred dollars. She usually took off the afternoon and evening to be with

Josh, but since he wasn't here, she'd asked Molly to let her work all day.

The bulk of her earnings would go toward her rent and savings, but some she'd take with her on Sunday when she went to see Josh so he wouldn't have to pay for anything. That would show him she wasn't looking for him to take care of her, just love her.

She was topping off Lance's coffee when Will came in. She greeted her hero with a genuine smile. "Hey, Will. Sit wherever you like. I'll be right over."

He rushed to her and took her elbow, leading her away from Lance's table. "If you still want a ride to the school, we need to go now," he whispered.

"Now?" Panic charged through her. "You said Sunday."

"The plan changed. Sorry, but it's now or never."

Her gaze swept over the crowded café. Her leaving would reduce the amount of money she'd earn, put Leanne in a bind, and risk her job. But this was a true life or death situation.

****

Josh flipped off the TV. He couldn't concentrate on anything that was on because all his thoughts were a hundred and twenty miles east, where Charleigh was.

How many times during this worst week of his life had he thought about calling her at the café to say he loved her and didn't want to break up? Or asking to borrow Will's pickup so he could go home to her and make things right between them? Millions of times a day, at least, but his damn pride stopped him, every time. And now, after a week of being without her, he was as riled as a trapped cougar.

Even if he had to walk, he had to go home. See her.

Talk to her. Hold her. He realized he hadn't handled the conversation well and wanted to apologize, wanted to explain himself, wanted to ask her to move in with him. Mostly, he wanted to tell her he loved her and never wanted to be apart from her again. Unfortunately, by the time he'd come to his senses that Friday after classes, Will was already gone. He had no other way to get to Charleigh.

He wasn't in the mood for company so he almost ignored the knock at the door but at the last second decided it might be important. His friend Travis, a redhead wrapped around him, stood at the door.

"Hey, Josh," Travis said. "Sorry to bug you on a Saturday morning so early."

"No problem. Come on in," he said and shut the door behind them. "What's up?"

"Well, see, the thing is— uh, this is my girlfriend, Lissa, by the way."

The redhead smiled, and Josh nodded.

"See, Lissa's in town for the weekend. And Eugene, my douche roommate? Well, he was supposed to be going home but changed his mind. And now, Lissa and I can't…you know."

Travis lived in the dorm that had two beds in one room while Josh and Will and two other guys had their own bedrooms connected to a shared living space. He knew where this conversation was going. And it might work to his advantage.

Josh crossed his arms over his chest. "That sucks, man."

"Yeah. Um, see, I was wondering if you'd be willing to trade rooms, just for the weekend. Lissa's leaving Sunday afternoon."

"What's it worth to you?"

Travis looked at Lissa. "Everything." He turned back to him. "Whatever you want, man."

Josh knew exactly how his friend felt. He'd do anything to get to spend the weekend with Charleigh. "An emergency came up at home, and I need to borrow your pickup."

"You want my pickup?" By the sound of Travis' voice, you'd think Josh had asked for a kidney.

Lissa slid her hand into Travis' pocket and pulled out his keys, handing them over.

After a quick stop at the store for a token, Josh took off toward home, the need to get to Charleigh making his foot heavy on the gas and his heart light in his chest.

****

Charleigh followed Will up the stairs to his dorm room. The apartment-like room was quiet. She thought Josh would be playing video games or watching TV or studying or something. He never slept late. Maybe he was out.

Will pointed to a closed door down a short hallway. "That's his room." He opened the door opposite it and went inside.

She opened Josh's door and stopped dead in her tracks. It was dim, blinds and curtains shut tight, but she clearly saw the redhead bouncing on top of Josh, heard the grunts and groans of pleasure coming from both of them.

Heart dropping into her stomach, she turned and ran out of the apartment, down the stairs, and away from the building. She didn't know where she was going or how she was going to get home, but she knew she had to get away from that room. From that sight. From Josh. Before she broke down completely and did something outrageous. Like strangle him and the girl riding him.

Will's voice calling her name penetrated the red fog of despair wrapped around her, but she didn't stop running until he caught her arm and pulled her to a stop. "Charleigh, what's wrong?"

Her breaths coming in short and choppy, she tried to speak, to explain, to answer his question, but couldn't find the words. She shook her head and let the tears fall. Will didn't ask for details, just drew her in, hugged her, and held her tight while the rest of her world crumbled.

****

Josh rushed into the café and looked around the crowded space for Charleigh and only saw Leanne in the middle of chaos, hustling from one table to another. He went to the kitchen. "Molly, where's Charleigh?"

She flicked her cigarette butt into a sink of slimy water. "Off with Will Simms for the weekend, leaving me short-handed." The smoke curling from her mouth poisoned each damning word. "I've a right mind to fire her scrawny little ass over it."

Why in the hell would she be going somewhere with Will? And for the weekend? "You know where they went?"

"Do I look like her secretary?" she groused and pounded the bell. "Order up, Leanne!"

He dogged Leanne as she delivered food and asked her the same question.

"I don't know, Josh. She just said it was a life or death emergency, then packed a bag and took off with

Will."

Josh stumbled to Travis' pickup in a fog and called Will's phone. No answer. Texted him. No response. After fifteen minutes of fruitless tries, he headed to the Simms ranch. He hadn't even shut off the pickup before Wyatt stormed out of the house with his shotgun, threatening to shoot. Josh headed back to town, parked in front of the café, and continued to call and text Will. A sick feeling in the pit of his stomach told him something was very wrong.

****

Charleigh and Will rode home in silence. It suited her fine. The last thing she wanted was to talk about the disaster that had destroyed her life.

"I'm leaving," Will said out of the blue.

Her gaze left the dull, five-shades of brown flatland streaking past her window and landed on his profile. "Leaving what?"

"School, the ranch, the state. Going to California."

"Why?"

He shrugged. "New start."

She closed her eyes and sighed heavily. "Man, I could use one of those."

"Because of what happened with Josh?"

"That's part of it."

"What's the other part?"

She had to tell someone. Why not Will? He was leaving and wouldn't tell anyone. "I'm pregnant. With Josh's baby. And he doesn't want us."

"He said that?" His voice was incredulous, like he didn't believe it. Like she was when Josh had said it to her.

"I told him I wanted marriage and kids, and he

said, 'Well, it won't be with me.' And he's already with another girl. He doesn't want us."

Will pulled off the road, shifted into park, and drew her into a hug.

"Hey, it'll be okay," he said, his hand slowly caressing her back.

She pulled out of his hug in frustration. "How will it be okay? I have a baby on the way and no one to help me. I can't work and take care of a baby, and I don't make enough money to pay for daycare. I don't want an abortion, but even if I did, I don't have the money to do it. I don't know what to do, Will."

His answer was swift, his voice unwavering. "You could come with me."

"How would that help?" she said. "I'd be in the same situation but in an unfamiliar and more expensive place."

"You'd have me."

"What are you saying?"

He took her hand, brought it to his mouth, kissed it. "Go to California with me. As my wife."

"*Wife*?" She shook her head in confusion and withdrew her hand from his. "That's… Will, that's crazy."

"With me you'd have a husband and your child would have a father. What do you have in Chismes Point?"

Without Josh, she had nothing, no reason to stay in town. "Why would you do that? I'd be nothing but a burden."

"You wouldn't be a burden. I…" He licked his lips. "I love you, Charleigh. Have since the day I met you."

His admission wasn't a surprise. She'd always

sensed he had feelings for her. But still it jarred her to hear him admit it. "You know I'm in love with Josh, despite everything."

"I know."

She squeezed his hand. "Will, I really appreciate what you're offering. You don't know how much it means to me, but no."

"Why not?"

"It wouldn't be fair to you, married to a woman who loves another man, raising a child who isn't yours. How could you be okay with that?"

"I'll love your child because it's yours. I'll love it like it was mine." He cupped her face. "I'll take care of you both like you're my world. Because you are. I promise."

For a half a minute, she let herself consider his offer. But the implications of it, what it would mean, pushed aside the haze of relief swirling in her heart and cleared her mind. Accepting his offer would close the book on her and Josh. How could she do that when the tiny spark of hope still alive in her heart allowed her to believe the break between them could still be mended?

"Charleigh. Do you have *any* reason to stay?"

Her mind flashed the image of Josh with that girl in his bed, and that tiny spark fizzled and died. The truth was harsh but clear. Josh was gone. She'd lost him. And having lost him, she'd lost everything. Nothing else in her life meant anything to her. Not her job. Her apartment. Her aunt. Her few friends.

She shook her head.

"Having no reason to stay is a good reason to go." He leaned in and kissed her forehead then held her gaze in his loving one. "Go with me."

****

Will sat in the pickup, waiting for Charleigh to pack. He'd offered to help, but she said there was so little, she could handle it herself. Worry raced through him as he thought about her up there, the memories of Josh swirling around her, trying to change her mind about going with him. He grabbed the door handle, ready to run up the stairs and make sure it didn't happen. But then his cell rang.

It was Josh. Again.

He ignored it. Again.

He had listened to and deleted the dozen or so other messages his friend had left. Deleted his many texts. His conscience was demanding he tell Charleigh the truth. That it hadn't been Josh in bed with that redhead. That Josh was here looking for her. That he was out of his mind with the need to find her and right the wrongs that had separated them.

Yeah, he should tell her. But if he did, she'd go back to Josh. She was about to be his. They were going to have a life together. He was the better man for her. Better than Josh ever could. But he'd never get the chance to prove it unless they got out of here before Josh showed up and ruined everything.

As if his ears were burning, Josh called again. The sound was an ice pick to Will's conscience. He was about to give in to the little voice and answer it and confess all when Charleigh came out with her possessions in a box, her stuffed backpack slung over her shoulder.

Even in the throes of despair, she was beautiful. Everything about her mesmerized him, from the way that wild storm of hair floated around her head like a halo, to the sound of her laughter, to the fun and energy she infused in everything she did. With her, he could finally pull a full breath of air into his lungs and his heart could finally beat strong and steady. With her, he could finally live the life he was meant to. With her, he was a complete man.

From the moment they'd met, he knew he'd found the one, his other half, but she'd chosen Josh. But today, she had chosen him. And he wouldn't let her go, no matter how much his conscience clawed him.

"Sorry, Josh," he muttered. Muting his phone, he jumped out and helped Charleigh into the pickup.

He dialed her aunt's phone number for her so she could tell her she was leaving town and never coming back. Then, the last tie to their old life severed, they raced out of town toward their new one. He'd never been happier. And he'd spend the rest of his life, use the last breath in his lungs, making sure she and her baby—their baby—were happy and cared for.

****

No one knew where Charleigh went, only that she said she wasn't coming back. Josh was out of ideas and filled with a deep, dark desolation the likes of which he'd never felt. His only hope was that the love between them was too strong to allow her to leave town for good without calling to give him a chance to fix things or at the very least to tell him goodbye. Unless she had never really loved him. The more time that passed without hearing from her, the more it looked like that was the case.

****

Will and Charleigh stopped for gas outside Vegas before making their final push into California. While she was in the store buying snacks, he filled the gas tank. As the pump clicked out the gallons, he was again relieved his credit card had worked. He'd half expected the old man to freeze the account the second he'd pulled out of the drive.

Thankfully it had bought them gas, food, two gold wedding bands, a quickie wedding in Vegas, a nice dinner, and a night in a decent hotel. Hopefully, it would hold until they arrived in California and got settled. If it didn't, they could tap into his savings, which would keep them afloat for a while. But money wasn't the only problem worrying his mind.

They were married, but the union hadn't been consummated. She said she needed time to get to know him before being intimate with him. He said he understood and didn't press her, but it was a reminder that he didn't really have her. Yet.

And although he was certain he'd made the right decision taking her, his conscience wouldn't let up about what he'd done to Josh. The right thing to do was to call him, let him know he'd never get Charleigh back. He owed his best friend that much.

He set the pump hose back into its slot and capped the tank. A glance into the store window showed Charleigh adding items to her small basket. Taking a deep breath and releasing it slowly to steady his nerves, he made the call.

"Where the fuck are you?" Josh growled his greeting.

"Vegas."

"Is Charleigh with you?"

"Yeah, but—"

"Bring her home. Now."

"There's nothing for her there."

"I'm fucking here!"

"Josh, Charleigh and I…" He looked at the gold band on his left hand. "We're married."

"Bullshit." The choking sound in Josh's pained growl told Will his words had all but knocked the breath from his lungs. "She loves me. She'd never marry you."

The guilt that had jabbed Will since he made the decision to lie to Charleigh and to steal the only person who meant anything to Josh flared at hearing the pain in his friend's voice. Despite what had happened between Charleigh and Josh, they loved each other, and by marrying her, taking her away, he had destroyed whatever chance they had to be a family with their child.

He'd betrayed all three of them—his best friend, the woman he loved, and their child—and the cold lump in the pit of his stomach told him the decision would haunt him for the rest of his life. But he wouldn't take blame for their failed relationship. That was on Josh. He's the one who had put this situation in motion, not taking care of her the way she needed and deserved. Remembering that helped him justify his actions and firm his voice.

"I warned you it would happen," he said.

"Put her on the fucking phone."

"She's mine now, Josh."

"God damn you to hell, Will Simms. Put her on the fu—"

Will hung up just as Charleigh came out of the store. And he turned the phone off.

****

Charleigh wrestled with her thoughts on the long drive. She should have called Josh, let him know she had left with Will. It didn't feel right, just leaving with no word. And especially leaving before telling him about the baby.

But her brain pushed back the desires of her heart, reminding her that he wouldn't care whether she was gone or not. He'd shown his true feelings by leaving her, by staying away, by fucking that girl. What choice did she have but to start a new life? With someone who did want her.

She looked at Will, her husband, sitting beside her in the pickup, jamming to the Sewernuts, then to her lap, where her finger and thumb twisted the gold band on her left hand. Her heart clenched. But not in love and happiness of a new bride. Not that she wasn't grateful to Will. She was. Because of his kindness she wouldn't have to raise her baby on her own.

At the reminder, she set her hand on her stomach. *I'm doing this for you, little one. So you'll have a mom and a dad who love and want you. For the rest of my life, I'll do whatever it takes to make things good for you. I promise.*

Though her head told her she'd made the right decision—the only decision—her heart was screaming that she'd regret not telling Josh. It was saying she should have pulled him out of that bed and screamed her news in his face, made him tell her to her face he didn't want her or the baby. But she hadn't had the courage to hear his answer. *I don't want you. I don't love you. I don't want that baby.*

And now, it was too late. She was married and headed to California.

43

But like a brand, a tattoo, her love for Josh Flores was forever, whether she wanted it or not. Whether *he* wanted it or not.

Chapter Two

August, almost six years later

Josh Flores braked his pickup to a stop in front of the Simms house and wondered for the umpteenth time why the hell he'd agreed to come. Nothing more than his own morbid curiosity at work. His thankfully departed father always said his curiosity would be the death of him.

Ruby Winters, the Simms housekeeper, had called him last night, saying Wyatt urgently needed to see him.

Wyatt.

He spat the name from his mouth out the open window. The old man was a selfish, conniving, underhanded asshat. Besides Wyatt being the father of his mortal enemy, bad blood had flowed between the Simms and Flores families for twenty plus years, and he could think of no business between them that hadn't already been fought over and finished. Yet he was here, in spite of his misgivings.

Abruptly, with the thought in mind of getting an unpleasant task done, he opened the door.

The Simms' dog, apparently having a keen ear and sharp eye for trespassers, darted from behind a hawthorn bush, barking ferociously, determined to protect his territory and his master's property.

Josh spoke firmly to the dog, who backed away a distance but was relentless in his aggressive stance, growling menacingly as Josh stepped toward the house.

That's what you get for being curious—a hunk out of your leg from a devil dog.

The screen door pushed open, and Ruby stepped out onto the porch, wiping her hands on her apron. "Brutus, hush up," she scolded.

Brutus slunk back to the cool of the bush, a low rumbling in his throat the whole way.

"Hello, Josh," Ruby said, a welcoming smile on her face, which he returned.

"How've you been, Ruby?"

"Oh, you know." She brushed the back of her hand across her forehead. "This unending summer heat's getting to me, but otherwise, I can't complain." She held the door open for him. "Come on in. He's anxious to see you."

He stepped inside, wiping his boots on the mat, removing his cap, and hanging it on the rack alongside several other weather- and sweat-stained hats. "What's he up to this time?"

"I reckon he'll tell you soon enough. How about a cool glass of sun tea before you go in?"

"Appreciate it, Ruby, but no thanks." He wanted to get this meeting over with and be gone. If it wasn't considered rude, he'd have kept his cap on in order to make a quicker getaway. Being in the Simms house made him sick to his stomach.

She led him into the kitchen, where the mouth-watering smell of just-baked chocolate chip cookies hanging in the air welcomed him with a hug.

"I know you can't say no to my chocolate chip

cookies," she said. "If I remember right, they're your favorite."

He gave the motherly woman a half grin. She had brought him casseroles and baked goods once a week for a month after his dad passed two years ago. Hands down, she made the best chocolate chip cookies he'd ever eaten. "Yes, ma'am, they are, but I better pass."

"All right then, I'll show you in," she said and led him down a short hallway toward what he remembered were bedrooms. "I hear you and Beth Powell are dating."

"Uh, well…"

His two-week-new friends-with-benefits arrangement with his long-time friend was supposed to be a secret. Leave it to Ruby, the community's repository of all gossip, real and invented, to have somehow acquired that juicy piece.

Dammit. He didn't like people knowing about his personal business, especially his nearly nonexistent sex life, but in a town the size of Chismes Point, there was no getting around it. Busybodiness was on page one of the playbook.

Ruby's light chuckle said she understood the situation. Fortunately, she didn't speak any more about it, just stopped at one of the bedroom doors and softly knocked.

A feeble voice answered, "Come on in."

Josh wasn't sure what he'd expected, but the frail, bony body propped upright by pillows in the huge four-poster bed wasn't it. Where was the devil incarnate? The iron fist? The cold-hearted bastard that had tortured the Flores family?

Wyatt rolled watery, yellowed eyes toward Josh as

Ruby plumped his pillows and adjusted the covers, and he felt his hatred for this villain wane ever so slightly.

"You need anything before I go, Wyatt?" she asked.

"You go along, Ruby. I'm fine."

"I'll be in the kitchen if you need me."

Josh had never heard Wyatt speak so softly and kindly to anyone. Clearly, the two held some affection for each other, if only friendship.

As she passed Josh, she whispered, "Don't stay too long. He needs his rest."

"No, ma'am."

"Good of you to come, boy," Wyatt said as Ruby closed the door behind her. "Pull that chair up here by the bed so we don't have to shout across the room at each other."

Josh did. "Heard about your illness," he said as he sat. "Must be hard." Lung cancer was fast whittling away the old man's days, but Josh felt no need to mention it by name.

"Can't change it. Best get on with the necessaries. Which is why I asked you here. Got a proposition for you."

Josh refrained from asking any questions that would give Wyatt the impression he was interested in any Simms proposition. Not that Josh's disinterest would stop the old man from freeing whatever snake was slithering around in his head.

"As you know, Will died six months ago. Cancer took him." A sadness not diminished by time or blunted by his own innate contrariness clouded his face, and he looked away, out the window. "Never expected that, him being so young—a month shy of twenty-four years when he passed. I'm right glad my Ellie wasn't here to see her son put in the grave."

The awkward moment of silence had Josh wanting to jump out the window, but Wyatt soon cleared the emotion from his throat and returned to the business at hand.

"Anyhow, it got me thinking about who's gonna take over this ranch when I'm gone." He shook his head. "I for damn sure ain't gonna let it go to the state. My ancestors sweated and toiled over and tamed this piece of prairie, making it a legacy worthy of the Simms name."

Josh couldn't stop an eyebrow raise at the comment. The place was pretty run down, he'd noticed as he drove in. Leaning fences in need of repair, the barn and house needing paint and fixes, and other dilapidation that spoke of neglect.

Wyatt caught the subtle gesture and raised his chin in defiance. "Oh, I know it don't look especially prosperous around here now. After Will ran off with that gal, I just didn't have the heart to keep things fixed up."

That gal. *His* gal. Charleigh. *CC*. At the mere thought of her, her essence spiraled up in his chest like wisps of smoke, caressing and awakening longings he'd never been able to kill and bury. He roused his stores of old anger to keep them at bay and refocused on Wyatt's voice.

"But that's no never-mind now. The important thing is, there's about fifteen hundred acres of grazing land, a section in hay that's made a tolerable crop so far with another cutting coming up next month, a section of wheat just harvested that earned a tidy sum, and a section ready to be planted. Plus, I got nearly a thousand head with the Bar S brand on 'em. I got a little savings squirreled away, too. You know how tight we cattlemen can be, never spending nothing if bailing wire and duct tape'll fix it."

"There a point to all this boasting?"

The biting comment drew a heated look from Wyatt. "I'm getting there, you impatient—" It was as if a powerful source had sucked the breath from his lungs. He melted into the pillows, his eyes wide, his breath coming in gasps.

Josh leaned in, his hand out. "I'll get Ruby."

Wyatt waved the offer away, took a few deep breaths, and eventually calmed himself enough to speak. "My point is, there's enough to keep this place going for years to come if it's run by someone with a speck of sense. That's where you come in."

Josh's radar immediately switched to high alert. "Where I come in? I'm sorry for your predicament, but whatever's cooking in that head of yours, don't even think about getting me involved in it. I know you too well to get pulled into any of your schemes."

The old man's face took on a wounded countenance. "Aw, now, Josh, don't be so suspicious. I got a plan that'll benefit both of us if you'll just hear me out." Taking Josh's silence as agreement, he continued. "You know that piece of land I bought from your daddy?"

Josh stiffened as the banked flame of old anger stirred to life at the careless mention of the source of the bitter dispute. His eyes hardened. "You mean the land you stole from him."

"Dang it all, boy, I didn't steal nothing. I came to

that land fair and square."

"You took advantage of a desperate man in a dire situation to get your hands on the best section of land in the county, and when it came time to honor your agreement, you reneged."

"Now, you lookie here, I held up my end of the bargain. I gave him the money he needed to get your baby sister them medical treatments that mighta saved her life. It was your daddy that didn't hold up his end and pay me back when he said he would."

"He was an hour late because his pickup broke down. Any decent human being would have still honored the agreement."

"First of all, he was over six hours late and smelling of whiskey. And second, we had an agreement. He broke it. A man that don't keep his word ain't no kind of man."

That wasn't the story his dad had told, but knowing his father's problems with alcohol made it plausible. Still, family loyalty was stronger than logic.

"Mighty convenient that neither of you signed a contract, but *you* ended up with the land. In a battle of Simms word against Flores, we didn't stand a chance. And you knew it."

"I won't have you calling me a liar in my own damn home, boy." Wyatt's fists pounded on the bed as the words spilled hotly from his mouth.

A taut silence fell on the room, both men momentarily rendered mute in uncompromising points of view. It was a futile quarrel, one Josh had vowed he would not be drawn into. Especially now, when it was too late to rectify past mistakes

He exhaled slowly, consciously relaxed his

clenched jaw, and settled his fists on his thighs. "If you asked me here to rehash ancient history—"

"It's the future I want to talk about." Wyatt licked his dry, parchment lips. "When I'm gone, Derrick will inherit everything, but I'm worried that momma of his won't—"

"Who is Derrick?" Josh interrupted.

Wyatt's lips slowly rose into a grin. "My grandson."

"Will's?" Josh choked out the word as chills skated over his body.

He nodded. "Turned five this month, I believe."

Well, goddamn. Charleigh had a child with Will. A child that should have been *his*. *Theirs*. He swallowed against the pain as the crack in his heart widened a little more. She'd wanted a husband and a baby. And apparently it hadn't mattered who with. She hadn't wasted any time getting pregnant either, he thought, doing the math in his head—the month she left.

"Right now, my foreman can ramrod the cowhands," Wyatt continued, pulling Josh back into the present. "Get the work done under my instructions 'til my number's up. But I need somebody more experienced to take hold to keep it going and to help Charleigh learn how to run this place."

Josh shook his head, feeling a rip in his gut about where this conversation was going.

"I can see you're getting mighty impatient, Josh, so I'll skip the particulars and get to it."

If only that were so. Josh's insides were itching like a colony of ants had taken up residence there. God, he needed to get out of here. Memories of Charleigh, both good and bad, were smothering him, making it hard to breathe.

"You're a little on the green side to be running a spread the size of the Flying F by yourself, but talk has it you're doing a fine job. That it's in better shape than it's ever been, even when your granddad was running it, which is saying something. So I'm gonna trust you with something that means more than a mite to me. And it ain't an easy thing to do, turning to a Flores for help. But there's no one else I trust."

Josh shot him a hard look and steeled himself, knowing this was the moment of truth. "What makes you think you can trust me?"

"Your top-notch reputation, and…" Tears welled up in the old man's dark eyes, and his throat bobbed in a hard swallow. "My boy said I could."

Will had talked about this plan with his father? Vouched for his integrity?

While that should have pumped his pride, it didn't. It just added to his mistrust of this ridiculous proposition. "What do you want, Wyatt?"

Wyatt cleared his throat and took a rattled breath. "I want you to marry Charleigh."

For a moment, Josh went numb. The next he shot to his feet. Giving Wyatt a go-to-hell look instead of spewing the foul words he wanted to say, he made for the door.

"If you marry her, I'll give you Antelope Spring."

Josh halted at the door. A fierce hope surged inside his chest at the words but died the moment it was born. In its place, a hot resentment settled in against Wyatt for concocting this cold-blooded plan with his son to manipulate an end more to his liking. He obviously was desperate to protect the Simms legacy. But that didn't entitle him to dangle Antelope Spring like a carrot on a stick to ensnare him into helping carry out his scheme. Well, it wasn't going to work. He would not be a player in the old man's drama.

Especially if it meant marrying Charleigh Cooper.

Make that Charleigh *Simms*.

The idea was preposterous beyond belief. No way in hell would he saddle himself to a sham marriage with that deceitful woman, even if it meant getting Antelope Spring.

He strode back to the bedside, his eyes hard as he regarded Wyatt. "If I married her, I'd have the whole goddamned Simms place, and even that's not enough of a reason to induce me to marry her. Nothing—no reward, no gain, no promise—will ever induce me to marry her," he said, his words spoken slowly as though to a two-year-old. "I'm sorry about your ranch. I'm sorry about your son. I'm sorry you're sick, but I can't help you."

"Oh, sit down, boy," the old man demanded. "I swear, you hop around more than that ol' one-legged rooster I used to have." His lips twisted. "Cougar got him, I expect. Maybe coyotes."

Drawing himself up tight, Josh throttled his irritation. More than anything, he wanted out of this bedroom, out of this house, out in the air where he could breathe. It smelled like mistakes and death in this tight box. But he resumed his seat.

"Believe you me, Josh, I understand your reluctance to marrying that gal." His voice was softer, almost kind, and Josh didn't trust it for a second. Then the old devil's cloudy eyes sparkled. "Must have been quite a blow to your manhood, her dumping you and running off with Will the way she did."

Ah, there it was. Silence flooded the space between them, giving the memory of that day time to pry the fresh scab off his never-healed wound before he could wrestle it back into place.

"I'd say I dodged a bullet, ridding myself of a deceitful woman."

"Fair enough." Wyatt pulled in a slow breath, studying Josh with narrowed eyes. "What if there was a way you could get Antelope Spring without marrying her? You interested in talking about that?"

Short of marrying Charleigh, there wasn't much he wouldn't do to regain title to Antelope Spring. "I'm listening."

****

Josh pushed back into the worn leather chair that had been his dad's and his granddad's before that. He propped his feet on the scarred oak desk that held a similar ancestry, kicked back, and considered the hand fate had dealt him.

He'd known Wyatt had little time left. Still, he'd been surprised by his death a week after their insane conversation, figuring the old cowboy would cheat death as easily as he had cheated the Flores family.

Josh's thoughts returned to their last meeting. Wyatt must have been desperate to come up with the ludicrous idea of having him marry Charleigh. Plan B—working with her and her son for a year, teaching them to run the ranch—was better. But not by much. Even the possibility of getting Antelope Spring wasn't enough of a draw to put himself through that hell.

He'd rejected both schemes and stormed out, Wyatt cursing his name before falling into a coughing fit that surprisingly hadn't taken his last breath right then and there.

But the man didn't give up easily, as evidenced by the fat envelope on his desk, delivered by the Simms lawyer, Horace Wilcox, the day before. Wyatt had sweetened the offer and made it legal by executing a contract in which Josh would earn a sizable salary and a bonus up front to manage the Bar S for a year and teach Charleigh and Derrick how to run it, at the end of which Antelope Spring would be his. All he had to do was sign the contract.

What he hadn't expected was Wyatt's final manipulative tug at his heartstrings. Derrick's inheritance was contingent upon Josh's agreement to become the Bar S manager. If he didn't, the ranch would be put up for sale with the assets going to various charities and the state. Ruby and the remaining hands would be out a job, and Derrick, the only Simms heir, would receive little more than a couple thousand dollars.

He had to admire the old man for knowing which buttons to push to get him to do as he asked, for knowing that if his hunger to reacquire Antelope Spring wouldn't convince him, his conscience would. But Wyatt had underestimated his aversion to being in close proximity to Charleigh. The thought of spending a year with Will's widow and son left him sick to his soul.

If he refused to sign, Charleigh would lose everything. Just payback due a betraying woman. The matter of the boy, though, pricked at his conscious, and he had to ask himself whether he could willingly allow Will's son to lose his inheritance. His legacy.

The five-year-old was an innocent child who didn't

deserve to be caught in the crossfire of the manipulating adults around him. He deserved a chance to preserve his family legacy. Like he, himself, was trying to do.

That said, Charleigh's possible return brought up the past and all the feelings he had tried hard to kill. Her leaving, and with his best friend, had almost destroyed him. He'd never forgiven either of them, and that anger and grief had moved in and cemented a large chunk of his heart. How could he work with her?

Despite his hesitation, the payoff the deal would bring—the opportunity to reclaim Flores land, to right the wrong done to his family, to fix up the homestead his great-granddad, Amado Flores, built nearly a hundred years ago—was stronger than the dread that froze his insides when he thought about again seeing the woman who had destroyed him.

His choice was clear.

He grabbed a pen and signed over his soul to the devil.

Chapter Three

"What do you mean, Derrick owns a ranch?"

Charleigh blinked at Aaron Romero, attorney at law, seated behind his massive, immaculate mahogany desk. She couldn't have been more stunned if he'd told her Derrick had won the million-dollar lottery.

"Your father-in-law, Wyatt Simms, named your son as the sole heir of the Simms estate—the acreage, the main house, outbuildings, livestock, tack, machinery, crops in the field, right down to his socks and underwear, if you want them." He chuckled at his own joke.

Charleigh shook her head in wonderment at the possibility that her son owned everything Will had abandoned. It made no sense. Why would Wyatt do that? He had disowned Will and never acknowledged Derrick's existence.

"This is almost too much to absorb." She was still in disbelief yet almost dizzy with relief that their financial struggles of the past year might be behind them.

"Obviously, as a five-year-old, Derrick is incapable of assuming the responsibilities of running a ranch. Therefore, as his mother, you'll be instrumental in carrying out the terms of the will. It will be you who acts in his place."

Run it? Oh, hell no. She had no plans to go back to

that shithole. She'd sell it as fast as she could to the first person foolish enough to buy it. The sale of the Simms assets would be a way out of their poverty-stricken lives and set them up financially for years to come. It was the kindest thing the old man had ever done for his son.

"However," the lawyer added, "the will includes several stipulations that, if not fully satisfied, will affect Derrick's right to inherit."

Ah. Strings. Now *that* sounded like the Simms patriarch Will had told her about. "What kind of stipulations?"

"The primary stipulation is that you and Derrick live on the ranch for a year and acquaint yourself with the full scope of the inheritance before you're allowed to place the ranch and its assets up for sale."

Charleigh's heart skidded to a hard halt. "We have to live there?"

"That's correct."

"Surely, there's some way around that." No way in hell would she live at Chismes Point again. "I just want to sell it."

"If you don't abide by this condition, Derrick won't inherit."

"This is insane." Full-blown anxiety shot her from her chair, and she strode to the windowed wall and looked out on the morning bustle below, arms tight around herself to still her trembling caused by her racing memories. She'd spoken too soon. This wasn't Wyatt doing a kind thing for his son's widow and child. It was his last chance to punish them. "I don't know a thing about ranching. How can I possibly fulfill the terms?"

"Mr. Simms contracted an experienced ranch manager for a year to help ensure your success. This manager has full authority to operate the Bar S as he sees fit and has a responsibility to educate you and Derrick in the basics of ranching and to see to your welfare."

"After that year, then what?"

"If you and the manager satisfy the conditions, and he feels you're ready to take over, then Derrick's inheritance becomes final. You'll assume full legal rights to manage the assets without oversight until Derrick reaches adulthood. You can sell it or run it."

Relief warred with worry in her stomach. "I'm relieved to know an experienced ranch manager will be there to guide us and take care of things. But I'm concerned the inheritance hangs on the whims of a stranger."

"Rightfully so, but realize that you're in this together. If one of you fails, you all do."

"And Derrick loses everything."

Aaron nodded. "All but twenty-five hundred dollars."

"What does the manager gain by giving up a year of his life?"

"He'll be well paid for his time, of course, and will acquire title to a valuable piece of Simms property."

It would be a huge gamble, moving back to Chismes Point. Vulnerability lived there, with much to lose and secrets placed at risk. The wrong decision could have disastrous consequences. Yet, how could she deprive her son of his inheritance, of his future? How could she not consider any reasonable way out of their precarious financial condition?

Besides, Josh was probably long gone. Probably well into his degree at that Colorado vet school he'd talked about. Regardless, no way in hell would he still be hanging around the place he'd always referred to as the ass crack of New Mexico. He'd been as eager as she to get out of there.

Feeling calmer at that revelation, she returned to the chair and sat. Her choice was clear. "Where do I sign?"

The lawyer slid the stack of pages to her and handed her a pen. "At the red flags."

The pen felt cold and weighty in her hand, but she gripped it firmly and flipped through the document to the first flag. A chill raced up her spine, almost like a warning, halting her from signing her name.

A valuable piece of property, the lawyer had said. The most valuable piece of land on the Simms ranch was Antelope Spring.

Her gaze flit up to Aaron's. "What's the name of the manager Wyatt engaged?"

He flipped through his copy until he found the page he needed. "Flores. Joshua A. Flores."

Energy flushed from her body in a tsunami, the pen dropping from her hand, her body collapsing against the back of the plush leather chair with a groan that came from the depths of her soul. Her hand flew to her forehead where a sharp ache flared from the exploding memories.

Josh? Oh, God, no! She couldn't go back to Josh, see him every day. He'd take one look at Derrick and know he was his son and that she'd kept Derrick from him. He might be angry enough or spiteful enough to try to take him from her. Even if she were able to keep

Derrick's parentage a secret, how could she put her life and his in Josh's hands? She couldn't. Wouldn't.

Aaron pressed a paper cup into her hands. She drank the water down in one greedy gulp.

"More?" he asked.

She shook her head, her body still numb.

He resumed his seat and tented his fingers on his desk. "The probate process takes time…" He jumped right back in as if there hadn't been this inconvenient little interruption. "But provision has been made for you to take possession of the house immediately. And there's an account for living expenses you can access without the manager's approval."

A house. Money for living expenses.

As the meaning of his words sank in, the fear gripping her eased slightly. To have a home to call their own rather than the dilapidated over-the-garage studio. A place safe from the gangs and drugs and crimes of the city. No constant worry of whether she could put food on the table and pay the bills. Money to pay more on Will's medical bills. A better life for Derrick.

Almost as if he had witnessed her dread dissolving, the lawyer picked up the pen she'd dropped and held it out. "It's yours, Mrs. Simms, all for the affordable price of your signature."

The price of signing her name to that document wasn't just her signature. It was her soul. But for Derrick's sake, she had to consider all options.

If she refused the ranch, they'd get twenty-five hundred dollars, which might be enough to pay to file for bankruptcy or maybe pay a lawyer to work a deal with the creditors so that she could pay a lessor amount to Will's medical bills each month. The option wouldn't provide the security they'd get from selling the ranch, but it would protect her heart and sanity—and her son—from the man who had broken her so thoroughly.

Accepting the ranch would give her and Derrick long-term financial security and a new future, one where every day was not a struggle to survive. But it would require her to sacrifice her soul for a year and risk…everything.

She'd made Derrick a promise before he was born that she'd do anything to ensure he had a good life. She hadn't been doing that great of a job of keeping that promise lately. For his sake, her choice was clear.

She took the pen from the lawyer and signed over her soul to the devil.

****

Josh lifted the mare's hoof and tucked it between his knees to hold it steady and within reach until he could affix the new shoe. Fast and agile, Zia was able to read the rambunctious intentions of the most skittish steer almost before the bovine itself knew. He needed her back in service quickly.

He glanced up briefly when his foreman, Joaquin Ruiz, aka Quino, rode up.

"*Los hombres tienan hambre,*" Quino said, dismounting. "*Esta lista la comida?*"

"Tammy Jo said the food would be ready in two minutes, but that was ten minutes ago," Josh mumbled around the nails between his lips.

"I keep telling you to get Ruby," Quino said. "Her food's delicious. Tammy Jo's gives me gas."

Josh grinned. They'd all noticed. The man was noisier than a popcorn maker. "I'll broach the subject with Ruby and the new owner when I go over there tomorrow to start lessons."

"*Estan alli?*"

"Sometime today."

Quino pulled off his hat and scratched the three black hairs atop his pale head. "After that long trip, they'd likely appreciate time to settle in. You know how women are about getting their stuff around them situated just right."

No, he didn't. But it didn't matter. They needed to get started right away. They only had a year, and that wasn't near enough time to learn all they needed to know. More than that, he couldn't wait to satisfy his curiosity about Charleigh and who she was now.

But he wasn't going to explain that to anyone, even Quino, who had worked for the ranch longer than Josh had been alive and had been privy to many a Flores family secret.

"You wanna go on up to the house and check on the food?" he said, changing the subject.

"*Claro, joven.*" Quino headed that way, and Josh returned his attention to the job at hand.

Zia leaned her rump into his shoulder while he nailed the shoe, partly for balance but mostly for the comfort of human contact. Now that's something he understood. The crazy things a body was willing to do to satisfy the need for a little close human contact.

Like his arrangement with Beth.

They say one person in a relationship always cares more than the other. That dubious honor fell to her. She'd been dropping hints for weeks—after someone had told her Charleigh was coming back to town— about turning their friends-with-benefits relationship into something substantial. Not that she wasn't a nice gal and good in the sack. He just didn't see it going anywhere, so only one of his organs was in it...and it wasn't his heart. He no longer had a heart capable of caring that much, just a constant ache marking where it used to beat. Thanks to Charleigh.

He had just tapped in the last nail and dropped the mare's leg when Quino came out of the house with his cell phone, which he'd left in the kitchen to charge while he shoed.

"*Telefono.*"

He removed his ferrier's apron and took the phone. "Flores." He headed deeper into the barn to hang up the apron and put away the tools.

"Josh, Horace Wilcox here. Thought you'd like to know that Charleigh and her boy just left my office, headed to the Simms place. I told her you'd be contacting her next week to talk about a schedule."

"I plan to head over there in the morning for the first lesson."

"Well, as ranch manager that's your business, certainly, but they're pretty tuckered. You might want to give them a few days to get their legs under them."

"It's important we get started right away."

"Yes, but—"

"'Preciate the heads up, Horace." He ended the call and exited the barn.

Quino was leaning against the fence, listening to his conversation. "Guess you'll be spending a good chunk of your time at the Simms place from now on."

Josh nodded. "I'm counting on you to take care of things around here when I'm gone. Hell, you'll probably do better without me around."

65

Quino grinned. "Most likely. Me and the boys'll take care of things. Getting all those calves rounded up and shipped off will keep us hopping the next few weeks. Good thing you hired a couple extra hands."

Because of his added obligations to the Bar S, Josh had hired two men to do his work here. All the ranches in the area usually shared labor for big things like roundup, but he didn't want to be left short in case some of them backed out, like last year. Now, in the last week of September, both the Flying F and the Bar S ranches were in full swing getting their cattle ready for market.

Josh glanced up, judging the angle of the sun. "We're burning daylight. Let's finish up the east pasture before nightfall."

"*Vaminos*," Quino said.

Josh pulled on his leather gloves and mounted Zia. As he and Quino rode out, Tammy Jo was loading the food into the pickup for the hungry crew.

All afternoon, Josh's mind kept drifting the ten miles away to the Bar S and its new owners. To Charleigh.

The woman's essence had lingered inside him all these years, like a recurring dream, a brand, a scent he could never wash off. He wondered for the hundredth time today how she'd changed in the years since she'd packed up and left town with Will. Older, of course, but he could get no farther than the honey eyes, the curly golden hair, and the lush body of the eighteen-year-old that had been his whole world. Longings stampeded in his gut, shoving aside the pain of old wounds and flooding his body with memories, strong and bittersweet and real enough to taste.

Annoyed with himself for not being able to stop thoughts of her from clouding his concentration and interrupting his work, he pulled off his hat, pushed back his sweat-slicked hair with one hand, and shoved his hat back on. With greater focus, he concentrated on the work before him, but soon the sound of the cattle, the smell of the dirt and shit, the sight of the organized chaos in front of him faded and was replaced by an image of her, of him, their last night together.

He closed his eyes and let the memories, the feelings, come, let them flood his system and drown him. Just for one sweet indulgent moment or two. The taste of her kisses, the sound of her voice and her laugh, the fullness of her breasts, the feel of her legs wrapped around him, the ecstasy of being inside her tight heat, her core gripping and stroking him… God, he remembered it all. Every detail. Still. With her, he'd known the deepest happiness. Without her, he'd known the deepest agony.

The sound of a horse nickering at his side jerked him out of the quicksand of memories, and he opened his eyes to see Quino beside him, staring at him from his mount. The knowing look in his foreman's twinkling green eyes pissed him off. How many times had the teenaged Josh been on the receiving end of that stare and a sharp chastisement about daydreaming of Charleigh when he should have been working? Too many times. But Josh was no longer a kid who needed to be kept on track.

Quino leaned over and squirted a neat stream of tobacco juice into the nearby scrub brush. "That's some powerful thinking you're doing. *Estas bien?*"

Truth was, he wasn't all right. Even though time

had stitched up the wounds caused by Charleigh's leaving, all the memories her return was stirring up were ripping open the stitches, making him feel everything from that time. Instead of answering his foreman's question, he straightened in the saddle, squared his shoulders, and anchored his hat more firmly on his head, down close to his eyes.

Hardening his face and his voice, he responded, "You need something, *viejo*, or are you just taking another break?"

****

Every mile that took Charleigh closer to Chismes Point, closer to the ranch, closer to Josh, knotted the ball of anxiety in her belly tighter. Crawling through the tiny town, she mused that the place hadn't changed much in six years. Her guess was it wouldn't change in another sixty.

However, two notable changes were that the café where she'd worked, and lived, was now a flower shop, and a new prefab building near it housed a roller skating rink. A dozen or so people milled about among the few stores squatting along the main street, and several residents in pickups crept along the worn road, but otherwise it was as slow-paced as ever.

No one in this town-that-time-forgot would be welcoming her with open arms. But that was okay. She hadn't come back for them. She'd come back for the same reason she'd left—for Derrick's sake.

As soon as she passed the town limits sign, she floored it, wanting to arrive in Wilton before Horace Wilcox closed up his law office for lunch.

Get through this year, then you're free became her mantra on the way there, trying to make herself believe it. By the time she reached Horace's office half an hour later, she had calmed a bit. Blowing out a tense breath, she climbed from the small moving truck, helped Derrick out, and went inside to cement the details of their sentence.

The sun was into its descending arch in the sky when they finally pulled into the yard of the Bar S ranch. She cut the engine and stared out the bug-splattered windshield at…home.

Constructed of stone and timber, the low, rambling house was more modest than she had imagined it would be, and it struck her as odd that in the two plus years she'd lived in town she'd never seen it. She'd heard of the million-dollar Simms ranch, though, and had expected a domicile that better matched the family's reputation for arrogance. Not that it mattered what the house looked like. They wouldn't be here that long. Besides, it was a veritable mansion compared to where they'd come from. And she was grateful for it.

Just when she'd reached out to open the door, a shaggy black dog darted from behind a bush that grew alongside the house, barking furiously and leaping up at the car door. Startled, she locked the door. Then felt stupid that she thought to lock the door against a dog.

Derrick's eyes opened wide. "Will he bite us?"

"I don't know," she said as the dog paced at the door.

A moment later, the door to the house opened and a tall, slim older woman in a plaid western blouse, faded blue jeans, and a flowery apron stepped out. "Brutus, stop your yapping," she hollered at the dog, who obeyed.

Displaying a friendly smile, the woman approached

the truck, and Charleigh rolled down the window. "He won't bite," she assured them. "He's just making noise. You're safe to get out."

Not at all convinced of that, Charleigh cautiously opened the door, keeping her eyes on the dog, and got out. Derrick scampered out on her side, and she pulled him behind her, placing herself between him and the animal that was tracking their every step, growling low in his throat.

The woman, as friendly as the dog was hostile, stepped toward them. "You must be Charleigh Simms and Derrick. I'm Ruby Winters, Bar S housekeeper. Glad you folks finally made it. Been expecting you."

Ruby led them up the porch steps and into a mudroom. An assortment of cowboy boots and galoshes in various stages of wear lined a metal shelving unit with hats, sweaters, coats, and overalls hanging from pegs. Along one wall was a washer and dryer as well as a freezer.

Charleigh took off her shoes and made Derrick remove his, too, keeping to their no-shoes-in-the-house rule. From there, they moved into a large kitchen, bright with yellow curtains and flowered wallpaper covering the walls. The rich aroma of coffee scented the air. At Ruby's urging, she and Derrick took a seat at the well-used dining table that dominated the far end of the room.

"You two must be hungry from your long trip," Ruby said.

"We grabbed something quick in town," Charleigh responded. Although truth be told, only Derrick had eaten. Her stomach was still in knots, making the idea of food or drink unpalatable.

"A cup of coffee at least? Fresh-brewed not ten minutes ago."

Accepting the offer of a cup of coffee seemed the right thing to do. "That would be nice. Thanks."

"And for you, cowboy?" Ruby asked Derrick.

"Um, no, thank you. I don't like coffee." His voice was low and thin, and Charleigh could tell he wasn't sure what to make of his new home.

"Well, now...would a sody pop be more to your liking?"

Soda being a rare treat for Derrick, his wide blue eyes shifted to Charleigh—who nodded—then back to Ruby. "Yes, please."

"Such good manners. Just like your daddy." The housekeeper brought their drinks, set the cream and sugar on the table, then poured a cup of coffee for herself and sat across the table from Charleigh, who stirred cream and sugar into the dark brew and took a sip.

"Well, now, how's the coffee?"

"As delicious as it smells. Thank you, Mrs. Winters."

"It's plain ol' Ruby. And you're certainly welcome. Supper won't be ready for another hour or so, so how about a cookie? Made 'em just this morning. I don't mean to boast, but they'll knock your socks off clean to Texas."

Charleigh declined, but Derrick took one from the cookie jar offered him. She usually didn't allow sweets before dinner, but this was an unusual situation. A little comfort in the form of a homemade cookie seemed appropriate. From the way he devoured it, he agreed with Ruby's assessment of their level of deliciousness.

"Did you know my dad?" Derrick asked Ruby, polishing off the cookie in three bites.

She nodded, sadness in her eyes. "Will was a good boy, and so talented with his drawing. My oatmeal cookies were his favorite, too." Winking, she held out the cookie jar to Derrick.

"Actually, my favorite's chocolate chip, but I like these, too." He proved it by taking another. "Mom, how come you and Dad never lived in this house?" He glanced around. "It's much better than ours."

Charleigh nearly choked on the swallow of coffee. "That's a story for another time. Right now, we need to get our stuff unloaded from the truck." She pushed back from the table.

"But I haven't finished my sody pop."

She cringed at how quickly he had adopted the vernacular. The last thing she wanted was for him to soak up this place and become part of it. They were staying just long enough to satisfy the contract and sell everything, then they'd get as far away from Josh and this place as possible.

"You can finish it in your room while you unpack. Just be careful not to spill it."

Despite Brutus' patrolling, the three of them had the truck unloaded in less than half an hour, everything piled in the kitchen, ready to be sorted into their respective rooms. Boxes in hand, Charleigh and Derrick followed Ruby down the hall to a small bedroom. A twin bed with a blue bedspread was pushed against the back wall, a dresser sat against another wall, and a window with curtains of the same blue as the bedspread looked out West, to the way they'd come.

"This is your room, Derrick," Ruby said. "It was

Will's when he lived here. He slept in that very same bed there, of course Josh—Josh Flores, your ranch manager—fitted it out with a new mattress and bedding. You'll be comfortable enough, I expect."

"I never had my own room," he said as he looked around curiously. Spotting a baseball glove on the dresser, he wandered over to it. "Was this my dad's glove?" He brought it to his nose, as if he hoped to smell Will in its stiff leather.

"Sure was," Ruby said. "And that trophy there, that was for having the best calf in show at the county fair. He wasn't much older than you when he won it."

"Wow," Derrick murmured, running his finger across the name plate on the base of the trophy that spelled out Will's name.

What Ruby didn't say was that Will had only *showed* the calf in the competition. He hadn't lifted a finger to raise it because he'd hated everything about ranch life. He hadn't wanted to even show it, but his dad insisted. The win had meant nothing to him, the trophy representing his father's controlling nature. Or at least that's what he'd said.

Charleigh dropped her arm around Derrick and kissed the top of his head. "We're burning daylight, puppy. Get your stuff put away."

He nodded and moved to explore the closet.

With a soft smile and shake of her head, she left him to inspect his room. On her way out the door, Will's high school baseball team photo on the wall caught her eye. Her gaze went first to Will then to the boy he stood next to—Josh—and her heart ping-ponged off her rib cage.

If that's how her body reacted at just seeing Josh's

face in a photo, how would it react when they met face to face, their eyes and souls assessing the other for changes, searching for a glimpse of the person they'd been? She'd find out soon enough when he came over to start their lessons. Hopefully, she'd have a few days to prepare herself, mentally and emotionally.

She wasn't happy about having to see him again, and likely he felt the same, but she was committed to being civil to ensure the success of their working relationship. That commitment would require her to rein in the pain of betrayal that had, over the years, become as part of her as her skin and not let it push her to do something that would end their arrangement before it began. Something satisfying, like punching him in the balls as payback for what he'd done. Civility was the plan, and she'd stick to it for Derrick's sake.

"Ready to see your room?" Ruby asked behind her, pulling her out of her moment.

"Sure." She ran a fingertip over the smiling faces of the two men who had shaped her life and asked one for strength to get through the coming year with the other. Then, following Ruby back to the kitchen, she grabbed her suitcase and one of her boxes. Ruby grabbed another two boxes and led the way down the hall from Derrick's room to another bedroom.

"This was the guest room," Ruby said and set the boxes on the floor. "Josh thought you'd be more comfortable here than in Wyatt's room at the end of the hall that's now the guest room."

Charleigh silently gave thanks to Josh. She wasn't a superstitious person, but the thought of sleeping in the room where her father-in-law had died was unsettling.

She set her things on the floor, too, and glanced

around the room. The faint smell of paint lingered from the pale green walls. Curtains—cream and the same pale green—hung from the window and lent light to counterbalance the dark wood of the bed and dresser. At the rear of the room was a small bathroom that also smelled faintly of paint. Also pale green.

Had Josh remembered green was her favorite color? Or had it been a random choice of the person he'd hired to do the painting?

"Well, it's certainly beautiful, and that bed looks so comfortable I can hardly wait to climb in. Thanks for all you've done to make us feel welcome."

"Oh, pshaw. It's Josh who deserves the bulk of those thanks. He's the one who made sure your rooms were in good shape before you arrived. Such a nice young man. And those eyes of his." She lowered her voice to a whisper. "They're enough to make a woman melt right outta her clothes, if you know what I mean." Ruby fanned her face.

Unfortunately, I know exactly what you mean. To hide her flushing face, she grabbed her suitcase, plopped it onto the bed, and unzipped it. She cleared her throat of the uncomfortable memories blocking her words. "I'll be sure to thank him."

"You'll get the chance soon enough, I reckon. Well, I need to finish up supper, but if you need anything, just holler," Ruby said.

Charleigh smiled her thanks. "I will."

In a surprise move that shook Charleigh to her toes, Ruby pulled her into a motherly hug. The scents of cinnamon, vanilla, and coffee wafted into her nose— scents she had associated with home when her mother was still alive.

"You and your boy are home, Charleigh. With family. Where you belong. Everything's going to be all right now." With that prediction and a pat on her arm, she left the room, her scent and her words remaining.

Everything's going to be all right now.

Charleigh dropped onto the edge of the bed, then flopped back on the mattress. She wished she could believe the words. They would be comforting. But she wasn't convinced. And Josh was the sole reason for her doubt. Just because he had gone to some trouble to ensure their comfort didn't mean she could soften her heart to him. He'd proven he couldn't be trusted. And time usually only strengthened a person's less-attractive characteristics.

She stared up at the ceiling, seeing Josh's face clearly. His smile and blue eyes that could, to quote Ruby, make her melt out of her clothes. If she and Derrick were to survive this year unscathed, she would have to guard her heart against Josh. And she would. The scars on her soul would be her armor, would remind her that he was not a man who could be trusted. She would not allow him in again.

With renewed determination buzzing through her, she jumped up and got to work unpacking and finding a place for her meager belongings. That done, she was preparing to go to Derrick's room to check on his progress when Ruby poked her head in.

"Charleigh, Josh just called to say he'd be here at seven o'clock tomorrow morning to start your training."

The statement flipped Charleigh's stomach up into her throat. She was nowhere near ready to face him. And it rankled that he'd just deliver a message and expect her to obey.

"I'm sorry to ask, but would you mind calling him back and telling him I can't meet with him until Monday. It's been a long trip, and Derrick and I need time to settle in."

"Of course." Ruby left the room, only to return a few minutes later. "He, uh, *insists* that you be ready at seven in the morning for training."

Charleigh's temper flared to the surface, obliterating every drop of anxiety and straightening her spine to its limits. "He insists? Who the hell does he think he is?"

A smile tugged at Ruby's mouth and in her sparkling brown eyes. "He thinks he's the ranch manager."

If she gave in to his demands once, he'd run roughshod over her from here on out. She would not allow that. He would not push her around. "Ranch manager, yes. My boss, no."

"He's still on the phone. What would you like me to tell him?"

"Tell him I said to go—" She stopped herself from finishing that sentence. It would set a bad tone for her and Josh's working relationship and give Ruby the wrong impression of her. She revised the sentence and delivered it calmly. "Please tell him he's welcome to join us tomorrow *evening* for a cup of coffee and a couple of chocolate chip cookies if that's still his thing, but training is going to wait until Monday."

Chapter Four

Josh drummed his fingers on the Simms' kitchen table where he'd sat since six fifty-five that morning. Ruby topped off his coffee, again, and he checked his watch, again. Seven twenty-five, and Charleigh still wasn't up.

He considered himself a patient man, but this insolence made his blood boil. He had to control the situation with her from the get-go, or they'd butt heads over his every decision. If they were to succeed, she must be made to accept her obligations, both to the Bar S and to him.

Her arrogance in having Ruby deliver her dismissive message last night rankled more than he wanted to admit. Only his own dog-tiredness had kept his ass at home instead of driving straight over and having it out with her then. But he needed to be fresh—in mind and body—to deal with her. Not that a night's delay had revived him all that much. The few hours he'd spent in bed had been wasted ones, filled with thoughts of her, followed by dreams of her.

He checked his watch against the clock on the wall that showed seven twenty-eight. He'd give her two more minutes. If she hadn't made an appearance by then, he'd march into her room and drag her ass out of bed.

Or join her in it.

Fire, quick and hot, licked through him at the thought of awakening her like he used to, with deep kisses and slow strokes.

Either action would get her out of bed and ensure she learned the first lesson of running a ranch. Country people had to be early risers to stay ahead of the never-ending chores, and self-indulgent sleeping habits would not be tolerated.

****

Charleigh rolled over in the bed and stretched big. For the past nearly six years, she'd shared a pull-out couch with Will, and then with Will and Derrick, then with Derrick. To have an actual bed all to herself was pure heaven. After she'd managed to dispel thoughts of Josh and fall asleep, it had been the best night's sleep she'd had in years.

She wanted to snuggle into the warmth of the comforter and grab another few zzzs. But thoughts of Josh and their coming year trickled into the remains of her slumber, dispelling it. Enticing aromas of coffee and frying bacon conspired with her thoughts to push her from bed.

After washing up, she peeked into Derrick's room and found him snoring softly. She kissed his forehead, at once hopeful for their future and yet fearful that it could go horribly wrong with Josh in the picture. Ironic how she'd once put him in the picture to calm her, and now that he *was* in the picture, it terrified her.

Leaving Derrick to his dreams, she padded to the kitchen, eager for a cup of coffee. One foot in the kitchen and she froze, every muscle in her body tensing except her heart, its thundering beat a warning that she was seconds from imminent danger and should flee or prepare to fight. Josh sat at the kitchen table, scowling at her, his melt-her-clothes-off blue eyes sparking with emotion as they gripped hers.

Her eyes quickly cataloged every detail of him, from the trace of dark stubble on his tanned jaw to the way his thick hair invited her fingers to run through it. From how the faded western-cut denim shirt he wore stretched tight over his wide shoulders and chest to how it fit looser at the waist where it tucked into his jeans. From the tight faded jeans that hugged his long muscular legs to how it hugged the swell between them.

He was still Josh, yet so much more—harder and more muscular than the eighteen-year-old had been and just as magnetic and catch-your-breath handsome. Pure, unadulterated desire fired to life in her body, shoving aside the anger she'd cuddled like a security blanket for years. She swallowed, trying to still the irrational desire racing through her, but her errant brain shot into overdrive, pumping out memory after memory, each one of them an image of her tangled around him.

Memories swirled between them and around them like ghosts, making her head swim, her knees weak, her body heat. The way his eyes raked her from head to toe made it impossible to think of anything but those memories. His gaze paused on her bare, exposed thighs, making her wish she'd taken the time to get dressed instead of coming out in the soft, faded green T-shirt she'd slept in for the past six years, making her wish she'd reined in her stampede of curls instead of leaving them to run wild down her back.

Silence stretched an eternity across the gap between them as each scrutinized the other. It was the same tense, aching, thick-with-emotion silence they'd left each other in. One of them had to break through it. She'd take the upper hand and do it. As Ruby had reminded her last night, this was her home now. Doing so would also give her an opportunity to set the tone, the expectation, that their business arrangement was a partnership, not a dictatorship, and that it didn't have to be an antagonistic one.

"Good morning, Josh."

The sound and taste of his name on her lips lifted them into a soft smile and set her heart to fluttering, but she was pleased that her attempt to make her voice sound strong but cordial had worked.

But then the man she'd loved with a scorching, all-consuming passion rose fluidly from the table, and she felt anything but strong and in charge.

"Good *afternoon*," he said.

His voice, low, hard, and laced with sarcasm, vibrated through her, tightening every muscle in her body.

"Better have your watch checked," she said and forced her legs to move to the cabinet for a mug, then to the coffee pot warming on the stove. "It's barely seven-thirty in the morning, nowhere near afternoon."

Relieved she hadn't scalded herself pouring the coffee, she moved back to the cabinets, trying to recall which one held the sugar. Luckily, it was door number one. She wasn't even going to attempt to find the cream in the fridge. Or Ruby, who was nowhere to be seen.

"Might as well be, for all the time you've wasted," he snarled.

So, that's the way he was going to play it. No civility. Just an iron fist. *Challenge accepted, asshat. Bring it on.*

"What are you doing here?" She stirred sugar into the coffee she couldn't possibly get down, watching the spoon go round and round instead of making eye contact with him.

"To lay down the rules," he said. "The first being that you and your boy haul your asses out of bed at the same time as the rest of the people on this ranch."

Her face flushed at his suggestion she was lazy, but as she turned and met his eyes, she fought to keep her gaze strong and voice confident. "Ruby told you last night I wouldn't be available for training until Monday, yet here you are, barging into my home, uninvited, wasting my time."

His eyes narrowed. "It's not your home yet, so don't get too snug."

"It's not yours either, so don't think you can charge in here whenever you feel like it, throwing your rules around."

He strode toward her, halting mere inches from her, the angry line of his lips placed threateningly close to hers, the ice in his eyes trying to freeze her in place, a tangible stream of fire coursing between them, eager to sear something.

Irrationally, given the circumstances, she longed to run her mouth across his, kiss away the hostility, make things right between them. Make him laugh like she used to be able to. Grip his hair and pull him in for a scorching kiss that would make him forget what had put him in a snit. But that tactic wouldn't work now, not this time, not in this reality.

"Something you need to remember about me," he said. "I don't tolerate insolence from those under me."

Under him? The asshat! "First of all, I'm not *under*

you. I'm a *partner* in this business arrangement. And second, I don't tolerate being bullied. *You* need to remember *that*."

He stepped closer, forcing her to step back to avoid touching him. The counter digging into her lower back and his wide chest all but crushing her breasts halted further retreat. He took the mug from her hand and set it behind her, then settled his palms on the counter on either side of her, trapping her, his eyes pinning her in place as effectively as his body was.

Her breath fluttered up in her throat at the force of his physical presence. Her nipples beaded hard against her shirt at the feel of his chest and hips and thighs against hers, of his breath against her mouth, and there was nothing she could do to stop the raging and unwanted reaction.

Though it was torture staring into his eyes, she refused to drop her gaze. She bit her tongue to stop the desire flowing through her at the scent of him, the feel of him, the remembered taste of him. After all this time, after what he'd done to her, how could it still be there, the same desire, tugging at her?

Because, you fool, it never left. But it hadn't been this burning, churning volcano in years. Now, in an instant, it was back, alive and ready to blow, eager to destroy everything in its path.

He leaned in, his knee easing between hers, his mouth settling near her ear. Lightning raced through her veins, breaking apart her breath in her throat. Her body remembered this, being this close to Josh, and was fighting to open up to what it knew should come next.

"Don't fuck with me, Charleigh." Josh kept his voice to a low whisper. "I promise, you won't like the results. I'm no longer the gullible boy you had wrapped around your little finger."

His harsh tone cracked her reverie like a fist to an eggshell, and though it took every ounce of will she could muster to stand her ground against him, she leaned back at the waist to face his hard stare. The subtle move thrust her pelvis against his, and she swore she felt the bulge between his legs harden. The surprising reaction shot an arrow of lust and power through her.

"Believe me, Josh, fucking with you is the last thing I want to do. And by the way…it's Mrs. Simms to you."

His eyes and face drew even harder. For a split second, he looked like he was going to slam his mouth onto hers in a punishing kiss that would make her regret crossing him and make her body and soul bend to his will. But then he dropped his hands to his sides and stepped back.

"Have it your way, *Mrs. Simms*." He said the name like it left a bad taste in his mouth. "Today. Monday morning you'd better be ready when I get here at seven. If you're not, you can pack your bags, and you and the boy can go back to whatever hell you came from, because I'm not going to waste my time if you're unwilling to me meet me half way."

He spun away from her and stormed toward the door.

She couldn't hold her tongue on a final stinging retort. "Pull off those shitkickers the next time you come into my house, Flores. I'm not here to clean up your messes."

Charleigh stayed on her feet until she heard the

screen door slam shut, then she stumbled to the table and dropped heavily into one of the chairs. Elbows propped on the table, she leaned her head in her hands. Seeing him again had shocked her more than she thought it would. It had zapped her strength, melted her bones, and popped open the stitches from the never-healed wounds in her soul.

All she wanted to feel for him was indifference, not white-hot passion. What she wanted to remember was the pain of his betrayal. But she remembered so much more. His kiss, his smell, his taste, his touch, the feel of him deep inside her as their bodies loved. It was all there in the pleasure that had rumbled through her like an earthquake when his body had pressed into hers. How could she hold her own against the force of nature that was this man?

Oh, Will. What have I gotten us into? I shouldn't have come here.

Ruby appeared from wherever she'd been and set the abandoned mug of coffee and a carton of cream in front of her, then took a seat next to her.

"When Josh's dad, Sam, took sick three years ago, Josh gave up his dream of becoming a vet and came home to take care of him and run the ranch. Took it over fully when Sam died months later. It's never been more successful. There's a drive in Josh to succeed that most men don't have. And he's got the smarts and gumption to back it up. That single-minded focus has made him a little rough around the edges, socially speaking, but Wyatt couldn't have picked a better person to help you run this place."

With a pat to Charleigh's shoulder, she crossed the floor to the stove. "Now let's get some breakfast in you.

Two eggs or three?"

"Thanks, Ruby, but I'll fix myself something when Derrick gets up," she said as her mind wrapped around the news Ruby had relayed. He had given up his dream for the ranch he said he hated and wanted to escape, but he hadn't been willing to give it up for her or his son. It was good reminder.

And what the hell was that comment about him being wrapped around her finger? He had it backward. She'd been the gullible one wrapped around his finger, so tight it had almost killed her when she'd been forced to rip herself from him.

****

"Why the fuck did you agree to this? It'll never work," Josh yelled to the windshield as he slammed the gear into second and the old pickup bumped and swerved over the rutted dirt lane that led to the pasture where Cole and the cowhands were working the roundup. His frustration was as much for himself as it was for the situation with Charleigh.

It had been a kick in the balls to see her standing there, as badass as ever yet somehow more vulnerable, and a little too thin, in that ragged, too-big T-shirt. She was even more beautiful than she'd been at eighteen. Maturity had sharpened her curves, sculpting a stunningly and incredibly sexy woman.

When she had strolled into the kitchen, her wild storm of hair sweeping down her back to her waist and across her breasts, her face still soft from sleep, that T-shirt showing off miles of long, smooth, tanned leg, he'd lost the ability to breathe—and think, since the bulk of his blood supply had rushed south of his belt buckle. A flood of memories had rushed in, memories of long-ago mornings he'd awakened next to her, her looking just like that.

Contrary to every grain of common sense he possessed, he had wanted to greet her not with harsh words but with a soul-connecting kiss. He'd wanted to seize her, pull her into him, and grind his body and mouth against her, drink her deep, fill his empty soul with her sweetness. Hell, in all honesty he'd wanted to do much more. Wanted to push that shirt up around her waist, lift her by her spread thighs, and thrust himself deep inside her as he had in that other life. His body remembered her, instinctively knew she was his and what he was supposed to do with her.

The unearthing of these memories pissed the hell out of him. All he wanted to feel for her was indifference, not lust. All he wanted to remember was her betrayal. But he felt and remembered so much more…so much of it good. His own weakness was what had caused him to lash out as he had, saying the first hateful thing that sprang to mind. All that reckless action had done was drive the wedge between them securely into place before they'd even had a chance to remove it.

Though he regretted his behavior, he was worried. If Charleigh didn't take hold and do her part, he didn't know what he'd do. Despite his threat, he couldn't force her from the ranch. Well, he could, but then he'd lose his last shot at Antelope Spring.

He rolled down the window, inhaled fall sage and piñon, hoping the spice in the rushing air would cleanse his mind of the mistakes of his youth, the memories of Charleigh, and the puzzling image filling his brain.

The T-shirt she'd been wearing was well-used,

frayed at the edges, faded to a soft green similar to the color of the paint he'd chosen for her walls, the logo on the chest barely visible. He'd recognized it instantly. It was the university-branded T-shirt he'd given her their last night together. She'd kept it. Worn the shit out of it. Why? What the hell did it mean?

Chapter Five

Derrick strolled into the kitchen minutes after Josh slammed out the door. Leaving Ruby to her chores, which at the moment was putting together a huge pot of green chile stew, Charleigh prepared their breakfast. Derrick dove into the bacon, eggs, and homemade biscuits and jam like he hadn't eaten in a week. In truth, it had been longer since he'd eaten this good. After cleaning up from breakfast, she dressed and spent the next several hours going over household tasks and schedules with Ruby.

At eleven o'clock, Ruby announced it was time to get dinner—apparently the noon meal—for the men working the roundup. She put Charleigh in charge of making sandwiches from thick slices of homemade bread and slabs of Bar S roast beef while she poured the green chile stew that had been bubbling on the stove into a two-gallon thermos. Thermoses of coffee and water and a plastic container of both chocolate and butterscotch brownies rounded out the meal. They boxed up everything and loaded it into the back of a ranch pickup. Charleigh didn't see the rental truck, which likely meant the hands had taken care of getting it back to town.

With Ruby present, Brutus was agreeable to simply eye them and not attack. He stayed in the shade and let loose an intermittent half-hearted woof as they climbed in and headed south along a rough dirt lane that had them bouncing all over the seat.

The large pasture was the scene of much activity. To Charleigh's untutored ears, it sounded like total cow chaos, with the frantic bawling of cows and calves splitting the air. Several large, metal holding pens were roughly arranged around the perimeter of the pasture, enclosing calves or cows, or both.

Several cowhands were astraddle horses, driving small groups of cattle toward one pen or another, occasionally hollering or flapping a rope to prod them along. Other men were separating calves from their mother cows and driving them through a chute. Josh worked alongside the others but appeared to be supervising the activities, because he occasionally gave direction to one or more of the hands, then observed another group, giving them direction as well.

At the pasture gate, Charleigh got out to open it, then closed it behind the pickup as it lumbered through toward where the men had begun gathering. They watched with hungry anticipation as she and Ruby dropped the tailgate and started spreading out the food. One man, about her age, approached her and held out his hand.

"Howdy, Miz Simms, I'm Cole Ledger."

Horace had told her that Cole was the Bar S foreman. "Good to meet you, Cole. Call me Charleigh."

"Ma'am," he said and touched his hand to his hat. "Didn't figure I'd see you today. Me and the boys wanted to give you time to settle in before we came around."

"Hi, I'm Derrick." Her son held out his hand to Cole, who took it.

"Hey, there, bud."

"Are you a cowboy?" Derrick asked, awe tinting his voice.

Cole chuckled. "I reckon so."

To the rest of the men, Cole introduced her as "the new boss, Miz Simms." After a flurry of hat tipping and "pleased to meet you, ma'ams," they tucked into the food.

Never having been this close to cows or to cowboys before, Derrick stared at everything in wide-eyed amazement. Some of the hands engaged him in conversation, and before long he was firing questions at them, his inquisitive nature ruling over his anxiety about the unfamiliar surroundings.

Josh was the last to come in, and her gaze tracked his every step. The determined set of his jaw marked a man used to doing things his way. His aura of aloof self-reliance and proficiency was immensely compelling. The woman in her felt it and instinctively responded to it on a visceral level. She tore her gaze away when his eyes met hers but returned to him while he filled his plate and quickly ate. Alone.

A half hour later, the men thanked them for the food, then drifted off to resume their duties. Ruby and Charleigh had packed up and were climbing into the pickup when Josh approached them.

"Charleigh. Just a moment," he said, his tone cool. "Since you're here, I'll explain the operation that's underway. Walk with me."

"I think Ruby's ready to get back to the house," she said.

He turned to the housekeeper. "No need to wait, Ruby. She'll ride back with me."

"I'm staying, too," Derrick said and stepped forward, stationing himself like a guard between Charleigh and Josh as if he sensed the man was a threat. Inquisitive and perceptive, her son.

Josh nodded his agreement, but she cupped a hand on Derrick's shoulder. "I'd rather you go back to the house." She looked questioningly to Ruby. "If it's okay with Ruby."

"Why, sure." Putting her hand at his back, Ruby started to lead him toward the pickup. "You and me'll whip up a batch of your favorite chocolate chip cookies."

"Hold on, son," Josh said to Derrick, his eyes flickering over him, then back to Charleigh. "This is an opportunity for the boy to learn as well."

Josh calling Derrick "son" spurred everything inside Charleigh to scream a resounding hell no. Swallowing it back, she responded calmly.

"I'd rather put off Derrick's training until I get more acquainted with our surroundings, so I can guide him, too."

Josh's eyes flashed, and he anchored the brim of his hat to his eyes, as if trying to mask or hold in the irritation and whatever other emotions flared within the blue depths. "Suit yourself." He walked away, toward the farthest pen of animals.

She helped Derrick into the pickup. After giving him a hug and a reminder to mind Ruby and to read two books, aloud, and practice his writing while she was gone, she stepped back and watched them drive off. It left her feeling more than a little panicked—and angry at Josh for bringing this up again when she'd already told him they needed time to settle before starting their training. But she was here, and she didn't want to get into an argument in front of the hands and make a bad impression.

"We're into the fall calf roundup," Josh jumped in when she'd caught up with him. "Last month, we separated the bulls from the cows. Now we're separating the calves from their mothers. Each calf is weighed and graded. The entire process takes—"

"Graded?"

"The process of deciding which calves will be retained as ranch stock and moved to a winter pasture and which will be placed in a holding pen for a short fattening-up period."

"For market?"

"For market."

Charleigh watched one of the hands separate a bellowing calf from its mother. The mother fought tenaciously to protect her baby. But it was a losing battle. The hand expertly maneuvered the calf into the pen where it was weighed and determined to be market bound.

A future decided in seconds based on a number.

She knew enough to know that this was the way of things on a ranch, but all she could think about was how she'd feel being separated from her child, never seeing him again. A knot of distress sat in her throat when she remembered that Josh might have the power to do that to her, to separate her from Derrick as neatly as that cowhand had separated the calf from its mother. Which was why he could never know Derrick was his son.

Realizing that Josh had stopped talking, she looked up to find him frowning at her, likely from reading the mother-emotions on her face. But then his gaze dropped to her hands clutching his sleeve. It was her touch that had earned that annoyed glare. She snatched her hands away, and his eyes returned to hers.

"Ranching is a business, Charleigh. You need to toughen up about every aspect of it, or you're never going to make it."

Anger surged at the ridicule and intolerance in his words, tone, and glare and evaporated any embarrassment she had experienced. "Don't let my empathy for the suffering of living things and my inexperience in this profession make you think I'm incapable. I'm tougher than you think, and I'll do whatever I have to do to make sure my son has a secure future. And unlike that mother, I won't lose."

She must have gotten through to him because, after that, he patiently explained every step of the process and answered all her questions without commenting on her reactions to them. She had to hand it to him. He made the complex information understandable, and she soon found herself engrossed and asking questions, eagerly awaiting his responses and the strum of his voice in her ear.

An hour or so later, they ended up back at the chute with the scales.

"As each calf is weighed," he explained, "we enter its ear tag number into a spreadsheet. The tag was placed on the calf at birth so we could identify which cow dropped the calf."

"Why is it important to know which cow dropped which calf?"

"We like to know which cows produce superior calves so that inferior mothers can be—"

"Put on birth control?" she teased.

A smile twitched at the corner of his mouth, lit his eyes, but he kept a rein on it. "Culled."

"Of course."

"We also cull the cows that don't produce at all."

"Sounds like the females are put to a pretty high standard of performance. What do the males contribute, other than their DNA material?"

"Steers are sold, too, and bulls are replaced every two years or so to keep the line strong."

"We're in the business of breeding."

"Yep." He nodded. "That's it for today. I need to check on the same work going on at my place. I'll give you a ride home." He left orders with Cole for the rest of the day, then led the way to his pickup.

Climbing into Josh's bucket of bolts was like climbing back in time. The pickup had been the one he'd driven when they'd been together. The bench seat had always been lumpy and cracked, but to two love struck teenagers, it had been a veritable love nest. It had absorbed their secrets, their scent, their imprints, the very essence of their love—probably still held them deep in its material flesh, a time capsule preserving a divine moment in time.

Did Josh feel her, smell her, think of her every time he climbed in? Nah. That was too sentimental a notion for someone as heartless as him.

They bounced down the washboard lane in silence except for the creaking and groaning of the pickup's suspension, Charleigh holding tightly onto the door handle. The vehicle and the road seemed to be conspiring to bounce her into her rightful place on the seat—right next to or on top of Josh—but she resisted with all her strength.

Then the pickup hit a particularly rough patch, and she was jarred loose from her death hold on the handle and thrown across the seat where she smacked up against him, her breasts pressed into his arm. At the last second, she caught herself from landing in his lap by bracing her hand high on his thigh, way too close to his crotch.

The heat simmering in his gaze matched the heat in her cheeks and seemed to say that he remembered the many times she had intentionally and eagerly pressed against him, had straddled him in this pickup, inviting him to take her breasts with his hands or his mouth.

"Rough road," she said and scrambled back to her side of the seat, taking a tighter grip on the handle.

As they pulled up to the house, she was preparing to hop out of the pickup and run inside before Brutus noticed her, but Josh spoke, halting her escape.

"We'll bring in another batch from the Davis pasture on Monday," he said as he shifted into neutral. "Your only job tomorrow is to have Cole show you around the various outbuildings."

"Does he live in the bunkhouse?" she asked.

Josh nodded. "He and Owen and Emmett." He stared out through the dirty windshield of the pickup, a gritting movement in his jaw, and adjusted his cap a little closer to his eyes, a move that used to mean that he was guarding his emotions.

She opened her mouth to say something to fill the silence but couldn't think of a thing. He didn't seem interested in chatting either. "Well, see you Monday," she said finally and reached for the handle.

He reached across her, his face close to hers, his arm across her breasts, not touching her but the sparks arcing between their bodies making it feel like he had.

She grabbed his arm. "What the hell are you doing?"

"Opening your door."

"I can open my own door, thank you."

He leaned back in his seat and motioned for her to go ahead.

She grabbed the handle and pulled. The door wouldn't budge. She tried again. And again. Several times. Nothing worked. She'd never had trouble opening it before. The smirk that had appeared on his face grew as did her frustrations. "What's wrong with this damn door?"

"Not a damn thing. It's just particular about who touches it." His tone told her he wasn't going to help her until she begged him for help.

She'd die before she asked him for help. She kept trying, sweat beading on her face the more she did. She rolled the window down. It stopped half way. Not enough room to climb out.

Well, shit. "Josh."

"Charleigh."

"I seem to be having trouble opening the door."

"I noticed."

"Instead of just sitting there *noticing* my distress, you could've stepped up to help me."

"I tried to help you, but instead of trusting me, you freaked out—"

"I did not freak out."

"—thinking I was going to kiss you or grab something."

She scoffed loudly to refute his accusation, but that's exactly what she'd thought. Worse, he knew it.

Even worse, the way his eyes flicked over her breasts when he said *grab something* caused her nipples to peak harder against her thin shirt, showing that that's what they'd thought, too.

"I promise you, *Mrs. Simms*, I'm not interested in doing either."

His insulting tone infuriated her and sharpened her tone to match. "And I'm relieved beyond words. Now would you please open the damn door so I can get the hell out of here?"

"Well, since you asked so nicely." He leaned toward her again, arm stretched across her chest, hooded eyes locked on hers. "I'm just going for the handle, sweetheart, nothing else."

For as long as she'd known him, his use of the term *sweetheart* had never been an endearment, only a slur. His voice, a sarcastic whisper on her face, said that hadn't changed. But it was a shock to be on the receiving end of that term.

He grabbed the handle and jerked it hard, the movement causing his arm to brush against her hard peaks. Her breath caught in her throat at the sparks it triggered.

The door swung open and cool air rushed in, hitting her flushed body, and Josh eased back to his side of the seat.

"You're welcome," he said.

Mumbling a curt "Thanks," she was about to climb out when Brutus appeared at the open door, growling and blocking her exit. She scrambled across the seat, right next to Josh. Brutus then jumped up into the pickup floorboard, his front paws on the seat, and barked. With a muffled shriek, she scooted into Josh's lap, straddling him, and leaned against his door, grabbing for the handle and pulling it. But this door was as particular as the other.

"Never thought I'd see this again," he said.

"See what?" She kept working the handle.

"You straddling me in this pickup." His low, silky tone drew her eyes to his, and his gaze held hers in a way he used to, and she couldn't look away.

"I'm just trying to get out of a difficult situation," she said and was surprised at how breathless she sounded.

"Like when you ran off with Will?"

Her lips parted, and her eyebrows furrowed at his words that seemed to suggest he thought she'd run off for no good reason.

"Mom? What are you doing?"

At Derrick's voice, she twisted on Josh's lap toward the house. Derrick had come out and was staring at them from the porch, cookie in his hand, chocolate streaking his mouth.

Interested in the opportunity for fresh chocolate-streaked meat, Brutus jumped out of the pickup and ran toward Derrick.

"Oh, God. Get out, get out," she said, frantically urging Josh to open the door and let her out, but the door was already swinging open as if he, too, had sensed her urgency. She scrambled out, him behind her, and took a step toward Derrick. "Get inside," she called out.

He rushed inside to safety, letting the screen door slam to, and Brutus turned toward her. Keeping her eyes on the dog, she backed up and ran smack dab into Josh. He shifted her behind him and knelt, stretching his hand out to the dog. Talking softly but firmly, Josh urged the dog toward him and away from the door.

Still growling, Brutus inched his way over and hesitantly sniffed the back of his hand. Josh slowly set his hand on his head and scratched his ears. Soon, the old dog leaned into the touch and plopped down on his haunches next to him, his tongue lolling out of his mouth.

"Go on in the house," Josh said quietly to her. "Move slowly."

Charleigh gave man and dog a wide berth as she made her way slowly to the door, eyes peeled for the impending attack. Brutus stayed put at Josh's side but kept his eyes on her, too, as if waiting for his opportunity.

Derrick pushed out through the door and jumped into her arms. With a final glance at Josh, she carried her son into the house, letting the screen door slam shut behind them.

****

Josh watched mother and son enter the house. Giving Brutus a final scratch, he stood and climbed into his pickup, shutting the doors. Brutus trotted back to the house and slumped down on the porch in front of the door, as if he were sulking because he was barred from the house.

He knew how the bristly mutt felt. He also would never be invited inside that house to partake in the love and laughter that emanated from the screen door alongside the tantalizing smell of Ruby's chocolate chip cookies. The warm welcome-home feeling was something he hadn't felt in a long time. And something he wasn't likely to feel in the near future. At least not in that house. Not with that woman.

After a moment contemplating the surprisingly sharp prick of that reality, he shifted his pickup into gear and pointed it toward his ranch, thoughts of Charleigh haunting him. Of course, that was nothing new. Every fucking time he climbed into this pickup, her ghost assailed him. Pieces of her—her scent, echoes of her laughter and sighs, her fingerprints, her very essence—were everywhere, filling every crack in the lumpy seat, in the hazy film that streaked the windows, on the faded radio knobs and buttons.

Over the years, he had learned to ignore her ghost. But having her sit in the pickup beside him, in the flesh, having her straddle his hips, was an assault his body was finding impossible to ignore.

Before he headed into the pasture where Quino had the hands at work, he fished his phone from his pocket and texted Beth to see if she was up for an unscheduled but sorely needed visit tonight.

****

That night, Charleigh realized she'd have to postpone her training on Monday to register Derrick for school. She dreaded another confrontation with Josh but could think of no way around it. Getting his cell number from Ruby, she called him.

A woman answered on the second ring.

Surprise thickened her tongue and flipped her stomach up into her throat, and for a moment, she couldn't speak. "I'm...I need to speak with Josh."

"He's in the shower."

Her eyes squeezed shut tight at the news, like a reaction to being punched in the stomach. "I'll call back later." She hit the end-call button.

Instead of throwing the phone across the room like she wanted, to feel the satisfaction of having it smash to pieces against the wall, she dropped down onto the couch, her stomach spinning with jealousy and distress.

He was with another woman.

She knew it was a possibility, that he'd have a woman, maybe even a wife and kids, but she hadn't realized it would hurt this much to confirm it.

The phone was still gripped in her hand when he called back. She delivered her news matter-of-factly and, as she had anticipated, he wasn't happy.

"I'd planned for you to take over for Emmett entering spreadsheet data, which would free him up for other duties."

"I can still make it," she said, "probably before ten."

Josh released an irritated huff. "Look, I realize you have responsibilities to the boy, but you have responsibilities to the ranch, too, and you can't take time off every time he needs some little something. Ranch work can't wait."

Even after all these years, he still knew where all her buttons were and how to push every single one of them, and she was in no mood for him right now.

"First of all, my son's name is *Derrick*, not *the boy*. Second, I haven't forgotten any of my responsibilities, and I certainly don't need any reminding. I just need a chance to get us settled in. And third, Derrick always comes first. I'm his mother. That's my most important responsibility, and I'd appreciate you not berating every decision I make regarding him."

"I'm not berating anything. I know we're both uncomfortable in this ridiculous situation, but I don't want us to fall into the habit of looking for excuses to avoid each other. That's all I'm saying. This will only work if we both do our part and keep our personal feelings out of it."

"I don't have any personal feelings other than wanting you to cut me some slack where Derrick is concerned and stop trying to bully me into complying with every demand that crosses your mind."

"The only demand I've made is that you fulfill the obligations you agreed to. If you can't do that, I'll call Horace in the morning and tell him the deal's off. You won't have to waste time getting *Derrick* registered for school, because you'll both be gone before the week is over."

The need to strike back at his rude and hurtful attitude was instant and strong. "You wouldn't do that. You must have wanted Antelope Spring pretty badly to agree to this *ridiculous* situation. You'll lose it for good." Her biting tone would probably rain down his wrath on her, but she couldn't temper it.

"You must have more to lose than I do, sweetheart, if you agreed to come back to this shithole."

Charleigh clamped her mouth shut on a rough scoff. She wasn't going to have that talk. But he was right about her lack of choices. Without this ranch, they'd be homeless. On the streets of this shithole.

He took advantage of her silence to bark his next order. "When you're done, come to the holding pasture where we were today." He hung up before she could respond.

Chapter Six

Charleigh left Derrick's classroom with more than a little trepidation about entrusting her son to this school, based in no small part on memories of her own rough time in a Chismes Point school. Having Josh back then had gotten her through the difficulties. She hoped Derrick would find someone, too.

Whether it was the memories of those days with Josh on the loose or the unseasonable warm October weather, the cab of the pickup grew stifling on the drive back to the ranch. She shrugged out of her hoodie and rolled the window down. The air blowing in filled the interior with the aroma of sage and piñon, scents that triggered memories of making love with Josh in his parked pickup, windows down to let the country air cool their heated, naked bodies.

To clear her mind of those images, she turned her attention outside the window, to the borrow ditches alongside the narrow two-lane road where summer's last sunflowers were tenaciously shining their faces up to the sun, determined to survive. Beyond that, cattle— her cattle—dotted the fields, grazing on dried grass. Another couple of months would likely bring snow, but right now, the weather was perfect, the sun bright in a cloudless blue sky.

She thought about stopping at the house to change out of her jean skirt, short-sleeved blouse, and sandals into jeans, a T-shirt, and sneakers, but she was ahead of schedule getting to the pasture and wanted to show Josh she was a woman of her word. It wasn't like she'd be riding a horse, roping, branding, or anything active today. She'd be sitting at a table and keying in numbers on a laptop, activities appropriate with her clothing. Decision made, she continued on.

As before, the area was alive with activity and the sound of bellowing cattle. Dust boiled from the hoofs of horses and milling bovine. Bringing the pickup to a halt by the gate, she climbed out. Cole tossed her a wave and a smile, jogged across the hard, stubbly ground, and opened the gate for her.

"Hey, Miz Simms."

"Cole, I told you, it's Charleigh."

"Yes, ma'am." He gave her a quick once-over. "You're looking mighty dolled-up for ranch work."

"I just came from getting Derrick registered for school, and I didn't want to waste time changing clothes."

"That itchy to get to work, are ya?"

She spied Josh in the pasture astride his horse. His eyes met hers in a lingering glint before he rode off in pursuit of a rambunctious calf, lasso twirling overhead. "You bet," she answered.

"Well, then, let's get you at it."

Cole took her elbow and escorted her to where the folding table had been set up, the laptop on it, a folding chair beside it. He explained her task and after ensuring she had no questions, left her and joined the other hands.

He weighed the calf in the chute, called out the tag number and weight, then pushed it through to the holding pen. She entered the figures into the spreadsheet and tried not to dwell on the fact that many of the figures she wrote represented a little calf she likely was sending to its death.

The morning passed slowly with nothing to do but listen for numbers, note them, and shoo away flies. The higher the sun rose, the hotter its rays beating down on her bare head became. She had acquired a good base tan from living in California, but her head, face, and arms were stinging after a couple hours in the intense direct sun, and she was wishing she'd grabbed Will's old baseball cap. She'd wanted to preserve it for Derrick, but tomorrow she'd bring it to preserve her skin until she could buy her own hat and some sunscreen.

At eleven-thirty, Ruby's vehicle lumbered up to the gate with the noon meal. Charleigh opened the gate for her, then helped Ruby set up. After the hands had filled their plates, she filled her own and dropped down in a patch of shade created by one of the pickups, grateful for a half hour's respite from the sun.

Cole approached her, plate in hand. "Mind if I join you, Miz Simms?"

"Cole, I'm going to fire you if you don't start calling me Charleigh," she teased.

He grinned and nodded. "Yes, ma'am." He settled beside her and took a bite out of his fried chicken. "So, is it all you thought it would be?"

"Ranch work, you mean?" At his nod, she grinned. "To be honest, I didn't know enough about ranching to even form an expectation."

"Well, you got yourself a fine teacher in Josh. And me and the boys will be glad to help however we can."

She took a bite of macaroni salad. "You wouldn't happen to have another hat in your pickup I could use this afternoon?"

He grinned and shook his head. "I noticed your face was redder than a cooked beet, but I'm too much of a gentleman to point it out."

She grinned back. "Are you enough of a gentleman to give me your hat?"

He sheepishly dropped his eyes to his plate. "No, ma'am, I ain't."

She laughed. "That's all right. I'll tough it out today."

"Begging your pardon, ma'am, uh, Charleigh, but it might be better for you to call it a day 'til you get a proper hat and clothing."

"No, really, it's not that bad," she said, waving away his concern. "Besides, I want to do my part."

"Doing your part's all well and good, but having a heatstroke doing it is another." His eyes searched the area for a moment, then he whistled through his teeth and called out, "Flores."

No, no, no, don't come over here

But Josh was already making his way over, a frown on his face. Did the man ever smile?

Out of the corner of her eye, she saw Cole nod his head toward her. "Charleigh's probably had enough sun for today."

Josh turned that frown on her. "Where's your hat?"

"I don't have a hat."

His eyes scanned her outfit from her thin cotton blouse and jean skirt to the sandals on her feet. "Is this your idea of how to dress for range work?"

"I don't have any range clothes either."

"Why the hell not?"

"If you remember, I only got here three days ago and you've been threatening me with dire consequences if I dared deviate from carrying out your orders." Embarrassed to be dressed down in front of Cole and the other men in hearing distance, her response was sharper than she normally would have allowed it to be.

"You've known for weeks you were moving here. Why didn't you buy the right clothing before you left California?"

Not for anything in the world would she tell him that she'd barely had food money. Buying clothes, especially expensive cowboy boots and hats, had been the least of her worries. "Since I've never done this kind of work, I had no idea what we'd need."

"But common sense told you it was a miniskirt and sandals?" Before she could respond, he turned to Cole. "Tell Emmett to take over for Mrs. Simms."

"Will do." Cole said and sat there, continuing to eat.

Josh kept his gaze locked on him. "Now would be a good time."

Cole's gaze went from Josh to her, then back to Josh. "You bet." He stood and headed toward a group of cowhands.

Josh reached down and took hold of her arm at the elbow. "Let's go."

She stiffened, refusing to budge an inch. "Where?"

"Into town for the right gear."

She pulled her arm from his grip. "It's not your responsibility to take me shopping."

"Having the right gear is part of your wellbeing. And your wellbeing is my responsibility."

108

"Make me a list, and I'll buy what I need this weekend."

He crouched down next to her, his knee on the ground beside her thigh, his hand braced beside her head on the pickup she leaned against. The scent of sweat and dirt, cow and horse, hard work and…Josh…ignited goosebumps all over her body, and she drew in a sharp, quick breath.

He leaned in, his mouth at her ear. "You either get up on your own and get in the pickup, or I'll pick you up, throw you over my shoulder, and carry you there."

His warm breath teased her nipples to high, tight points in her bra cups. "You wouldn't dare," she whispered back.

He eased back to stare into her face, the smirk on his lips and in his eyes saying *try me*.

It wasn't just anger that curled her hands into tight fists. It was the need to stop herself from reaching up, grabbing his face, and pulling that smirking mouth to hers. She licked her lips, and his gaze captured the movement. When his eyes lifted back to hers, there was a different fire in them that she recognized, and it turned the air between them thick and pulsing until she couldn't breathe. She had to get away. The only way to do that was to give him what he wanted.

"Fine," she said, the word whispering from her mouth, brushing his lips.

He licked his lips, as if taking her word, her breath, her taste into his mouth. "Fine, you'll walk? Or fine, I'll carry you?"

A part of her wanted to risk the danger of choosing the second option, just to test him. If they'd been alone, she would have. But with witnesses, she'd play it safe.

"I'll walk."

The expression on his face seemed to say he wished she had chosen the second option. He stood and offered her his hand to help her up.

She thrust her plate into his hand and scrambled up on her own as gracefully as she could without flashing anyone.

His hand at her back as if he thought she'd bolt, he trundled her over to where Ruby stood by the ranch pickup, accepting thanks from one of the hands for the food.

Josh handed Charleigh's plate to the housekeeper. "The Flying F hands are in the south pasture today. You know how to get there to take them their dinner?"

Ruby nodded. "Quino filled me in last night when he dropped off the check."

"Good. I appreciate you being willing to take on extra work. The hands were talking mutiny if we didn't get them your food."

She chuckled. "No trouble at all. Charleigh was agreeable, so why not. I'm tickled they like my cooking that much."

"I'll check in with you tonight to see how it went. But right now, Charleigh and I are headed into Wilton to buy gear. You need anything while we're out?"

"I don't reckon so, but I appreciate you checking."

"I'll have her home before supper."

Ruby barely had time to nod before Josh led Charleigh to his pickup. Once she was in, he slammed the door, then climbed in on his side, slammed the door, and fired up the engine.

Fuming at his highhandedness, she waited until they were out of earshot of the hands, then she let him have it. "You asshat! How dare you treat me like that in front of Cole and the men. You're supposed to educate me, but all you've done is bully me, criticize me, and embarrass me."

"Educating means correcting your behavior," he shot back in the same tone. "I do that by being direct and honest, not by blowing sunshine up your miniskirt and making you feel good."

She fought the urge to tug on her skirt, which wasn't that short, dammit. "Well, congratulations, you haven't sent any sunshine my way. Not once. All you've done is make me feel stupid and burdensome."

"What do you want? To be carried around on my shoulders like some princess?"

"I want you to show me some respect."

"You *earn* respect around here. It's not something that's handed out, like goodies at Halloween."

"And you're saying I haven't earned it."

"You haven't done shit to earn it."

"I also haven't done shit to earn your hostility, but that's all you've given me since I got here." She glared at him, trying not to let emotions overwhelm her. "I'm running completely blind in this unfamiliar, uncomfortable situation that I didn't initiate, and you're punishing me for it. And that's just plain hateful. And if you plan to use this method of *educating* with my son, I swear you'll never get near him."

"Jesus, Charleigh, I'm not punishing you. Ranching is a tough business, and I wouldn't be doing my job if I sugarcoated everything for you."

She crossed her arms, then uncrossed them when she felt herself being jostled toward Josh's side of the seat. Using her hands to brace herself, she'd made a mental note to talk to Cole about getting this damn road graded. "Bullshit. You *are* punishing me, and we both know why."

"Why?"

"Those personal feelings you mentioned the other night. Wyatt put you in this situation where you had to see me again, and you're punishing me for it because you…" The words stuck in her throat, and she turned away from him and stared out the side window, swallowing hard.

"Because I what?" he demanded.

"You hate me." Damn frustration for making her voice crack.

He didn't answer. He didn't need to. The truth was written on his angry face, in his tense body, his fist gripping the wheel, his jaw working. She'd seen it that first morning, too, when he looked at her with eyes as cold and hard as a glacier.

Josh hated her.

The man who had once been her warm, safe world hated her. The hard truth saddened her but also worried the hell out of her. Not even a week together and all they'd done was fight. Would they even make it a year?

"I don't hate you," he said a minute later, no sarcasm sharpening the edges of his tone. "This is new to me, too…teaching someone how to run a ranch who has never set foot on one until a few days ago. And yes, our history makes it more complicated."

She hadn't thought about it from his point of view. Two greenhorns, one a five-year-old boy, thrust into his charge, along with managing one of the largest ranches in the state—and managing his own—and dealing with whatever emotions might be left over from the days when they'd been lovers and their sudden heartbreaking ending. The new perspective pushed her to formulate a solution.

"Let's call a do-over," she said, looking his way. It was how they'd resolved the few arguments they'd had when they were together. It was how she and Will had done it, too, although Will had usually just given in to keep the peace.

"What do you have in mind?" he asked.

"You promise to be kinder and less overbearing in your lessons, and I'll promise to be… I don't know. What do you want from me?"

"Obedience."

"Obedience?" She scoffed. "Yeah, right. You going to tie me up with your rope? Lash me with your whip? Torture me with your spurs? Is that what you're into these days?"

His eyes went back and forth from the road to her. "Dammit, Charleigh. I don't mean it that way."

"Then what do you mean?"

"I want you to do what I tell you to do, but I want you to do it because you recognize that I have your best interests in mind."

"You're talking about trust."

"Yes."

"Trust, like respect, has to be earned," she said.

"You don't trust me?"

She had trusted him—implicitly, blindly, stupidly—and it hadn't turned out well for her. Now he expected her to put her and Derrick's life in his hands? She wasn't sure she could give him that much free rein. "How can I? I don't know you."

His mouth drew tight, as if her revelation upset

him. But what was the feeling behind it? Anger? Frustration? Disappointment? She studied his profile but couldn't decipher it.

Then he braked the pickup, downshifted, and turned toward her, pinning her with his gaze. "You used to trust me."

Yes, she had...before he left her when she'd needed him the most and cheated on her when he'd told her he loved only her. "Things have changed." *Understatement.*

"So much that you'd think I'd hurt you? Or your boy?"

He meant physical pain when it was emotional pain she worried about. But clarifying that distinction would only open old wounds and drive the wedge between them deeper. Truth was, despite their passionate past and their rocky present, she knew he wouldn't ask her to do something that would harm them. So she'd try. Try to trust. Because they could accomplish more if they weren't fighting. It wouldn't be easy, for either one of them, but knowing they were in it together, both trying, both working toward the same goal, might somehow make it more doable.

"How about I promise to try to trust you with all things ranch related," she said.

"And stop questioning everything I say," he fired back.

"I'm going to question you, Josh. That's the way I learn. I'll try to be less—"

"Antagonistic?" he said.

"Reactive."

He stuck out his hand. "Shake on it."

Shaking on it also had been part of their resolution,

114

followed by hot sex.

She slid her hand into his. It was rough with evidence that he worked long, hard hours. Day in, day out. Evidence that he knew what he was doing. His hands hadn't been this rough when he'd been hers, but even back then, the work-laid callouses had provided just the right amount of friction on her soft skin to flick her desires into full-on lust in a matter of moments.

Even now, after so long, her body knew the proper reaction. Her nipples rolled up into hard points that reached out to him, the sudden action tugging on her womb and releasing a tickling arousal between her legs to prepare it for what it thought was next—sex with Josh.

Somehow, the pickup cab was getting smaller and tighter and hotter, making her lungs work double-time to squeeze out breaths. It didn't help that they weren't shaking hands. They were holding hands. And each other's eyes.

The pickup lurched forward, demanding his attention and breaking their connection. The after-effects of being locked in Josh's heated gaze brought on a sudden shiver, and she turned away and stared out the window but was unable to focus on anything in her line of vision. Thankfully, he didn't talk. He just shifted into gear and headed on.

At the main highway, he turned west toward Wilton. Some miles down the road, however, he swerved off the paved road onto a gravel road, rumbled over a cattle guard, and headed back north. She remembered this road. It was one they had sometimes driven down to get to a cutoff route where they went to park and make love when they couldn't go to the pond.

"Where are you going?" she asked. "This isn't the road to Wilton."

"That look in your eyes made me think you'd like to check out one of our old haunts." He grinned and winked at her.

"What?" The little crack in her voice, her rounded eyes, and the chills stampeding up her thighs revealed her full-blown panic at his idea.

He laughed. "Relax. I'm joking. You used to have a sense of humor."

She reached out and slapped his arm. "You used to be funny."

A grin still on his face, he explained. "This work pickup is too slow and uncomfortable for an hour's drive to town, and with no belts, it's not street-safe. I'm headed home to pick up other transportation." He shot her a sideways look. "That okay with you, Mrs. Simms?"

His teasing tone surprised her, pleased her. He was trying. "As long as you don't take too long, Mr. Flores," she replied in the same tone. "We're burning daylight."

Burning daylight had been one of his sayings when they were together. Whenever she was running late, his go-to way of telling her to hurry up was, *c'mon, baby, we're burning daylight.* His little grin and sideways glance told her he remembered. It lit her up inside. Damn his sexy hide.

The road swept through shrubby brush intermingled with gamma and other grasses and slowly curved west toward a towering, rocky, sandstone escarpment. After a while, the road lifted and cut into a boulder-strewn area of prickly pear cactus and small, stunted piñon, arriving at last on a more or less level straightaway that stretched toward a cluster of buildings at the foot of the escarpment.

The two-story Spanish colonial had been built to stand the test of time. Roof tiles a rusty orange capped an off-white stuccoed structure and blended in with the rich sandstone backdrop. A short driveway split off from the gravel road and snaked up toward the house while the main road proceeded north for a short way before dropping down into a small depression and leading to a number of outbuildings.

He'd never talked much about the home his great-grandfather had built for his bride nearly a hundred years ago, other than he couldn't wait to get away from it. And she'd never seen it when they were together. He always said he didn't want to run into his dad, who was usually drunk and in a foul mood. But she had always harbored the suspicion that it was because he was ashamed of his home or ashamed of her.

By the look of the place, it had been her.

"Josh, it's beautiful here. The way you always described it, I was expecting a shanty of sticks and stones in a pile of dirt and weeds."

"I've been updating it," he said as he pulled the pickup around to the back of the house and stopped at a detached three-car garage.

She didn't even flinch when he reached over and opened her door. They got out, and he went into the garage, momentarily reappearing behind the wheel of an SUV. He opened her door before she could, and she climbed in and buckled up.

Minutes down the road, a thought struck her. She glanced at the clock on the dash. Twelve-eighteen. "Is that the right time?"

He glanced at it, then his watch. "Yeah."

"I have to go back home."

"Why?"

"Derrick gets out of school at one o'clock. We won't have time to get to Wilton and back by the time he gets home at two."

"Ruby'll be at the house."

"Today was his first day at his new school."

"So?"

"It's important for me to be there to share it with him." She put her hand on his arm. The spark in that simple touch burned her hand like she'd been branded, and she jerked it back. "Josh, please don't fight me over this. Derrick and I will drive in on Saturday and do our shopping. I promise."

"We'll pick him up so he can get some clothes, too."

"That's not—"

"It *is* necessary. The boy—Derrick needs clothes, too. Besides that, he and I need to get acquainted." He shot her a questioning glance. "It's either call Ruby to watch after him, or you and I pick him up. Those are your options."

"I don't remember you being so bossy."

A grin sparkled in his eyes. "And I don't remember you being so disagreeable to everything I suggested."

There was a time she'd been agreeable to most everything he'd wanted from her. And had done it eagerly. "Get Derrick."

"As you wish."

"Except…"

He released a sigh. "What?"

"The checkbook's at the house."

"The ranch has an account at the store we're going to. You can charge everything you need."

With no more excuses handy, Charleigh settled back and tried to ignore Josh during the drive to Derrick's school, but the man positively radiated masculine potency. Try as she might, she was powerless to keep her eyes averted.

With the driver's window rolled down to catch the fall air and one elbow stuck out the window, he effortlessly steered the SUV down the road as casually indifferent to his effect on her libido as he was to the condition of the battered, sun bleached, sweat-stained cap pulled low on his brow. She felt helplessly drawn to how his jeans, faded to a soft blue the color of his eyes, gripped his long, strong legs. And the way they lovingly cupped the hefty bulge between his legs was a work of art.

From the top of that thought, it was an easy hop to wondering about his sex life and the woman who had answered his phone. Was it just sex between them? Or were they committed? She wanted to ask, but she'd die first.

More than any other single thing in the world, she wanted to reach across the cracked seat and touch him. Wanted to scoot over next to him, flip his hat off, and run her fingers through his hair the color of sun-kissed wheat, like she had when he was hers. Wanted to run her hands over the muscled chest and stomach and beyond as she had when he had welcomed and encouraged her caresses. Wanted to feel the heat of his body burn against hers. Wanted to see if he still tasted the same, felt the same, kissed the same, loved the same.

He caught her staring. She looked away but couldn't stop her rapid pulse, couldn't cool the heat blooming in her face and in her body. For the rest of the ride, she willed her gaze to stay focused on the fence posts streaking past and not on the man beside her she wanted to strip, straddle, and ride to completion.

****

Josh was acutely aware of Charleigh in the seat beside him, red faced and so goddamned beautiful it made his chest hurt. Being this close to her had ramped up his libido to a point that all he wanted was to stop the pickup in the middle of the road and yank her into his arms. Taste her lips and her hot skin. Slide off her panties and pull her onto his lap, so she could straddle his hips and envelop his throbbing hardness like she'd done hundreds of times. And ease this damned need that had burned inside him for nearly six years.

But he wouldn't do that, not even if she initiated it. She had left him, become someone else's wife and had a child with him, and it still ate at him like a cancer he'd never been able to get rid of. But, oh, he had loved her. More than anything in his life. He'd been scared to admit how much. To her. To himself. And it had cost him.

But how could she love him so completely for over two years and after a single, stupid fight, and without a single word, a simple goodbye, a hastily written note, leave him? What kind of woman did that? He'd asked himself that question thousands of times and had never been able to answer it to his satisfaction.

Now that she was here beside him, within arm's reach, a finger touch away, he could ask. But he'd die first. Because he wasn't sure he could handle hearing her answer. That she'd never really loved him, that he had been only a pawn in her plan to get a husband who'd get her out of her dead-end life. When he wouldn't play, she simply moved on to a more profitable choice.

Not that it mattered now. She was part of his past, and these longings in his gut were merely echoes of that past, remnants of a fantasy, a stain that couldn't be lifted. But he didn't hate her as she'd accused. Far from it, he decided as he wondered yet again how it would be to have her in his bed once more, bucking under his body, moaning his name as she came.

He arched his hips up slightly to try to adjust the hard-on in his jeans that was wondering why the hell it wasn't already inside her. He'd seen the need sparking in her eyes. He'd seen her nipples pucker against her shirt earlier, and he could smell her sweet arousal. She smelled the same. He bet she tasted the same. He licked his lips. After all these years, he could still taste her. Damn. It was as clear as his hard-on. He wanted her. Maybe if he took her to bed, satisfied the craving, he'd see the desire end.

Not fucking likely.

Their fragile do-over agreement might help them work better together, but he wasn't holding his breath. It was obvious she was still too feisty of a woman to bow to his every wish, even if it was for her own good. But she said she was willing to try. And she'd shaken on it.

But then, she'd also promised to love him forever. Clearly, she was a lying, cheating woman who didn't know shit about keeping her word.

Chapter Seven

Josh pulled to a stop in front of the elementary school, and he and Charleigh climbed out just as a group of kids ran out of the building toward a half dozen parked yellow school buses. A couple of minutes later, Derrick walked out with a blonde girl about his age, and Charleigh headed toward them. The little girl hugged him then ran off toward the buses. When he saw Charleigh, he ran to her, a bright smile on his face.

"Hey, puppy." Charleigh hugged him, then with an arm around his shoulders, led him the few feet to where Josh leaned on the front of the SUV. "How was school?"

Derrick's smile vanished the second his steely, unblinking gaze zeroed in on Josh. "Fine."

"Do you like your teacher?" Charleigh asked. "Ms. Barnes?"

"Sure."

"What did you guys do today?"

Derrick's gaze left Josh and settled on his mother. "Why is he here?"

Josh had seen that look in others eyes often enough in his twenty-four years to know what it meant. The emotion in that boy's crystal blue eyes was pure, unadulterated suspicion.

Charleigh stepped in as if she had read it in his tone. "This is Mr. Flores. You saw him the other day.

Remember? He's managing the ranch and helping us learn to run it."

Sizing Josh up carefully, Derrick stepped forward and manfully stuck out his little hand, more because it was expected than because he wanted to, and grasped Josh's in a firm handshake. "Hello, Mr. Flores."

Yep, definitely suspicion in that low tone.

"Derrick," Josh said with a small nod. "Call me Josh."

The boy said nothing, just kept eyeing him as if he had three noses and they were all breathing fire.

"Josh is taking us to Wilton so we can buy some ranch clothes," Charleigh said.

The kid's surprised gaze flew to her. "We have money?"

Her sunburned face turned even redder. "Let's get you buckled in," she said quickly and bustled him into the backseat.

Josh wasn't quite sure what Derrick's comment meant, but he tucked it away, with the few other pieces of disjointed information he'd collected about Charleigh. Soon, he'd have enough pieces to see the full picture about her and her life, why she was really here, and why she had left him. And he needed the full picture before he could decide whether he could trust her. Right now, he didn't trust her any more than Derrick trusted him.

During the drive into Wilton, Charleigh tried to engage Derrick in small talk, but he was too busy giving Josh the stink eye in the rearview mirror to have any of it. If this sullen behavior was what Josh had to look forward to for the next year, it wasn't going to be a pleasant time for any of them, especially Derrick, because he wouldn't put up with that shit. He didn't know what kind of a father Will had been, but based on Derrick's behavior, he'd been indulgent and lax.

It was a relief when they pulled up in front of the store. The three of them hit the boys' clothing section first, selecting jeans, shirts, socks, and underwear, as well as leather gloves, a work hat, a jean jacket, and a winter coat. As each article of clothing was added to the pile, Derrick's eyes grew wider and searched Charleigh's face as if verifying she actually intended to buy it all.

Josh had wandered several aisles over to inspect kids' boots when he overheard Derrick bargaining with her.

"Mom, I really, really need new shoes for school. If I put some other things back, can we get them?"

This was the boy's second comment that suggested his family didn't condone excessive spending habits. It was something Josh could identify with. His family had been land rich but cash poor, which meant they wore clothing not until it no longer fit well, but until it fell apart. Even then, a new use was often found for it from dust and grease rags to quilt squares.

The Simmses had never suffered such problems. So why was this rich Simms boy acting as if getting new shoes and clothes was like winning the lottery?

Derrick held out one sneakered foot. "These are too small, and when I run, my toes hurt," he said to Charleigh. "And some guy in school pointed at them and called me a hayseed. The other kids laughed. What's a hayseed?"

Josh rejoined them. "Better pick out new sneakers while we're here," he told Derrick. You're about to grow out of those."

Derrick looked up at him, eyes wide, mouth open. "I get work boots and sneakers?"

"You can't wear work boots to school. People'll get the idea you're a hayseed."

"What's a hayseed?" he asked.

Josh settled his hand on Derrick's back and steered him toward the shoes. "Something you'll never be if I have anything to say about it."

For some odd reason, he already felt a protectiveness toward the boy. And as long as he was responsible for his wellbeing, he'd be damned if Derrick would go through the teasing he had in elementary school because he had to wear beat up work boots and threadbare jeans.

Along with the sneakers and work boots, they selected a pair of dress boots that Derrick insisted he'd never need. Josh then helped Charleigh select the items she'd need. She acquiesced on every item he suggested until they came to her jeans. He argued with her about the style and fit she'd chosen, saying they were for work not a fashion show. She argued it was none of his business what size or kind she wore. He gave in, but the argument had ratcheted up the tension between them.

When he had inadvertently followed her into the lingerie section, she rounded on him and shot him a stop-right-there glare.

"Are you going to pick out my bras and panties, too?" she said, the words heavy with annoyance. "Make me model them so you can tell me whether you think they fit?"

Because he was a red-blooded man who appreciated the beauty of a woman's body, especially hers, which had fit his like it was made for him, her idea had an immediate appeal and lifted a wicked grin to his lips as his gaze crawled over her.

Charleigh's curves appeared as luscious as they'd been when his hands and mouth had free rein to explore every inch of them. His hands itched now to reach out and weigh her breasts in his palms, cup her rounded hips as he fit her against his angles, grip her perky ass as she rode his erection.

But he wasn't stupid or entitled, so he made do with eyeballing her physique. Since she didn't look like she'd put on an ounce of weight over the years, despite having given birth to Derrick, it was a safe bet that her bra and panty sizes hadn't changed.

His hazy gaze met her steamy glare. "You're a 36D in bras and a small in panties. Color is up to you, Mrs. Simms."

Leaving her with her mouth agape, he turned and retraced his steps to the menswear section to put some space between them before he shocked them both and took her up on her dare. While he was here, he'd pick out a shirt for himself. The season for get-togethers was coming up, and he didn't want to look like a hayseed either. Besides that, he needed time to settle the desire that had flared throughout his body as his eyes had traveled down the mine-filled memory lane.

As the three of them headed toward the SUV with their packages, the aroma of grilling burgers coming from the café down the way caught Derrick's attention.

He rushed over and peered in through the window. "Mom, I'm starving. Really starving."

"Ruby will probably have dinner—uh, supper— ready when we get home," she said. "And we already spent a lot of money."

Derrick's face dropped, but he didn't argue.

"You know, I could go for a burger," Josh said to Derrick, rubbing his own growling stomach. "Your mom and I skipped dinner."

Derrick's mouth lifted into a hopeful grin, but he still looked to Charleigh for permission.

He was the most well-mannered kid Josh had ever known, but Josh wondered about the tight rein Charleigh and Will had to keep on him to get him that way. Kids needed an amount of freedom, with a gradually lengthening lead rope, so they could learn to properly handle freedom when they got older. Without practice, in small, manageable steps, they'd never get good at managing their lives.

Not that he was an expert on kids.

At Charleigh's hesitation, her eyes going to Josh's, he somehow inherently knew she was silently asking about the money. Three comments about money. *Three trees is a forest.*

He nodded briefly and winked. "My treat."

"No need to do that," she said as if the thought of him buying her anything was abhorrent.

"Call Ruby, tell her you won't be home to eat." If his tone couldn't settle the matter, maybe his pulling open the door and guiding her in would.

Derrick needed no convincing. He flashed Josh a full-fledged genuine smile and sauntered in. "I think we need fries, too."

Josh grinned back, glad for this breakthrough with the boy. Food. Of course. It's what had worked with him as a kid. "You bet."

Only a few of the dozen or so tables and booths

were occupied, so they had their pick. Josh chose the booth that gave them a view of the street and the SUV with their packages locked inside. His granddad had told him a man needed to sit facing the door so he can protect his family, his possessions, and himself. Charleigh and Derrick weren't his family and he wasn't worried about being robbed, but the long-ingrained habit was too strong to ignore. He slid in.

"Let's wash our hands," Charleigh said to Derrick, her hand on his shoulder stopping him from climbing in beside Josh.

"Josh isn't washing his hands," Derrick said.

She looked at Josh, lifted an eyebrow, the message in the gesture telling him he needed to be a good role model.

He slid out of the booth. "I was just headed that way."

"I'll go with you," Derrick said.

Charleigh quickly countered the idea. "I'll take you."

"Mom, I'm five years old. I'm too old to go to the girls' bathroom."

"He can go with me," Josh said and headed that way, Derrick beside him.

"Do you need help?" Josh asked him when they got to the bathroom and he saw Derrick stretching up on his toes to reach the faucets and soap.

"No, thanks."

They washed up in silence.

When they got back, Derrick climbed onto Josh's side of the booth. Wanting to face the door, Josh slid in beside him. Glancing around, he saw Charleigh at the café's phone, probably calling Ruby. She watched their booth like a hawk, like she didn't trust him with Derrick.

Derrick picked up one of the menus the waitress had left and looked it over like he was reading it.

"You know what you want?" Josh asked, opening his own menu but watching Derrick.

The boy pointed one little finger to the word *hamburger* in the kids' section of the menu. "A cheeseburger with fries and a soda if Mom says okay."

"You can read?"

"Sure. Watch, I'll show you." He stood on his knees and moved closer to Josh, pointed to different words on his open menu and read them. "Hamburger. Fries. Cheese. Eggs. Milk. And mmm, pie."

He got them all right. "That's real good. I couldn't read 'til I was in first grade."

"My mom taught me," he said and plopped down onto the seat. "I can write some, too, but my spelling sucks."

"Think you're going to like school?" Josh asked.

Derrick shrugged.

"Maybe after you meet some friends."

"Oh, I already have a friend. Her name is Nikki. She shared her cookies with me at lunch and played horses with me at recess. I wanted to play basketball, but the guys were asshats."

Josh stifled a grin at the "asshats" comment. No doubt about where he'd learned that word. "I went to that school, too."

"Really? Did you like it?"

Truth was, he had hated being trapped inside all day. His favorite part of school had been recess. "It was all right. I didn't much like having to sit still and be inside all day."

"Me neither. It makes me itch."

"Makes you itch?"

"Yeah, like ants are in my pants." Derrick squirmed on the seat to illustrate. "Ms. Barnes said I was the fidgetiest boy she'd ever seen."

Josh laughed and, without thinking, his hand settled on Derrick's head and tussled his hair. "My teachers told me the same thing."

"But don't tell my mom, okay? She wants me to like it."

"I won't tell."

Charleigh slid in on her side. "What are you guys talking about?"

"School," Derrick said.

"How about you come sit with me?" she asked Derrick.

"I wanna sit with Josh this time."

"Oh. Okay."

The look in her eyes said she was disappointed Derrick had chosen to sit with him, but her tone didn't hint of it. He admired that, and that she didn't say anything to make him feel guilty or force him to move.

When the waitress took their order, Derrick ordered for himself, acting more grown up than he'd imagined a boy of his age would. Charleigh changed his order for a soda to milk.

"I like all my new stuff," he said after their order was placed. "Thanks a lot, Josh."

"You're welcome, but thank your mom. She paid for it."

"Thanks, Mom."

"You're welcome, puppy."

Josh nudged Derrick with his elbow. "Why does your mom call you puppy?"

"'Cause I always wanted a puppy, but we couldn't have one, so me and Dad became puppies."

Josh's gaze went to her for clarification.

"They crawled around the house, barking and panting, wrestling, lapping water from a bowl on the floor, and eating crackers they called bones from a plate." She shook her head. "They only answered to the name puppy. And it stuck. With Derrick, anyway."

"I don't do that anymore," Derrick said in a serious tone and met Josh's eyes, looking a little embarrassed that he'd think he'd do such a childish thing.

Josh had known going into this business arrangement that hearing stories about Charleigh's life as a family with Will would be part of it, had known it would rekindle his anger and pain, but the emotion surging at Derrick's stories today wasn't so much anger but jealously. And it pissed him off that he was jealous of the perfect life Will had built with Charleigh and Derrick.

His lover and his best friend had betrayed him. He didn't want to forgive them, and he sure as hell didn't want to hear their damned fairy tale stories. Especially from Derrick, the product of their love, the evidence of their betrayal.

But the more Charleigh and Derrick talked, the more Josh found himself engaged, wanting to know… everything. Which wasn't like him.

The situation was odd in other ways, too. Since Charleigh had left him, he'd lived a solitary life, his grief at losing her closing him off. Even now, though he was becoming more involved in the community out of necessity, for the most part, he was a loner, which meant he ate his meals alone.

Occasionally, Quino joined him to make sure he was eating, but that duty never involved a lot of talking. Sometimes, he and Beth ate food during their so-called dates, but he considered that activity more foreplay, or afterplay, not mealtime, and his goal was to keep her lips busy with things other than talking.

Sitting with Charleigh and Derrick, listening to them talk and laugh, he realized his solitary habits had dulled the edges of his social skills. However, neither mother nor son seemed to notice he was out of practice and just continued to pull him into the conversations.

Not that he'd want this chatter all the time, but if he was being honest, this moment was…not terrible. Derrick had decided Josh wasn't some kind of monster, and Charleigh seemed more relaxed than she'd been earlier. Was it because of the new purchases? Their new peace settlement? Or just an act for her son's sake?

When the waitress brought the food, Derrick grabbed the ketchup bottle and drew a line across the plate of fries. "This side's mine," he said, looking at Josh. "That side's yours."

Josh's eyes flew to Charleigh. She had done the same thing when they were together so he wouldn't eat them all. She grabbed a fry from *their* side and fed it into her smiling mouth.

"Hey, Josh," Derrick said around a bite of burger. "What did the momma cow say to her baby cow?"

"I don't know. What did the momma cow say to her calf?"

"Moooooo."

The engaging grin on Derrick's face would have

been enough to make Josh play along, but the joke was funny in a juvenile way and clever because it was relevant to his new life. He laughed, then Derrick did, then Charleigh.

The few other diners turned to stare at them. To them, the three of them probably looked like a happy family enjoying a meal together. During their time here, even he had relaxed and begun to feel like they were a unit. It had his mind playing a dangerous game of what-if. What if he and Charleigh had stayed together? Maybe by now they'd have a couple of kids. And at the end of a meal like this, they'd go home. To their ranch. Put their kids to bed. Then go to their bed. He'd unhook her 36D bra, slide off her small panties, and make love to her, his wife. *His wife.*

She'd wanted to be his wife, have his kids, and he'd shot her down. Then lost her. Today, he had a taste of what he'd missed out on and what Will had enjoyed. The regret of it sat like a lump in his stomach, but that didn't mean he was ready to forgive her.

****

Except for the light from the dash softly illuminating Josh's face, darkness closed around them, making the interior of the vehicle feel intimate. Desire teased up Charleigh's back and down her thighs and brought a soft smile to her face as she remembered other times in another darkened vehicle with Josh. Burning kisses and feverous touches. Hastily kicked off boots and shoes. Jeans and shirts turned inside out as they were yanked off. Laughter. Moans. Fun. Love. So much love.

She hadn't just loved Josh back then, she'd liked him, enjoyed his company. Today reminded her why.

Her smile dimmed when she recalled that Derrick had enjoyed Josh's company, too, because the last thing she wanted was to have Derrick get used to having him around. He'd only be with them for a year, and it wasn't to be a father to his son.

"I saw you, you know." Josh's low voice dragged her out of her thoughts.

She turned to him. "Saw me? What do you mean?"

"At Will's funeral."

Her heart banged against her spine, stiffening her back against the seat, her smile vanishing altogether. She looked away. For the past few hours, she hadn't thought about Will once, about the uncertainty and emptiness left by his death. Now it all came flooding back, pushing out the sweet moments of today, making her feel ashamed for enjoying them.

"I didn't know you were there," she said. Will's request to be buried at Chismes Point had surprised her, but she'd done as he asked. Only Wyatt and a preacher had attended.

"I was chopping ice in one of the watering tanks across from the cemetery. There was a bad storm that day."

She'd never forget the roar of the wind in her ears that day, the slash of the ice blades on her face, the feel of the frozen ground beneath her knees.

"You stayed in the cemetery a long time," he said.

When she didn't respond, he prompted.

"I guess you were having trouble saying goodbye?"

She glanced into the back where Derrick slept. "I'd said my goodbyes as his illness took a little more of him every day. But when I got to the cemetery, knew he was in that box and would never again..." She released a breath from her tight chest. "It was my last chance to say everything I should have said before."

Mainly she had thanked Will for being there for her when she needed him and apologized for not being there for him the way he deserved.

She turned toward Josh, ready for the disdain she was sure she'd see on his face. "I'm sure you find that silly."

His eyes were soft on hers, kind. "I'm not heartless, Charleigh."

The way he'd interacted with Derrick today said he was not heartless, despite how she remembered him on their last night together.

"I know," she whispered on a sigh. "Sorry."

His thumb softly strummed the steering wheel. "He's been gone almost a year."

Eight months. "Almost."

"Have you thought about getting married again?"

The months following Will's death had left her thinking about nothing but putting food on the table, paying bills, and taking care of Derrick. But she didn't have to do any deep thinking to know that if she did marry again, she wanted it to be for true love and not out of desperation. True love would be hard to come by, especially in this place, and right now, she didn't have the time or energy or desire to put into making it happen. "No."

"What about Derrick? A boy needs a father." The soft tone of his voice suggested he'd meant the quiet words as concern, but they were a knife to her chest. Her son did need a father. But Will, who wanted to be his father, was dead. And Josh, who was his father, hadn't been interested, and certainly wouldn't be interested now.

"Oh gosh golly darn. Turn this thing around and head back to the store. I knew I'd forgotten to buy something." Sarcasm dripped from each word. "Since you're an expert at knowing my size, maybe you can choose a husband that fits me just right."

"Retract your claws, sweetheart. I wasn't criticizing."

"Look, Josh, I agreed to trust you on ranching business, but I'm telling you right now, you don't get a say in how I conduct my life or raise my son."

The rest of the drive home carried no more talk of marriage, Derrick's need for a father, ranch business, or anything else. That wedge was snuggly in place, and it did all the talking.

When they pulled up to the house, she thought he'd let her handle Derrick and the packages on her own then race away. But he turned off the engine and got out. Brutus welcomed them with bristled growls, but when Josh greeted him firmly but friendly, the dog quieted. Josh opened the back door where Derrick sat buckled in.

Before she could get out and move around to that side, he had unbuckled the seatbelt and picked Derrick up in his arms. Seeing Derrick in Josh's arms rushed panic through her suddenly trembling body. Not that she was worried this one touch would miraculously peel back the veil of secrecy to reveal their father-son connection. It was that the touching moment made her feel guilty. Reminded her of all she had taken from Josh, from Derrick. Golden moments like these. A father carrying his sleeping son to bed after a fun family outing. Will had done it, of course, but to see it

136

happening with Josh was a jab to the heart.

"Give him to me," she whispered, frantic to get her son out of his arms.

He nodded toward the house and whispered, "Get the door."

Instead of standing in the dark, arguing, attempting to pull Derrick from his arms like she wanted to, she hurried ahead and opened the door, then ahead again to open his bedroom door.

She pulled back the covers, and Josh laid him on the bed and pulled off his new sneakers that he'd insisted on wearing right out of the store. She tried to tug off his jeans so he'd rest better, but he rolled over onto his side.

"Leave him be," Josh said when she tried again. "You'll wake him."

He was right—to continue would be to risk waking Derrick—but that didn't stop her from wanting to lay into Josh for telling her what to do. Instead, she bit her tongue and focused on what was best for her son. Fighting with Josh in the middle of his bedroom wasn't it.

She pulled the blankets up over her son, brushed back his hair from his forehead, and kissed him. When she straightened and turned, Josh was right there and her body bumped against his. Him in front of her, the bed behind her, she couldn't move.

Oh, please, Josh, move back so I can breathe.

"He's a great kid." His low voice was sincere.

"Thank you."

Hesitantly, he lifted his hand and brushed it down her hair, crown to tip, tugging the ends to stretch the curl that fell past her breasts, like he used to.

Her eyes fluttered closed for a moment, and she shivered. She swallowed and brought her gaze up to his. They breathed together in that tight, silent moment for so long she thought her legs would collapse.

He dropped his hand. "I'll bring in your things."

He left her standing in the dark, trembling and alive from his closeness, from his familiar touch and voice, everything in her wishing he had pulled her to him and kissed her. Palmed her breast. Ground the need in his jeans against hers.

Just once.

Just for old time's sake.

Just to satisfy her need to know whether he still felt and tasted the same.

Just because it had been over a year since she'd had sex.

Just because she was hungry for the feeling of being loved, hungry for the touch of a man. Hungry for Josh.

A minute later, he was back in the kitchen where she waited, their packages in his hands.

"Where do you want these?" His curt, no-nonsense tone was back.

"Here's fine. I want to wash everything."

He set them down where he stood, then turned and headed for the door. "See you in the morning."

"I'll be ready," she said.

He was out the door when she realized she had to tell him what today had meant to her. She rushed out the door as he was climbing into the SUV.

He saw her and climbed out. "You need something?"

She joined him at the SUV, making sure to keep

the open door between them. "Thank you for today, Josh. It's the most I've heard Derrick laugh in a long time."

"Like I said…his wellbeing is my job." Without another word, he climbed in, started the engine, and when she moved away, he shut the door.

So, that's how it was. She and Derrick were nothing more than responsibilities to him, like torturing the cattle, breaking the horses, fixing fences. It was good she knew that.

After he disappeared from sight, she went in, contemplating how different the boy she'd loved was from the man she didn't know. And mourning the difference.

****

Only after Charleigh had gone inside did Josh focus his eyes on the road, his mind back on their afternoon in Wilton. It had been better than he imagined it would be. In fact, it had been great. He liked the kid. He had a quirky, dry sense of humor unusual for a five-year-old—not that he had any idea what was normal for a five-year-old—and had made him laugh. Like when he'd talked about how being stuck in a classroom made him itch, how he'd drawn the line of ketchup in the fries, and how he told that lame cow joke.

But something about the boy puzzled him. He felt a niggling familiarity with him, as if he'd met him before. He'd studied his face, stared into his eyes, trying to see Will in him but couldn't. Thank God he couldn't. Seeing Will in Derrick would be an everyday, in-his-face reminder of Charleigh's betrayal.

Strange thing was, he couldn't see that much of Charleigh in him either. Where had those blue eyes come from? Hers were amber, the color of honey, and Will had dark, almost black eyes. A recessive gene kicking in? He thought he remembered her once saying her mom had blue eyes. That must be it.

Driving back home with her beside him, the kid asleep in the back, had been comfortable. Before he'd ruined it with his questions, destroying almost every bit of good will they'd created. Standing in Will's old room, in the dark, with her, putting her son to bed, an odd feeling came over him that had sent tingles up his spine, a feeling that he belonged there with her. With them. It had made him reckless, reaching out to touch her, stretch her curls, like he used to.

Despite his lingering lust for Charleigh, he would not insert himself into her life or the boy's any more than he had to for their agreement. He wasn't that stupid. The last thing he needed was to get wrapped around her little finger again. He had made mistakes with her, but he'd long ago done as his granddad had instructed and turned his mistakes into lessons learned.

But he would take hope from their small success in ending the day on a more or less agreeable note, and he would build on that, one day at a time, so he could fulfill the terms of Wyatt's will and accomplish his goal of bringing Antelope Spring back into the Flores family…even if that family now consisted only of him.

That's all he wanted from this disaster waiting to happen.

Chapter Eight

Derrick was up and showered when Charleigh went into his room the next morning to wake him for school.

"You're up early," she said.

"I want to make sure I'm ready right when Josh gets here."

"Why?"

He shrugged. "I want to talk to him."

"What about?"

"Mom." The sigh and eye-rolling tone said he'd had enough of her questions.

Lately, she'd been seeing more of these signs that he was growing up and needing space to explore his own ideas and interests. She wasn't anywhere near ready to let go, but she was trying to loosen her grip.

"I washed your new clothes last night. They're in your drawers if you want to wear them today."

"Thanks." He pulled out a pair of his new jeans and a new shirt.

"You're welcome. Well, I'll have a shower and meet you at the table for breakfast."

Fifteen minutes later, she was showered and dressed and in the kitchen. Derrick wasn't there, and Ruby was clearing away his breakfast dishes.

"Ruby, where's Derrick?"

"He heard Josh's pickup pull in just now and shot outta here like a jet."

Charleigh glanced at the clock. Barely seven-thirty. They'd negotiated her start time to right after Derrick caught the school bus at eight. Why was Josh so early? She went to the door to find out.

Josh was getting out of his pickup, and Derrick was headed down the porch steps to him when Brutus charged out from behind the bush, barking.

"Derrick!" She rushed out the door to grab him and pull him back inside the house, but he ran to Josh, launching himself at him. Josh swung him up in his arms just as the dog got to him.

"I think Brutus wants to eat me," Derrick said, his voice shaky, his arms wrapped around Josh's neck.

"Nah, he just doesn't know you," Josh said. "It's time you guys got acquainted." He looked at her where she stood, back tight against the screen door, ready to run in if she had to. "Charleigh, ask Ruby for the bag of dog treats."

"You're rewarding him for that behavior?"

Ruby opened the door and handed her a small bag.

Charleigh took it, held it to her chest.

"Bring them over," Josh said, humor in his voice. "He won't bite."

"That bark says otherwise." She tossed the bag to him, and he snatched it out of mid-air.

He tried to set Derrick down, but the boy clung to him, arms and legs and hands. Josh knelt on one knee, setting him on the ground beside him. "It'll be okay. I'm right beside you."

Derrick released his death grip on Josh but kept one hand clutched to his sleeve.

"Speak softly and calmly to Brutus," Josh said. "Show him you're a friend, not a threat."

"Hi, Brutus," Derrick said, his voice hesitant. "Hey, boy."

"Good. Now put your hand out, slowly, fingers curled under, and let him smell it."

Derrick shook his head.

"Like this." Josh demonstrated the move. Brutus stopped barking and crept forward, then stretched out to sniff his hand. Josh then lifted his hand to the dog's head and scratched his ears.

"Okay, your turn," he said to Derrick, who gingerly did as instructed. Brutus sniffed the offered hand. Then Derrick put his hand on the dog's head next to Josh's and scratched his ears. Josh opened the bag, pulled out a treat, and handed it to Derrick. "Give it to him."

Derrick took it and held it out to Brutus by the tip. The dog cautiously sniffed the snack, then took it and ate it. He then dropped to his haunches, licked his lips, and woofed for more.

Josh handed Derrick another one. When Brutus swallowed that treat, he shifted closer, sniffed Derrick's hand, looking for more, which Derrick was quick to supply.

A few treats later, and the bond between boy and dog—and boy and man—had begun.

"All right, that's enough." Josh sealed the bag. "He'll get a belly ache if he has too many."

Brutus stepped forward and licked Derrick's face.

Derrick laughed and reached out to hug the dog as if they were old friends. He grinned up at Josh. "I think he likes me."

"I think you're right."

"Mom, it's okay. He's nice now."

Charleigh appreciated Josh's patience and

determination to help Derrick face this. To see her son learn this important lesson from his father touched her heart. "That's great. But you need to come in now and get ready for school."

"I just have to grab my backpack."

"And wash your hands and brush your teeth," she added.

"Bye, Brutus." He loved on the dog, all fear seemingly vanished. "We'll play when I get home from school. Don't forget you like me, okay?"

Full of confidence, Derrick left Josh's side and strutted into the house, leaving her alone with Josh, his gaze on her, his hand rhythmically scratching Brutus on one floppy ear. Thoughts of how his hands had always caressed her as gently flooded her mind and heated her cheeks.

"I thought you liked dogs?" he said, his voice low, light, teasing, bringing her out of her erotic memories.

"Not ones that want to eat me for breakfast."

A heart-stopping half-grin lifted one corner of his lips. As he eased to standing, she was again reminded of the many times that mouth had brought her such exquisite pleasure. The mouth that now pleasured another woman.

"Fortunately for you, Brutus prefers these bacon treats over pretty women." He tossed the bag to her, like she'd done to him.

She caught it, grinned at his compliment. Or joke. She wasn't sure which. "You're early. I still need to get Derrick to the bus stop."

"I came over early to talk to him about starting his chores."

"What kind of chores?"

Before he could clarify, Derrick and Ruby came out.

"Bye, Ruby," Derrick said and hugged her.

"I packed a special little treat for you in your lunchbox."

He grinned. "Really? What is it?"

"It's a surprise."

"I can't wait 'til lunch!"

"What do you say to Ruby for thinking of you?" Charleigh reminded him.

"Thank you!"

"You're welcome." She patted his back. "See you this afternoon."

"'Kay," Derrick said and sauntered over to Josh's pickup and stood by the door.

"Puppy, I'm driving us in our pickup," Charleigh said.

He grabbed onto the door handle. "But Josh came over early to drive me to the bus stop."

The look she and Josh shared said that hadn't been his initial intent, but his small shrug said he was going with it. He went to the pickup and opened his door. Derrick scrambled in and settled in the middle of the seat, leaving Charleigh little choice but to get in or be left behind. To argue against it, like she wanted, would only cause upset, and she didn't want Derrick to start his day with upset.

"When you get home, we'll have a talk about the chores you need to do every day before and after school," Josh said to Derrick as they bounced down the road to where the bus would pick him up in the mornings and drop him off in the afternoons.

"What kind of chores?" he asked. "Like dumping

145

the trash?"

"That, and other stuff, like feeding Brutus, the chickens, the horses, and the yearling, collecting the eggs—"

"Isn't that a little much?" Charleigh said.

"Nope." Josh's answer was swift and sure.

"I can do it, Mom," Derrick insisted before she could argue. "I'm pretty strong."

The bus was a short distance away when they got to the stop. Josh shut off the engine, and they climbed out. Charleigh knelt beside Derrick to give him a final hug and kiss and words of encouragement.

He looked up at Josh. "Do you have your phone with you?"

"Yep."

"Would you take a picture of us?"

"Sure." Josh fished it from his pocket.

Charleigh hugged Derrick, pressed her cheek to his, and Josh aimed it at them.

"I want you in the picture, too," Derrick insisted to Josh.

Derrick's desire to have Josh in the picture raked across her heart, but she swallowed the emotion and shifted to allow Josh room to join them. He knelt at Derrick's other side, put his arm around him, lightly resting his hand on Charleigh's back. It felt like a hot branding iron pressed against her skin and made her body tense up at his closeness.

Holding out his phone, Josh centered their faces in the screen. "Say, cows' knees."

Derrick laughed and said cows' knees, and Josh snapped the picture.

"Can I see it?" Derrick asked.

Josh showed him, and he stared at it. "I'm locking this picture up in my brain so I can see it when I miss you guys today."

Over Derrick's shoulder, Charleigh's gaze zoomed in on the picture, on the blue eyes and right cheek dimple that Josh and Derrick shared. Didn't Josh see the resemblance? It was only a matter of time before he or someone did.

The bus rolled to a stop in front of them, and the door flung open. "Morning folks," the bus driver said, a cheery older woman with a round freckled face and bottled red hair shorn close in a pixie cut.

Josh held up his hand. "Morning."

"First day for the little one?"

"First day riding the bus."

"Well, I'll take real good care of your boy."

Instead of explaining her mistake, Josh just nodded. "'Appreciate it."

"Bye, Mom." Derrick hugged her, and she held him tight.

It was almost more than she could take. Her stomach was turned inside out at the thought of letting him get on that bus and leave her. For some reason, it was harder today than it had been the day before.

"Have a good day," she whispered to disguise the tears in her throat. "I love you."

"Love you, too." He left her arms and turned to Josh, hugging him.

Josh patted his back. "No ants in the pants today."

Derrick grinned. "I'll try."

She felt a prick of jealousy at what sounded like an inside joke between the two of them.

Derrick turned, faced the bus, then walked slowly

but resolutely toward it, head high.

She stepped forward, planning to go on board and help him find a seat and get settled, hug him one more time. But Josh grabbed her arm to hold her back. When she looked at him, he shook his head.

"It'll tell him you think he isn't capable of doing it on his own."

Their son climbed the steps, never looking back. They watched him walk down the aisle, only the top of his head visible through the windows, and claim a seat. His little face appeared at a window, a nervous little grin on his mouth, his eyes wide, and he gave a little wave.

She and Josh waved back. "Now he knows, and you know, and all the kids on that bus know that he is. It's good for him, Charleigh. It's one lesson out of many he needs to learn on his way to becoming a man."

"I'll drop him here at two o'clock," the driver said and, with a salute and a smile, shut the door.

Derrick gave another little wave, and they waved back as the bus continued down the road, taking him from her. She turned away from the bus, from Josh, and let the tears fall.

Josh was suddenly behind her. Right behind her. "He'll be okay." His kind, low-spoken words tangled in her hair, and the heat radiating from his body tingled up her spine, comforting her without a single touch.

"Mastering little lessons like these will prepare him for the big ones he'll face down the road. You help him best by letting him try."

Unable to speak without releasing all her emotions, she nodded.

The sudden feel of his hands lightly cupping her

shoulders shook her to her core. Part of her wanted to lean back against him, drop her head on his chest, accept the comfort of his arms. But she couldn't allow herself that small weakness. Not from him.

Wiping her eyes with the backs of her hands, she left his embrace, walked to the pickup, opened her door, and climbed in.

****

Josh watched the bus until it was out of sight. While he'd believed every word he'd said to Charleigh, watching Derrick maneuver this necessary hurdle on the long path to manhood brought up surprising flutters of apprehension in his stomach as well as memories. He and Will had sat together on that first scary bus ride, and when they'd arrived at school, they'd recognized every face in their classroom and most of them in the school. Derrick was alone. Knew no one.

New situation, new people, new school… It was a lot for anyone to handle, especially a five-year-old boy. But the kid was brave, gotta give him credit for that. Charleigh and Will had done a good job with him. She was a bit overprotective, but clearly she loved him and would scrap with the devil himself to protect him.

Would it ease her mind to know he'd be there for Derrick, too, to guide and protect him? For some reason, he wasn't sure it would. She didn't seem to like the two of them interacting on a personal level, as if she believed he was intruding.

He climbed into the pickup. She stared out the side window, probably trying to control her emotions. She had always hated crying in front of him as much as he hated seeing her cry.

It would be a hard day for her, as much of a lesson

for her as it was for Derrick. They'd both get through it and be stronger for it. Even if he could protect them from the discomfort, he wouldn't. Growth was painful but necessary. And there was a hell of a lot of growth up ahead for both of them. He'd see to it. It was what he'd signed on for.

Hitting the starter, he headed to the holding pen, where he hoped Cole had the hands already at work.

The image of Derrick's brave little face peering out the bus window stayed with him the rest of the morning. Now and then, he'd pull out his phone and look at the picture he'd taken of the three of them. Tonight, he'd print it for Derrick so he could take it to school with him if he wanted. He would print it for Charleigh if he thought she'd want it. The look on her face when Derrick said he wanted him in the picture told him she might not.

For a second, he swore he saw her eyes darken, her mouth tighten, a shade pass over her face. It had passed as quickly as it had appeared, but it loudly and clearly said she didn't want him around her son for anything other than work issues. It bothered him that she didn't seem to trust him with the boy.

He stared across the field to where she sat at the table, entering the numbers Cole called out. As if she sensed his eyes on her, she looked up, met his gaze from under the bill of the new pale straw cowboy hat she had insisted on buying even though he'd told her she needed one more suited to the coming winter weather. Even from this distance, he saw the rosy blush creep up her chest and neck to her face under his direct stare. But she held his gaze until Cole called out another number, only then letting her attention return to her work.

He'd love to know what was going on in her head. Back when they were together, he'd been adept at reading her unspoken thoughts and emotions. Either she'd gotten better at hiding them, or he'd lost his ability.

Hopefully, trust and time would resolve whatever issues she had with him being around her son. But whether it did or not, he was going to be around. For a year. So she might as well get used to it and stop fighting him on everything.

Taking a final look at the picture, he put his phone away and got back to work. But still Charleigh filled his mind. And by the time the two of them left that afternoon to pick Derrick up from the bus stop, he realized his first assumption about her being back in town was right on—he was fucked. That twisting in his gut was him getting wrapped around her again. And her son, too.

****

"Your animals depend on you for everything—food, water, shelter, care," Josh said as he walked Derrick through the chores that afternoon, Charleigh at his side. "If you don't take care of them, they'll die. That's not only an unnecessary cruelty, but a hit to your finances as well."

"I won't let them die, Josh," the boy said. "I promise."

"I know."

More than an hour later, the chores done, Josh prepared to leave.

"I'll be here every morning at seven to guide you through your chores, then again in the afternoon to do the same thing until I feel you're capable of doing it on your own."

"Okay." Derrick nodded, and Josh was impressed at his rapt attention and seeming willingness to do the work the right way.

He set his hand on Derrick's head. "Okay. Well, I got work to do at home, but I'll see you tomorrow...at what time?"

"Seven o'clock," Derrick said.

Josh held out his hand for a fist bump, and Derrick obliged. He then turned his gaze to Charleigh, who stood a little apart from them, arms crossed over her chest in a stance that used to mean she was bugged. If that was the case, him asking why would only worsen the situation, so he didn't. He nodded to her. "See you tomorrow."

She nodded back.

As he headed to his pickup, he heard her tell Derrick to go on in and start on his homework. When he'd gone in, she rushed toward the pickup. "Josh, can I talk to you for a sec?"

He stopped, the open door between them. "Yep."

"That's an awful lot of work for a five-year-old, especially first thing in the morning. He needs to be well-rested going in to school, not already tired from a day's work."

"A day's work?" He hadn't meant to punctuate the statement with a sarcastic scoff, but that's what came out. "I did twice that every morning and afternoon and still managed to go to school, do my schoolwork, and participate in extra-curricular activities."

"And I remember you falling asleep in class a few times, too."

A wicked little grin lifted his mouth. "That wasn't from doing chores. Leastwise, I never considered staying out late to make love to you a chore."

A blush bloomed high in her cheeks and across her chest at his comment, and her nipples pearled up toward him. Clearly, he'd embarrassed her. Realizing he'd been out of line with that comment, he stared down at the ground to give his grin and ill-chosen words time to dissipate. "Once he gets the hang of it, it'll take him a half hour at the most."

"If I see him struggling, I'm going to help him," she said, her voice tight.

"If you see him struggling, tell me. It means I didn't do a good enough job of teaching him to do what needs to be done. Do not do it for him. He'll get the idea that hard work is dealt with not by trying harder but by letting someone else do it. Is that the lesson you want to teach him?"

"No," she said through gritted teeth, showing her irritation.

"Anything else you need to talk about?" His tone mirrored hers.

"No."

He nodded curtly. "Good."

Without a word, she stormed into the house, firmly closing the doors.

He climbed into his pickup and went home to check on the work his men were doing, the only thought on his mind that Charleigh was driving him batshit crazy. Like riding a green-broke filly, they'd be going along on a straight line when all of a sudden she'd buck and throw him on his ass. It was like she couldn't stand it when they were getting along and had to do something to make herself feel the anger that seemed to make her more comfortable around him. He needed time to reset from that kind of bullshit.

He pulled out his phone and texted Beth, feeling the need to sink into some of those benefits attached to their friendship. It riled him to admit it, but being around Charleigh, working with her, had him horny and on edge all the time, despite his attempts to shame himself not to be. He had absorbed her into his skin like a drug—the little blue pill, to be exact—even though she was totally off limits. For so many reasons. But it was a perfect storm to develop a painful case of blue balls. Hence, his second visit to Beth's this week.

Later that night, he showered and headed to Beth's. On his way there, he stopped at the post office to check the mailboxes for both ranches. Surprised to see a thick stack of mail in the Bar S box, he pulled it out and rifled through it. Several envelopes were from collection agencies, addressed to Charleigh and Will.

Josh's mouth twisted with irritation. So Charleigh doesn't pay her bills. Well, shit.

It was his job to protect the ranch. Leaving it open to hungry creditors could put it in danger. He needed to get the full story, but he doubted he'd get it from Charleigh. Pulling out his phone, he called a private investigator acquaintance and asked him to check into her background, with an emphasis on her financial situation, and rush it.

He stuffed the mail into his glove box to give to Horace later and went on to Beth's even though he knew he shouldn't because his mind wouldn't be fully on her. But his body needed a hard release in a soft, uncomplicated woman.

Chapter Nine

Charleigh Simms was ass-over-teakettle in debt. Or so claimed the private investigator's report that arrived several weeks later. It charted her and Will's fall from financial stability stemming from the medical bills incurred during Will's illness. His twenty-five-hour-a-week job as a tattoo artist and her forty-to-fifty-hour-a-week job as an at-home medical transcriptionist hadn't stretched enough to allow them to buy medical insurance, so with Will's illness and subsequent death, Charleigh was on the hook for all of the debt.

It was all she could do to keep a roof over their heads, food on the table, and the lights on in the over-the-garage studio smack dab in the middle of gangland, but she'd paid a little every month on medical bills. The pictures that accompanied the report made it clear they'd lived a meager existence, with only the most basic necessities. They'd had no vehicle, no phone, no cable, no TV, no gaming devices, just an old borrowed computer Charleigh used for work.

The landlady, a Mrs. Yawber, commented that they had eaten a lot of mac 'n' cheese and hot dogs, and that she had given them fruits and vegetables from her garden when she could…for the sweet little one, of course.

Most of the community had always believed Charleigh had left him for Will to snag the Simms

Sophia Ryan

wealth. Part of him had believed it as well. Anger, and no small amount of guilt, stabbed through him, thinking about her living like that all those years, doing without. Because of Will.

The son-of-a-bitch must have been too proud to ask for help from his dad. And too lazy to find another job with more hours so he could have taken better care of his family. He'd sat back and let Charleigh do the heavy lifting, then left her penniless and in debt. Now he understood why she'd come back here. It offered a way out of her debt and provided a safe home for Derrick. A better life for both of them.

He called Horace, explained the situation, and asked him to negotiate pay-off amounts and pay them. He wouldn't let Charleigh know he knew, but Horace would tell her the bills were taken care of. It would put her mind at ease, and maybe she could relax around him and start to enjoy her new life now that the last tie to the old one was gone.

She and Derrick wouldn't have to struggle like that here. Ever. He'd make damn sure of it.

****

As the weeks passed, Charleigh more and more came to admit that coming to the Bar S had been the right decision.

She was getting the hang of things and found that she enjoyed the physical work and being outside. Derrick was doing well, both in school and at home. And out of the blue, Horace called to let her know that Will's past due medical bills had been paid in full from the estate.

What also brought her relief was that she and Josh had fallen into an easy routine that was relatively free of drama, unlike their earlier interactions, which had been so up and down she felt like a yo-yo being yanked on a string.

Except for weekends, he appeared at seven each morning and spent the time with Derrick, watching him do his chores, guiding him. He patiently went over everything with him, praising him when he did well, correcting him when he missed something. He soon progressed to inspecting them after the fact, but he still came by early to take Derrick to the bus stop and spend time talking with him, answering questions.

She was amazed how easily Derrick got up in the morning, rushed out to do his chores, with her by his side, and then came in and got ready for school. All without reminding or prodding or grumbling. He looked forward to Josh coming by to grade his efforts and wanted to do his best to please him. He beamed when he earned one of Josh's smiles, pats on the back, fist bumps, or words of praise.

Derrick had been over the moon when Josh instituted horseback riding lessons on Saturday mornings until he learned he would not actually climb onto a horse until he had learned basic horse safety and operation. Josh started by teaching them the names of the horse's parts, then progressed to grooming, haltering, leading, saddling, and riding safety. Only then did he allow them to mount the horse and ride, but in the corral, instructing the horse to walk, trot, lope, stop, and back. Josh was at their side through it all, ready to correct and praise their efforts.

In late October, cattle buyers sent semitrailers to haul their stock to market. Josh had involved her in every step and every decision along the way, making her feel every bit his partner in the sale. She was pleased by the amount of money they'd earned, an amount he'd said was above average. If that was true, she credited him for it.

The annual fall event in town on the last day of October wasn't to celebrate Halloween but to celebrate the conclusion of the roundup, the last big ranching job of the year. Derrick was disappointed there was no trick or treating until Ruby assured him that the candy would flow like water at the dance/carnival. From that moment on, they were going, and Derrick roped Josh into taking them.

For Charleigh, the event didn't just mark the end of a successful roundup. It marked, almost to the day, the six-year anniversary of her leaving Josh. Not that she needed reminders of that time. The memory was a permanent occupant of the small dark hole in her heart.

****

Derrick's school friends pulled him away to play, leaving Josh and Charleigh to wander over to the dance floor, where most people had congregated. Josh was pointing out various people he thought she needed to know when she felt a hand on her shoulder.

"Charleigh Cooper?"

She turned to see Lance Barton, the huge grin on his face and sparkle in his eyes saying he was happy to see her. Lance had always been kind to her when she lived here and had always left her a generous tip at the café.

"I thought that was you." He pulled her into a bear hug. "Looking as gorgeous as ever, darlin'. Good to see you."

Feeling smothered by his tight embrace, she kept

her hands at his stomach, trying to insert some breathing room between them. "Good to see you, too."

"Give her some air, Barton," Josh growled, as if reading her mind.

Lance ignored him but let her go. "It's been what, six years? Almost to the day if I remember right."

"Something like that. I hear you're the vet in town now. Congratulations."

"You keeping tabs on me?" He grinned like the idea of that pleased him.

"No. Josh mentioned it."

"I still can't get over you moving to California and marrying Will Simms." He chuckled. "Nobody saw that one coming." In an instant, the mirth faded from his face. "My condolences on his passing, by the way. About a year now, right?"

"Almost."

"And now you and Josh are running the Bar S together with your son. Wow. Time does change things. How about a dance to catch up?"

She had been trying to decipher the meaning behind the jealous scowl that had fixed on Josh's face the moment Lance joined them. She didn't even have time to enjoy the idea that it might be jealousy. Beth Powell, former miss rodeo queen, joined them and slid her arms around Josh's waist.

"About time you got here, cowboy," she cooed.

Flames of jealousy plumed hot and high as Charleigh realized it had been Beth's voice she'd heard on the phone the night she'd called Josh. *Dammit, Josh!* Of all the women he could have been with, he had to choose her, the girl who had constantly slutted after him in high school.

Then Beth reached up on tiptoes and planted a wet kiss on his lips. Everything inside Charleigh wanted to yank Josh away from Beth and kick her ass like she'd done in high school to remind her that he was hers, and only hers. Only, he wasn't hers. Not anymore.

Josh pulled back first, his eyes darting to hers. For a second, she swore she'd seen guilt in those eyes, an apology. But then he looked away and she couldn't be sure what she'd seen.

"Hello, Charleigh," Beth said, a satisfied grin on her just-been-kissed mouth that very clearly declared, *he's mine now*. "I heard you were back in town."

"Beth. I'm surprised you're not in L.A., serving as the shrink to the stars. Wasn't that always your goal?"

A practiced, fake smile lifted the woman's pink-glossed lips. "How sweet of you to remember." She rubbed her hand on Josh's chest and stared adoringly up into his face. "I found much more satisfying pursuits right here at home."

Charleigh stopped herself from throwing up on Beth's pink boots that, dammit, were pretty cute, but couldn't stop herself from rolling her eyes that she suspected had turned a nasty shade of green since Beth had joined them. The ugly truth smacking her in the face was that seeing Josh with a woman, *any* woman, made her body buzz with crazy.

She needed to get away from them before she did something to embarrass herself. "Well, I'd love to hear all about it, but Lance just asked me to dance." Her gaze paused on Josh long enough to give him a *you gotta be kidding me* eyebrow lift, then slid to Lance. "Ready?"

"*Years* past ready, darlin'."

He put his hand at her back and led her to the dance floor with such speed it seemed as though he thought someone would stop him. He danced her around the floor in smooth, well-practiced steps, talking incessantly, but she couldn't recall one thing he said because her mind was on Josh and what he and Beth were doing. She knew the exact moment they'd joined the couples on the dance floor and couldn't keep her eyes off them.

"I'm glad I didn't bet the farm on it." Lance's comment drew Charleigh's attention from Josh.

"I'm sorry, what?"

"I said I never thought I'd see you in this town again."

"Oh. Yeah, I guess it's an odd situation."

"Odd doesn't begin to cover it. The two most scandalous things that ever happened in this town centered around you and Josh…first your ditching him to marry Will, and now you're coming back, son in tow, to run the ranch with him. It's a head scratcher all right."

Since no one but her and Will knew the real reason she'd left, she wasn't surprised everyone blamed her for the breakup. And she wasn't in the mood to set them straight. She'd be leaving in eleven months. What difference would the truth make?

"I tell you what, the stories flying around about what might have happened with the three of you has kept tongues wagging and lips flapping for six, long years. I don't suppose you want to put an end to all the speculation?"

"What happened is between Josh and me."

He grinned. "You might want to tell him, darlin',

because he doesn't know why you left him either. Leastways, that's the story."

Even though Josh didn't know she knew about his cheating, the fight they'd had should have made it clear why she'd left, and it wasn't like he'd bothered to try to get her back. Well, if he had any questions, he could damn well ask her himself. She'd be glad to tell him the truth. Well, some of the truth. But no way was she telling Lance, or anyone else, anything.

He chuckled at her lack of response. "Well, if you don't want to comment on the old gossip about you and Josh, maybe you'd like to comment on the newest?"

"Not really."

He made a show of zipping his lips, but the longer he kept quiet, the more it drove her crazy.

"All right, tell me," she said, convinced it was better to know than to wonder.

He grinned. "That before the contract is up, you and Josh will have—as the womenfolk say—rekindled your love."

A too-harsh, too-fake laugh burst from her lips. "That's completely ridiculous. Josh is with someone, and I'm not interested."

"Appearances can be deceiving."

"What do you mean?"

"Well, I'm dancing with you, doing my darnedest to be charming and entertaining, but your eyes have been on him since we got out here. And he's been watching us like a hawk despite Beth's best attempts to monopolize his attention. And word is, their relationship is more of a *you scratch my itch, I'll scratch yours* arrangement, if you know what I mean."

"Josh and I are not rekindling anything." As the

162

words left her mouth, pain shot through her heart as if it were being jammed with a cattle prod for lying. She swallowed back the shock of it. "We have a contract that demands we work together for a year. End of story."

He grinned. "I'm real glad to hear that, darlin'. Real glad."

He didn't specify why he was *real glad*, and she didn't ask because she didn't want to know.

Over the next couple of hours, Charleigh danced with Lance a few more times, with Cole several times, as well as with a few teenaged boys she hadn't known from before and a few other men she had. The main thought irritating her brain like a burr all night was that the asshat hadn't asked her to dance. Not once. He was too busy holding Beth's hand. So she was surprised to see him join her as she left the floor with Cole toward the end of the night.

"Well, if y'all will excuse me," Cole said quickly when he saw Josh's scowl, which she'd noticed he'd worn all night.

"Having fun?" Josh asked once Cole had left.

"Sure," she lied. "You?"

"Sure."

The one-word responses plunged them into silence.

"Where's the queen?" she asked a moment later.

"Bathroom. Why?"

She grinned that he knew exactly who she meant. "No reason. Just surprised she'd let you go wandering off by yourself."

"What's that supposed to mean?"

A tall, lanky teenager approached her, saving her from having to respond. He stopped between them, grinning, his cheeks flushed, and his eyes dipping repeatedly from her eyes to her breasts and back. "Hey, Charleigh. You wanna dance?"

Josh grabbed her hand. "Sorry, Chase, I asked her first." He led her to the floor. "You'll thank me later," he whispered close to her ear. "He's a known toe-stomper."

"Uh-huh."

"Plus, I don't like the way he was looking at you."

"How was he looking at me?"

Josh put his hand low on her back and drew her in, carefully, slowly, then fully. "I figured you were proficient at deciphering the tongue-dragging look of a horny eighteen-year-old."

For a few, long moments, his eyes held hers, as if he was remembering how they'd been when he was the horny eighteen-year-old.

"It's been awhile," she said.

In a natural move, his hand drew hers down to settle against his hip, where it always had rested. The feel of his hip muscles flexing under her hand as they moved slid heat into her core, stirring and heating feelings best left cold.

The song ended and another started. And not just any song. Their song. The only country song she had liked. *I Cross My Heart.* The words to the song pulled up the feelings of when things had been perfect between them. The promises they'd made to each other.

They stared at each other, the look on his face mirroring the one on hers, showing that they both remembered. They were barely moving, shuffling on the floor in sync, one body, one heart, one breath. The warmth and solidness of his chest, the heat of him against her belly, her thighs, the comfort of his arms around her, was all so familiar, and it spiraled her away to the time when this place in his arms was her home. Her whole world. She gave in and rested her head on his chest, and he pulled her deeper into his embrace, stepping fully into the past.

She was well aware he wasn't hers anymore. Knew he didn't want to be. But for this moment, she would let go of the uncertain present and sink into the comfortable past, sink into him like she used to when he was her everything.

Urgent tapping on her shoulder some time later pricked her euphoric bubble, and she didn't have to turn her head to look to know who stood behind her with the lethal pin.

"I'll take him back now," Beth said, annoyance in every curt word.

Charleigh and Josh stopped. Her eyes met his, and they shared a look that seemed to say neither one of them was ready to end this two-step back in time, especially when their song was still playing.

"Thanks for keeping him entertained for me," Beth prodded when they didn't separate.

It took every ounce of strength inside her, but Charleigh started the slow, surprisingly painful process of leaving his arms. After a brief moment, when he held her firmly in place, as if he wasn't going to release her, he finally did.

Because there was nothing left to do but leave the dance floor, she did and headed toward the refreshment table to get something to drink, hoping someone had spiked the punch. On the way there, the teenaged toe stomper waylaid her and pulled her out to dance. By the time the song was done, a dozen sorries rang in her ears and her left big toe felt battered but not broken.

Josh didn't dance with her again for the rest of the night, didn't stray from Beth's side, her hand tight in his, but his eyes were on the dance floor where Charleigh was with whichever man had asked her to dance. She knew this because her eyes were on him, too.

Just when she didn't think the night could get any worse, it did. Beth rode home with them after the dance, sitting in the front seat, obviously going to stay the night with Josh.

Charleigh was going to have to learn to rein in the jealousy eating her from the inside out. Like it or not, Beth was part of his life. And because Josh was a part of her and Derrick's life for a year, she was going to have to get used to seeing the couple together.

It was going to be a long year.

"Hey, Josh…" Derrick spoke up from the backseat where he sat beside Charleigh. "We're still going riding in the morning, right?"

She spoke up before Josh could. "Derrick, another day might be better. It's been a late night, and Josh has company."

Josh's eyes met hers in the rearview mirror, and he wasn't happy. Neither was Derrick.

"But, Mom, it's our first real ride outside the corral. And he promised."

"I know, puppy, but sometimes plans change."

"Derrick, I told you I'd take you, and I will," Josh said. "Have your chores done, your horse saddled, and be ready to go at eight."

"Yes!" Derrick said.

"Josh, there's no need to leave your guest for a riding lesson that you can do at any other time."

"My guest can come along if she wants."

No way in hell would she allow Derrick to go riding with Beth and Josh, and no way in hell was *she* going on a ride with Beth.

"Derrick, Cole said he'd be glad to take us."

"I want Josh."

The sting of Derrick's adamant declaration shut down every argument she had other than the truth. *Don't love him, Derrick. He'll break your heart just like he broke mine.*

But she couldn't say that, and before she could come up with something else, Josh spoke again. "Riding lessons are my responsibility, Charleigh, not Cole's."

His words drew her gaze to the rearview mirror. Sparks flared in the blue orbs, and she could almost see the words *Is that clear?* blazing in them.

She tore her gaze away from his and responded with a puerile "Whatever."

The vehicle was skin-prickly quiet the rest of the way home. She had her seatbelt and Derrick's already unbuckled before Josh pulled to a stop in front of the house. She jumped out and lifted Derrick out, not even giving him a chance to climb out. After tossing a short goodnight toward the front to Josh and Beth, she hurried to the house, hand firmly on Derrick's back, wanting to avoid conversation and the hug he always gave Josh whenever they parted.

Josh jumped out of the SUV, too, leaving the engine running, headlights on, and rushed to the door before they could get inside. He barred it with his hand so she couldn't open it. "I need to speak with you."

"And I need to get Derrick to bed."

"Derrick, I need to speak with your mom. Go on in and get yourself ready for bed."

"Don't tell my son what to do!"

Josh eyes narrowed, then cut to Derrick and back to hers, sending her a clear message to cool it. Her gaze swung to her little boy. He stood there, mouth open, eyes wide, confused about what was going on and about what to do. She could tell he was upset by her and Josh's tense exchange, and it made her ashamed that Josh had noticed it before she had.

"Go on in, puppy. I'll be right there," she said, keeping her voice calm, adding a small smile. "Brush extra good and floss. You ate a lot of sweets tonight."

He nodded. "Bye, Josh," he said in a thin, little voice, and hugged him.

Josh patted his back. "See you in the morning, bud."

Derrick headed inside, and the second both doors shut, Charleigh and Josh faced off.

"What the hell's your problem," they said in unison.

He jumped in again before she could. "I promised I'd take him riding, and I mean to keep that promise."

"Not this time."

"Why the hell not?"

"Because your full attention won't be on him, which means he could get hurt."

"Anytime I'm with Derrick, my full attention's on him. I take the responsibility of his safety seriously."

"You can't, not if you're playing grab ass with the queen."

"You think I'd do that in front of Derrick?"

"You were doing it tonight in front of the whole fucking town. Why would an intimate little horse ride be any different?"

"You didn't seem to have a problem with him seeing you hang all over Barton, and Ledger, and all those horny teenagers."

"It was a dance. I danced. That's all."

"Yeah, I saw where Ledger's hand was."

"Oh, please," she said with an exaggerated eyeroll. "Cole's a gentleman who would never—"

"Cole's a red-blooded male who knows exactly what to do when the sexy woman in his arms is getting up in his business."

She almost choked on her tongue. First of all, how dare he? Second, did he mean sexy women in general, or that she was sexy? "I wasn't up in his business, and he doesn't think of me that way."

"Bullshit. And it's obvious you think of him that way, too."

"I most certainly do not!"

"It looked that way to me and everyone else at the dance. I warn you, Charleigh, if you're not interested in him as a fuckmate, you might want to back off the seduction routine before you get yourself in trouble."

"You asshat!" She shoved him, but his body was so rigid and solidly grounded in place he barely moved. "You're the one who needs to back off." She shoved him again with the same result. "My behavior doesn't need policing, certainly not by you."

She was ready to shove him a third time, but lightning fast, he caught her wrists and wound her arms behind her back, his arms around her waist, pulling her in and trapping her against his chest.

He was hard, tense, tight, a clock wound too tight that was about to spring. And so was she. They didn't speak, didn't break eye contact, barely breathed. But every breath she did pull in was of him. He smelled like home. Like happiness. Like pleasure. Like red hot passion. In that moment, it struck her as odd that lust could so thoroughly mask the scent of betrayal.

Their chests were rising and falling in unison, his hard chest scraping against her hard nipples, the length of their bodies pressed together in a tight, almost magnetic embrace, the friction between them sparking a fire that seemed to be melding them tighter together at the thin seam separating them.

Six, seven, eight years ago, this is the point where they'd be ripping each other's clothes off and settling their dispute physically. Carnally. Deliciously. Oh, God, she was ready for it. She hadn't realized how much she missed sex until she got around Josh again. Now, the hunger was constant.

"Be ready at eight," he said finally, in a ragged whisper. "You and Derrick, both."

"And if I'm not?"

"You really want to find out?" His words brushed like tongues of electricity across her mouth.

"Maybe I do." No maybe about it. She did.

At this moment, she wanted to push him until he punished her disobedience with that soft mouth, that hard body. And for a moment, when his head lowered, closer to hers, and his fiery gaze feasted on her mouth, it looked like he was going to.

She licked her lips, wanting to be ready for it.

He did the same and found her eyes again. Some

emotion she couldn't read flickered there. Whatever it was, it stopped him from taking her mouth, and instead pushed him to release her and take several steps back. But they stayed connected through their gaze, through their runaway, in-sync breathing.

"Do whatever the fuck you want, Charleigh." His words were sandpaper rough. "Like you always did." In a furious stride, he headed back to the SUV.

"Don't worry, I will." She yanked open the screen door.

"Good." He got in.

"Good." She pushed open the wooden door and went in.

They both slammed their respective doors.

Through the closed doors, she heard the SUV tear off down the road, spitting gravel. She wanted to scream but instead dug her nails into her palms and forced herself to breathe slowly and deeply to calm down before heading to Derrick's room to tuck him in and then straight into a cold shower.

What a jacked-up night this had turned out to be.

****

The fight with Charleigh had him revved up tighter than…tighter than those fucking hot jeans painted on her. The raging hard-on filling his jeans all night was because of her and the way her jeans showed off her tiny waist, little round ass, and long legs.

And that shirt. Lord almighty. He couldn't tear his eyes from it for not wanting to miss the moment those luscious breasts of hers popped the buttons on the sleeveless strip of thin white gauze she called a shirt. It never happened, as far as he knew. But if it had, it was probably that fucking Ledger who got to see it.

Goddammit! He'd have to have a talk with the foreman about boundaries with his new boss. He'd keep his hands off her or look for another job, by God.

And he'd keep a closer eye on the clothes she bought from now on. The skintight scraps she'd chosen would attract the wrong kind of attention from the wrong kind of people.

People like that pompous Lance Barton. He hadn't been shy about showing his interest in Charleigh in the past, and he hadn't been shy about showing it tonight either. And if his asshat of a brother ever even looked at her, he'd—

"Hey, do you mind slowing down a bit? I'm getting black and blue from all the bouncing around." Beth's voice jerked his gaze to the passenger side. She was hanging on to the door handle with one hand, bracing herself on the center console with the other. He'd forgotten she was even there. A glance at the speedometer showed he was going way too fast for this road. He eased his foot off the accelerator.

"Are you okay?" She slid her hand along the bunched muscles of his thigh, squeezed, and for some reason it irritated him further. "You look like you're about to pop a vein."

He didn't speak. Didn't dare speak, or it would all come out. Six years of it. And he wasn't into sharing his feelings with anyone, but especially the town shrink who'd be quick to psychoanalyze his every word, every tone, every inflection, every gesture.

"That was some fight."

"Everything is a fight with her. She never used to be like this back when..." He chopped off the rest of the sentence. He did not want to talk about the time they'd been lovers.

"Back when you two were *lovers*? No, because you and she both wanted the same thing—each other—and were getting it. Often."

"What do you know about it?"

"This little community has deep roots, shallow minds, and long memories. We all remember how hot and heavy you and Charleigh were before she ran off with Will."

Hot and heavy. Understatement of the century. "Those feelings are dead and gone."

"Are they?"

"Yes."

"Oh, Joshua. You're smarter than the average cowboy, so I'm surprised you can't see what's right before your eyes. She obviously still has feelings for you, and I…think you do, too."

His stomach bobbed up into his chest, smacking into his heart and triggering a rough scoff from his throat. "You had a front-row seat to the fight we just had. And it's like that all the fu—all the time. I don't know what that is, but it sure ain't love."

"Well, I never mentioned *love*, but you can't deny there's something still between you two. Your words are intimate, personal. They're coming from deep inside you where all the memories and emotions live. It's clear you left things unsettled, and it's all coming out in passion-filled squabbles like the one tonight. You're not able to make love to each other, like you really want, so you make war. It's classic."

"Good to see you putting that psych degree to use, Beth."

"Doesn't take a psych degree to see what tonight

was about."

"It was what it's always about—her countermanding my every decision just to piss me off."

"It was about jealousy. Plain and simple."

There was that dismissive scoff again, but it didn't do any good convincing him to believe it. And it didn't convince Beth either.

"She was jealous you were with me," she continued, "and you were jealous she was with any man. And by the way, she's right. Cole's not interested in her, and she's definitely not interested in him."

"How do you know?"

"You were so busy watching her, you didn't see him with Teri Barnes in the corner. And you didn't see the way she looked at you the few times you weren't looking at her. Lance, on the other hand, is interested in her. Very interested. But she's not. Not yet anyway."

His brain picked through Beth's crazy theory for flaws, holes, solid evidence that it was all horse shit. Frustrated at finding none, when the road to his house came up, he kept going.

"Are you uninviting me to our sleepover?" she asked.

"I won't be good company tonight."

A rough sigh exited her mouth. "I knew this would happen."

Although she muttered the words, he heard them clearly, heard the strong emotion that fueled them. A sick sixth sense told him more was coming, so he didn't ask for clarification.

"I've never made any demands on you, Josh. I've accepted your terms for our relationship, even though I want more."

At her clipped words, he kept his eyes glued to the road ahead. The last thing he'd wanted tonight was to have a relationship talk with a woman he was just having sex with.

What a jacked-up night this had turned out to be.

"I'll do anything for you," she continued. "Fight for you, if I have to, but when I see her so easily seducing you back into her life, I have to wonder whether I even have a chance."

"That's not what she's doing."

"What I saw tonight says otherwise. How you danced with her? It was like old times."

"I danced with her *once*, out of obligation as her ranch manager. It would have looked strange if I hadn't."

"You danced *every* dance with her."

"I spent practically the whole night glued to your side." He tried to keep the frustration out of his voice, but he heard it weaving through every word.

"Your body was with me, but your eyes were on her, your attention was on her. In your mind, in your heart, you were there with her, holding her in your arms like you used to. I saw it on your face. I saw it on hers."

"What the hell do you want from me, Beth?"

"I want you to tell me you're not getting back together with her."

"I told you, before she even came back to town, that she and I—"

"Say the words, Josh. Those exact words. I need to hear them come from your mouth before I believe you two are done. Because I know you're a man of your word."

He opened his mouth to say the simple words that

would appease her when a sharp pain in the vicinity of his heart burned like he'd been rammed with a hot branding iron. The jolt jerked his body and snapped his mouth closed. The words refused to budge, as if something deep inside him knew there was no truth to them and wouldn't let him lie.

His head didn't for a second believe that he and Charleigh would get back together, not after the hell she'd dragged him through. But his heart—his broken, lifeless heart—was racing at the thought.

Beside him, Beth released a choking sob. "Oh, God."

He glanced at her. Her chin was quivering, and a glint of tears shone in her eyes. It pushed him to reach out and take her hand in his. Even if their relationship was no deeper than casual sex, she was a friend and he didn't want to hurt her.

"We're not…getting back together." As the low, weak words left his mouth, the pain in his heart intensified, as if in punishment for lying.

Beth didn't respond.

"Okay?" he asked, squeezing her hand.

She nodded.

"Look at me, Beth."

She faced him.

"Okay?" he asked, his voice soft.

She clutched their linked hands in her other hand and pulled them to her mouth. She kissed his hand, then looked at him, smiling tearfully and nodding. "Okay."

They made the rest of the drive hand-in-hand but in silence except the radio playing low on the rock station Derrick had asked him to set it to on their way to the dance. He should have turned it off. It kept his mind focused on Charleigh and the feel of her body in his arms on the dance floor, not just tonight, but before, when she was his and there was no question that he was the only man who'd hold her in his arms, both on the dance floor and off.

He remembered how back then they'd kissed through entire songs on the dance floor until the chaperones made them stop. He remembered how she'd brazenly pulled him out of the building and to his pickup. He remembered how they'd made love by the light of the dashboard, the radio turned up to a loud rock station to drown out her cries of pleasure. They'd had something special back then, him and Charleigh. At least he'd thought they had.

Beth was right about one thing. Things between them were unfinished. They'd stay that way until he found out why Charleigh had left him.

As he walked Beth to her door, he somehow knew this was it for them. Though tonight wasn't the time to say it. She was feeling vulnerable. And she'd jump to the conclusion that his decision was related to her theory that he still loved Charleigh, when the truth was, he and Beth were at different places as far as a relationship went.

"Why don't you come in," she said, all sex and smiles again. "We can talk more about things. Or..." She cupped his crotch that surprisingly wasn't showing any interest. "We can *not* talk. And I can instead help you release the tension that's been wrapped around you all night." She caressed him purposefully through his jeans, encouraging him to stay. "I guarantee you'll feel like a new man afterward. I won't even make you stay the night."

"Tempting, Beth, but another time."

She retracted her hand and set it on his chest alongside her other one. "Sure."

The disappointment in her face and tone weren't enough to get him to change his mind. About anything. "'Night," he said and brushed a kiss on her cheek. He turned to leave, but she grabbed the front of his shirt, keeping him in place.

"Talk things out with her. Put the past to bed. For your own happiness and wellbeing, but also for the boy's. It's not good for him to see the two most important people in his life fighting."

"Two most im— What makes you think I'm one half of that equation?"

"Anyone with eyes can see that little boy idolizes you. A black hole opened up in his life when his father died, a hole his mother can't fill, no matter how loving and attentive she is. He's been searching for someone to fill it ever since. He's picked you."

He shook his head in denial. "My only role in that boy's life is to teach him and his mother how to manage the ranch they inherited."

"Like it or not, you're his father figure, and he's looking to you to show him what it means to be a man. He's watching everything you do. Is arguing with his mother the example you want to set for him?"

He said nothing. At least not aloud. He did, however, silently curse Wyatt Simms for putting him in this damned situation. And Will Simms, for taking Charleigh away from him. And Charleigh, for leaving him in the first place. And himself for...for a lot of shit. But Derrick was an innocent bystander in all this and didn't deserve the sharp end.

As much as he liked the kid, he had his own issues to deal with. Like taking care of two ranches and not getting burned by his residual feelings for an old flame. Tonight, holding Charleigh in his arms, her body cemented into his, it was almost more than he could do to keep from slamming his mouth down on hers and pressing her up against the door and taking her. Right there on her front porch. Hard and fast. And he still knew her well enough to recognize the fire in her eyes that said she'd wanted that, too.

So some embers of attraction still burned between them. It would be a mistake to fan them. It could negatively affect Derrick. He was fragile right now, even after nearly nine months since his dad died. Though she didn't show it, Charleigh probably was, too. And if things went south between them, like before, she might dissolve the contract. Derrick would get hurt, and he'd lose Antelope Spring for good. Best thing for all of them was for him to keep his distance for all but his job. It would keep them all safe.

Beth patted his chest. "You give it some thought, cowboy, and if you need help, you know where I am." She leaned in and gave him a lingering kiss on the mouth that almost had him reconsidering leaving.

On the way home, he thought about all Beth had said and begrudgingly admitted she had some solid points. Not that he even for a second entertained the idea of taking on the father-figure role, but if he did, what then? Who would fill that footprint at the end of their year? Cole? Lance? Some other man? Bitterness that tasted a lot like jealousy raged through him at the idea of watching some other man insert himself into Derrick's life, into Charleigh's.

If tonight was any indication, she wouldn't have any trouble finding one. She was a young, smart, beautiful, sexy, desirable, and now-rich woman. That dynamite combination would have the available men prowling around her for more than just a turn around the dance floor. He'd seen that tonight. Felt it in the air. And as much as he hated to admit it, the thought of it ate at his insides. It didn't matter that she no longer was his or no longer wanted to be his, she had been, and the feeling of her belonging to him still saturated every cell of his body.

As he pulled up to his house, the idea that won out was that he had given his word—and signed a legally binding contract—to teach Derrick and Charleigh how to run the ranch. That would include teaching Derrick what he needed to know about being a man and keeping the wolves away from Charleigh…for her own good and for the good of her son and his inheritance.

When someone suitable could take over, he'd make the break and let Charleigh and Derrick go on with their lives. Without him. Because that would be better for them. And him. But in the meantime, no way in hell would he even entertain the idea that he and Charleigh still loved each other. Besides being too ludicrous, it was also too painful.

Chapter Ten

Charleigh and Derrick were at the barn, saddling their mounts when Josh arrived shortly before eight. Derrick ran to him as he climbed out of the pickup.

"Mom said you might not come, but I knew you would," he said, a grin a mile wide on his face as he slipped his hand into Josh's.

Josh's heart ached at the small but weighty gesture. The trust it displayed. The admiration. He felt ashamed of himself over last night, arguing with Charleigh in front of him, and because the boy hadn't been sure he'd show up or keep his promise. If there was one lesson he'd teach Derrick, it was that his word was his bond.

"Of course. I always keep my promises. A man's word—"

"Is his bond," finished Derrick.

Josh grinned down at him. "Where'd you learn that?"

"You."

Pride beamed like a sunburst inside his chest. Is this what fatherhood felt like? Seeing your child learn life's lessons thanks in part to your time and effort? If so, it wasn't a bad feeling.

"Okay, wiseacre, let's see how well you remember the rules of riding I taught you," he teased as they walked to the barn where Charleigh was saddling a third horse. For him. "If you get any wrong," he said to

Derrick, "I won't let you ride today."

"I won't get any wrong. I been practicing."

"All right. Start with your eyes."

Derrick recited each rule, pointed to the respective parts of his body as he did. "Keep my eyes up and looking where I'm going, shoulders back, elbows in, butt in the seat, heels down, toes in."

Josh nodded. "Why do you keep your heels down?"

"So my feet don't go through the stirrups and to help me balance."

"Good. What do you do with the reins?"

"Hold them light, not tight, thumb up the reins, and don't drop them."

"What do you do if your horse takes off?" Josh said as they reached Charleigh, who was tightening the cinch on the saddle of his mount.

"Hold on tight," Derrick said. "Don't yell or cry. And pull back on the reins." He illustrated his words with motions. "…back and back and back, hard."

Charleigh smiled at her son's explanation, and Josh's heart flipped a few times in his chest. Her smile wasn't for him, but he was in its radius so the effect was the same. It brought a small smile to his face and bloomed a huge one inside his chest.

When she met his gaze, he winked and asked Derrick his final question. "You mount the horse from which side?"

"Duh," he said and rolled his eyes. "Left."

Josh knocked the front of the boy's hat down over his eyes. "You're ready."

Derrick shuffled his hat back and beamed up at him.

"Good job," Charleigh said and hugged Derrick. "You remembered everything."

"Josh is a good teacher."

"Yeah. He is." Her calm, steady gaze held what looked to him like an apology. Maybe it was just reflecting what was in his eyes.

Her gaze cut to Derrick, and she smiled. "Since you're so good at riding now, maybe you could give me some pointers."

"Sure."

Josh checked the saddles on all three horses and, finding everything sound, he mounted. He was impressed at the way Derrick scrambled his way up into the saddle, not asking for help. At the way he grasped the reins in his left hand and seated himself deep. At the way he did a body check, like he'd been instructed to during their previous lessons, to make sure to remind himself of proper positioning until it became second nature. Charleigh mounted, too, in a strong, graceful arc that said she'd been practicing as well. Then the three of them headed at a walk toward the dirt road that would take them to open pasture.

On a ranch, horseback riding wasn't just a pleasure activity. As a rancher, Derrick would need to saddle up to check on his stock and on his land in places beyond the reach of a vehicle. Josh would use this ride, and future rides, to show Derrick his land until he was so familiar with every blade of grass, every rock, every tree, every hill and valley that he could see it clearly in his mind when he closed his eyes at night to sleep.

****

They rode for an hour, Josh taking Charleigh and Derrick through the various lessons they'd learned in the corral, him watching carefully to make sure they were doing it right.

The air was cool, the sun warm on her back. Fall had claimed this land almost overnight, leaving a rich color palate of ochre sunflowers bending stiffly to the ground, fans of dusty green sage, dry tawny grasses waving underneath a windswept cornflower blue sky. Being out in it, feeling the soothing, steady rhythm of the warm horse beneath her, hearing the melodic birdsong from the fields invigorated her, helped her see the appeal of country living. Not that country living was all about pleasure rides.

She had learned a lot from Josh in the month they'd been here. Enough to know that this kind of downtime was for her benefit and Derrick's. He was giving up a year of his life to fulfill the contract. Ruby was right. He was the best man for the job. But having him around so much was hard on her heart.

Her gaze fixed on the man ahead of her, riding beside her son. *His* son. Their son. The two were chatting on like they'd known each other forever. Derrick's voice drifted back to her, cheerful, animated...happy. She tried to remember a time when he'd been this happy and couldn't. Even during the time before Will had gotten sick. Being on the ranch, being around Josh, had switched something on in Derrick, given him a sense of security and confidence he'd never had. His new life swept away the grit of worry that had permeated their old life in California, and he was enjoying all it offered.

He was quickly becoming every bit his father's son, a fact that pleased her as much as it worried her. It would be hard on Derrick when they left here when the year was over. But leaving was for the best. She couldn't get involved with Josh again. And that thing that had happened between them last night…well, it had told her that might be where they were headed. If he'd kissed her—

Josh laughed at something Derrick said, refocusing her thoughts.

"Mom, me and Josh are hungry and ready for a snack," Derrick said.

"Who says I brought snacks?" she teased.

"You always have snacks. You know I'm a growing boy."

She chuckled. "Lucky for you, I do."

They dismounted and tied their horses to the fence. Charleigh pulled a bag of snacks and a thin blanket from the saddlebags. She spread the blanket on the ground and sat.

Josh sat, too, stretching out his legs, crossing them at his ankles, and leaning back on his palms. Derrick mirrored his position.

She pulled a bottle of sanitizer from her pocket and squirted some into Derrick's hand, then Josh's and hers. Then she opened the bag and laid out snacks and bottles of water.

As Josh and Derrick ate, they talked about horses, the weather, cows, school, guns, and more while she mainly watched, listened, and choked on her guilt.

A while later, the snacks gone, Charleigh gathered up the trash and put it into a plastic bag. Josh grabbed the blanket and tossed her the end of it to help shake it out and fold it. Derrick ran to the horses and scrambled up onto his, eager to show Josh how capable he was.

The second he was seated, a bird flew out of the

tall grasses nearby, spooking the horse. The little mare skittered sideways, then bolted off across the pasture.

"Oh, God, Josh!" Charleigh screamed, helplessly staring at the horror playing out before her. Josh dropped the blanket and ran to his horse.

****

His heart pounding in his throat, Josh swung up into the saddle and raced after Derrick.

As a kid, a year younger than Derrick, he'd been the one on a runaway horse, and it had been terrifying, all that powerful horseflesh racing out of control under him, sweeping him along. Panic had consumed him, erasing from memory all the lessons his granddad had taught him about riding. The fall had broken his arm.

If anything happened to Derrick...

Leaning forward in the saddle, he spurred his horse faster, and soon caught up to and rode alongside the runaway. Derrick's face was white with fear, his blue eyes wide, his mouth open, his little hands gripping the saddle horn for dear life, his legs wrapped as tight against the horse as they could.

The right thing to do was to grab the loose reins and turn the horse, slowing it, then stopping it, but everything in him was set on getting Derrick out of harm's way. Leaning over, he snaked his arm around him and lifted him out of the saddle, into his arms. The mare raced on, likely headed toward the barn and food.

Derrick clung to him but didn't cry. He just held on. Tight. As tight as Josh was holding him. Josh could feel Derrick's little heart pounding against his, his shaky breaths. Smell the sun in his hair, the fear on his skin.

The thought that this boy could have been hurt

scared him more than he'd ever been. God, he'd never forgive himself. Charleigh would never forgive him.

"You hurt?" he asked, fighting to keep his voice calm and matter of fact.

He felt Derrick's tentative head shake. "No, sir."

He reined in, stopping his horse. Dismounting, Derrick still in his arms, he knelt, setting the boy on his feet. He held him by the shoulders and looked him in the eye.

"I'm proud of you, son. You held on. You didn't scream or cry." He nodded. "You did good."

The color was coming back into Derrick's face, and he wasn't trembling as much, but his eyes wouldn't leave Josh's. "But I dropped the reins."

"Next time, you won't. Because you'll turn this mistake into a lesson. Think about what went wrong and how you're going to prevent it next time."

Charleigh's horse ran up at that moment and slid to a halt. She vaulted off and ran to Derrick, his hat clutched in her hand. Falling to her knees, she pulled him down into her arms and rocked him. "Baby, are you all right?" Her voice was shaky, which meant she was on the verge of tears. Not that he blamed her.

"Yeah, Mom." Derrick responded in a nonchalant tone, as if a runaway horse was a common occurrence for him.

"Charleigh, he's fine," Josh said, lending credence to Derrick's claim. "He handled it like a pro."

Her eyes were on fire with fear and anger when they met his. "Don't you dare trivialize this, Josh Flores. He could have been killed."

"It was my fault," Derrick jumped in. "I accidentally dropped the reins. I shouldn't have done that. That's one of the rules."

Josh mounted his horse. "Derrick, give me your hand."

Charleigh bolted to her feet and held Derrick back when he stepped forward to obey him. "Why?"

"He lost his horse and needs to go get it."

"Are you out of your mind? He's not getting back on that horse. Or any horse. Ever."

"Mom!" Derrick sounded more afraid of not getting to ride again than he was about remounting the out-of-control horse. His gaze grabbed Josh's as if appealing to him for help.

"He must, Charleigh. After something like this, he has to get back on right away or the fear will be the last thing he remembers.

"No."

"I'll be right there with him."

"Josh, he's—" She swallowed hard.

He didn't know what the rest of her sentence would have been, but he could guess. *He's just a baby. He's not ready. He's all I've got.* He understood her fears, but damned if he'd let her—or Derrick—give in to them. Fear could paralyze if allowed a foothold. "I'll take care of him, CC. I promise."

He was surprised to hear her nickname flow from his lips, and she was, too, judging by the look she gave him, eyes wide and soft. She bit her trembling lip against the meltdown he knew was going on inside her.

At her barely perceptible nod, he held out his hand to Derrick. She let her son go, and he eagerly went to Josh and gripped his outstretched hand. Josh hauled him up into the saddle behind him. She handed Derrick his hat, and with a grin he put it on. Without further discussion, he and Derrick rode off to capture the runaway horse.

The trust it took for CC to let her son go with him was huge, and the weight of that gift warmed him to his very core. He meant what he told her. He'd take care of this boy. Give his own life to keep him safe. And he'd do the same for her. Because he…

Because it was his job.

****

Charleigh followed several feet behind Derrick and Josh, her heart heavy. Will had never questioned her parenting decisions. Josh challenged everything. Thing was, she knew he was right, about most things. What was more, she knew Derrick was safe with him. But it didn't alleviate the tornado in her stomach or the anchor in her heart.

Their laughter floated back to her, releasing another wave of emotion that flooded her system— jealousy. She'd never felt this way before, with Derrick, anyway. She had been everything to her son, especially after Will died. Now, more and more, she had to share him. With Josh. The man who had broken her heart. The man who hadn't wanted them. The man whose care for them was contracted and would end when the year was up.

Almost as troubling as the ever-present anxiety was the ever-growing joy. He'd called her CC. Something he'd called her when they were together and wanted to remind her how much he loved her. What did his calling her that mean now? Was he using his old tricks to get her cooperation? Or did it mean something else?

She didn't know. But one thing she knew for sure…she would have to take care not to allow herself to get swept up in him again. It wouldn't be easy. Like last night, when he'd pulled her to him. She had felt his passion, smelled it, seen it in his eyes. If he had kissed her, tried to take her right there on the porch, she would have been powerless to stop him. Because, despite it being a colossal mistake, she still wanted him. As much as she always had.

But then making mistakes with Josh was old hat. What was it that he used to say about turning your mistakes into lessons? It wasn't something she had learned. At least with regard to him. She had Derrick to watch out for, his future to protect, so she'd be more careful not to do anything to put that at risk. Getting involved with Josh again would do that. She was sure of it.

They captured the runaway mare at the gate that separated the pasture from the road, and Derrick rode home on her with no further incidence. Back at the barn, Josh had Derrick talk them through the unsaddling and grooming routine, a few times correcting him, immediately, both telling him and showing him the right way, and making him repeat it.

The horses taken care of, Derrick raced inside to wash up and get something to eat. He was always hungry, and fortunately there was always enough food to eat now.

Charleigh and Josh stood side by side, arms folded atop the tailgate of his pickup.

"Thank you for saving him," she said.

"I know you don't believe it, but he handled it well. Most novices panic and fall off. I did. Broke my—"

"Left arm," she said, remembering the story.

"When you were four."

He nodded.

"If he did well, it was because of your training," she added.

"He's a fast learner. But one of these days, he will fall off. And get hurt. It's all part of the learning process."

"Josh, I want you to know that when I disagree with you about Derrick, I'm not trying to be difficult and I'm not saying I don't trust you with him. I'm just trying to protect him the best way I know how. That's my responsibility, and I take it very seriously. He's everything to me, he's all I have, and I'll do whatever I have to do to protect him. From anything or anyone who could hurt him."

He brushed her elbow with his and left it there. "I won't hurt him, CC. I promise."

Whenever he called her CC, her legs went weak at the knees, and her breath burned up in her lungs, scattering like sparks to melt her heart. Add his touch to the mix and she was toast.

"You might," she said. "Unintentionally, of course. He looks up to you." She lifted one brow. "Worships you, really." In fact, Derrick's constant *Josh said this, Josh said that, look what Josh taught me, me and Josh are going to this and this and that* and on and on wore on her. "And it worries me."

"Why?"

She met his gaze, wanting to show him how serious she was about this. "The separation will hurt him."

"The separation?"

"When the year is up."

"I'll still be around."

"But we won't."

He stiffened, making her wish she'd chosen her words more carefully. "So you're selling," he said, his tone controlled and flat.

"I don't know for sure yet, but even if we stay, it won't be the same. You won't be around, not like you are now." She turned her attention to a flake of paint on the tailgate and scratched it with her fingernail. "And knowing the heartache that's coming for him makes me anxious and reactive."

Josh anchored his hat down close to his eyes and looked away. "Guess I'd feel the same way if he was my boy."

Her heart froze in her chest at his words and heat took her face. The words "he is your boy" were on the tip of her tongue and tried to squeeze through, out into the fresh air, but she reined them in. "I'm glad you understand."

"Would you feel better if I transferred some of my training duties to Cole?"

No! "Why would that make me feel better?" Her fingernail worrying at the paint chip finally flicked it off, leaving her free to look him in the eyes.

"Derrick could bond with someone who's on site now and will be in the future, so if you did decide to stay—"

"Do you want to do that?"

"No. It doesn't feel right, seeing as it's my job." He scratched his neck. "I'm just trying to address your concerns."

"I didn't bring this up because I wanted a change in our situation. I brought it up so you'd better understand why I act the way I do. Plus, the contract is pretty clear, and I don't want to do anything that would risk invalidating it." She pushed back from the tailgate. "Let's leave things as they are. Whatever happens at the end, he'll get through it. He's tough."

"Like his mother."

Was he complimenting her? Or ridiculing her? Didn't matter. "I am tough. I've had to be."

His lips lifted in an amused smile. "You say it like it's a new development. You've always been tough."

When they'd been together, she'd had a reputation for being the toughest, most badass girl in town, refusing to take shit from anyone. But in truth, it had been an act. She'd been nothing but a scared little girl who'd lost her parents and had no one to love her. No one but Josh. And he'd been everything to her, the reason she'd been able to survive.

But now, she was genuinely tough. The struggles she had endured had demanded it. She'd survived her parents dying and leaving her, Josh leaving her, childbirth, Will dying and leaving her, being a widowed mother with no support and little money, and starting a new life that demanded she risk exposing her most vulnerable secret to the man who had left her when she'd needed him the most.

That he had seen that strength in her—and commented on it—made her proud. But he still had no idea what she'd been through or who she was now. For some reason, it was important to her that he understand that. "I'm not the same girl you knew, Josh."

"And I'm not the same guy."

She'd seen that right off. That man who'd threatened her in her kitchen her first morning here was

Josh yet so much more. Like a pencil sketch, he had been fully colored in. It was the same for her. Losing him had broken her into a million pieces, and when they'd finally reassembled, they hadn't come back together in the same way. She was a different person now. A stronger person. It probably was the same for him.

The realization that they'd both grown, changed, in the years apart from each other also exposed the idea that maybe they could build a relationship as the adults they were now and let go of the baggage carried by the kids they'd been. Maybe they could see each other through new eyes.

The crash of a dish falling to the floor in the house and a loud "uh-oh!" enabled her to drag her attention away from his eyes. "I better check on him before he destroys Ruby's kitchen."

She started toward the house.

"CC." He caught her arm at the elbow and eased her back around to face him. He looked at her like he was going to say something else on their previous topic, but then he didn't. He let her go. "I'm headed out to check on the hands repairing a section of fence line. It would be good for you to go with me. See how it's done."

"Sure. You want a sandwich or something first?"

He pushed his hat back on his head and rubbed a hand over his hard stomach. "I could eat," he said, a little half grin lifting his mouth. Like father, like son.

Minutes later, the three of them set off in Josh's pickup, eating on the way the sandwiches Ruby packed for them, and for the rest of the day, she and Derrick got a lesson in the art of mending fences.

****

Dusk was on them by the time Josh got Charleigh and Derrick home. He was beat, and he knew they were, too, but there were chores to do. Part of him wanted to tell them to go on in and relax. But he didn't. They needed to know that being tired wasn't a reason to skip work or unload it on someone else. Ranching was a hard life, and they needed to understand that.

Charleigh was right. He wouldn't be here for them as much when the year was up. They'd have to do it on their own. It was his job to make sure they could. Or maybe help them to realize they couldn't and guide their best decision for their best future.

After supervising the chores and refusing Derrick's daily invitation to join them for supper, he headed home for a hot shower, cold beer, and whatever meal he could scrounge up from the measly contents of his fridge.

All afternoon, he'd thought about what Charleigh had said about Derrick worshiping him. It mirrored what Beth had said. And today, working the fences he'd seen it in Derrick's every action. The boy watched him like a hawk, emulated him, whether it was how he wore his hat or stood or what he laughed at or what he did. He even walked like him and had picked up some of his mannerisms and expressions.

Clearly, the boy absorbed everything he said and did, like a sponge soaking up water. He was a great kid, always asking questions and listening attentively to the answers, and a hard worker, jumping in eagerly and cheerfully to whatever the task required. He'd miss this daily contact with Derrick, and with Charleigh, when the contract was up. The thought left him cold inside.

He pulled up in front of his house. It was dark and

quiet, lacking the warmth and joy of the Simms house, but there was comfort in the fact it was his and in knowing it wasn't Will's. Being in that place creeped him out, memories good and bad chasing him like demons.

He went inside, stripped down, and jumped into the shower. Feeling more clear-headed, he grabbed a long-neck from the fridge and plopped down into the desk chair. Flipping open his laptop, he entered the search words "father figure to boys." Dozens of sites returned, and he selected one after the other, scanning the research. The responsibility inherent in the role settled in his gut like a boulder.

It's confusing and distressing for a boy to bond with an adult and then suddenly no longer have him in his life.

A father figure needs to be someone who regularly invests time in the relationship and participates in activities that interest him.

A father figure is a symbol of security for a boy that enables him to grow into a strong, decent, loving man, and a productive member of society.

Boys who don't have a father or a male role model in their lives have more addictions and high-risk behaviors than those who do.

Jails are filled with men who didn't have good male role models during their formative years.

He kicked back in his chair and took a long pull on his beer. It would be detrimental to Derrick's wellbeing to end the relationship. So, no matter what it cost him, he'd continue in the role placed on him.

He'd do it for Derrick, because he was a good kid and because he'd lost his father too young. He'd do it for Charleigh, because for some reason he felt the need to make her life more comfortable. He'd do it for himself, because it felt good to be needed, because this might be as close as he'd ever get to being a father, and because he knew how it felt to grow up without a positive father figure. He'd maintain that role until Charleigh found the boy a real father. Or left town. Then he'd let go. Of both of them.

His mind wandered back to Wyatt's initial proposal for him to marry Charleigh. Maybe he shouldn't have been so quick to dismiss it. The matter would be settled. She would have a husband, Derrick would have a father, and he'd have a family. For better or for worse. For now and always.

Odd how the thought didn't leave him as cold as it had all those months ago.

Chapter Eleven

While Derrick was in school, Charleigh explored every corner of the property with Josh as they fed the cattle and checked for and repaired downed fences. Every day, she loaded jugs of water, thermoses of coffee, and plenty of food in a cooler so they wouldn't have to come back in to eat, and, after dropping Derrick at the bus stop, struck out across the pastures to do their work.

Josh also used that time to point out which pastures were for grazing, which were cultivated for growing feed for the cattle, and which were dedicated to growing wheat for sale. He'd also given her homework—learn about the two crops, from how to grow them to how to the market them.

They were at the last pasture for the day before picking up Derrick, forking hay from the pickup for the cattle and filling the troughs with protein pellets when Josh's stomach growled loudly for the third time.

"I'm so damn hungry I'm ready to eat these protein pellets," Josh said, filling the trough with another can of the supplemental food.

Charleigh scooped her can into the bag, too, and poured the pellets into the other side of the trough. "You had four of Ruby's pancakes this morning, two eggs, bacon, and two biscuits with peach preserves."

"Two and a half biscuits," he corrected, grinning.

"Derrick gave me half of his second."

"I think you and Derrick have holes in your legs where the food falls out," she said.

Derrick had been so relentless in his attempts to get Josh to have breakfast with them every weekday morning that he finally gave in. Breakfasts, and even some suppers, had been a standing date since, and between the two of them, it was hard to know who ate more. Derrick was his father's son.

She hadn't gotten used to eating such a big meal that early in the morning, so come noon time, she was hungry.

"He sure can put it away," he said. "I remember being his age and always hungry."

Her stomach growled loudly, and Josh scooped up a pellet and lobbed it at her. "Sounds like you're ready to eat, too."

She caught it. "I could eat. But not this." Grinning, she threw it back at him, which he swatted into the trough. "C'mon, let's see what Ruby packed for us today."

He lifted the bag of pellets and set it back into the pickup bed, and she set their tin cans alongside it. He opened the tailgate, jumped into the bed, and pulled the cooler forward so they could dig in. They sat next to each other on the tailgate, and she squirted sanitizer into his hands then hers.

"I want to start shooting lessons for you and Derrick this Saturday after our ride," he said as she opened the cooler, pulled out the food Ruby packed for them, and set it on the bandana she had spread out.

She had never been around guns, and the thought of using one on any living thing turned her stomach. So did the idea of her five-year-old son being forced to face that decision. "Absolutely not." She handed him a sandwich, then picked up her own and bit into it.

"What is it you're objecting to?" he said, digging into his. "The timing? Or the idea?"

"Shooting. Guns."

"What would you do if a cougar or a coyote came into the yard and cornered Derrick? What if some stranger showed up at night and you and Derrick were alone in the house?"

She grabbed the water jug and poured them each a cup of water. "Unlikely scenarios." She handed him his.

"But possible," he said, drinking his down in one long gulp and holding it out for more. "I'd feel better knowing you and Derrick were acquainted with the business end of the gun."

She refilled it, and he nodded his thanks. "Well, you can relax because we both know that much."

"Shooting is part of what you need to know as a rancher," he said around a bite of the second half of his sandwich. "You don't need to be a sniper, but you do need to know the basics—how to set and release the safety, load and unload, shoot." She opened her mouth to argue when he jumped in. "I thought you were going to trust me about ranch stuff?"

She had promised to trust Josh with all things ranch, and she'd keep that promise. If he thought shooting was a necessary skill, then she would heed his advice. Even if the idea rubbed her every sensibility wrong. Anything to protect Derrick.

She released an exasperated sigh. "What are we talking...pistol? Rifle?"

"We'll start with the rifle."

"Okay, but under protest."

He grinned. "Got it. Any more sandwiches?"

She pulled one from the container and held it out to him. "And a condition."

"No. I'm shocked."

At his teasing tone, she pulled back the sandwich as he reached for it. "I want to learn first, so when it's Derrick's turn, I'll be able to teach him with you, ease any fears he has, and make sure he understands the gravity of what you're teaching him."

She held out the sandwich, and he took it but didn't move to unwrap it, just kept staring at her, his blue eyes starting soft little fires wherever they touched.

"What?" she asked with a small self-conscious grin and wiped her mouth with her napkin for stray crumbs or glob of mayonnaise.

"Every child should be lucky enough to have a mother like you."

Pride ballooned in her chest at his comment. "That's about the sweetest thing you've ever said to me."

"You're a good mom, Charleigh."

Her face heated at his praise. "I appreciate you saying that."

He dug into his second sandwich. "Was Will a good father?"

Will had been more of a playmate than a disciplinarian, but there was no reason to share that with Josh. "Yes."

"I'm guessing you were the disciplinarian."

She almost choked on her sandwich at his expression of her very thoughts. "Why would you think that?"

"'Cause I know Will," he said with a scoff. "*Knew* Will. He was probably more of a playmate."

She kept eating to avoid the conversation.

"Did you guys have a good marriage?"

"I'm not talking about my marriage."

"Was it that bad?"

With each probing question, her appetite fled. "Just drop it, Josh."

"Charleigh, I'm just trying to understand."

"The *only* thing you need to understand is that you and I aren't talking about my marriage. And I don't want to hear about you and the queen or any of your other girlfriends."

"Were you in love with Will when you married him?"

"What did I *just* say?" She prayed each sharp-edged word that left her mouth would put an end to this conversation.

"I deserve the truth about whether you loved him when you married him. Give me that at least."

The implication was, of course, that if she had loved Will when she married him, she hadn't loved Josh. The trap was, it didn't matter what she said, he'd find fault with her answer.

If she said no, he'd accuse her of marrying Will because she wanted a husband, no matter who. Or he'd accuse her of being after Will's money. Which was so far from the truth it was laughable. If she lied and said yes, he'd accuse her of lying about loving him and accuse her of cheating on him with Will. She didn't want to hurt him by suggesting that her love for him had been a lie. Almost better he think she was a gold digger.

"Why all the deep thinking?" he said. "It's an easy yes or no question."

She looked at the half-eaten sandwich in her hand instead of at him as she searched for the right answer.

"Look at me, CC." His voice was little more than a harsh whisper but it was commanding.

She corralled her courage and faced him. He looked at her as if everything was riding on her answer to his question.

"Were you in love with Will when you ran off with him and married him?" he repeated.

She licked her lips to keep from biting them. "No. I wasn't."

His full lips thinned in anger. "So it was just a husband you wanted all along? Didn't matter who?"

"No," she said. "That's not how it was."

He kept going, as if he thought it was. "Well, congratulations. You made the better choice in Will. It got you this million-dollar ranch. That's a hell of a lot more than you would have gotten with me." He stood, tossed the remainder of his sandwich into the tall grass, and faced away from her, hands in fists at his sides.

She jumped off the tailgate and flung her sandwich into the grass, too. "Who the hell are you to judge me? You threw me away, like you just did that sandwich. And then I had no one. Nothing. When Will offered me a chance at a better life, I took it. If that offends your high and mighty sense of right and wrong, I don't really give a damn."

The fire in his eyes was hot when he spun back toward her. "I didn't throw you away. You kicked me out."

"Because you didn't want me!"

"I loved you!"

The vehemence and anguish in his voice shook her. He had loved her, a lot, but when she'd needed it the most, it hadn't been enough.

"Not enough to want a life with me."

"I was eighteen fucking years old, Charleigh. I could barely wipe my own ass. I wasn't ready or able to take on the responsibilities of marriage. And neither were you."

"You don't know that. In typical Josh Flores fashion, you decided what the *right* way was, and when what I needed didn't fall in line with your thinking, you bailed."

"You're the one who wasn't interested in discussing it, finding a solution that worked for both of us," he said. "You just flat-assed kicked me out and told me not to come back. Then a week later you...you fucking married my best friend."

The pain in his voice, in his gaze, worsened her own pain. "I only wanted you," she said. "You wanted someone else. I took the only solution available—to go on with my life without you."

Confusion twisted his features. "I didn't want anyone else."

She shook her head at his lie and turned to pack up their lunch items.

"Who?" he demanded.

When she ignored him, he grabbed her arms and turned her to face him, knocking the thermos from her hand. It fell onto the tailgate and rolled off into the dirt.

"You need to tell me who the hell you're talking about."

"I don't need to tell you shit." She pushed away.

The memory of him with that redhead in his room, in his bed, a week after they broke up, was almost as painful today as it was the day she'd seen it happen. She picked up the thermos and stuffed it into the cooler. "My thoughts, my feelings—past and present—are outside the boundaries of your managerial responsibilities. So don't even ask."

She expected him to fire back with some scathing retort or demand she explain the comment, but he didn't. She felt his eyes burning into her, and she couldn't keep from glancing up at him. There was a sad emptiness in them that mirrored what she felt inside. Regret that things hadn't worked out differently between them? That things were going so badly between them even though they'd once loved each other so completely it seemed as if they shared one soul? That they couldn't talk about their past for more than a minute without fighting?

But she didn't dare push him for an explanation. Because then she'd have to share her own explanation. And her own feelings. Being that vulnerable would bring down the corral she'd carefully erected around them.

Thunder rolled in the darkening clouds overhead, and a few spits of rain pinged her skin. "I'd like to go now. Derrick'll be home from school soon."

He didn't respond, but she sensed him behind her, his gaze burning into her as she put the lid on the cooler and shoved it deeper into the bed. She climbed into the pickup and slammed the door. Several seconds later, he slammed the tailgate, climbed in beside her, slammed his door, and drove toward home.

****

The wipers squeaked away the light drops of rain, but by the look of the sky up ahead, they were in for a downpour that would test the old blades.

Josh should have had them home by now. But the delay was worth it. He was piecing together a picture that said her and Will's marriage hadn't been a fairytale love story. But what had it been? Why had she married him? Because he wouldn't? To get back at him? Because she'd been desperate to get out of Chismes Point?

It hurt to think she'd married a man she didn't love just to get out of the life he'd left her in when he wouldn't marry her. It didn't surprise him that Will had asked her to marry him. But what the hell was that about him wanting someone else? He hadn't wanted anyone but her. Ever. He hadn't had a serious relationship since she'd left with Will. He'd had his fair share of hookups after he'd learned she was married, more to numb his pain than to find someone to replace her. But she couldn't know that. Had Will lied to her to cause trouble between them?

He'd make himself crazy thinking about it, thinking about all the what-ifs, especially the big one that was as part of him as his skin... How their lives would have changed if only he'd been able to give Charleigh the token she'd asked for that night.

Ah, hell. It didn't do any good to think like that. They couldn't change things. They couldn't go back. But if he knew the truth about why she left, maybe they could move ahead. The uninterrupted, no-holds-barred conversation he'd hoped to have with her about their past had turned into another argument. She was defensive and reluctant as hell to be honest with him.

It didn't help that he was just…angry, hurting. Still. After all these years. He had swallowed his grief when she'd left him, every bitter drop, and it had, over time, fermented into a steeping pile of anger. Having her here, day in, day out, was bringing into the light all the feelings from that day—the worst of his life— peeling back layers, making him face his memories. His mistakes. His truths. But he couldn't put the pain behind him unless he got her truths.

She was holding secrets. He was sure of it. Today's reveal was only the tip of the iceberg. He would get them out of her, even if he had to drag them out one at a time. It was the only way they both would ever get past what happened and be able to work together now and in the future.

Half way home, rain began to fall, light but steady. He was praying the bald tires on the pickup had enough traction to get them through the mounting mud when the pickup skidded right then stopped its forward motion, the tires spinning uselessly.

"Shit," he mumbled and slammed it into park.

"Hope you're packing kitty litter," she said.

He looked at her. Humor sparkled in her eyes and curved her lips into a soft smile.

Grinning back in spite of himself, he shook his head. "Not one bag."

"Mistakes, lessons."

It tickled him that she remembered his granddad's quote. "Smartass."

"So who're you calling to come rescue us this time?"

This time. So she remembered *last* time. She remembered a lot about their past. Like he did. There wasn't one memory of them that had faded from his brain.

"We're on our own." He opened his door. "Let's go."

"We'll get soaked."

"Fortunately, neither one of us is made of sugar."

She crawled out on his side, and together they gathered twigs, branches, gravel, pebbles, pretty much any natural detritus that was less slick than the mud. Armful after armful. Then they dug some of the mud away from the tires with a shovel he had in the back and packed the areas with the stuff that hopefully would give them the traction they needed.

"Let's give it a try," he said.

As they started toward the driver's side door, she slipped in the mud and grabbed his arm to keep from falling. He grabbed her to steady her, but then they both went down, her landing on top of him.

Her hands on his chest, she pushed herself up. "Sorry," she said then snickered.

"What's so damn funny?" he asked.

"You got a little mud on you." She streaked a finger down the length of his nose, laughing again. "It's a good look on you." The words choked out among the chuckles.

"You think so?" he said.

She nodded and kept laughing.

He grabbed hold of her and rolled them over so he was on top, then drew a mustache on her with his muddy finger. Laughing, lips closed, she turned her head back and forth to try to avoid it.

"Never seen you look better, sweetheart," he said, admiring his handiwork.

Eyes shining, she grinned. "Back atcha, cowboy."

As his gaze took in her face, everything came into sharp focus. The chill of the wet mud, the smell of the rain pattering down on them, the thin sheet of heat hoverboarding between his body and hers, the thudding of his heart against hers, the heaviness that had settled in his groin, gripping the base of his growing erection. Even muddy, Charleigh was beautiful. Even muddy, those lips of hers enticed him. Even muddy, her body fit perfectly under his. Even muddy, she was dangerous, making him forget things he shouldn't. Like her betrayal.

"We should get home." He rolled off her and, holding onto the pickup, climbed to his feet. Behind him, she rose to her knees. He held out his hand, and she grabbed it with both hands. After pulling her to her feet, he immediately released her.

"Let's give it a try." He headed to the driver-side door, she to the other. They both opened their doors and stared at each other from across the cab.

"We're going to get mud all over the seat," she said.

Her words triggered the memory of the last time they'd faced this very problem, prompting his gaze to snake up then down her body. In his mind's eye, he could see beneath the mud and clothes to the delicious, smooth curves.

He swallowed back a groan. "If you're worried about it, we could do what we did the last time we got stuck in the mud."

They'd gone to the pond to make love. When they started to leave, the pickup had gotten stuck in the mud because it had rained the day before. They'd tried

209

everything to get unstuck, but nothing worked. He ended up calling his dad to pull them out.

His dad had been fully pissed and half drunk when he'd arrived with a bag of kitty litter and a tirade of insults. He threw the bag into the back of the pickup, told Josh to get his ass home after dropping off the girl, threatened him with severe bodily harm if he got mud on the seats, then got in his pickup and left.

Josh had been mortified. To lighten the situation, Charleigh had suggested they take off their clothes before getting into the pickup so his dad wouldn't be pissed that they'd gotten it muddy. After pouring kitty litter behind and in front of the tires, they had stripped down to skin, hopped in, and driven right out. On the way home, they had explored each other with such vigor he'd almost driven off the road and gotten stuck again. The red on her cheeks said the memory ran through her head, too.

"We could, but let's use this plastic tarp instead." She pulled it from behind the seat and unfolded it.

Grinning, he caught the end of the tarp she'd tossed to him, and together they spread it over the bench seat and up the back, then climbed in. He cranked the engine, rocked the pickup forward, then back, forward again, until the tires found traction. On their way again, he called Ruby and asked her to pick Derrick up from the bus stop because they were going to be late.

****

"You know, there's always been something about that day that confused me," Charleigh said, still thinking about that day they'd gotten stuck in the mud and had to call his dad for help.

"What day?"

"The day we got stuck."

"What's that?"

"Why your dad was so mad."

"It didn't take much to piss him off, especially where I was concerned. But on that day, it was because he had to cross onto Simms land to get us. I wasn't supposed to be there, and the last thing he wanted was a run-in with Wyatt."

"It you weren't supposed to be there, why were you always taking me there?"

He grinned. "Because you were always begging me to go there."

She laughed because she knew he was right. Until she had moved into her apartment, the pond was the only place, other than his pickup, where they could be alone and make love, and nearly every day she begged him to take her there.

"You could have said no," she said.

He held her gaze so tightly it felt like he was crawling inside her, looking for the memories of that time, trying to see whether hers matched his. Then he let his eyes return to the windshield. "No. I couldn't."

He could have said no. It wouldn't have mattered to her. *Where* they made love was far less important than that they *could* make love. At the time, she hadn't realized the lengths he had gone to to make her happy. And now…today…he was giving a year of his life to help her and Derrick get the ranch. Horace had told her that if Josh hadn't signed the contract, Wyatt wouldn't have given the ranch to Derrick. But it wasn't like Josh was doing it solely out of the goodness of his heart.

"That land, Antelope Spring, that's the reason you agreed to Wyatt's plan, isn't it?"

He pulled the front of his cap a little lower. "One of the reasons, yes."

He'd long ago told her how the land had transferred from Flores hands into Simms hands. Reclaiming Antelope Spring and getting funds to renovate the family ranch was why he'd agreed to this agreement. But had the desire to see her again played any part in it?

"What's another reason?"

"That, Mrs. Simms, is none of your business." His teasing tone triggered a smile.

"Well, whatever your reasons, I'm glad you agreed." She reached across the seat and squeezed his arm. "And I'm glad you're getting back the land that belonged to your family. It's only right."

"Clearly, you don't understand the value of that piece of property," he said with a wry grin.

"I understand its value to you."

He looked at her. He didn't speak, but the light in his eyes spoke volumes. He had heard the sincerity in her quiet voice, and it made her happy.

Less than a half an hour later, they pulled up in front of her house and he turned off the engine.

A warm, golden light radiated through the windows of the house, giving it a cheery, welcome look on this cold, rainy day. It would be warm and dry inside. She could take a shower and put on clean, dry clothes. She could hug her son. Despite all that, all she wanted was to stay in the muddy pickup, with a muddy Josh.

The sound of the rain pinging on the metal roof of the pickup sent chills up her spine and covered her skin with goosebumps. In the past, she'd have scooted up close to Josh and let his arm around her chase away her chills. Let his kisses warm her even more. Let his touches light an inferno inside her that would steam up the windows. Then let his body extinguish the flames. That wasn't an option now. She knew it, but it didn't stop her mind from playing what-if.

"It's supposed to rain all day tomorrow," he said, breaking the silence between them. "After we get Derrick off to school, we'll stay in and go over the books."

"Okay."

He leaned toward her, and she thought he was going to open her door for her, but instead he took her hand and linked his fingers with hers.

Her gaze flew to where their muddy hands were joined on the seat, then up to his face.

"CC—"

A knocking on her window interrupted him and jerked his hand from hers. Derrick stood on the running board, staring in at them, grinning, holding an umbrella over his head.

She rolled down the window as far as it would go, to its half position.

"Hi, Mom. Hi, Josh," he said and waved.

Josh held up his hand in a small wave.

"You guys coming in?" he said.

"Yeah, puppy, I'll be right in.

"Ready for me to check your chores?" Josh asked him.

"Cole checked them. He said I did great."

"Good," he said.

"Ruby says you should stay and eat supper with us."

213

"Thanks, bud, but I got a lot of work waiting on me at home."

"How come you guys got mud all over you?"

Ruby stuck her head out the door. "Derrick, Nikki's on the phone for you."

"Okay, Ruby," he said then turned back to the pickup window. "Nikki wants to be my girlfriend, but I'm not sure yet." He hopped down and rushed toward the house, hitting every puddle as he did, until he was back inside.

Charleigh rolled up the window and turned to Josh. "You should join us for supper. It's Ruby's green chile stew and cornbread. Perfect for a night like this."

"I'm not eating a thing until after I shower."

"You could come back after your shower. We'll wait for you."

"Thanks, but I'll pass tonight." He leaned over, his hand reaching toward her again but this time settling on the door handle.

A rush of disappointment shot her hand out to grip his arm. "What were you going to say?" she whispered, his face right by hers. "Before Derrick showed up?"

He shook his head. "Not important." He yanked hard on the handle. The door creaked open, letting in the rain.

She caught it before it flopped open all the way. "Tell me. Please?"

He eased upright, away from her. "When we were together, was your favorite band the Sewernuts?"

The seriousness in his face, hearing the word Sewernuts come from his mouth, the question itself—it was all so absurd, she couldn't hold back a giggle. "What?"

"Was it your favorite band?" His tone sharpened a bit, and he looked irritated.

"No."

"Never?"

She shrugged. "I mean, you know, they were all right, and I liked that one song, but they were never my favorite." But they had at one time been Will's favorite. "Why?"

The hardness in Josh's eyes and in his expression eased at her admission, like it made him happy. "Just wondered."

"No. You don't get to ask a strange question like that without telling me why."

"Will said it was."

The smile left her face. She'd never said that to Will. So why would he say it to Josh? When had he said it? It didn't matter. What mattered is that he'd lied about it. "He was wrong."

"Good."

Their eyes stayed connected for a long moment until Derrick pushed open the screen door and hollered, "Mom, Nikki's mom wants to talk to you."

"I'll be right there," she called out, then turned back to Josh. "Guess I should go in."

"Guess so."

"See you tomorrow."

"Yep."

She wanted him to come inside with her or wanted to stay outside with him, but she climbed out, closed the door, and walked to the back to grab the cooler. At her front door, she paused long enough to give him a little wave, and her heart swelled when he waved back. She went in then, closing the doors on the oddly sad sound of his pickup driving away.

****

Will Simms was a lying son-of-bitch. Clearly, he'd been trying to make Josh mistrust Charleigh and their relationship. Trying to drive a wedge between them, break them apart, so he could have her. He'd made it so easy for Will to take her. Dammit! If only he'd kept his cool and dug a little to see why she was acting so out of character. If only she'd trusted him more and waited a little longer before jumping into a loveless marriage.

On the drive home, his cold, wet shoulders slumped under the weight of all the if-onlys and missed opportunities shaking loose inside him. He and Charleigh had both messed up, and he had a sinking suspicion those mistakes had cost them much more than their relationship.

****

Days later, after the ground had dried up, Josh and Charleigh drove to a pasture she'd never seen before. There were no troughs there to fill, no water tank to check, no cows as far as the eye could see.

"What are we doing here?" she asked after he'd shut off the engine.

"Welcome to your first shooting lesson."

Her stomach sank to her knees, but she didn't argue or try to get out of it. She'd given her word. She'd keep it.

He grabbed the rifle from the gun rack and ammo from the glove box, then they climbed out and sat on the tailgate. For the next half hour, he went over the names of every part of his rifle, had her repeat them, had her load and unload the gun, turn the safety on and off, and so many things she wasn't sure she'd remember it all.

"Ready to shoot?" he asked, taking the loaded gun from her hands.

"Sure." She wasn't sure at all, but knowing he was there to guide her through it calmed her nerves.

"Grab the target," he nodded toward the rolled up paper tube in the truck bed.

She did and followed him to a fencepost, where he attached the target, then walked the two of them several yards away from it.

"I'm holding the rifle in my left hand, and it's pointed down range." He pointed his right hand in the direction of the target to reinforce where down range was. "Put your left hand over my left hand."

She reached out and set her hand on his.

"Not like that. You need to get in front of me."

"Well, you didn't say that. Not very thorough of you, Flores."

He hooked his hand around her waist and guided her in front of him. His touch, the warmth of his body behind her, was going to make it almost impossible to concentrate on anything he said.

"I'm bringing my right hand onto the gun," he said, his voice low, not a whisper but soft at her ear, and it was doing crazy things to her insides. "Put your right hand over mine, keeping your finger *off* the trigger."

He held her between his arms, his front to her back, her hands on his. She couldn't help herself. She turned her head to face him, wanting to see his eyes, his mouth.

He met her eyes. "Keep your eyes down range."

A little grin sneaked out before she faced front.

"Now grip my hands. Firmly."

She did and forced herself to focus on the work at hand and not on him and the heat swirling through her at his touch, his closeness, his scent.

"Are you comfortable?"

They were too close. Little sweat beads of desire tickled at her hairline and between her shoulder blades and breasts. Her hard nipples were tight and tingling, tugging on her core. Comfortable? Hell, no. "Yes."

"Good. When I say 'now,' I want you to put your right finger on the trigger, but do *not* pull the trigger. Do you understand?"

"Yes."

"What did I say?"

Her huffed breath of irritation sneaked out before she could stop it, accompanied by an eye roll.

He took the gun from her hands and stepped back, away from her.

She spun around to face him. "What are you doing?"

"If you're not going to take this seriously…"

"I am."

"This is serious business, CC. I have to know you understand what I'm telling you."

"I know it's serious. But you don't have to talk to me like I'm a two-year-old."

"This is your first lesson. It's important that we go over every step slowly and carefully. A gun can take a life—yours, someone else's, an animal's. Its use is not to be taken lightly. You can't forget anything I've told you when you take a gun in your hand with the intent to shoot it."

"You're right. I'm sorry. I understand."

He returned to their positions, her hands on his, and

she could swear they were even closer than before. She tried not to lean back into him, but his body drew hers to him like a magnetic force.

"What's the last thing I said?" he asked.

"When you say 'now,' I put my finger on the trigger but don't pull it."

"Right. You ready?"

"Yes."

"Now" whispered out of his mouth, tickling her ear and whipping up a barrage of tingles that swarmed across her skin, head to toe.

She put her finger on the trigger, and the gun discharged. The action kicked her hard against his chest and expelled a surprised, "Oh, shit!" from her mouth.

"Dammit, Charleigh!"

She removed her hands from his and spun around to face him.

"You could have shot yourself. Or me," he said.

"I know. Sorry. The trigger is more sensitive than I thought it would be. Now I know. Let's try it again."

With a shake of his head, he drew her into place, and she put her hands on his.

"This time when I say 'now,' I want you to look down range at the target through the sight. When you think you have the target centered, put your finger on the trigger and gently squeeze it. After you do, you need to stay still and just move your finger away from the trigger. Nothing else. Do you understand?"

"When you say now, I look down range through the sight at the target, put my finger on the trigger, and squeeze it, gently, move my finger away, and stay still."

"Right. You ready?"

Her eyes were already down range, fixed on the

center of the target. "Yes."

"Now."

She squeezed the trigger. The gun discharged with a kick, but she was ready for it, and a hole ripped into the target at the center of the target. "Oh, my God, I hit it!"

"Finger off the trigger. Stay still."

She almost spun around and hugged him in her excitement, but she didn't because she didn't want to again make him think she wasn't taking this seriously.

"Josh, that was awesome!"

"Lower the gun."

She did.

"Take your right hand off."

She did.

"Now your left hand."

She did and turned to face him. She swore that was admiration gleaming in his eyes. Her hands in the shape of pistols, she poked him in the stomach, wanting to draw a word of praise from him. "I did good, huh," she said, flashing him a sassy grin.

He grinned, too. "Ready to do it again? On your own this time? Without me aiming it for you?"

She laughed at his suggestion that she'd only hit the target because of him. "You bet."

For the next half an hour, he critiqued her technique and analyzed her shots, which, more often than not, hit or clustered around the bull's eye. Through it all, he gave her feedback and encouragement.

"For someone who claims to hate guns, you're a surprisingly good shot," he said as they walked back to the pickup. "How do you explain that?"

The pride in his voice bloomed joy in her heart. "I

have an excellent teacher."

"Yeah, that's it," he said, a grin on his face.

He had her unload the gun, check it, and set the safety.

"If the gun's unloaded, why do I have to set the safety?" she asked.

"Because people make mistakes." He put the gun away. "Better safe than sorry."

From that day on, he started every lesson with a quick recap of the basics, having her explain everything to him, then they spent the rest of the hour before leaving to get Derrick perfecting her technique. When she was proficient with the rifle, he moved on to the shot gun. Then the pistol.

When he decided it was time to start Derrick's lessons, she'd be skilled enough to help. She wasn't just blowing sunshine up his boxers when she'd said he was an excellent teacher. He was, and not just with shooting. She was lucky to have him, and more than once since she'd arrived, she'd sent up a silent thanks to Wyatt for choosing Josh.

She couldn't learn everything she needed to know about running the Bar S in the remaining ten months, but because of Josh she would learn enough to continue on alone, if she decided to stay.

Chapter Twelve

Ruby set the basket of made-from-scratch rolls on the table between the perfectly browned turkey Josh had just carved and the sweet potatoes Derrick had insisted needed more marshmallows. Josh set the dish of cornbread stuffing between the mashed potatoes and green beans while Charleigh poured the iced tea. Ruby set the gravy and cranberry sauce in an open spot on the laden table, and Derrick added serving spoons to all the dishes.

As the four of them gathered around the table and took their seats, Josh realized he hadn't seen a spread this big for Thanksgiving since his grandmother had still been alive.

"As the head of this household, Charleigh, would you like to say the blessing?" Ruby asked before they could dig in.

"Um, well..." Charleigh's gaze zagged to Josh as if suggesting he should do it.

He shook his head. "Don't look at me."

He, like her, hadn't been raised in a religious family, so things like prayer, other than said silently between him and God, hadn't been a part of life.

"At school, Ms. Barnes had us go around the circle and say something we're thankful for," Derrick said. "How about we do that?"

"Great idea," Charleigh said, looking relieved.

"And since it was your idea, how about you go first?"

"Okay. But it's going to take time 'cause I'm thankful for tons of stuff."

To chuckles, he got up and went to Ruby and hugged her. "I'm grateful for all of Ruby's delicious cooking. Especially her chocolate chip cookies."

"I'll second that," Josh said and everyone chuckled.

Ruby hugged Derrick. "Does my heart good to see a healthy appetite on a boy."

He went to Josh next. "I'm thankful for Josh 'cause he teaches me lots of cool stuff and rides horses with me. And he makes me not miss my dad so much." Derrick hugged him. Josh hugged him back, surprised at the lump in his throat.

Derrick then went to Charleigh. "I'm thankful 'cause I have the best mom in the whole world and 'cause she brought us to this ranch where I love it a lot." He kissed her cheek and hugged her. "And 'cause I love you."

She hugged him tight. "Love you, too, puppy."

He returned to his chair. "Who wants to go next?"

Ruby spoke up. "Well, I'm thankful you folks came here and gave me the chance to stay on, doing what I love. I'm even more thankful you've treated me like family, not hired help."

"You are family," Derrick said. "Like a grandma. And that's another thing I'm grateful for, that I have a grandma."

Charleigh took Ruby's hand and squeezed it. "We're the lucky ones that you stayed."

She squeezed it back then looked at Josh. "I'm also thankful Wyatt had the good sense to choose Josh to help you and Derrick find your place here. He couldn't have chosen a better person for the job. Don't you agree, Josh?"

"Well, I'm sure there were plenty others just as qualified, but I'm glad he chose me. The opportunity to eat your delicious cooking was too good to pass up." Through the chuckles, he continued, his gaze including Derrick and Charleigh. "My granddad always said that if we have food before us, family beside us, and love between us, we have everything we need. Because Wyatt chose me, I'm closer to having all that than I've been in a long time."

Derrick got up again and put his arm around Josh's shoulders. "I'm glad grandpa Wyatt chose you, too. You're part of our family, like Ruby." He turned to Charleigh. "Right, mom?"

Charleigh's eyes on Josh's sent his heart bouncing through his chest. The soft, warm light in that honey gaze told him she felt the same way.

"Right," she said with a nod and a smile.

"Your turn, Mom," Derrick said.

"You've all said everything I was thinking," she started, "but I'll add this. Family isn't just about blood. It's about having people in your life who care about you and who you care about. Derrick and I have that here, with both of you, and it means everything to us." She squeezed Ruby's hand. "Thank you." Then she took Josh's hand, squeezed it. "Thank you."

"What about me?" Derrick asked.

She grabbed him up and squeezed him, kissing him on the nose. "And I have the best son in the whole world."

He giggled and squirmed to get away. "Okay, can

we eat now?"

She let him go with a chuckle. "Yes, I'm starving."

As she unfolded her napkin and set it on her lap, her eyes met Josh's again, and she smiled at him like she used to when she was happy and his…and happy to be his.

Family. Only Charleigh and Derrick were related, but it did feel like the four of them had combined into a family-like grouping. He cared about them. And they cared about him. And like she'd said, that was family.

But then a thought burned in his brain that made the food in his mouth taste like ash. *It was temporary.* In ten months, the contract would be fulfilled and another lucky man might be sitting at this table, leaving Josh as unnecessary and unwanted as a holey and outgrown pair of boots, and no longer considered part of this family.

The thought tore him up inside. He set his fork down, the food on it forgotten.

"Don't you like the sweet potatoes?" Derrick asked him.

Josh smiled and shook off the negative thoughts. "Needs more marshmallows," he teased and forked the bite into his mouth. His comment drew a laugh from…his family.

"See, Mom, I told you," Derrick exclaimed with a laugh.

As Josh pulled up in front of his house that evening, he exited his pickup but got only as far as his porch, unable to force himself to enter the dark, empty, lonely house. He dropped down onto the bench swing and stared out into the dark, his mind and body still riding the happiness high that fired up in him every time he was with Charleigh and Derrick. A goofball grin on his face, he replayed the day in his mind, analyzing every word, every look, every action.

They'd called him family. Derrick meant it. That he knew for sure. Charleigh certainly acted like she meant it.

But she'd fooled him before.

That small vine of doubt that creeped in through a tiny crack got a foothold and spread until he felt it smothering the warm rush he'd worn all day. It switched the track playing in his head from Charleigh's sweet words to his dad's bitter voice telling him, *Get your goddamned head on straight, boy, before you lose it.* It had been his dad's go-to phrase for warning Josh off whatever foolhardy path he was on.

It was a reminder that the fairy tale holiday he'd just enjoyed with Charleigh might be nothing more than fantasy. She needed him now because of the contract, but as soon as it was up, she'd be gone, and he'd be out.

Until he knew her secrets and knew for sure what path she had chosen, he'd remind himself of this reality every day so he wouldn't allow himself to get embedded in her life.

Suddenly tired, physically and mentally, he pushed to his feet and headed inside to bed. As he stared at the picture of Charleigh on his nightstand, the spark of warmth returned, and he knew he'd fail that self-imposed mission.

****

Josh pulled in front of the Simms' house the Sunday after Thanksgiving. Ruby's car and Cole's pickup were nowhere in sight—probably both at church—but from outside the house, he could hear rock music blasting. He grinned. He had never been able to cure Charleigh of her rock addiction and switch to country like everyone else in the two hundred and fifty-mile vicinity. It was an affliction her son shared. Whenever Derrick was in the pickup, he'd switch stations and blast it.

Josh would have knocked on the door if he thought they'd hear it. Knowing they wouldn't, he just went in. He'd have to talk to them about locking up when they were alone in the house. Even in this remote area, it was important to be cautious.

Fighting the desire to shove his hands over his ears, he headed to the living room, the epicenter of the noise. Wyatt was probably spinning in his grave at the *music* blasting from the old Westinghouse radio.

Derrick, still in his pjs, was singing into a banana something about not being able to feel his face when he's with someone. And Charleigh, wearing that faded T-shirt of hers, was dancing and singing along. The flash of pink panties kept Josh's eyes glued to her shaking behind.

All too soon the song ended, and mother and son collapsed on the couch, laughing, as another, equally raucous song started. Josh turned off the radio, and their eyes flew to where he stood.

"You two should go on TV with that act."

Charleigh shot to her feet but stayed by the couch, her face red. At his catching her dancing and singing? Or at catching her in that T-shirt that barely covered her sweet little ass? She tugged the hem of the shirt down as if to make sure she was covered, but he'd already seen those pink panties and couldn't stop thinking about the parts they barely covered.

"Josh!" Derrick jumped off the couch, ran to him, and hugged him. "What are you doing here? It's Sunday."

The kid liked routine, and he always noticed and questioned when something was off. Just like Josh did.

"I thought you and your mom might like to pick out your Christmas tree today."

Derrick's eyes rounded. "This early?"

"When do you usually get it?"

"Christmas Eve eve."

"Oh. Well, if you'd rather wait."

"No, let's get it now," Derrick said quickly, jumping up and down.

"If it's all right with your mom."

Derrick turned to her. "It's okay, Mom, right?"

"Sure," she said.

"I'll go get dressed," he said and was out of the room like a shot.

"And brush your teeth and hair," she called after him.

Derrick's departure left a hole in the air and quiet seeped in. Josh knew he had to say something to get his mind off her body beneath that shirt. His shirt.

"When my grandparents were still alive, we always got our tree the first Sunday after Thanksgiving, so it's been on my mind. But I don't want to change your family traditions."

"No, it's fine," she said. "Thanks for thinking of it."

They couldn't take their eyes off each other.

"So," he said. "You still don't like country?"

"I like it as much as you like rock."

He nodded toward the radio. "I liked that song that

was just playing."

"Oh, really?" She set her hands on her hips and tipped her head to one side in a flirty move he remembered meant she didn't believe him. "What did you like about it?"

What did he like about it? His gaze left her face and did a slow crawl downward, over her breasts, the curve of her waist where her hands made the shirt dip in, her long, bare legs, then reversed direction and came back up to her flushed face.

He liked seeing the way her body moved to it.

Liked seeing the pleasure it brought her.

Liked that it captured how he felt when he was with her, that she'd be the death of him but he wouldn't do anything about it because it felt too good. So good he was numb.

But he couldn't say any of that. So he went for the laugh. "That it's over."

As he'd hoped, she laughed, the sound of it wrapping around his heart so fully he could feel it double-beating.

Derrick came back into the room, tucking his long-sleeved western shirt into his jeans, because Josh did, his hair sorta combed. "Mom, you're not dressed."

"Just gotta pull on my boots."

He looked at Josh, shook his head, and rolled his eyes. "Girls are so weird."

"You have no idea, bud."

She rushed to Derrick, grabbed him, flipped him to the floor, and tickled him, making him giggle. "For your 411, girls rule."

With that, she got up and headed toward her room, not even trying to hide the full-blown smile on her face as Derrick laughed at her insult.

This was the Charleigh he remembered. Full of fun, eager to laugh and tease and love. She was as intoxicating today as she'd been when they'd been together. More, even, because she was more comfortable in her own skin now. And his mission to fight his craving for her would take every ounce of willpower he could muster.

Falling for her again might be disastrous. Not just for the two of them, but for Derrick. But as his body buzzed—from her presence, her voice, her smile, her scent—he knew he couldn't stop it from happening. Knew he didn't want to stop it.

****

Josh headed deeper into the property, not toward town as Charleigh thought they would.

"Is there a tree lot operating on my property I don't know about?" she teased as they bumped over the little-used path.

"We're not going to a lot," Josh said.

"Then how're we getting a tree?" Derrick asked.

"We're cutting our own."

"Oh, Josh, no. Let's don't cut down a tree," she said.

"Someone cut those trees at the lot," he countered.

"Yes, but they're doing it to make a living, and they've already cut them."

"Culling a tree in the spot I'm headed to will benefit the surrounding trees."

Derrick, who believed everything Josh said, took no further convincing. "Mom, I want to cut my own tree this year. Just this once. Please?"

She wasn't as convinced, but she'd give Derrick

this experience, this memory. Because next Christmas... Next Christmas they might not have this opportunity. Josh's year would be up, the contract fulfilled, Antelope Spring back in Flores hands, and he would be less interested in spending this kind of time with them. Or maybe she and Derrick would have sold the ranch and left town. Whichever scenario came to be, this moment was unlikely to come again.

Josh stopped at a sloped area with piñon trees clustered among scrub and boulders, and they climbed out of the pickup.

"Got your gloves?" he asked Derrick as he retrieved his own from his back pocket and pulled them on.

"Yep." Derrick pulled his from his pocket, too, and tugged them on.

"Good." Josh pulled a hacksaw and a chainsaw from the tool box in back and the three of them headed into the trees.

"You know anything about picking a good Christmas tree?" he asked Derrick.

"Yep. Me and Mom chose ours every year. Dad carried it home for us. Except for last year 'cause he was too sick. Then he went to the hospital and died."

Derrick's comment took her back to the Christmases with Will. They'd never had the money for a lavish Christmas. They bought their tree so late because they could get it at a deep discount. Which meant they got the leftover trees no one wanted. The far-from-perfect ones that were misshapen, half bare in areas, half dead in others.

But the three of them were just happy to have a tree, which they'd decorated mostly with homemade ornaments and a few Will had picked up on the cheap at garage sales, like Derrick's favorite, the silver star with his birth year imprinted on it.

Now, they were getting the best tree Derrick ever had. Thanks to Josh.

They inspected nearly every tree before deciding on a six-footer that came as close to perfect as any she'd ever seen. Josh showed Derrick how to use the hacksaw on the tree trunk then let him do it, delivering the lesson that the things you work hard for are more valued and appreciated than the things that come easy.

Derrick sawed away, moisture dotting his serious face after a few minutes. More than half the way through the trunk, he stopped, and wiped the sweat from his brow. "Okay, I got it started for you, Josh," he said, panting. "How about you finish it off?" He held out the hacksaw.

"Thanks, bud." Josh took the saw, but then dropped it to the ground. He winked at her and started the chainsaw, making quick work of the tree.

"No fair," Derrick exclaimed and picked up the hacksaw.

Josh chuckled. "Let's get on home."

She held out her hand for the chainsaw, and Josh handed it to her. Then he grabbed the trunk end of the tree and pulled it toward the pickup, her beside him.

"Guys, wait," Derrick said, rooted in place at the stump. "We need another one."

"Puppy, there's not room in the house for two," she said.

"No. One's for Josh's house."

"Oh…well, I'm not getting one," Josh said.

"But where will you put your ornaments and your

presents?"

"It's just me at home. Doesn't seem worth it."

At that moment, the sad reality punched her in the gut. Josh was all alone. No family. No significant other. No one. She was alone, too, except for Derrick. Together, the three of them weren't alone. Together, they were family.

As if he sensed the same thing, Derrick went to Josh, took his hand, tipped his head back to look up at him, his father, the man he obviously loved and admired.

"This can be your tree, too," he said. "You can bring over all your ornaments, and we'll decorate it. You can have Christmas with me and Mom and Ruby."

Her son had always had a caring and loving heart the size of the universe. She was proud of that trait, even as part of her wished he hadn't extended the offer to Josh.

The day-to-day work, she could handle. It was structured. Contracted. But to be together in scenarios like family holidays was saying they're choosing to be together because they want to be together. Thanksgiving had shown her how hard the fantasy—the three of them together as a family—was on her heart because it gave her a glimpse of what might have been. Thinking like that could leave her vulnerable to another heartbreak. But not for anything would she hurt Josh and upset Derrick by retracting the offer.

Josh got the tree into the bed, then they climbed into the pickup and headed home. Derrick found a station that was playing Christmas carols, and on the way, she and Derrick sang along with the ones they knew. Josh was strangely quiet.

When they arrived home, Derrick ran into the house while Charleigh and Josh unloaded the tree.

"If you don't want me involved in your holiday, tell me. I'll find a way out of it," he said as he lifted the tree out of the pickup. His tone was curt, and he wouldn't meet her eyes.

"Do you want to get out of it?"

He leaned the piñon against the house. "I don't want to horn in."

"You're not, but if you don't want to join us, just say so." The prickle in her tone matched his.

He met her gaze, his eyebrows furrowed. "I didn't say I didn't want to."

"Then what's the problem?"

"You tell me."

"God, just tell me what you're talking about," she said.

"I saw your face when Derrick invited me to share the tree and have Christmas with you. You were pissed."

"I wasn't pissed," she snapped back. Really, she wasn't pissed. What she felt was more complicated than pissed. Anxious. Scared. Thrilled. She checked her tone. "I was worried he'd put you on the spot. You do a lot for us that falls outside the parameters of the contract. Like getting us this tree. I don't want you to feel like you have to. I mean, I know you have a life that doesn't revolve around us and this ranch."

"If I didn't want to do it, I wouldn't have."

"Okay. Well, thanks." She nodded. "Derrick really wants you to join us."

"Do you?"

"I said I don't mind."

"That's not what I asked, CC. Do you want me there?"

Despite her trepidation, she wanted him there. For Derrick, because Josh was his father. For Josh, because Derrick was his son. For her, because…because she still loved Josh and was a glutton for punishment as long as he was the one doling it out.

The yes rolled off her tongue just as Derrick charged through the door, jumped off the porch, and landed beside them. "Ready?"

Josh finally tore his gaze from hers and addressed Derrick. "You get your decorations, I'll go get mine, and we'll get 'er up."

"I'll help you," Derrick said, skipping toward the pickup.

Panic gripped Charleigh. "Derrick, how about you stay here and help me find our decorations?"

"You put the box in the hall closet, 'member? I got some stuff I need to talk to Josh about."

"Stuff? What stuff?" She spoke the words to Derrick, but she was looking at Josh, silently asking him as well. He shrugged and opened the pickup door.

"Guy stuff," Derrick said and scrambled in.

Josh cocked his head and grinned, winked at her. "Guy stuff."

Everything inside her said to stop this. Not because she didn't trust Josh with Derrick, but because she didn't trust that Derrick wouldn't slip up and reveal family secrets.

She'd used the long drive here from California to prep him for what to say and what not to say on various topics, but he was only five and a half. And the burden of their many secrets was a heavy one. But if he gave away too many clues about the state of their family—the bills, the lack of food, lack of money—Josh might be able to add the pieces together into a picture of reality that he'd ask her to explain. And no way could Josh find out that Derrick's birthdate wasn't in August, but in May.

Before she could devise a drama-free way to say no, the pickup was flying down the road toward the Flying F, Derrick and Josh waving goodbye from their respective windows.

Chapter Thirteen

The pickup bounced down the road toward the Flying F, Derrick chatting on about their last horseback ride, their next ride, and the horse he'd like to have while Josh sat listening and wondering what *guy stuff* the five-year-old wanted to discuss. He never knew what Derrick was going to say, and more often than not, he was caught off guard by his questions. Many of them of a personal nature.

"How come you call my mom sissy?"

Josh grinned. "Not sissy. CC. The letters."

"How come you call her that?"

"When I met her, her last name was Cooper. Because her first and last names started with C, I called her CC."

"My dad called her LeeLee. Were you and Mom friends?"

He nodded. "I went to high school with her."

"Were you friends with my dad, too?"

"Your dad and I were best friends when we were kids."

"Was my mom and dad boyfriend and girlfriend then?"

"You should probably ask your mom about that stuff."

"She won't talk about the time before her and dad moved to California."

Huh. "The way I remember it, your mom and dad were just friends back then."

"Was Beth your girlfriend then?"

"No."

"Did you have a girlfriend?"

If he said yes, Derrick was going to ask who. And then he had to decide whether to lie or tell the truth. Lying didn't sit right with him. Never had. His only option was to derail his train of thought.

"Why are you so interested in girlfriend/boyfriend stuff? You thinking about getting a girlfriend?"

"'Member how I told you Nikki wants to be my girlfriend? I told her I wasn't ready to settle down."

Josh stifled a chuckle. "That's smart. Get to know all the girls, figure out what you like before you settle down."

"That's what Mom said."

"Your mom's pretty smart."

"Yep. But now Nikki is sad."

For the next few minutes, Derrick talked about Nikki's sadness, his other friends, and the asshats at school. Then, out of the blue, he said "Can I tell you a secret?"

Josh shifted uncomfortably on the seat. He had a feeling this conversation was about to cross into the awkward zone. "Sure."

"You won't tell my mom?"

"I don't like keeping secrets from your mom. If there's something wrong or something you're worried about, I know she'd understand and help you."

"I did something. And she'd be really mad if she knew."

"You rob a bank?"

"No," Derrick said through a grin.

"Is it something that could hurt you or others?"

"No, sir."

"Then you're probably fine."

"Will you tell my mom?"

"I don't know, bud. I'll have to hear it first."

Derrick looked at him as if deciding whether he should trust him with his weighty secret.

"See, Mom has this box. It's made of a bunch of different colors of wood, and it has a black curly tattoo on the top. She hides it, but last year I found it. I showed it to her and asked her if I could see what's in it. She took it away from me and told me it was hers and only hers and that I'd be in big trouble if I touched it again. Her voice was mad, but she was crying. I told my dad about it when we visited him in the hospital, and he said he wasn't allowed to touch it either, but that it was okay because we're all allowed to have secrets. Then he cried."

Will cried? About the box? Or about secrets? Josh didn't know which, but he was certain that box was the one he'd made in shop for Charleigh. It had taken him months to get it just right, with all the different types of wood he'd used. He'd burned the Flores brand into the top as a way of saying she was his. He'd given it to her that first Christmas they were together.

"You get into it?"

"Not that day. But when we moved here and were unpacking our stuff, I saw where she hid it. That day you and her came home all muddy, I took it out before she got home and I looked inside."

He shouldn't ask, but he was going to. "What was in there?"

"A necklace with a silver heart, a couple of old flowers, some papers tied with a blue ribbon, two pieces of a Christmas tree, her favorite snowflake ornament, a keychain, a heart-shaped rock, a candy wrapper with a helmet on it, and a picture."

All the things he'd given Charleigh over the two years they'd been together. And that picture? It had to be the one he'd taken after they'd made love for the first time. The same picture that had sat on his nightstand since he'd learned she was coming back to town. She'd kept everything. Down to their first condom wrapper.

"Did you read the papers?"

"No. I knew I couldn't tie the ribbon back so good, and she'd know I got in there."

Thank God for small favors. His face heated just thinking about the love notes he'd written to Charleigh. "Smart choice."

"That picture was you and her. You guys were smiling and hugging, with your cheeks together." He patted his cheek at the word. "And you and her didn't have clothes on, but she was wearing that necklace that was in the box."

Josh's eyes were on the road, but his mind was on the day he'd taken that picture. His phone camera had captured them from the waist up. His arms around her, hers around his, chests together, hid most of her breasts, but hell yeah, they were naked, wearing nothing but each other's love, kisses, and touches. God, he'd loved her, especially that day. He'd never been happier in his whole life.

"Was Mom your girlfriend?"

"Yeah." The one-word answer was out before he

could stop it. Warmth rushed over him at hearing it out there, at being infused in memories of a time that being able to say she was his had meant everything to him.

"She looked really happy in that picture," Derrick said. "I never seen her that happy. Ever. I think my mom loved you a lot."

Josh licked his lips, unsure what to say. She had been happy. At least he'd thought so…up until the day she kicked him out of her life and married Will.

"Did you love my mom?"

The gate open, this response exited easily. "Yeah."

"Do you still love her?"

He slammed the gate on the third *yeah* before it could escape. "Things are different between us now."

"If you loved her once, you can love her again. You can make her happy like she was in that picture."

"We can't go back."

"But—"

"Derrick, I won't tell your mom about you getting into the box, but you need to stop talking about the two of us being together. It's not going to happen."

"Don't you like her?"

"Yes, I like her, but you need more than liking to…" He ran his hand over his face. "Listen," he said and gave the boy a sharp look. "You need to drop this. Got it?"

"Yes, sir." His voice cracked a little like he was trying not to cry.

Shit. He hadn't meant to be so hard on him. This talk about him and Charleigh and their past and the knowledge that she'd kept everything he'd given her had knocked him off balance.

She had left him, married his best friend, never

contacted him in all her years away. Yet she had kept every memento of their love…kept them secret, sacred, just for her. Why? What did that mean? The possibilities scrambled his brain, but the last thing he wanted to do was take it out on Derrick.

He stretched out his hand and settled it briefly on the boy's head. "What's Santa bringing you for Christmas?"

"Um, I wanted a real gun, but Mom said Santa's elves don't make real guns, so I'm gonna ask for some other things."

"What kind of things?"

"Things I want to keep secret, just between me and Santa."

Josh grinned at Derrick's secrecy. "If you write your letter tonight, I'll mail it for you when I'm in town tomorrow."

"I already wrote it."

"Oh, yeah? By yourself?"

"Mom spelled out Merry Christmas for me, but the rest of it I did by myself. Some of the words I didn't know how to spell, but Santa knows what I mean."

"You bet he does."

"Can we listen to the radio?"

"Sure." He reached out and turned it on. It was still on the rock station Charleigh had turned it to, the artist belting out a rockin' rendition of *Santa Claus Is Coming to Town*.

Derrick scooted forward on the seat toward the radio. "What station do you like?"

"Punch the first button," Josh said.

Derrick did, then sat back, nodded his head to the music, and sang along. "*Body like a backbone, driving with my eyes closed...* Josh, what does body like a backbone mean? Like a skeleton?"

"No, he's saying, body like a back road."

"Oh. You mean bumpy, like our road?"

"Uh, well—"

"And how come he's driving with his eyes closed? Isn't that kinda dangerous?"

"Yeah, real dangerous."

"And what does hips like honey—"

"I thought you didn't like country?" Josh jumped in to quickly change the direction the conversation was going.

He shrugged. "I like it now. But don't tell Mom. She still hates it."

Josh was still grinning at Derrick's singing— which, fortunately, was now to a song that didn't require translation—when he pulled up at his house.

They got out, Derrick beside him and glancing around curiously. "I like your house."

"Thanks. It's been in my family for almost a hundred years."

"Who gets it when you die?"

"Hadn't thought about it." Josh opened the heavy oak arched door he'd put in last year, and Derrick strolled in like he was the lord of the manor.

"Let's get that box," Josh said and led the way to the bedroom that had, at one time, been Jessie's but was now storage, as were the two other bedrooms on the top floor. He rummaged through the boxes, opening a few until he came to the one with the remaining few Christmas ornaments he'd been able to save during one of his father's destructive, drunken rants.

Box in hand, he looked around for Derrick, who

was peering into Jessie's crib. He joined him at the rail. "Ready?"

Derrick looked up at him. "Did you have a baby?"

"This was my sister's bed."

"Does she live here with you?"

"No. She died when she was a baby."

"Sorry. I don't have a brother or sister either. What's her name?"

"Jessica. I called her Jessie."

They looked into the crib, each letting their own thoughts silence them. Josh wondered why Charleigh and Will hadn't had more kids, but he wasn't going to try to wrangle personal information out of a five-year-old who probably hadn't been privy to that decision.

"Can I ask you one more question?" Derrick said, breaking the dusty silence.

The look in the boy's eyes, the tone in his voice, told Josh his question wouldn't be about their mutual lack of siblings. "Is it about me and your mom?"

He nodded.

Josh had already prepared the "no" when Derrick spoke up. "Last one today. I promise."

He gave the boy his strongest stink-eye stare. "Last one."

"If you loved her and she loved you, how come you didn't marry her?"

Derrick's gaze was locked on his, waiting for an answer. No way was he going to explain that he could have married her but messed up his chance or that she dumped his ass to run away with Will. He went with the raw, basic truth.

"She married your dad instead."

"Did that make you sad?"

His chest tightened at the old pain of learning that Charleigh had married Will. Sad? Hell, it had ripped his fucking heart out and stomped it into the dry plains dirt.

He swallowed to settle the throbbing mass of pain, but it had no effect, so he cleared his throat and spoke around it. "Let's go. Your mom's waiting." He headed for the door.

"You could marry her now."

The almost pleading in the boy's little voice brought Josh to a full stop. He turned back. Derrick's blue eyes met his, and they shared a connection in that sad gaze that seemed to say they'd both lost out.

"Then I could be your son, and me and Mom and Ruby would live in this house with you and be a real family. And none of us would ever be sad and alone ever again."

The words so closely mirrored Josh's fantasies of late he couldn't find the words to respond, even to make it clear—to both of them—that no way in hell would it happen.

"I gotta pee." Derrick broke their connection.

Josh led him to the bathroom that was in his bedroom since the others in the house weren't working due to his slow attempts at DIY renovation. When Derrick finished, they hopped into the pickup, the box of ornaments between them, and talked about safe topics on the way home.

Out of the blue, Derrick started crying. Feeling a bit panicked about why he'd gone from happy to bawling in a matter of seconds, Josh stopped the pickup and settled his hand on the boy's shoulder. "What's wrong?"

Derrick looked at him, tears rolling down his

cheeks. "I miss my dad." He scooted over to Josh, stood on his knees, and put his arms around Josh's neck.

Josh awkwardly patted his back. "I know." He couldn't think of a thing to say to comfort him that didn't sound stupid. So he just hugged him, letting him cry through it on his shoulder.

When tears slowed to sniffles, Josh drew a clean handkerchief from his back pocket and handed it to Derrick. "Wipe your face and blow your nose."

He did and handed it back to Josh.

"Put it in your pocket. Ask your mom or Ruby to wash it for you, then keep it in your pocket, clean, at all times."

"Yes, sir." He hiccupped.

"Now then. You wanna tell me what set off the waterworks?"

"That song." He pointed to the radio.

"That song makes you think of your dad?"

He nodded. "And I miss him."

"Was it his favorite song or something?"

"No. He didn't like country."

"Then what about it reminds you of him?"

"Sometimes my mom would be really sad, and she would lay on the bed and listen to it and cry. My dad would lay down with her and hug her and whisper stuff to her. After it was over, he'd turn off the music and kiss her and tell her 'I love you,' and she'd feel better."

That song was about a man whose woman was still in love with her old flame. The implications had him reeling. Was that old flame him? Had Charleigh been in love with him throughout her marriage to Will? Had she been crying over him? If so, and if she loved him so damn much, why had she left him for Will? He couldn't ask Derrick any of those questions, but he did ask, "Why was she so sad?"

He shrugged. "My dad said sometimes girls just need to cry out all their sad to make room for their happy again, and we have to make sure not to do anything to make them sadder."

"Does she still lie on the bed and cry?"

"Not since we got here. She's mostly happy. I think it's 'cause you're here."

He had no clue what to say to that hypothesis. She did seem happier now than when she'd first arrived. But that didn't necessarily mean it was because of him. Did it?

This relationship with Charleigh was a field of goddamned bindweed. No sooner would he pull up an answer to one question than another five questions would surface. But he'd figure it out, get all his questions answered. Somehow.

"Don't tell my mom I was crying, okay?" Derrick said, wiping his nose again with the handkerchief, then tucked it into his pocket. "I don't want her to be sad."

Josh now knew that Derrick's overprotectiveness of his mother and her feelings had been Will's doing. Him not wanting to do anything to upset her, encouraging their son to be as cautious. Both of them tiptoeing around her like she was a fragile pane of glass, afraid to do or say anything that would risk her breaking. Or them from getting cut. It wasn't healthy that he couldn't act like himself for worry that he'd upset her. That needed to change.

"I won't tell her. But Derrick, you shouldn't hide your feelings from your mom for fear of upsetting her. She loves you more than anything. And because of that, she wants to know what you think and feel and want. And you need to tell her, not hide it. Hiding your feelings is like lying. It's no good. Especially for people who love each other."

"But what if she cries and gets upset 'cause of me?"

"It could happen. But then you talk it out. She tells you why she's upset, and you tell her why you're upset. Then you find a solution that works for both of you. It's the only way to have a strong, honest relationship."

"Like you and me talk about stuff?"

He grinned. "Yeah." Like he and Charleigh used to. At least until that last night. If he'd taken his own advice, he might not have lost her.

Charleigh was outside when they pulled up. The tree was already in the stand, and she was crouched in front of it, tightening the screws that would hold it upright and secure for the duration of the holiday.

Derrick climbed out on Josh's side and ran to her. "It looks great, Mom," he said, excitement glowing on his face as he hugged her, all traces of his meltdown vanished.

She hugged him, too, then stood and grabbed the tree, testing its stability. "It's still a bit wobbly."

"Josh can tighten it. He's real strong. Huh, Josh."

Her laughing eyes met Josh's. "Okay, He-Man. Have at it."

He handed her his box of ornaments. She took them and stepped aside as he crouched down. Derrick joined him, right by his side.

"You wanna hold the tree still while I tighten?" Josh asked him.

"Yes, sir," Derrick jumped up and reached a little

hand through the branches to grip the trunk. "Mom, tell us if it's crooked."

She positioned herself behind Josh so she could eye it straight on. "A little to the left."

Derrick moved it slightly to the right.

"Your other left," she said. "There," she called out when he'd moved it enough. "Perfect."

Josh tightened the screws then stood, gripped the tree, and shook it to make sure it was secure in the stand. He stepped back, even with Charleigh, to scrutinize it.

Derrick joined them, squeezing in between them, a hand in each of theirs, tying them together, making them a single unit. The feel of belonging elated Josh even as it alarmed him. Suddenly, he wasn't sure he was ready for this family-centric project. Especially after the conversation he'd just had, the secrets that had been revealed.

He removed his hand from Derrick's and stepped toward the tree. "Let's get it inside."

Derrick rushed to the door and held it open while Josh carried the tree into the living room, and Charleigh rushed ahead of them. "There, in the corner," she said, pointing to the empty corner between the window and the fireplace she'd cleared while they'd been gone.

It was where he'd envisioned it going when he came over this morning to invite them to get a tree. He carried it to the spot Charleigh indicated and set it down while she turned on the radio and set it to a station playing Christmas music.

Derrick dug into their box of decorations, which Charleigh had set on the floor by the table, pulled out a string of multicolored lights that had been carefully looped into a lariat shape, and handed the plug end to Josh. "We gotta plug them in first to make sure they work," he explained.

Josh plugged them in and was surprised they all lit up. His family had bad karma with Christmas lights and had needed new strings every year. When it was just him and his dad, they hadn't bothered with lights. Or a tree. Or gifts. Or a holiday.

He unplugged the string, and he and Derrick wrapped them around the tree, Charleigh following behind them to rearrange the bulbs on the branches.

Next came the ornaments, most of them homemade. One by one, Derrick hung them on the tree, telling Josh the story behind each one. When they were all up, Derrick handed Josh's box of ornaments to him. Josh pulled one out and was about to hang it when Derrick stopped him. "Tell us the story about it."

"Oh, well, most of them don't have much of a story." He'd never felt more on the spot, having to talk about his failed family. But because it meant something to Derrick, he'd do it.

He held up the tarnished-with-age silver star that looked like a sheriff's badge. "This one was my great-granddad's. His dad made it for him the year he was born, and he brought it with him from Spain when he moved to Texas and then here to homestead." He fingered one point of the star, remembering the pride in his granddad's voice when he told the story of the star every Christmas until his last.

"He handed it down to his son—my granddad—who handed it down to his son—my father—who handed it down to me." In Josh's case, it was less of a hand-down and more of a saving the star before his dad broke it in half during one of his explosive episodes. After that, Josh had hidden the remaining few keepsakes in a box in Jessie's room, a room his father hadn't entered since the day they'd buried her.

Derrick stood next to him, eyes on the star, fascinated with the story. "Can I touch it?" he asked in almost a whisper.

"Better than that, how about you hang it on the tree?"

"Really?"

"Yep." Josh held it out to him.

Derrick took the star and placed it on the tree, right next to the ornament he'd said was his favorite—a star with the year he was born imprinted on it.

"It looks perfect," Derrick said, smiling at the star hanging on the tree next to his.

****

Charleigh was in the middle of a meltdown at the tender moment, made even more poignant by the fact that neither knew they were father and son and sort of continuing the tradition that started generations ago. It ate at her heart, expanding the ache that would stay until the secret came out.

Josh pulled out the next one, a crystal snowman, which had a similar look to the crystal snowflake he'd given her their last Christmas together.

"This one came from my mother's side of the family," Josh said, Derrick at his elbow taking it all in. "Their name was Olsson. Her people were from Sweden. She said it was her grandmother's and had come with her when she moved to America with her new husband."

The star on the tree, the snowman in his hands, the

other ornaments in the box—they were physical evidence of where Josh came from. Where Derrick came from. It was important, and she'd die if Derrick accidentally dropped the delicate crystal ornament.

"Josh, I think you should hang that one."

He held it out to her. "I think you should."

The way he stared at her, his eyes bright with pleasure, a warm little half smile on his lips, rushed heat over her cheeks and a smile to her lips. She took the snowman from his hand, the tips of her fingers burning hot where their hands touched, and hung it on the tree in a prominent spot. He moved on to the next one.

Derrick was mesmerized by Josh's stories and ornaments, even the less inspiring ones, like the clothespin Rudolph he'd made in first grade and the small green felt stocking he'd made in 4-H when he was nine that had his name written in glitter.

She wasn't unaffected by them either. To see pieces of his history, to see something he'd made with his own two hands, was like getting a peek at the boy he'd been. It warmed her heart and gave her a better understanding of the man she loved and had created a child with.

****

Josh and Charleigh didn't have enough lights or ornaments between them to fill such a big tree, and neither of them had a tree topper, but it didn't matter. It was pretty magical as it was. After the last item from his box was up, Charleigh went to the tree to plug in the lights.

"You guys ready?" she said. "Drum roll."

"Wait, Mom," Derrick said. "You didn't hang your

snowflake."

"I'll do it later." Her cheeks flushed, she waved away Derrick's words as if she were trying to stop him from talking about it.

Was it the snowflake he'd given her their last Christmas that, according to Derrick, she kept in her special box? The snowflake, along with the snowman, were the last surviving pieces from a set of four. Giving the snowflake to her had been his way of saying she was unique and that she was part of his life.

"We can't plug in the lights until it's up," Derrick insisted. "That's the rule."

"This year, I'd like to check out the lights first," she said.

Derrick wasn't having it. "But it's your most favortest one."

"Derrick, I said later."

The boy's eyes darted to Josh's before cutting back to Charleigh's, and the look in them said he was about to have a meltdown. "It always goes on last," he said, his voice small but resolved. "Before we turn the lights on."

Mother and son stared at each other for a long, prickly moment. Clearly, it was a tradition that Derrick did not want altered, despite their being in a new place this Christmas. Maybe because of it. And clearly she didn't want to bring it out because Josh was there and he'd know the significance of it.

He was impressed with how Derrick wasn't holding back. But he felt bad that they were both tense and upset at a time they should be happy. He put his hand on Derrick's head. "Hey, bud, maybe your mom wants to put it up alone, without you and me around."

"No. It's our tradition. And it's important."

Charleigh spun on her heels and stormed from the room.

He and Derrick looked at each other, both wondering whether she was coming back. But moments later, she was, the snowflake in hand. Her face red, her eyes avoiding his and Derrick's, she hung it on the tree between his star and Derrick's and above the snowman.

Then, she faced him, eyes vulnerable, lips pressed tight, back straight as a board, almost daring him to say anything.

The things he gave her meant something to her. The bubble of joy bursting inside him at that reality prevented him from saying anything, but some of it leaked out to lift a smile onto his face.

Derrick, his smile a mile wide, rushed to her side and hugged her. "I love you, Mom."

She put her arms around him. "I love you, too." She kissed the top of his head. "*Now* can we can plug in the lights?"

"Yep." He ran to the light switch on the wall. "Get ready, Josh." Once Josh was in place at the tree, Derrick turned off the overhead light, and Josh plugged in the string of lights.

The three of them joined in front of the tree, words unnecessary as the glow of the lights and the sparkle of old memories represented in the ornaments they'd hung formed new memories involving the three of them in this place. His ornaments mixed with theirs perfectly. Sparkling the brightest was the snowflake in the center, gathering and reflecting the lights and the shine from the stars flanking it.

Derrick took his hand again, connecting the three

of them, like the snowflake did the other ornaments. This time Josh didn't pull away, just held on, not wanting to let go.

"I'm starving. Can we eat now?" Derrick said, scattering his thoughts.

"I'm starting to think you got a hollow leg, boy," Josh said.

"Ruby says growing boys like me are supposed to eat a lot."

Josh laughed. "Ruby's right. How about we grab something in town? My treat. We need to get a tree topper and some Christmas lights for outside anyway."

"Really? Yes!" Derrick ran to the mudroom to pull on his boots and coat.

Charleigh shook her head, a smile on her face. "Who's going to hang all those outside lights?"

He reached out and stretched one of her long curls. "*We* are," he said and released it.

****

Josh pulled to a stop in front of Rogers' General Store. Charleigh unbuckled her seatbelt and turned to help Derrick unbuckle his, but he had already done it and was scampering out on Josh's side of the pickup.

"Welcome, folks," Mary Rogers called out from behind the counter at the front of the store.

"Mary," Josh said with a nod, and Charleigh and Derrick said hi.

They made their way to the Christmas decorations aisle and were discussing the rather limited choices when…

"Hello, Josh."

They all turned at Beth's voice behind them.

Josh's cheeks flushed, and he looked

uncomfortable at the interruption. "Beth."

At Beth's initiation, the two of them moved into that awkward tentative hug people do when either they don't know each other well or they used to.

Derrick glared at them, a scowl on his face that suggested he was about to loudly protest the interruption.

The interruption annoyed Charleigh as much as it did Derrick, but she didn't have the right to do anything about it. She put her arm around Derrick. "Let's look for a topper," she said and led him farther down the aisle, giving the couple privacy.

She tried to keep Derrick occupied with the ornaments, but he kept looking back at Josh and Beth. She picked up an angel a little farther down the aisle. "What do you think about this for—" She turned to show Derrick, but he was walking down the aisle toward Josh.

"Josh, are you done? We need your help."

Charleigh joined them. "Puppy, it's rude to interrupt people when they're talking. Josh will help us in a minute."

"But, Mom. He's here with us, not her."

"Come on."

As she led him away, she heard Josh tell Beth, "Well, I'll let you get to your shopping."

"Why don't you come by tonight?" she asked. "You can help me string some lights."

"Oh, uh, thanks, but I have plans."

Charleigh bit her lip to tether the smile that reared at his comment.

"Well, another time," Beth said.

"Sure," he said.

They did the awkward hug again, then Josh left her and rejoined them.

Charleigh met his eyes. "If you'd rather string her lights tonight, we can do ours on our own."

"Mom, no," Derrick said, his brows furrowed. "He said he would help us. And a man's word is his bond. Right Josh?"

"Right."

She held up her hands in surrender. "Okay, fine. Heaven forbid a man ever changes his mind."

They discussed the pros and cons of various light styles before selecting several boxes of big, colorful lights that Josh thought would be enough to string around the roof and the fence circling the house. They couldn't find a suitable topper, so Josh said he and Derrick would make a star for the top. After grabbing a bite to eat at the café, they headed home.

After several hours working as a team, they got the lights up just before dark. Charleigh looped her arm around Derrick, who stood between her and Josh.

"Well, what do you think, bud?" Josh asked as the three of them admired their efforts.

"It's beautiful!" Derrick exclaimed and hugged him. "I love you, Josh."

Josh's eyes rounded in surprise, and his hands hovered awkwardly over Derrick's back before finally settling lightly on him. His awestruck gaze lifted and tangled with hers.

Having received many I love you's from Derrick over the years, she recognized the emotion flooding Josh at this special parent-child moment and knew the reason for the look of pure, powerful, helpless love in his eyes.

"Ruby's gotta see this." Derrick ran into the house to get Ruby, who had left the last string for them to put up so she could get supper going.

Charleigh moved closer to Josh. "You okay?"

He nodded.

"'Cause you look a little shook up."

"I'm…"

"If it makes you uncomfortable that he says that, I can talk to him."

"No one has said those words to me since…" He reached out and took her hand in his. "Since you."

She squeezed his hand, comforted that he had reached out, that he'd needed her comfort.

Memories of the time they'd loved each other— and had shown it and said it freely—zinged back and forth between them. She wanted to pull him closer, close enough to taste him, to hear his heartbeat, to feel his breath on her lips, and was ready to make her move when he made his first.

Keeping her hand in his, he looped that arm around her waist and drew her in, slowly as if to give her time to pull away if she chose to. When she didn't move away, he lifted his other hand and brushed it down her hair, crown to tips, and tugged the end of one long curl to stretch it. The curl sprang back when he released it, and he grinned, as if the action made him happy. His hand then rose to her face and cupped her cheek. She arched into his touch, and he brushed his thumb across her bottom lip.

As they stared into each other's eyes, she wanted to say something, something magical that would speak right to his heart and make him understand what being with him meant to her. But when she saw that look in his eyes, saw his tongue dart out to wet his lips, saw his head lean in toward hers, she realized that words could wait. Because that look, those signs, pointed to one thing. He was going to kiss her. And heaven help her, she was going to let him.

Or she would have had Derrick not pushed out the door right then, Ruby trailing behind him.

Instead of coming together in slow, hot fusion of lips and bodies, she and Josh separated abruptly.

Ruby, hugging Derrick, admired their handiwork. "Oh, my! This house hasn't been dolled up like this in years. Y'all did a right fine job."

Derrick excitedly described all the work they'd done, giving Josh and Charleigh a little credit, too, and Ruby marveled appropriately.

****

As they ate supper, Ruby regaled them with stories from the Christmas event she and the fundraising committee were putting on. Charleigh had helped her with some baking and crafts and had, surprisingly, enjoyed it. Not that she was going to make it a habit.

"Me and Mom are going," Derrick told Josh. "How about you come with us?"

"If it's all right with Charleigh," Josh said.

Three sets of eyes zeroed in on her.

"Of course."

While Derrick was on a roll, he also convinced Josh to take them to the Christmas tree lighting ceremony in town, which was the coming week, and his school concert the week after that.

She and Derrick were spending more and more time with Josh doing non-ranch activities. Although she wondered how he was going to explain to Beth his lack

259

of availability this holiday, she didn't let it deter her from accepting his offer to accompany them to those events. As long as he was game, she wouldn't do anything to deter his interest because being with Josh was what she wanted.

As Josh was leaving for home, Derrick handed him his letter to Santa to mail. Charleigh got Derrick's shower going then walked Josh out.

"Thanks for today," she said as they stood together at the side of his pickup. "Derrick had so much fun."

"Did you?"

Her face flushed from the memory of the almost kiss in the glow of the Christmas lights. "Yes. Did you?"

His arm crawled around her waist. His other hand rose to the back of her head, his fingers digging in her hair, not hesitantly, but confidently. She was sure he'd seen the yes in her eyes from earlier, and he wouldn't have to look too hard or deep to see that it was still firmly in place.

His whispered "yes" brushed her mouth, preparing her for the kiss she knew was coming. As he eased her head closer to his, she couldn't seem to catch a breath. Anytime she found one, her pounding heart broke it apart.

"I'm glad," she whispered and licked her lips.

Their lips were on their way to paradise when the porch light came on and the door opened.

"Well, goddamn," he cursed under his breath and released her, stepping back.

She stifled a chuckle but not a grin as Ruby came out, carrying a bag of trash.

"Lands sake," she said. "I didn't know anybody

was out here. Josh, I thought you'd left already."

"Headed that way," he said, his voice rough. "Here, let me get that for you." He lifted the bag from Ruby's hands and set it in the pickup bed to toss on his way out.

"Appreciate it. I confess it spooks me heading to the trash bin this late since I heard Frank Collier chased off a cougar just last week. The thing nearly got the drop on him from his own trash bin. Happened before he knew it. Luckily, he made a big ruckus and scared it off."

Josh had told her and Derrick about it at lunch, saying that, although cougars typically don't look at humans as prey, they will if they're hungry enough. He also warned her that children are at a higher risk for being attacked than adults.

He nodded. "Keep the gun loaded and handy and don't let Derrick wander too far off alone," he said to both of them but looked long at Charleigh.

At that moment, she was grateful he'd taught her to shoot. If a dangerous animal came into the area, it would be up to her to protect them. And she could, thanks to him.

"We'll be careful all right," Ruby said.

Charleigh wanted Ruby to go back inside so she could give free rein to the kiss that had been pulsing between her and Josh all day, but the woman stood there, almost like she knew what they wanted to do and was mother-henning her.

"Well…guess I'll go. 'Night, Ruby." Josh touched the brim of his hat toward Ruby, then settled his gaze on Charleigh. "CC."

"'Night," she said, holding his gaze and her breath

and giving him a little *next time* smile.

Finally, he broke eye contact, climbed into his pickup, and headed out.

Ruby went back inside, but Charleigh stayed on the porch and watched as he stopped at the trash bin. She stayed until his pickup cleared the gate and disappeared down the road toward his place.

She could feel his almost kisses tingling warm on her mouth. She licked her lips and could almost taste them. Missing him, a solid ache sitting south of her stomach, she went inside and, for the rest of the night, wondered what those almost kisses meant and prayed it wouldn't be the last time he tried.

****

At home, settled on the porch swing with a bottle of beer, Josh pulled out the letter to Santa Derrick had given him to mail. Normally, he'd respect the boy's privacy, but if he was to get him what he wanted for Christmas, he'd have to read it.

Hi Santa.

I haf bin a gud boy.

Wat I wot the mostist for Christmas is Mom and Josh to get mereed.

Mom wud be so happy cuz she has Josh. I wud be so happy cuz I haf a Dad. Josh wud be so happy cuz he has us to love him.

If yu cant get me thet, I wud lik a reel gun or a sooper soker gun or remot contolr pickup or legos. Or a hors.

Thank you.

Merry Christmas to yu an yor famle.

Love Derrick Simms Flores

PS I live on the Simms rench an I reely wat mos to

haf Josh for my Dad. Pleeze!

The scrawled words blurred before his eyes, and the letter fell from his hand and floated to the floor. He brought his hands to his face, holding back the emotion threatening to break loose and tumble out. He lodged his fingers on his eyelids, which stopped the tears but didn't keep the ache in his heart from leaking out and flooding his body.

"Charleigh." Her name whispered out between the regret wracking his body.

When they were still together and he was having a bad day, he'd whisper her name. The sound of it brought him a sense of love and peace and filled him with the comforting, energizing certainty that, with her by his side and in his heart, he could do anything.

The sound of her name now filled him with the same euphoria. And the truth. Despite how much she'd hurt him, he still loved her. And he loved her kid. Will's kid. The walking, talking evidence of her betrayal. The boy that should have been their kid—his and Charleigh's.

What was between him and Charleigh wasn't over. Couldn't be. Not when he still felt this need, this hunger, this love for her. The question was, what was he going to do about it? Could he do this to himself again? Put his happiness in her hands? Did he even have a choice?

The love of a lifetime is worth a million tries to hold on to it.

His granddad's words rang true and clear in his ears. He knew what he had to do.

Chapter Fourteen

The community center was decorated to the hilt for the holidays, everything trimmed in red and green and sparkling snowflakes, which Charleigh had helped with. Ruby had roped her into other behind-the-scenes tasks as well, so she felt like she'd played a small part in creating the Christmas wonderland.

Her best understanding was that every fundraising event was pretty much the same—a cookie-cutter event that included a dance, baked goods sale, and sometimes an auction. Not that there was anything wrong with that setup. If it worked, it worked. But if she were involved, they'd shake things up, do different themes and activities to gear up more interest and support.

She had mentioned it to Ruby, who said it was a great idea and that she should come to the next fundraiser planning meeting. She'd said she'd think about it, but if she wasn't going to stay around, she really had no business getting involved in community issues.

Derrick ran off to join his friends, and she and Josh stood together at the edge of the dance floor, talking. Whenever it looked like a man was coming to ask her to dance, he grabbed her hand and led her to the floor.

"You don't want me dancing with other men?" she teased him after the sixth time.

"Do you want to dance with other men?"

"Not particularly."

He grinned and twirled her twice before pulling her closer against him. "Then shut up."

His teasing tone made her laugh. "Bossy."

One song ended and the next had started when Lance tried to cut in.

Josh glared at him. "Wait until we finish this dance."

"Waiting defeats the purpose of cutting in."

"Deal with it."

The two stared each other down, Lance's eyes finally darting from Josh to her, signaling that he was backing down.

"Charleigh, just so there's no confusion, I get the next dance." With a little smile, he tipped his hat and left the floor. He stood at the edge, legs-spread stance, arms crossed over his chest, watching their every move, like he was primed to intervene if Josh tried to twirl her away.

"Asshat," Josh muttered as he drew her back in and resumed their dance.

"You could tell him no," she said.

He shook his head. "That's not my ring on your finger."

If removing the ring would remove any barrier to his keeping her in his arms for the rest of the night, then there was only one thing to do. Easing her hand from his, she removed her ring, slid it into the little pocket of his snug, black jeans, then went back into his arms.

"Whoa. Living dangerously there, Mrs. Simms," he said.

The glimmer in his eyes made her heart speed up. "How so?"

"With that ring off, you're saying loud and clear to every man here that you're available. And I can't stop them."

"Why can't you stop them?"

"It would be saying you're mine."

"What does it say that you and I haven't danced with anyone but each other tonight?"

"It says this is our last dance for the night."

"Then let's enjoy it." She leaned in to kiss him, but he pulled back.

The light and heat in his gaze clearly said that he wanted the kiss that had been teasing between them for weeks as much as she did. She'd hold his gaze until he told her why they weren't getting it.

"Charleigh, if I kiss you here, it'll confirm what everyone is thinking—that we're back together," he whispered, answering the question he must have seen flickering in her eyes.

"But we're not."

"That only makes it worse."

"I don't follow."

"We're not together, but we're kissing on the dance floor, like we did when we were together."

"So, I'm some kind of slut for kissing you?"

"What you are is the owner of the area's largest ranch, community member, employer, mother, widow. Your behavior shapes how these people see you, which shapes how they talk about you, how they treat you, how they interact with you, whether they trust you or like you. As long as you're here, you need them. And you need them to have a good impression of you. Not just for you, but for your son, your ranch, your employees. And it's the same for me."

His lecture on proper behavior annoyed her to no end, but she didn't want to ruin their night with a fight, and she really didn't want to leave his arms before she had to.

Forcing back her pride and anger, she went with amused and let a little grin lift the corners of her mouth. "Well, that sucks for you, Flores, seeing as how you've been trying to kiss me for weeks," she said, just enough sass in her tone to show her displeasure and disappointment. "That kiss would have knocked your socks off clear to Texas."

His responding ghost of a grin said he was relieved she'd gone with amused instead of wildcat pissed like she'd been known to do back when they'd been together.

"I don't doubt it," he said. "Want your ring back?"

What she wanted was this. His arms around her, holding her close. Him. "I just want to enjoy our last dance," she said and tucked her head against his shoulder, where it had always belonged when they'd danced.

The song could have lasted to morning light and still would have been over too soon. Josh held her through the last notes of the song, through the slim space of quiet that followed it, and through the beginning notes of another song, stretching out their last dance as far as it would go. Despite his lecture, his behavior showed that he, like her, would be happy if the two of them could stay like this all night.

But then Lance showed up to claim her as promised.

And as promised, Josh released her and walked away.

Lance danced her around the floor to the lively song, talking about his day administering vaccines at the area's only equine ranch. She heard only half of it because her attention was on Beth pulling Josh onto the floor. The jealousy that galloped through her wasn't surprising. She would never get used to seeing Josh with another woman. What was surprising was the old desire to kick Beth's ass if she stole that kiss from Josh that should have been hers.

"Charleigh, I gotta ask…are you and Josh back together?"

The comment shifted her attention back to her dance partner. She didn't want to give Lance the idea she was available, but she couldn't say she was with Josh. "Why would you think that?"

"Men have been lined up to dance with you all night long, me included, but every time they get near you, he pulls you out to dance. I had to come out here to get a chance with you. And even then, it was like pulling teeth to get him to let you go. And, well, the way you two were dancing reminded me of when you were together."

"Josh and I work together. We're friends."

"Good. Real glad to hear that. Because I'd like to see you. And not as friends."

Her ringless finger tingled, confirming that Josh's warning about removing the ring had been right on the mark. Before she could think of a gentle rebuff, the song was over.

"Thanks for the dance." She left his arms and turned to leave the dance floor.

He caught her hand. "Now that I got you, I was hoping to hold on for a while. Another dance?"

"Rain check? I need to go to the ladies' room."

"I'll take you."

She set her palms on his chest to stop him. "Lance, I haven't needed help going to the bathroom for quite a few years," she said, trying to disguise her annoyance with lighthearted teasing. "I'll be back."

She rushed to the bathroom, but instead of going in, she headed down the hall to the exit.

Pushing out the door, she pressed her back up against the wall and gulped in the cold night air, hoping it would cool her flushed and tingling skin from the idea racing through her mind. Did everyone think she and Josh were a couple again? Did Josh want it? She smiled, remembering those almost kisses from a few nights ago, the way they'd danced tonight.

Did she want it?

Elevating their friendship to a lovership would complicate things. Could they manage it without ruining their partnership? Without getting hurt again?

If they did get back together, could she leave him at the end of the contract if she decided not to stay? Would he go with her?

The sound of the door handle being pressed gave her a two-second warning to scurry around the corner of the building. If Lance had come looking for her, she didn't want to be stuck in the moonlight with him, discussing his desire to be more than friends.

"I thought it would be nice to talk out here, away from prying eyes and flapping tongues." The sweet-tea voice belonged to Beth.

Charleigh didn't need three guesses as to who was with her.

"It's pretty cold out. Maybe we should go back in."

Right on the first guess. Josh.

"I'll warm you up," Beth said.

When Charleigh and Josh had been together, he'd kept her warm with hugs, kisses, and caresses. That damning moment of silence suggested that the same thing was going on between him and Beth.

"I miss you, Josh," Beth said. "We haven't been together since October."

"Yeah, I've been pretty busy."

"With her?"

"With work obligations."

"She's looking more and more like a preference than an obligation."

He didn't respond. Was he nodding? Thinking? What? *Say something, dammit!*

Beth released an audible sigh. "Are we over?"

He was slow to respond, but when he finally did, his words were low and kind. "We're still friends, Beth. Like we always were."

"Friends, but with no benefits and no plans for a future together."

"You and I are at different places right now—"

"Don't give me that bullshit, Josh. It's because you're back together with her."

"Charleigh and I work together. We're friends."

Laugher bubbled inside Charleigh that she and Josh had given the same answer to the question about their relationship status.

"Why don't you just admit that you two are involved again?"

"Because we're not."

"Oh, please. Everybody knows you are."

"Everybody's wrong."

"You took them to the tree lighting and to her boy's school concert. You helped put up their lights and decorate their tree…the tree you took them to cut down. You spent Thanksgiving with them and will probably spend Christmas and New Year with them as well. You're running around town with them all the time, acting like a happy little family. And everybody's gossiping about you two drooling all over each other on the dance floor tonight."

Charleigh was amazed at the efficiency of the gossip chain in this town. These people didn't miss a thing.

"We were just dancing," Josh insisted.

"No one else will tell you the truth, but I will because I care about you," Beth said, negating his attempt to unravel the story before it grew legs. "Charleigh and Derrick Simms aren't your family—as much as you might want them to be—and they never will be. That bitch came back for one reason—to get the Simms' fortune. She needs you now because you're part of the contract, but the second she gets what she wants, she'll drop you, just like she did before. And when she does, don't expect me to pick up the pieces of your broken heart again."

The sound of the door being yanked forcibly open was followed by it banging closed. Charleigh figured it was Beth who had gone in, not Josh, but she didn't know. Then she heard something that let her know for sure.

"Charleigh." Josh whispered her name on a long, drawn-out note. At first, she thought she was busted, that he knew she was there, eavesdropping. But when he said her name again, in almost a plea, she realized he

271

was just saying her name, like she said his when she needed to evoke his essence, his strength.

When the door squeaked open again a few tense minutes later, she peeked around the corner in time to see it shut with a soft clink. She was alone with her thoughts again, one stronger than the others. Maybe Josh wanted her and Derrick to be his family.

"Josh," she whispered into the quiet night and made a wish on all the points of shimmering light caught in the ebony net of velvet overhead that the right answers would materialize. Shaking her head at her silliness, she pulled open the door and went in. This time, she stopped at the bathroom. When she came out, Lance was there, leaning a shoulder against the wall, arms and ankles crossed.

"I was about to send in a search party, darlin'," he said with a grin that no doubt had charmed many a darlin' out of her panties.

He put his hand low at her back and guided her to the dance floor. She didn't see Josh, but Beth was in a huddle of friends, a couple she recognized from school.

She and Lance had just started dancing when his brother Randy slapped him on the back, stopping their dance.

"Hey, bro. Damn fine job stealing Charleigh from Flores."

"Get lost, Randy," Lance said, annoyed with the interruption.

"Oh, c'mon. Just one little ol' dance. I'll give her right back." He pulled her hand from Lance's and grabbed her up in his arms

Lance stood there for a few seconds, steaming about the situation, then walked off the floor, his stance showing he was pissed.

"Just like old times, id'nit, sweetness?" Randy said, his hot breath smelling like yesterday's whiskey as he danced her around the floor in a sloppy, drunken fashion.

"How so?"

His glassy gaze left her eyes and crawled downward, tucking into her cleavage. A low and vibrating mmm rumbled from his leering lips. "That pretty little dress makes me feel funny in the pants. Like that little pink uniform you used to wear."

"Behave, Randy, or you're gonna be feeling nothing but pain in the pants."

He chuckled. "Just as sassy as ever. I'm real happy that hasn't changed." The grin still in place, he continued. "So tell me…since you're not with Flores, you gonna give one of us Barton boys a shot this time?"

"Everyone else in this town thinks Josh and I are together," she said before she could stop herself. "Why don't you?"

"Oh, hell, girl, if you were with him, you wouldn't be dancing with anybody else."

Randy might still be a peanut butter brain, but he was right on the money about that. She nodded.

"Since we both agree that your ex-lover isn't taking care of your womanly needs…" His hand slid to her butt and squeezed. "Let's move on to discussing who's the best man to help you with that."

"Not you." She shoved out of his arms and walked away.

He caught her hand and pulled her back to him. "We haven't finished our dance."

"Yeah, you have." Josh pulled her away from

Randy, put her behind him, then stood toe to toe with the asshat. "Keep your hands off her, Barton."

The alcohol coursing through Randy's veins obviously giving him false courage, he muttered something she didn't hear but that Josh must have heard clearly because he punched Randy, who fell to the floor.

At some point, the music had stopped, and the sheriff had joined them. "What's going on here?" he demanded.

"Randy was harassing me," she said when Josh remained quiet. "Josh stopped him."

The sheriff shook his head. "You know the rules, Josh. We have zero tolerance for fighting."

"You also have zero tolerance for drinking, but Randy's drunk," Charleigh said. "You should be thanking Josh. He was doing your job, resolving the problem."

"I don't doubt it, young lady, but you should have come to me with your complaint, let me handle it proper. Josh, you and Randy both have to leave."

"Oh my God, you're frickin' kidding me," she exploded at the injustice of the situation. "Josh was defending me. Why is he being punished?"

"Best get your little woman's mouth under control," he said to Josh, then he and another man pulled Randy to his feet and escorted him toward the door.

"Little woman?" she exclaimed and started to follow him to give him a piece of her mind about his sexist word choices and archaic attitude when Josh gripped her arm to hold her back from doing anything that likely would just cause more trouble.

At the same time, another hand gripped her other arm.

"No reason you have to go," Lance said at her side. "I'll be glad to take you home after the dance."

A little scoff was out before she could stop it. "I'm going home with Josh." At Lance's dejected look, she tacked on, "Thanks for the offer, though."

Josh set his hand at her back and led her away from Lance, away from the dance floor. "Let's find Derrick and get the hell out of here," he whispered to her.

Their son was headed toward them, his coat on, their coats in his hands. They'd both unquestioningly chosen to go with Josh. As it should be. They were family.

****

By Josh's silence, the way his jaw was working, and how heavy his foot was on the gas pedal as he headed home, Charleigh knew he was still fuming over how the night had ended. So was she.

He had done the right thing and was punished for it. That backward sense of justice rubbed her wrong, making her again unsure whether she could ever live here happily. The one good thing that came from tonight was that he'd stuck up for her, in front of everyone at the dance. That had to mean something.

"Sorry I ruined our night," Josh said finally, his voice still tight with anger. "Something else you guys want to do?"

"Let's stop and look at the stars," Derrick suggested. "Me and Mom and Dad used to do that. Remember, Mom?"

"Good idea," she said with a nod in Derrick's direction in the back seat. It had been a source of free entertainment for their family that brought them closer. Will had checked out books from the library about constellations so he could learn about them and teach Derrick.

Will had constantly gone above and beyond to show Derrick a good time. When she had once commented on it, Will said that he wanted to make sure Derrick knew how much he loved him so when he found out that his *real* dad didn't want him, he would know for sure that Will had.

Josh pulled down one of the side roads between his place and hers, and they all got out and lay on the hood, covering up with a blanket he kept in the vehicle.

"Derrick, I want you to know it was wrong of me to hit Randy," Josh said after they'd gotten settled.

Derrick turned to face him. "How come you did?"

"He said some hateful things."

"Was it about Mom or me, or you, or Ruby?"

"Yes."

"My dad said that sometimes a man has to fight to protect his family."

"Your dad was right. But sometimes you can protect them without fighting. That's usually the better way. I should have just told him to knock it off, then gone to the sheriff and let him handle it."

Derrick seemed to accept that decision, because he dropped the subject and moved on to telling Josh about the constellations. She was surprised by how much he remembered. She also was surprised by how much Josh added to the conversation. It was shortsighted and insulting of her to assume he knew little beyond topics pertaining to ranching.

Some time after Derrick fell asleep, Charleigh

looped back around to the topic that had been on her mind all night.

"What did Randy say that made you hit him?" she whispered.

"You know how he is."

"Tell me."

He looked at Derrick.

"He's asleep and can't hear us." She wasn't sure if she wanted to know but she *needed* to. She needed to know what would make Josh, a man who typically had a firm grip on his emotions and actions, mad enough to hit someone.

"He said if I wasn't man enough to take care of your womanly needs, I needed to step aside so someone else could."

"Ah, so it was Randy questioning your manhood that made you mad," she said.

"It was his disrespect for you and his arrogance in believing he deserves someone like you. Plus, I don't like him putting his hands on you."

A warm, satisfied smile took her lips. "Well, I don't like you fighting, but thanks for sticking up for me."

"No problem."

"He said pretty much the same thing to me, which is why I pushed away from him."

"Asshat," he muttered. "I should have hit him harder in high school to make it clear you were off limits for eternity."

She chuckled. "As I remember, you did. Several times."

"Clearly not hard enough."

"Lance asked me whether you and I are together,"

she said a minute later. She hadn't decided until that moment to tell Josh what Lance said. But she wanted to know what he'd say about it. Whether he'd tell her about Beth saying the same thing. Whether bringing it up would open the conversation for them about being together.

"People asked me the same thing." He sighed. "Guess we better slow down on being together in public."

His comment cut her to the quick. He'd been trying to kiss her for weeks, danced with her most of the night, stuck up for her in front of everyone, hit Randy for disrespecting her, and still he insisted they hide whatever it was that was going on between them.

Well, she wasn't willing to be that woman who was good enough to kiss in private, but not good enough to kiss in public because of what people might think. She wasn't sure what pissed her off more—that he was okay with hiding their relationship or that he was putting her needs last again.

"Seriously?" she said. "You're going to let the town busybodies dictate our behavior?"

"We just had this talk, Charleigh. Do I really need to explain again how it is here?"

"No, I got it the first time, thanks. What I don't know is why you're okay with it."

"It's the way it is whether I'm okay with it or not. Why does it bother you so much? It never did when you lived here before."

"It didn't bother me then because I had you, and because you didn't care about what people thought about us either. It was you and me against them. But now—"

"You still have me. I'm responsible for you and Derrick, and I take that responsibility seriously."

"That doesn't mean you're obligated to fight our battles."

"It means I'll do whatever I have to to protect you."

"I don't want you to have to protect us from what people think about us." The tenor of her voice rose and sharpened with every word. "I want you to agree with me that Derrick growing up in such a narrow-minded community where he's under the microscope for everything he does and says and is shamed for it if it runs counter to their skewed norm is wrong and harmful. But clearly you're not going to do that because you're fine with it. And that's why Derrick and I can't stay here."

Josh rose up on his elbow. "So everything I'm doing, everything I'm teaching you and Derrick is just to satisfy the contract, not because you want to build a life here?"

"The option to sell is in the contract, and I mentioned early on I was leaning that way."

He sat up. "It's late. I should get you home." He slid off the hood.

She slid off, too, grabbed his arm to stop him and made him face her. He just didn't get it, and for some reason, it was critical to her that he do. "You know I hate this place. Why are you acting so surprised and pissed that I want to get out of here?"

He pulled away from her grip. "Whether you go or stay is up to you, but you can't run from your past. It always catches up with you, demanding to be addressed."

"This has nothing to do with my past and everything to do with my future. And Derrick's. The only reason I came back to this shithole was to satisfy the terms of Wyatt's will so I could sell everything and provide a secure future for my son."

Well, shit. She'd just backed up Beth's accusation, and the pain of it flickered in his eyes before he could blink it away. She hated to play any part in helping prove Beth right, but she owed it to Josh to be honest.

"Yeah, well, just remember, you need me to sign off on that," he said.

"Sign off? On what?"

"On whether you've fulfilled the terms of the will. Read our contract, sweetheart. Without my signature, you can't assume full ownership, which means you can't sell."

"I've done everything you asked of me. How dare you suggest—"

"No, you haven't."

"Name one thing."

"Derrick."

Panic pricked the length of her body. "What about him?"

"I get a couple of hours with him every day. That's not enough time to teach him what he needs to know."

"He has school. That's more important than—"

"It's kindergarten. He doesn't need to be there, drawing circles and squares and singing his ABC's. The kid can already read and write, for fuck's sake. First grade is soon enough to force him to sit in a classroom all day. I need him with me if I'm to do my job and teach him what he needs to know about ranching."

"Education and socializing with kids his own age

are more important than him learning about a life he's never going to have."

"Something wrong with being a rancher?"

"I want more for him."

He reared back like her words had clocked him on the chin. "So this life isn't good enough for your son?"

"That's not what I said. I want something different for him. You used to want something different, too, Josh. What happened to that?"

"Life happened. I had responsibilities and obligations, and I accepted them, like a man. But more than that, I have a legacy here that deserves to be upheld for the next generation."

"Well, Derrick has other plans than fulfilling someone else's legacy, and they deserve to be realized, too."

"What plans does he have at five, other than eating, riding horses, and playing?"

"That's none of your business. I'm his mother, and until he gets old enough to make those decisions on his own, I make them for him. Me. Not you. And what I want—"

"And what you want is to sell his ranch and make him leave everyone in his life that at Thanksgiving *you* called *family*."

"I don't want to leave the ranch," Derrick said behind them, halting her heated response.

In unison, their gazes spun to the SUV where Derrick sat on the hood, eyes wide, looking at her and Josh.

He climbed off and joined them. Standing at Josh's side, he took Josh's hand in his and faced her. "I want to be with Josh and have him teach me ranching. That's more important than school. More important than anything."

Anguish rocked her back a half step. She was losing her son to his father, little by little, and it hurt like hell.

She crouched down in front of Derrick and took his other hand. "But when we sell the ranch, we can go anywhere, do anything we want. Like we talked about."

"I just want to stay here." He pulled his hand from hers and wrapped both arms around Josh. "With Josh. He wants us to stay with him, too." He looked up at Josh. "Right, Josh?"

Josh's arm settled around Derrick's shoulders, and he met his eyes and nodded. Then two sets of blue eyes pinned her with the same determined gaze.

Feeling outnumbered and way too vulnerable, she hauled herself away from them to the passenger side of the SUV and climbed in.

No one talked on the way home. Even Derrick seemed to understand that talk wasn't the best thing at the moment. For Charleigh, the quiet gave her a chance to isolate and analyze the words they'd all said tonight and try to figure out how she felt about them and determine the next steps. Particularly troubling was Derrick's bond with Josh.

Her son loved her, she knew that, but if she insisted on selling the ranch and leaving Josh, doing what she thought was best for his future and hers, would it cause irreparable damage to their relationship? He'd made it clear he loved Josh, wanted to stay with him. With Josh saying he wanted that, too, her chances of convincing Derrick this wasn't the place for them had all but disintegrated.

Josh said he wanted them to stay, but did he mean it? And as what? Neighbors? Friends? Something more? She had to find out. The truth could determine what happened next. It could change everything.

"Derrick, go on in and get ready for bed," she said when they arrived at the house and had climbed out. "I'll be right in."

"Don't fight again. I don't like it."

"We're just going to talk. Now, go on in."

He hugged Josh. "Can you come over tomorrow?"

"We'll see."

At any other time, his answer would have been yes, but tonight's response likely was based on his uncertainty about how their coming talk would play out.

Derrick went in, and Charleigh shut the doors and turned to face Josh.

"CC, I wouldn't have brought it up if I'd known he was awake and listening. I don't want to come between you two."

His apology was sincere, and she knew he'd said everything he had only because of what she'd said about not wanting this life for Derrick. She had insulted his profession, his livelihood, his legacy, the value of the task he'd been given to teach her and Derrick, to impart his knowledge. Of course he was going to be defensive. He had his pride. His feelings. And she'd stomped them under her boot heels.

"Sorry," he mumbled and turned toward the SUV.

"Hold on, Flores," she called out before he could climb in. He turned back to face her, wariness in his eyes as she approached him. "You ruined my one night out, first by getting us kicked out of the dance, then by ganging up on me with my son. I'd like to know how you plan to make it up to me." She stopped in front of him.

"You got something in mind?" he said through that little half grin that made her heart flip.

"Of course."

"I'm not surprised. Name it."

"Dance with me."

"No music."

"You have a radio."

"And it's tuned to Country."

"That's all right."

His eyebrow lifted in surprise.

At her grin, he leaned into the SUV, inserted the key into the ignition, and turned it to make the radio come on. Country lyrics about playing with fire and getting burned floated out the door—a warning?—and surrounded them.

He took her hand in his, led her a few feet away from the SUV, and eased her into his arms. They danced in the dirt, slowly, closely, sharing their heat.

"Josh, I'm sorry for what I said earlier. I didn't mean that ranching and your job with us aren't valuable and honorable and important, but I know that's how it came across. Forgive me?"

"Forgiven," he said, his soft tone telling her he meant it.

"I want you to know, I'm impressed with you, with your knowledge and skills, your integrity, your commitment to your work and to us. Derrick and I are lucky to have you with us for this year."

"Compliments? Keep it up, Cooper, and I might get the idea you like me."

"Careful, Flores. Ideas like that could be dangerous."

Their being this friendly—dancing, almost kissing, spending time together—could be dangerous. It could destroy everything they were working for. But right now, right here, in his arms, moving to the music as one, she wasn't worried about the danger. She wasn't worried about anything but staying in his arms, where she was safe, warm, peaceful, and had everything she needed and wanted.

"Aren't you the one who used to say a little danger keeps things interesting?" he asked.

"Actually, that was you," she said with a grin. "I just agreed with you."

He released a long-suffering sigh. "You were a helluva lot more agreeable to my ideas back then."

She chuckled. "That's because you used to have some damn good ideas."

He chuckled, too, and they settled closer to each other, her head on his chest, and danced.

The first song had ended, moved into the second, maybe third, but he hadn't let her go, and she hadn't moved away. She never wanted this to end, except to move on to a more dangerous level. Like kissing. Like touching. Like—

"Are we okay now?" he whispered against her hair, bringing her mind back to the reason she was in his arms.

She licked her lips then looked up, capturing his gaze. "Almost."

Without warning, she leaned in and kissed him softly on the mouth, elevating the level of danger between them. It wasn't the deep, lingering, languid, soul-connecting kiss she wanted, but it was good enough, a taste that hopefully would whet his appetite for more, would let him know she wanted to go there. Because she did. No matter the danger. No matter how complicated it got between them.

"Goodnight," she whispered against his lips.

She had left his arms and turned with the intent to head to the house when he caught her arm and tugged her back to him, drawing her in snug against him, anchoring one hand in her hair. Then his mouth claimed hers the way she'd wanted him to since that first morning she'd arrived. And, oh God, was it good. If she'd been wearing socks, they'd have reached Texas by now.

His mouth knew hers. Her mouth knew his. Together, they knew how to give each other maximum pleasure from each hot touch and wet glide. And for one dizzying moment, she forgot how to breathe, how to think, how to do everything except feel, except get drunk on his taste and touch.

Wanting to get lost in the exhilarating danger wrapping around them, she arched into him with a hungry little mewling that had him gripping her butt and trying to mold her even closer to his hard body. Her hands gripped his hair to hold his mouth to hers like she needed him to breathe.

Then, as if they'd reached that invisible but buzzing line that marked the point of no return, he eased out of the kiss, brushed his lips over hers once more, then pulled back and looked into her eyes. His heated gaze suggested that what he wanted was to cross that line, pick her up, carry her to her bed, and do all the things she'd been thinking about.

She didn't want to leave him, but she had to or she'd end up pulling him into the house, into her bed, and letting him.

Lungs aching with the breaths she hadn't used during the kiss, she rocked back a step. "Thanks for tonight," she whispered. "For everything."

He nodded.

Weak-kneed, she walked toward the house.

"Why did you come with me instead of letting Lance take you home?" he asked when she stepped onto the porch.

She turned around. "I wanted to come with you."

He strode forward in a slow measure that allowed her time to appreciate his hard form, his full lips that tasted like sin, his desire pulsing toward her. She wanted it all. Was ready to take it all.

Stopping a foot from her, he pulled her wedding ring from his pocket and took her left hand. His eyes never leaving hers, he slid the ring into place.

Before she could voice the disappointed "Why?" clanging in her heart, he explained. "You're safer with it on."

"Maybe I don't want safe."

"What *do* you want, Charleigh?"

His need-you gaze was locked so tight on hers, she swore she could feel him inside her mind, strolling through every naughty, delicious want blooming there, each one more colorful and intoxicating than the one before. He knew her well enough to know exactly what she wanted—their bodies locked into each other, giving pleasure as only they could.

But they weren't alone. Ruby and Derrick were in the house. And she had never been a quiet lover, at least not with Josh. And the more sensible part of her knew the move would be a disaster. Tonight, she'd go with safe.

"I'd settle for another kiss," she said.

"Settle? That doesn't sound like the Charleigh Cooper I know."

He wanted to kiss her again. She knew it. Knew his signs. What she didn't know was why he wasn't taking the step that would give them what they both wanted. Maybe he needed a little push. She took her cue from the song on the radio.

"Are you gonna kiss me or not, Flores?"

Desire burning in his eyes, he brought her hand to his mouth and pressed a kiss to her palm, then flicked it with the tip of his tongue like he used to do on her…other body parts. The breath that had balled up in her chest shuddered out on a sigh, desire flooding her system, drawing every muscle in her body tight with need for more of him.

The disappointment that burned through her when he released her hand rocked her. To try to disguise it, she asked the question she needed the answer to. "Did you mean what you said? That you want Derrick and me to stay?"

When he didn't respond right away, she dropped her disappointed gaze to the tip of his boots. "You said it not to hurt Derrick's feelings."

His finger tucked under her chin and lifted it to face him. "I said it because it's the truth."

Her heart pinballed against her ribs at his truth, and she cupped his face, leaned in, and pressed a sweet kiss to his lips.

"Does that kiss mean you're staying?" he asked

when she pulled back.

"The way country music's growing on me, you never know."

To the sound of his chuckling, she went inside the house and shut the doors on the best mistake she wished she'd made.

****

Josh wanted to go after Charleigh, break down the door even if she'd hadn't locked it, grab her up, and carry her to her room and satisfy that need burning in her eyes and through her body. But the more sensible parts of him didn't want to mess up the smooth path they were finally on. And he'd die from the damaging effects of blue balls before he'd make love to her in Will's house. That's for damn sure.

Fortunately, after those kisses, he couldn't feel his legs. After a minute of standing there, likely looking like a love-sick hayseed, he stumbled to the SUV, climbed in, and headed home, a grin on his face the entire way, knowing she'd be in his dreams tonight.

Only, he couldn't sleep.

Image after image of their night flashed before his eyes, and the feel of her in his arms, against his body, and the taste of her kisses on his lips kept his libido raging on high. At the same time, his struggle to decipher what her actions and words meant gnawed at his brain.

She'd kissed him when he'd admitted he wanted her to stay, but she hadn't outright said she was staying. Was there anything he could do or say to make her stay? If there was, and if she named it, would he be able to do it? The biggest question of all was, could he trust her enough to allow her back into his life?

Tired of uselessly chasing sleep, he sat up and flipped on the bedside lamp to read. But as he reached for the veterinary manual on the nightstand, Charleigh's face smiling at him from the picture of the two of them stole his attention. He picked it up, ran a fingertip across the mouth that he was happy to know still tasted as delicious as a wet, ripe cherry. The picture was proof that everything had, at least in that heartbeat of a moment, been perfect between them. He remembered that day like it was yesterday. It was burned into his soul, a permanent brand he'd wear into death.

Derrick was right. They looked happy and in love because they had been. And for longer than that day. Could they be again? His granddad used to say that when you lose something important to you, it's sometimes because you weren't ready for it yet, but that if it comes back around, it's a sign you are ready. In other words, sometimes timing made all the difference.

Maybe tonight was a sign that he and Charleigh were now ready for each other.

Frustration and desire gripping him in a tight fist, he set the picture back in place and headed to the bathroom for a cold shower and temporary relief.

Chapter Fifteen

After Christmas Eve dinner, Charleigh, Derrick, Ruby, and Josh had settled into the living room to open presents, then Ruby and Charleigh went into the kitchen to bring in dessert and coffee, leaving Josh and Derrick to discuss their gifts.

"I like my belt," Derrick said to Josh, who sat on the couch, watching the boy thread into his belt loops the new belt he'd made him.

"Next time we go into town, you can pick out a better buckle for it," Josh said. "A man needs to find one that's meaningful to him."

"Can I have one like yours?"

"This was my granddad's. It's the Flores brand, so it's one of a kind."

"You gonna give it to your son?"

The kid wouldn't let up. He was always talking up the benefits of a wife and kids and family. "I would, but as you know, I don't have one."

"Do you want one?"

"I probably should get a wife first."

"My dad said my mom was the best wife in the whole wide world."

"Your mom is pretty good at whatever she does."

"Yep." Derrick climbed on the couch beside Josh, stood on his knees, and put his hand on Josh's shoulder. "I asked Santa for my mom to get married again."

"I think your mom would say that's her decision, not Santa's."

"We'll see." He jumped off the couch and got the plaster handprint hanging he'd made for Josh and handed it to him before climbing back on the couch next to him. "Where you gonna put it?"

"Probably my office."

"We were only supposed to get to make one, but I told Ms. Barnes I had to make one for my dad."

Josh's mind pushed him to say *I'm not your dad*, to make it clear what their relationship was and wasn't, but his heart wouldn't let the words pass his lips. Truth was, it made him feel good that Derrick thought of him that way. His fingers felt the name Derrick had scratched into the plaster on the back, and it filled him with a father's pride. "I noticed you wrote Derrick Simms Flores on the back."

"You mad I used your name?"

"No. Just curious why you did it."

Derrick glanced toward the kitchen where Charleigh was busy arranging the desserts on a platter, then back at him. "I like to pretend you're my dad," he whispered, his blue eyes hooked to his, his hand on his shoulder.

The sincerity and love audible and visible in the gesture gripped Josh's heart.

"But don't tell my mom, 'k?"

Josh and Derrick had amassed several little secrets between them. Keeping secrets from Charleigh wasn't the right thing to do, but with a slow shake of his head, he accepted another one. With each one added, he felt their bond strengthen. Besides, telling her this latest secret served no purpose, might even hurt her feelings, so he wouldn't encourage Derrick to tell her.

"Come and get it," Ruby said as she and Charleigh came into the room, carrying trays of dessert and coffee, and milk for Derrick, and set them on the coffee table.

Josh set Derrick's handprint in the box he'd use to carry home his presents while Derrick jumped off the couch and rushed toward the dessert. He loaded up a plate with two snowman cookies, two chocolate chip cookies, two slices of pumpkin roll, two lemon squares, two frosted brownie, and two pieces of fudge.

"Whoa, puppy, that's way too much for you," Charleigh said.

"Oh, it's not for me. It's for Josh."

"That's too much for me, too, bud. How about you put half back, and we share the rest?"

"Okay." Derrick put some back and grabbed two forks.

Charleigh handed Josh a cup of coffee as Derrick scampered back onto the couch and settled next to him, plate in his lap, and handed him a fork.

"Derrick, did you open all your gifts?" Josh said after everyone settled in.

"Yep, I did."

"You sure?" Josh forked a bite of the pumpkin roll into his mouth.

"Yep," the boy said around his own bite of pumpkin roll. "I looked all under the tree, crawling."

"Well what's that poking out from behind the chair?"

Instantly alert, Derrick scooted to the front of the couch and looked around. "Where?"

Josh nodded with his chin. "Behind Ruby's chair."

Derrick thrust his plate to Charleigh, who had sat beside him on the couch, and raced to Ruby's chair, grabbed the tip of the long and narrow present wrapped in red and green paper, and pulled it out.

"What did you do?" Charleigh whispered to Josh, then set Derrick's plate and hers on the coffee table.

"You'll see," he said through a grin and set his coffee beside the plates.

"It's from Josh." Eyes wide and smiling, Derrick dragged the present back to the couch with both hands. "Wow! It's heavy." He set it on the floor and plopped down next to it.

Josh knelt beside Derrick as the boy ripped the paper off, then helped him lift the side flap of the box. Derrick's eyes lit up, his grin beaming.

"Yes! It's just what I wanted!" He lunged at Josh, hugging him tight, and whispered so only he could hear, "Thanks, Dad." He pulled back and jumped up and down, like Josh's heart was doing.

"Well, show us what it is," Ruby said.

Josh held open the flap, and Derrick pulled out a small rifle, a scope attached. In triumph, Derrick held the gun aloft with a shout.

"It's the one my granddad gave me when I was your age," Josh said, smiling almost as much as Derrick. "And it was my dad's before that. I had a scope fitted to it."

Derrick went to Charleigh and held it out so she could see. "Look, Mom. Isn't it the best?"

For half a second, she looked like she was ready to argue that he was too young, but instead, she stood.

"Excuse me, I'll be right back," she said, her voice tight, and rushed from the room.

Josh's gaze followed her. He probably should have cleared it with her first. Dammit. His surprise lost some of its luster at the knowledge he'd upset her at Christmas.

"It's not loaded," Derrick said to Charleigh's retreating back. "Is it?" he asked Josh.

"No. And it'll stay unloaded until you learn how to handle it, clean it, and take care of it. Your mom and I'll start your lessons after the holidays."

Derrick hugged him again. "It's the best present I ever had in my whole life."

"Glad you like it. But remember, it's not a toy."

He nodded and ran his hands along the gun, as if he couldn't believe it was real. And his.

****

Charleigh leaned against the bathroom sink, trying to breathe, trying to control the tears triggered by the touching gesture, of Josh giving Derrick the gun his granddad had given him. No one realized the weighty significance of his action. But she did, and it was a secret she carried on her soul.

Josh should know the truth. Derrick should know. They'd already lost nearly six years and shouldn't lose any more. But not knowing how Josh would react to the truth kept her from taking that leap. Would he be so angry at her for not telling him from the start that he'd break all ties and crush Derrick's spirit? Would he try to take Derrick away from her? Would he dissolve the contract?

She couldn't let any of that happen. Especially at Christmas. So she'd keep her secret. In nine months, Josh would go back to his life, and she and Derrick would leave. It was the best way. The only way.

Eyes red but dry, she went back into the living room, a smile on her face for Derrick, and took her place on the couch near Josh. "Derrick, can you show me your gun?"

Grinning, he stood in front of her with his gun. "It's a single-bolt .22, which means it shoots one bullet at a time." He pulled the bolt back to demonstrate where the bullet went, then rattled off the names of the parts that Josh had no doubt instructed him on in her absence.

Not for anything would she spoil his moment, but she would do her job as a mother and relay the importance of safety. "You know this is not a toy."

He laughed. "That's what Josh said."

She met Josh's eyes over Derrick's blond head. Her heart fluttered in her chest at the sweet don't-be-mad-at-me look in his eyes.

"He said you guys are gonna teach me how to shoot it after New Year's," Derrick added.

The two of them teaching their son. How incredibly right was that. "Sounds good, but for now, how about you put the gun down and let's read one of your Christmas books."

"Okay."

Taking his gun with him, he ran to his room and came back with two books. And the gun. He scrambled up on the couch between her and Josh and handed Josh the book Will had always read to him.

The surprise showing on Josh's face was panic kicking inside her. No, Josh should not read him *that* book.

"I'll read it," she said and reached for it.

"Dad always read this one to me. I'm used to a guy

voice," Derrick said. "You always read this one, remember?" He handed that book to her. Then, the gun across their laps, Derrick curled into Josh's side, like he used to do with Will, and Josh's arm went around him like it was the most natural thing in the world.

Josh opened the book and started reading. "I am your...parent, you are my child. I am your quiet place, you are my wild."

Listening to him read the sentimental words was a lesson in control for her fragile emotions. But she managed to keep it together and even get through the book Derrick brought her to read. The clock struck eleven as she finished the last page.

She kissed the top of Derrick's head and closed the book. "Time to get ready for bed."

"Can I stay up just a little longer? Please?"

"Santa won't come if you're awake. He might just pass by our house."

"Okay. Josh, would you tuck me in after I get ready?"

"Sure," he said.

He flew toward the bathroom, gun in one hand, the books in the other.

"Well, folks, think I'll turn in, too," Ruby said and rocked forward and back several times to build the momentum to close the recliner and get up.

"Merry Christmas," she said and hugged them, then set off toward her bedroom, leaving them sitting alone in the soft glow of the tree lights.

Josh slid his hand across the couch to Charleigh's and brushed her finger with his. "I should have checked with you before I gave him the rifle."

"Yeah, you should have. But I'll let it slide because

he's so happy."

"I had the same reaction when my granddad gave it to me. I would have slept with it had my mom not forbade it."

Her finger brushed over his. "Are you sure you want to give it to him?"

"If I wasn't sure, I wouldn't have done it. Besides, someone should get use out of it."

The suggestion in his statement squeezed her chest. "So, you still don't want kids?"

His hand slid over hers, and he linked their fingers loosely. "As I told Derrick, I probably need a wife first."

"You and Derrick were talking about kids and marriage?" His nod and shrug earned a little chuckle from her. "Awkward conversation?"

"Sorta."

"What about with the queen?" She thought she knew the answer, after eavesdropping on that conversation, and because of their kisses, but she had to make sure.

He captured her gaze and shook his head slowly.

Bubbles of relief burst through her, and she curled her fingers over his. "You're not seeing her anymore?"

He held her hand tighter. "Not since October."

She bit her bottom lip to staunch the smile. "Oh. Well. I'm…" She laughed. "Sorry, but I'm not sorry to hear that."

He chuckled. "You never liked her in high school either. Why was that, exactly?"

She'd had to threaten Beth a few times in high school for coming on to Josh. "You know why."

Before she could elaborate, Derrick rushed back

into the room. They let their hands separate seconds before he plopped down between them.

"Ready to tuck me in?" he asked Josh.

"Yep."

Josh scooted forward and Derrick jumped on his back, and they followed Charleigh to his bedroom. She pulled back the covers, and Josh set him down in the bed. Derrick lay down, and Josh pulled the covers up over him.

"Merry Christmas, puppy," she said and kissed him. "Love you."

"Love you, Mom," he said.

"Merry Christmas, bud," Josh said and tussled his hair.

Derrick smiled up at him, love shining in his eyes. "Love you, Josh."

"Love you, too." Seconds after the whispered, heartfelt but shaky words left Josh's mouth, Derrick rolled over onto his side, the content smile still on his face.

Hearing those words from Josh had always made her smile, too, like all was right with her world. Hopefully, Derrick wouldn't experience the heartbreak she had from loving Josh.

She flipped off the light, Josh pulled the door to, and they returned to the living room.

"I brought him a couple of presents from Santa," Josh said. "There're in the pickup. I'll be right back."

"Need help?" she asked, noticing he still wore the shell-shocked look of a man caught in the blast radius of an emotion explosion.

"Nope," he said, already headed toward the door so fast she wondered whether he'd just keep going when he got to his pickup.

Knowing he'd probably need some time, she did the last of the night's tasks. She pulled the super soaker water gun down from where she had hidden it in her closet and set it under the tree. Not that it could compare with the real gun Josh had given him. She wrapped the desserts and put them away. She rinsed the dishes they'd used and put them in the dishwasher, then started it. She poured most of the milk Derrick left for Santa down the drain then set the glass back on the coffee table. She grabbed the plate with the Christmas cookie Derrick had decorated for Santa and curled up on the couch to wait for Josh.

Hearing the door open, heralding his return, a feeling of comfort and relief washed over her. He entered the room, arms full of presents, and the light in his eyes as they met hers said that whatever confusion he might have been feeling when he left had resolved itself. Going to the tree, he set a blue remote control pickup, a pack of batteries, and a container of Legos next to the water gun.

"That's exactly what he wanted," she said. "How did you know?"

"I talked to Santa," he said through a grin.

He settled next to her on the couch, closer now that Derrick wasn't sitting between them, and rested his arm along the top of the couch.

He settled his leg against hers. On purpose.

He brushed his fingers over her shoulder. On purpose.

Since their kisses after the Christmas dance, he'd been touching her more lately. Just little touches—to her hand, her arm, her leg, her shoulder, her head, her face, her hair. They hadn't kissed again since the night of the dance—she liked to think it was just because they hadn't had a moment alone—but their new closeness thrilled and terrified her all at the same time.

The heat of his arm along her shoulders, the heat of his body alongside hers, sent a tingling warmth flooding over every nerve ending in her body that had her wanting to curl up against him all night.

She held out the plate. "Well, have your cookie, Santa."

He ran his hand over his muscled stomach. "I'm stuffed. Did you see how much shit he gave me tonight?"

"He decorated this for Santa. If it isn't eaten, his belief will be shattered. Besides, it's the parents' job to eat the cookies left for Santa."

"Yeah, but I'm not the parent, so it's all on you."

"After all the presents you brought tonight, you're playing the role. Eat up."

"I draw the line at drinking that milk." He nodded to the glass on the table.

"I poured most of it down the drain. The rest stays there to show that Santa was here. I'll half the cookie with you." She broke it in half.

Heaving a resolved sigh, he took his half and took a bite.

She held out the plate to catch the crumbs. "Make sure the crumbs fall on the plate. He'll get suspicious otherwise."

"That kid notices every detail," he said. "Can't get away with anything."

"Believe me, I know," she said and took a bite of her half.

"He reminds me of me at that age. My mom would get fed up with my questions and tell me to go ask my granddad."

"What did your granddad say?"

"He'd give me a chore."

She chuckled. "I appreciate how patient you are with him. His curiosity can be exhausting. But I never want to stifle it. So…thanks."

"You bet."

"Thanks, too, for helping to make this Christmas so special for him."

He finished his half of the cookie and turned toward her. "So… What's Santa bringing you?"

This. Right here. It was the best gift she could wish for. "I have a warm, safe home for Derrick. He's happy and healthy. That's all I need." She plucked a crumb form his shirt and dropped it onto the plate.

"Happy, healthy, and world peace don't count. If you could wake up in the morning and find your greatest wish set out under that tree, what would it be?"

What she'd always wanted. Josh. His love.

"I have everything I want and need," she said and took another bite of her cookie.

"I know something you really need." His grin suggested something naughty.

"Oh? What's that?"

"A new nightgown. That old T-shirt you sleep in looks like shit."

"Shut up." She returned his grin. "It's comfortable."

"It's the shirt I gave you the night I left, isn't it?"

"Yes." She broke their gaze, set the plate with her half of the cookie half-eaten on the table, and folded her legs under her.

"You've worn it all these years?"

"Yes."

"Why?" He gently massaged along her shoulder, setting off explosions of tingles throughout her body.

Wearing Josh's shirt had comforted her, made her feel closer to him, especially during her pregnancy. "I told you…it's comfortable."

"It didn't bother Will that you wore it?" His hand slid under the curtain of her long hair then rose to the back of her head, his fingers slowly massaging her scalp the way she loved.

"It never came up." Although Will had never said a word about it, she knew he hadn't liked that she'd worn it, because it was a physical reminder that Josh was always between them. But she hadn't been able to give up the comfort it gave her, even for her husband's comfort.

"Never?" Josh whispered, his fingers tangling in her hair, gently tugging, increasing her pleasure. "You wear your ex-lover's shirt to bed, and your husband has no objection? If our roles had been reversed, that shirt would have been ashes at the bottom of the garbage can the first time you tried to wear it."

"We agreed early on not to talk about you, so…" The words trickled out on a breath.

"So you just forgot about me?" His hand caressed the skin at the side of her neck where her pulse was going crazy.

"I said I didn't talk about you. I didn't say I forgot about you."

At his simple touches, desire for him broke from the box she'd carefully packed it in and swirled through her like a dust devil. She let her eyes flutter closed for an instant, wanting to just feel everything he was doing to her, willing him to lean in and put his mouth to that pulse, swirl his tongue over it.

"Look at me, CC."

Against her better judgment, she did. His lips were all but on hers. His eyes held hers, his lids half closed. She knew that look. It was a look that said *I'm going to steal your breath and blow your mind.*

"Were you in love with me while you were married to him?" he asked.

She swallowed, trying to bring moisture to her dry mouth, trying to find the yes to answer his question. Before she could respond, the clock struck midnight. Their gazes stayed connected throughout the twelve soft dings. He licked his lips and watched as she licked hers.

"Merry Christmas," they said in unison.

His hand cupped her face and eased closer, eliminating the slim distance between them until their mouths touched. She'd wanted another kiss since the night of the dance a week ago when she'd boldly, joyously kissed him. Three times.

His mouth. His kiss. His taste. His touch. That's what she wanted for Christmas. Every Christmas, every birthday, every wish made on falling stars and wind-strewn dandelions, every day since she'd met him.

She leaned into the kiss, taking it deeper, as deep as it could go, trying to swallow it whole. His tongue took hers, and her hands moved into his hair to hold him close. She groaned at the feelings heating her body.

The kiss tipped her world over, and she went with it, feeling the couch pillow beneath her head, Josh's body pressed deliciously into hers, his hardness fitting perfectly against her softness, her breasts submitting to his chest, her curves fitting into his angles like a matched set.

His mouth knew its way around her body and was intent on proving it. It moved first to that pounding pulse at her neck, his lips kissing it, his teeth nipping it, his tongue swirling over it, making her gasp, making her mind loosen its grip on reality. He moved on to nibbling her ear, kissing along her jaw, then traveling the slow way back to her mouth.

She knew what lay at the end of this path. And as much as she wanted it, she wasn't sure it was the right move. If they made love, it could destroy everything they'd worked for.

Just when she'd decided to throw caution to the wind, say the hell with it and give in to her long-held desire, he eased back from the kiss. Even in the semidarkness of the living room, she saw the desire burning in his eyes. He stared at her with those mesmerizing eyes, his breathing as labored as hers.

"This is probably a bad idea," he whispered.

"Probably."

"People are here…"

"And they'd ask embarrassing questions if they caught us…"

He grinned. "And you're really noisy when you—"

She chuckled. "Shut up."

"And it's Will's house," he said, grin gone.

"It's my house."

"It'll always be his house. And I don't want to make love to you here."

He didn't move away from her, and she knew it

would take little effort on her part to crumble his fragile hesitation like a Christmas cookie. But then he leaned in and pressed a soft kiss to her forehead, signaling that his decision was made.

He moved off her and sat back on the couch, not as close as before. She sat up, too, and for a time, they did nothing but stare at each other in thick, heated silence.

Missing his touch, she took his hand and set it in her lap. "I'm glad you joined us tonight."

"Thanks for including me. It was the best Christmas I've had in a long time."

The words "Me, too," slipped out before she realized that it suggested Christmases with Will hadn't been good. Turning toward him, she quickly moved into a question. "Tell me about your other best Christmases."

"I have two others."

"What's the first?"

"The year my granddad gave me that .22. I had just turned six and had pestered my family about wanting one since Will had gotten one for his birthday months before. My dad said we weren't going to waste money on shit like that. My grandma said I wasn't old enough. My mom said over her dead body."

"Ah…so ol' Rey played the grandparent's prerogative card?"

"Something like that. He'd saved the gun he'd given my dad when he was a boy, fixed it up for me. He told them I could handle it. He's the one who taught me to shoot."

"He sounds like a wonderful man. I wish Derrick could have known him."

"Why?"

When she realized what she'd said, her heart and stomach switched places, making her scramble for an answer. "Um, well, you always speak so highly of him."

He nodded. "He was the dad I wish I'd had."

She remembered Ruby mentioning that his dad had died a couple years ago. And that Josh had left college to run the ranch. Who'd been at his side to help him through his grief, through his challenges? She wished it had been her.

"I heard about your dad," she said, squeezing his hand. "I'm sorry. I know you didn't get along, but he was still your dad. It must have been hard to say goodbye."

"Not really." Yawning, he pulled his hand from hers and lay back on the couch at the other end, his head on the pillow, his eyes gazing at her through dark, spiky lashes. "Tell me about your best Christmas."

"I have two others, like you. The first is that last Christmas with my parents."

He nodded. They'd had this conversation years ago, so she didn't need to explain.

"And the second?" he asked.

"I'll tell you mine after you tell me yours."

He held his arm out to her, inviting her to lie beside him. "Come here, and I'll tell you."

Her heart skipped a beat at his request, his challenge. At her hesitation, he spoke again, in a voice that could bring down the stars from the sky. "I won't try anything, if that's what you're worried about. I just…I want to feel you beside me."

To lie beside him, in his arms, feel his heart beat against hers, inhale his scent into her lungs. She wanted that, too. In truth, she wouldn't mind if he tried something.

It would be dangerous to take this gift, but it was Christmas, and the universe had been kind enough to give her what she wanted most—him. How could she refuse? So she would take it. Enjoy it. For a little while at least.

"Call it a Christmas bonus for your loyal ranch manager," he added to convince her.

"You're already well paid for that."

"Then do it because we used to love each other."

Used to? Try still do. At least on her part. She stood and went to stand beside him. He scooted deeper back against the couch and turned his body to face her. She started to settle in, facing him, but he stopped her.

"It'll be safer if your back is to me."

"Safer for who?"

He grinned. "Both of us."

She settled with her back to him, laying her head in the crook of his arm and easing her body into his. His arms went around her, and she clasped his hand in hers. They shifted slightly to better fit their bodies on the couch and to each other.

"This doesn't feel safer," she teased at the feel of his hardness against her butt. "It doesn't feel safe at all."

"Thought you didn't want safe?" he teased back.

"Don't throw my words back at me."

"If you don't trust me, you can get up."

His heartbeat thumped against her back and hers thundered in her ears, their wild beats racing as one. Joy and trepidation rippled in tandem streams through her at feeling him this close. She wouldn't be getting up. Not yet. Instead, she sank into him, wanting to enjoy him while she could. Other than Derrick's happiness, health, and safety, this was the best gift she could have asked for.

"I trust you," she said softly. And she realized it was the truth. She did trust him. "Now, tell me."

He pressed a kiss to her head. "That last Christmas with you."

His words were little more than breaths that barely stirred the strands of her hair, but they were powerful enough to steal the air from her lungs and ping-pong her heart against her lungs.

She swallowed the pleasure tickling her throat so she could speak. "That's mine, too," she whispered without waiting for him to ask. She probably should have said Derrick's first Christmas or Will's last. But here in his arms, the truth was so close to the surface, she wasn't sure she could lie, even to save her heart and soul.

He rewarded her for telling the truth by tightening his arms a little more around her and kissing her shoulder where her sweater had slipped off. They didn't need to say anything about that last Christmas, the memories flowing between them more than enough to explain what had made it so special for both of them. Filled with peace, she snuggled more fully into him, closing her eyes in gratitude.

Tomorrow, they might go back to being hands-off co-workers and very-*ex*-lovers, so she would enjoy this tonight, mistake or not.

"Were you still in love with me?" he repeated his question from earlier, his voice a whisper in her hair.

Her eyes popped open. "Yes."

"Then why did you leave me?"

She swallowed the lump in her throat. "What I want for Christmas is for us to enjoy tonight and not talk about the past."

His long silence said he might not let it go. But then he released a sigh. "Okay. For now. But I'm not going to let it go until you tell me."

They both went quiet then, and she imagined he, like her, was thinking about the past. And while she trusted him, now wasn't the time to tell him her secret. This moment was her gift, dammit, and she didn't want anything to spoil it.

"I've decided that Derrick won't go back to kindergarten after Christmas," she whispered. "I'll homeschool him, which will give him more time with you. At least until August when first grade starts."

"Good. Thank you. I can help you with that if you want. I know you suck at math."

"Asshat," she said with a chuckle. "I can do kindergarten math."

He chuckled. "What about you staying here?"

"I'm not sure yet. But I am considering *all* my options."

"Fair enough."

For a time, they whispered in the dark of inconsequential things, memories, plans, then grew quiet as if both were content to sink into each other and the happiness they'd found in each other's arms this blessed night.

The temptation was strong to turn to him, lift her face to his, find his lips with hers, taste the sweet cookie on his tongue, swirl with him down into a whirlpool of bliss. Before she could take action, make her fantasy real, she felt herself drifting into a dream where she, Josh, and Derrick were a real family.

****

Charleigh was opening up about her life with Will, but the information Josh wanted most—the real reason she had gone with him—was still hidden. He would find out what she was hiding. But right now, every cell of his body was filled with memories of their last Christmas together, of being with her like this, and was celebrating.

He pulled her closer, wanting to feel all of her against all of him. He wished he hadn't promised not to try anything. It would be a natural next move to slide his hand under her sweater and cup her breasts, then pull the sweater and bra off and take those breasts, first with his hands, then with his mouth. Then kiss down her stomach. And lower. And keep going until she was crying out his name in pleasure like she used to under the flick of his tongue, the caress of his lips. The only thing better than hearing her come was making her come. The crotch of his jeans tightened at the thought.

But he'd promised her, and a man always kept his word, both to others and to himself. And he'd promised himself that if he ever got the chance to make love to her, he wouldn't do it in this house.

Feeling her low, steady breaths against his chest, seeing the small smile on her mouth, feeling her curves cup his angles, breathing in her scent, he was filled with an all-consuming peace for the first time since the last time she'd been in his arms this way.

In a while, he'd get up and drive home. It wouldn't be good for anyone to catch them like this. But for now, he was going to enjoy this long-wanted and hard-earned gift and pretend he belonged here with her, where he'd always wanted to be, and pretend that here with him was where she wanted to be.

A smile on his face, his heart thumping with joy in his chest, he closed his eyes and sank into the feel of her, the only woman he'd ever loved. The woman he still loved.

His last act before falling into a dream where Charleigh was his wife and Derrick was his son was to pull the crocheted afghan from the back of the couch and cover them with it so the chill wouldn't rouse them from their dream come true.

Chapter Sixteen

Josh blamed the swelling in his jeans on the soft, warm body wrapped around his and the hand full of mighty fine ass he instantly recognized as Charleigh's.

His eyes opened to slits against the dim morning light. Sometime in the night, she had turned to face him and their bodies had drawn closer, seeking out and finding each other easily while their consciences had slept. Her arm was low around his hips, her leg around his thigh, her crotch perfectly aligned with his. Memories of the way they matched, the way they fit, the way they loved made him smile.

He should wake her. Unwrap from her. But, God, he didn't want to. She was what he'd wanted for Christmas—this one and every other one since she'd left—and he wasn't giving it up. Not yet, anyway. He pressed a soft kiss to her forehead. It was then he saw a familiar pair of blue eyes staring at him from the edge of the couch.

Derrick stood there looking down at him, eyes wide, a grin the size of his whole head, his .22 in his hand.

Josh's sleep-fogged brain quickly sized up the situation. He and Charleigh were on the couch, knotted up with each other like a Christmas gift bow, had slept there all night, and it was now morning. Christmas morning. Having read Derrick's letter to Santa, he knew exactly how the boy was interpreting this scene.

"You and Mom slept together?" Derrick whispered.

As if the mother part of her brain was programmed to awaken upon hearing her child's voice, Charleigh stirred. Her honey eyes finding Josh's, she smiled and murmured "good morning" in that sexy, sleepy voice that took him back to those other mornings they'd woken up wrapped around each other. That look, that smile, that voice had usually been followed by an energizing session of wake-up sex.

"Good morning," Josh whispered back.

Her lips were on their way to greet his when Derrick said, "Merry Christmas, Mom."

His cheery little voice stripped the smile from her face and shot her eyes open wide. She bolted upright, pulling out of their embrace, and jumped up from the couch. Her movements jerked the afghan off him, but he grabbed a corner and dragged it back across his hips to hide the bulge in his jeans.

She tugged on her sweater that had somehow risen up in the night. "Did Santa come last night?" she asked, a hitch in her voice as she tried to staunch the questions she saw in her son's eyes before they exited his mouth.

Derrick's gaze cut from hers to Josh. "He sure did."

"Well, show me what he brought you." As she went to the tree, she ran her hands through her wild storm of curls, smoothing it back from her face and twisting it in a nervous gesture.

Derrick took Josh's hand. "C'mon, Josh, come see what else Santa brought me."

"I'll be right there."

Derrick left him and joined Charleigh at the tree. Josh willed his erection down before he stood and joined them. It was cold in the house, so he took the afghan with him and draped it across Charleigh's shoulders. Her eyes met his in thanks but quickly darted away, her red cheeks showing she was embarrassed by Derrick catching them together on the couch in such an intimate position.

"I can't believe Santa got me everything I asked for," Derrick said and hugged Josh, then Charleigh. "This is my best Christmas ever."

Josh's eyes met hers over Derrick's head, and they shared a smile. Somehow, this Christmas had landed on the *best list* for all three of them. Pretty damn magical.

****

"After breakfast, how about we try out my remote control pickup?" Derrick asked Josh as they polished off Ruby's stacks of buttermilk pancakes.

"After breakfast, you need to get on your chores," Josh said, setting his fork in his plate.

"But it's Christmas." Derrick's tone sounded a little disappointed that the fun was over.

"Chores don't stop for holidays," Josh said. "Your animals still need to eat."

"Okay. I'll go get dressed." Derrick set his fork down and headed to his room.

Josh touched Charleigh's arm when she picked up his and Derrick's plates. "I hope you're coming with us."

She smiled. "I'll put these in the dishwasher then get dressed."

The three of them did the Simms ranch chores, then went to the Flying F to do those chores. Quino had

315

already done most of them, but Josh took over for him. Afterward, he showered and changed, and they went back to Charleigh's. He and Derrick spent hours running the remote control pickup all over the front drive before Ruby and Charleigh called them in for Christmas dinner.

"So when are you and Josh getting married?" Derrick asked and shoveled a bite of enchiladas into his mouth.

Charleigh choked on her mouthful of iced tea at Derrick's words. Josh's fork clanged to the plate. Ruby's fork full of tamale hovered in mid-air on the way to her mouth.

"What are you talking about?" Charleigh said, wiping her mouth.

"Well, I asked Santa for you guys to get married, and this morning you were sleeping together, so that means you're getting married. I want to know when."

"We're not...not getting married," Charleigh insisted. Josh was amused by the panic in her voice and the bright red flush on her face.

"But you slept together," Derrick said.

"We were waiting for Santa, then accidentally fell asleep on the couch," Josh said, trying to defuse the situation before it got hotter.

"Did you guys have sex?"

"Derrick," Charleigh exclaimed, "that's enough. We don't talk about sex during supper, er, dinner. Or any meal."

Derrick eyed Josh, expecting an answer.

Josh shook his head. "We didn't."

"Well, why not?"

Barely containing a chuckle, Ruby got up from her

chair and strolled over to the stovetop and took her time cooking a few more tortillas on the griddle, her back shaking with mirth.

Charleigh sat rod-straight in her chair, face bright red, eyes downcast to her full plate, and forked a bite of beans into her mouth.

Josh steered Derrick into another topic of conversation, and the rest of the meal was filled with his chatter about this great Christmas and the horses and the shooting lessons that would begin after the holiday and the fact that he would be spending his days with Josh and Charleigh, learning about ranching instead of going back to kindergarten. He seemed genuinely happy about it, and knowing that Derrick wanted to spend time with him filled him with satisfaction.

Josh didn't run off after the meal but settled in the living room with Charleigh and Derrick to put together the puzzle Ruby had given him.

The phone rang, and Ruby hollered out "I got it" from the kitchen.

From the living room, they could hear her conversation. "Merry Christmas to you, Lance. Yes, she's here."

"I better get that," Charleigh went into the kitchen before Ruby could come into the living room with the phone.

Listening intently to the one-sided conversation, Josh discerned that Lance was inviting her to the New Year's celebration in Wilton.

"Does he call here a lot?" he whispered to Derrick.

Derrick nodded and scrunched up his face. "Sorta. When he calls and I answer it, he calls me *little*

317

cowpoke. I don't like that."

Sorta. What the hell did sorta mean? Once was once too often. "Little cowpoke?" Josh repeated and scrunched his face, too. Derrick laughed and added another puzzle piece. Then he jumped up. "I gotta pee." He ran to the bathroom.

Josh heard Charleigh turn down Lance's offer. He didn't hear her excuse, but he heard her goodbye. It shocked him how relieved he was.

"You not interested in spending the new year with Dr. Barton at what's being hailed as the party of the year?" he asked her when she rejoined him.

She met his gaze, the light in her eyes saying that his jealousy was showing and that it amused her. "Listening to my conversation?"

Her teasing tone annoyed him even more.

"It was hard not to, what with how loud you were talking and giggling." His attempt to keep his tone light and teasing failed, and it came out on the sharp side. But the thought that she might be interested in Lance bore a hole in his chest.

"I wasn't loud, and I wasn't giggling."

"So, is it the party or going with Lance that you're not interested in?" He was being pushy, but he had to know the truth.

"You sure are nosy today."

Ah, dammit, CC, just frickin' tell me! "I'm thinking it's Lance you're not interested in. Because, I mean, c'mon... Lance?"

"There's nothing wrong with Lance. He's nice, smart, interesting, good-looking—"

Her comment drew a quick scoff from his mouth. "He's what you consider good-looking?"

"Any woman with functioning eyes in her head would call *Doctor* Barton good-looking. And a good catch."

Well, son-of-bitch. "If he's so damn perfect, then why did you turn him down?"

"A couple of reasons," she said with a sly smile that said she knew exactly what her comments were doing to him.

"Like?"

"I'd rather celebrate at home with Derrick so I can kiss him at midnight. It's said that the first person you kiss at the new year is the person—"

"—you'll be with the whole year," he added, remembering that it hadn't worked for them.

"Something like that."

"And the second?"

Derrick plopped down between them, breaking their gaze and halting further discussion.

"Josh, I been thinking…if you want to take Mom to the party, I could stay home with Ruby. She said she doesn't like loud parties with people acting like idiots."

"Derrick," Charleigh said, "I've talked to you before about asking some guy to take me out."

"Josh isn't just some guy, Mom. You've seen each other naked, after all."

She blinked. "How would you know?"

"That picture."

Her eyes went round. "What picture?"

"Um…" As if realizing he'd just spilled the beans on himself, Derrick let his startled gaze dart to Josh, then back to her. "The one in Josh's house."

Thanks a lot, kid.

Her gaze speared him.

"Our pond photo," he explained.

Her eyebrows lifted. "You showed it to him?"

His eyebrows furrowed. "Course not."

"Then how did he see it?"

"He didn't show it to me," Derrick interjected. "It was just in his bedroom on the nightstand."

"Why were you in his bedroom?"

"I had to pee."

"When we went to get the ornaments, he had to go to the bathroom," Josh explained. "I'm renovating the others, so he had to use the one in my room."

He'd been looking at the picture every night since he'd learned Charleigh was coming back and had left it out on his nightstand. And now she knew he'd kept it...and had been looking at it. The truth of that fact showed in her shining eyes, in the large swallow that bobbed her throat.

"You kept it?" she whispered.

He nodded.

Her cheeks pinkened, and she licked her lips, which were quirking, as if trying hard not to give in to a full-blown smile. "I kept mine, too."

"Do you want to sleep over again?" Derrick asked him, thankfully changing the subject.

Josh wanted to say yes, but he didn't want to make Charleigh uncomfortable. He wasn't stupid enough to think that their one night on the couch meant they were headed toward some fairy tale ending.

"Thanks, bud, but I gotta get home, do my evening chores. In fact—" He stood. "—I should probably get going while I still have the light."

Derrick and Charleigh stood, too. "Me and Mom can go with you and help you again. You can get done faster, then you can come back over."

"Wouldn't you rather stay here and play with your toys?"

"No, I'd rather help you."

It was clear Derrick didn't want him to go. Josh looked at Charleigh, ready to ask her if she wanted to come with him.

"Derrick, Josh has things to do at home. He can't spend all his time here with us."

That wasn't at all what that look had meant or what he wanted. But obviously it's what she wanted—him to go home.

Derrick wrapped his arms around him and hugged him. "I want you to stay."

"I'll be over tomorrow," he said, trying to console him.

"Can you spend New Year's with us?" he said, then turned to Charleigh. "Can Josh spend New Year's with us?"

"He might have other plans," she said.

Derrick looked up at him. "Do you have other plans?"

He shook his head.

"So will you?"

"If it's okay with your mom." He looked at Charleigh. So did Derrick.

"Of course. We'd be glad for you to join us."

With a smile, Derrick let him go and jumped up and down a few times. Then he ran into the kitchen. "Ruby, Josh is spending New Years with us."

"Well, that's great news," Ruby said, patting his back then smiling at Josh and Charleigh as they walked into the kitchen right behind him. "You're not leaving already?" she asked Josh.

"Yes, ma'am. As you know, chores don't stop for holidays." He leaned in to hug her goodbye. "Thanks for the delicious supper."

"My pleasure," she said, adding for his ears only, "That boy sure don't like you none."

He grinned and wondered at the happiness filling his heart at her statement. "No ma'am. He don't."

In the mudroom, Derrick and Charleigh beside him, he pulled on his boots, coat, and hat, and they walked him out. They stood on the porch as he got into his pickup. They watched him drive away, Derrick waving, Charleigh behind him, arms around her son.

Seemed like the boy had grown a couple of inches since they'd arrived and seemed happier and more energetic. Josh liked to think he had something to do with it. He watched them in the rearview mirror until he could no longer see them.

Minutes after he got home, he was still sitting in the pickup, regret gnawing his gut. Truth was, he wished he was still there with them. Or, better yet, that they were here with him.

****

On New Year's Eve, Derrick conked out on the couch at eleven-thirty, his head in Charleigh's lap, his feet in Josh's. Josh's arm was around her shoulders, had been most of the night, his fingers playing in her hair, wrapping her curls around his finger, lighting matches to her libido with every caress.

Ruby had turned in minutes earlier, saying she couldn't keep her eyes open for another second. That left Charleigh and Josh to ring in the new year alone. The air in the room became heavy and hot and charged with anticipation, making her breath short and choppy. Something would happen between them tonight. She felt it.

The clock struck midnight. At the second ding, their eyes locked, and they whispered "Happy New Year" in unison. At the third, they leaned in, no hesitation from either of them, and kissed. Kissed like they'd both wanted it forever and had been waiting for the right time. That time was here, now, and eagerly she shifted and turned into him, putting her hand on his head, her fingers in his hair and pulling him closer.

"Is it Happy New Year yet?" Derrick mumbled, half asleep.

They broke apart. "Yep," Josh whispered, his eyes hooked to Charleigh's.

"Would you carry him to bed?" she asked, desire making her voice breathless.

Josh stood, picked up Derrick, and carried him to bed. She covered her son, kissed his forehead, and they left the room.

Getting no farther than the dark kitchen, Josh hooked her waist and drew her into him, kissing her again. Fully. She moaned and lifted her thigh, wrapping it around his leg and pulling him close. He pressed hard into her, and she arched into him, showing her eagerness for what they were doing. She had been ready to pull him into her bedroom when the phone rang loud in the quiet house.

He broke the kiss. "Better get that before it wakes everybody."

She rushed into the living room where they'd all been sitting and grabbed the phone.

"Happy New Year, Charleigh," Lance said, his

words bubbly and slightly slurred.

"Happy New Year, Lance." Her voice was less than enthusiastic at the interruption.

"Wish you were here. You're missing a great party."

She could hear cheers and music in the background. "Sounds like it."

"What did you and the little cowpoke do tonight?"

"Spent time as a family." She heard the door open, then close. Was Josh leaving? "Listen, Lance, I need to—"

"Let's get together for dinner next week to celebrate the new year together. Just the two of us. Who says it has to be the first day of the year?"

"Uh, well..." She rushed into the mudroom. Josh was gone. "Thanks for calling, but I need to go."

He chuckled. "You trying to get rid of me?"

"I don't want to keep you from your party."

"All right. Well, night darlin'. I'll call you tomorrow to set up a date."

"Okay, bye." She hung up and opened the door, ran outside. Josh's pickup was headed down the road.

She called his cell. It rang three times before he answered.

"Why did you leave?" she said, damning the neediness in her shaky voice.

"If I'd stayed, we would have done more than kiss on the couch."

He was right, but she didn't confirm it aloud. "And you didn't want to?"

His brake lights came on, and she heard the squeak that told her he'd applied the brakes.

"Tell me that's what you want, and I'll turn around

right now."

She wanted it. But she wasn't ready to admit it, especially since he didn't seem to want it enough to have stayed and tried to make it happen. And because it was probably a bad move. Before she could come up with a response, he closed the door on the opportunity.

"Happy New Year, CC," he said.

"It's what I want," she said into the phone, but he'd already hung up.

Into the crisp, clear air of the first day of the new year, she spoke the words of her heart. "I want you, Josh Flores. Only you."

It wasn't until later, when she was in bed, imagining how good it would have been to have him with her, that she realized he'd been the first man she'd kissed at the dawn of the new year. What would that portend for them? Happiness? Or more heartbreak?

****

"We're starting your shooting lessons today," Josh told Derrick a week into the new year as he drove with him and Charleigh out to the pasture where he'd held her shooting lessons.

Since the day after Christmas, he had been going over gun safety with Derrick, getting the boy used to his .22, instructing him on how to carry it, load it, unload it, check to see whether it was loaded, and so on. Today, he'd instruct him on how to shoot.

The trick to avoiding a dangerous situation was to slow down and make firing the gun a clear, orderly, repeatable ritual. It was the way he'd approached it with Charleigh, and it was the way he'd approach it with Derrick.

After forty-five minutes or so of instruction and

shooting, Charleigh ran her hand across Josh's back, then down his arm in a light caress. "I'll go lay out our snacks," she said, her way of saying Derrick had had enough for today.

He gripped her hand when it reached his and squeezed. "We'll be right there," he said through a smile and watched her walk to the pickup, watched her glance over her shoulder at him and shoot him one of her sexy smiles.

She'd been generous with these affectionate little gestures and kisses since New Year's. And he'd reciprocated. Although they were both careful about not crossing the line.

"Let's go see how I did," Derrick said, pulling Josh's attention away from the sway of Charleigh's perfect little behind.

"Where's your muzzle pointed?" Josh asked him.

"Down range," he said after checking and adjusting.

"All right. Let's go."

A couple of near-bullseyes marred the target, along with a few holes on the outer rings. As expected, several rounds missed the target, but Derrick was thrilled with his effort, and Josh was proud of him.

"I did good, huh?" He beamed up at Josh.

"You did well for your first time. You take after your mom." Kneeling, Josh pulled a pen from his shirt pocket and wrote on the paper target Derrick's name, the date, the distance, and the gun used. He removed the target from the bale, rolled it into a loose tube, and handed it to Derrick. "This'll help you chart your progress."

"I'm going to hang it in my room."

"Sounds good. Ready to eat?"

"Naw, I'm not hungry."

"What?"

Derrick laughed. "Just kidding."

"For a minute, I thought we were going to have to take you in for a stomach scan."

Laughing, they headed over to where Charleigh had spread a blanket and was setting out food.

"Do you have a dollar in your pocket?" Derrick asked on the way.

"Yeah, why?"

"I bet you a dollar that when we get to Mom, she's going to put sanitizer on our hands."

Josh chuckled, knowing he was right. "She's a stickler for clean hands all right. Has she always been like that?"

"Not 'til my dad got sick. Then we had to wash our hands all the time."

"When people are sick, like your dad was, their bodies aren't as strong and have a hard time fighting germs."

"That's what she said. But you and me aren't sick."

"She just wants to make sure to keep it that way." To change the suddenly awkward mood, he said, "You got a dollar to back up that bet?"

Derrick stopped and pulled from his pocket the crumpled single Josh had given him a few weeks ago, telling him that a man needed to always have a bit of cash in his pocket, just in case. He held it up to show it to him. "Do you?"

Josh pulled a dollar from his wallet and held it up. "You're on," he said, and they sealed their bet with a fist bump.

"How'd you do?" Charleigh asked when they got to her.

"I hit it a bunch of times," Derrick said proudly as he plopped down next to her.

Josh settled next to him as Charleigh pulled from her jacket pocket a small bottle of hand sanitizer.

"Hold out your hands," she said to Derrick.

Derrick shot Josh an I-told-you-so grin.

Josh chuckled.

"What's so funny?" she said, her gaze darting between them.

Josh shrugged. "Nothing." He handed the dollar to Derrick.

"Nothing," Derrick said and with a laugh, pocketed his win.

"Why do I always get the feeling you two are keeping secrets from me?"

"Just suspicious, I guess," Josh said.

"Yeah, just suspicious," Derrick echoed.

Grinning, and with a shake of her head, she squirted sanitizer into Derrick's hands and then into Josh's.

"Can we go shooting again tomorrow?" Derrick asked as they ate.

"You bet," Josh said.

"If you finish all your homework tonight," Charleigh added.

"I will."

Chapter Seventeen

Josh pulled off his hat and wiped the sweat from his brow, then put it back on. Two more blades to replace on the old windmill then he could head home for a shower and a cold beer.

Luck had been with him today. The blade hub and mechanical components would hold a bit longer. He'd go ahead and pick up the parts in town, and he'd bring Derrick over to help him fix it this coming week. The boy needed to learn about these types of mundane, never-ending chores that took up much of a rancher's day.

His gaze traveled the direction of his thoughts, to the Simms ranch, where Charleigh and Derrick were. Picturing them as he left them today after their standing Saturday ride and shooting lesson, he wondered what they were doing. Derrick was probably playing with Brutus or helping Cole with something in the barn, and Charleigh was probably helping Ruby with her latest fundraising activity for the school. She was becoming more involved in the community, not directly, but helping Ruby with the cooking, baking, crafts, and organization it required. Could that mean she was staying?

The quiet surrounding him pressed in on him, only the occasional whip of a bird breaking through his thoughts of Charleigh. And Derrick. Even when he was alone, like now, he could feel them around him, hear their voices.

His mind drifted back to the kiss Charleigh had given him in the barn today before he'd left. It still warmed his mouth and made his heart pound just thinking about it. And the way she'd pressed her body against him told him she wanted him as much as he wanted her.

In the two months since Christmas, they'd adjusted their do-not-cross line several times. They hadn't made love, but the desire was there. He had a feeling it was only a matter of time before they obliterated the line altogether. He was more than ready, the bulge in his jeans an almost permanent and painful fixture. But he wouldn't push her. He'd let her come to him when she was ready. Hopefully, the at-the-ready condom in his pocket would last that long.

The two of them were inching their way down a rocky path rife with land mines, but neither seemed eager to get off the path. The light shining in her eyes today when she pulled back from the kiss told him they'd go to the delicious end, risks be damned. And the risks were many. But that wouldn't stop him.

He needed her. As much as he always had.

And he was crazy about that kid of hers.

Because of them, he'd never felt so wanted and needed.

He hadn't planned to see them again today, but that didn't mean he couldn't. As soon as he got this windmill back in working order, he'd go back over, see if they wanted to go to dinner in town or maybe see a movie. Decision made, he set his attention back on the work at hand.

The last blade affixed, he gathered his tools, climbed down, and tested his handiwork. The blades spun smoothly in the gentle breeze. He loaded the tools into his pickup, then headed home to shower.

Brutus and a blaring rocking country song greeted him as he pulled into the Simms yard. Once in the house, he pulled off his boots and hat and headed into the living room to turn down the music. The sight welcoming him froze him in the doorway. Her back to the door, wearing only a towel, Charleigh stood at the desk, singing and dancing to the music as she bent over the books.

Knowing that a thin towel was the only thing keeping her body from his was doing crazy things to his own. Walking was hard, but he took the few steps to the radio and turned it off.

She spun toward the radio, the motion loosening her towel. He got a good look at her breasts before she caught and secured it. They were as full and firm as he remembered. It made his already swollen erection throb, made his lungs burn with the attempt to breathe.

"What are you doing here?" she said.

His eyes left her breasts and settled on her flushed face. "I wanted to ask you and Derrick to go to dinner with me."

"Derrick's not here."

"Where is he?"

"In town with Ruby."

They had the house to themselves, and every cell in his body pulsed with the implications. He couldn't speak but his eyes worked just fine. They took her in. Slowly. Thoroughly. Eagerly. Everything in him wanted to yank the towel from her body and drop it on the floor. But if he did, her body would be his. He licked his lips at the tasty thought.

As if she had heard his thought, she tucked the towel tighter around her. "I...better go get dressed." She started past him, but he held out his arm, catching her lightly at the waist.

He turned her toward him and ran his hands slowly up her arms, her rising goosebumps and trembling sigh telling him she liked it. He slid his arm around her and let his hand settle firmly on one rounded cheek of her sweet little ass, tucking her against him, letting her feel his hardness. His other hand rose to cup her face, his thumb brushing across her plump bottom lip.

"Charleigh..." The simple whispered plea unleashed a stampede of wants.

It happened so quickly he wasn't sure which of them had moved first. Her arms were around his neck, their bodies plastered together, head to toe, and they were kissing like they were trying to make up for all the years they hadn't been able to be this close. He marched her backward until she could move no more, her back firmly kissing the wall.

Keeping one arm around her waist to anchor her body to his, his other hand yanked off her towel, tossing it somewhere behind him. She didn't stop him, so he took the next step and cupped a hand around her breast. Her sweet moan in his mouth was the best thing he'd tasted in a long time. But he knew something even sweeter was available, and suddenly he was ravenous.

He kissed down her neck and chest to those breasts. Mouthing the hard rosy tips, he flicked his tongue over them, sucked them, nipped them to the applause of her soft groans urging him on. At the same time, he reached his hand between her legs and cupped and massaged her mound. She moaned his name and lifted her knee, wrapping her leg around his hip, opening herself to his touch.

Wasting no time, he slid two fingers in a V-shape back and forth on either side of the tight little stem of nerves in a slight pinching motion, again and again, then straight back, plunging into her sweet, swelled flesh. She was wet and hot. Because of him. For him.

Her low, rough groan triggered one from his throat, and he dragged his mouth back to hers and claimed it again, his tongue stroking her mouth as his fingers stroked her tunnel.

She reached between them and fumbled with his belt buckle, her frantic movements telling him she wanted him, too. He thought about shoving her hands aside and doing it himself, but he didn't want to take his hands from her, didn't want to drop the level of desire he was building inside her and risk having her come to her senses. He knew he had nothing to worry about when, in seconds, she had his jeans and briefs down enough for her hand to wrap around him.

There was no time for him to get as naked as she was. There was no time to give her the sweet, gentle caresses and tender, loving words she deserved. Their bodies were throbbing, pulsing, aching from years of needing to be connected. He knew her signs, knew that raw, hot sex was all she needed right now. Her kisses, her touches, her movements, her sounds, the moisture between her thighs said so.

The feel of her hand stroking him was enough to make him come apart right then, but he'd be damned if he'd miss this chance to be inside her. He lifted her and wrapped her legs around his hips. Without a word, a sigh, a breath, he slid into her wet heat, going in easily, going in hard, going home. At last.

A euphoric gasp rose in tandem from them at the connection.

****

A raging ache had surged inside Charleigh at Josh's first touch, but the feel of him so tight and full inside her had her gasping in pleasure. She had wanted this, needed this, for so long. Not just sex. Josh. She needed Josh.

Refusing to question this decision, she clutched her thighs and arms around him. With a low growl he cupped her ass and rocked hard against her, filling her fully.

Their mouths fused as tight as their bodies as he drove into her again and again, and she tipped her hips up to take him all. Harder, faster, pure need drove them upward to the plot of heaven reserved for only them. His body, his thrusts, his kisses demanded all she had to give, and she gave it eagerly, hungrily taking all he was giving.

A burst of sensation ripped through her, her muscles jerking and spasming around him, against him. She groaned a loud, rough breath that carried his name. He dropped his head back in a long, loud groan that joined hers.

Their breath labored, their bodies still cemented together, their hazy eyes met. Whispering her name, he pressed soft kisses to her face, her neck. Suddenly, he stopped.

"Ah, fuck," he breathed into her neck. His gaze rose to hers. "CC, I'm sorry." He shook his head. "I—"

The screen door to the mudroom squeaked opened and voices cut off the rest of his sentence. It was Ruby and Derrick, home from buying groceries, and Cole was with them, likely to help them carry in the groceries. They were still in the mudroom, removing boots and hats, but in short time, they'd be in the kitchen, steps from the living room where Josh had her speared to the wall. Derrick would have seen his pickup parked out front, know he was here, and head straight to the living room to see him.

She and Josh rushed apart, and it felt like a part of her body being ripped away. Shit! She couldn't go out there in a towel. She couldn't even find the towel! As if the thought had occurred to him first, Josh had already yanked off his Western shirt and was holding it out to her. She slid her arms in and snapped it while he fastened his jeans and his belt, leaving the T-shirt he'd worn under his shirt untucked.

At the moment she felt the evidence of their lovemaking trickle down her inner thighs, he also handed her his handkerchief. She tucked it up between her legs hoping it would hold until she could get to her room and clean up. At least his shirt was long enough to cover the important parts.

"Mom. Josh," Derrick hollered. "We're home." He was in the kitchen. She heard the rustling from Ruby unloading groceries from the bags.

Three sets of eyes pinned her and Josh in place when they slinked into the kitchen, her skin burning. Having Josh beside her should have made her feel better. But it didn't. All she could think about was that he'd said he was sorry he had sex with her.

She was sure they all knew what they'd done.

Well, Ruby and Cole, anyway. Although the way Derrick was looking them up and down, even he knew something was up.

"How come you're wearing Josh's shirt?" he asked then turned his suspicion on Josh. "How come your hair is all messed up? And your shirt's not tucked in. Have you guys been wrestling?"

The red on Ruby's cheeks said the housekeeper knew what they'd done, and when Derrick would have stepped closer, she held him back. "Let's wash the store germs off your hands," she said and led him to the kitchen sink to his protests that he didn't have any because he'd sanitized his hands in the car.

Cole stood statue still in front of them, arms crossed over his chest, glaring at Josh like he wanted to take him out back and kick his ass.

In a subtle move, Josh reached out his hand and threaded his fingers between hers, but she pulled away and rushed to her room.

He'd apologized for having sex with her. He regretted it. And now, she did, too.

He didn't want you then, and he doesn't want you now. Do you finally get it?

****

He'd just had sex with Charleigh. The only woman he'd ever loved. The one who'd broken his heart into pieces then betrayed him. If either of them should be feeling regret, it was him. But he wasn't. Unfortunately, it was clear she was.

He'd tried to tell her he was with her by reaching out and linking his fingers with hers. But she jerked her hand away so fast the band of her wedding ring scratched him, telling him that not only did she regret what they'd done, she blamed him for it.

And she was probably right. He had no business doing what he'd done. He was her ranch manager, not her lover.

But with everyone in the room, he could hardly ask her what was going on in her head and try to fix it.

Damn it. He should have kept his fucking jeans zipped.

Derrick rejoined him. "Where's Mom?"

"In her room."

He started to head that way, but Josh caught him— with the hand that hadn't been inside Charleigh. "Hey, bud. Your mom needs a few minutes."

"To do what?"

"How about you and I get one of those cinnamon rolls Ruby made this morning and eat it outside on the porch."

"You know I'm not supposed to eat sweets 'til after supper."

"It'll be all right this one time. We'll half it." He turned Derrick around and led him to the pan of cinnamon rolls on the counter. "You pick one out while I wash my hands."

Josh had to walk past Cole on the way to the kitchen sink. The foreman glared at him like a man ready to kick the ass of the man who was messing with his sister. Josh brushed past him, and Cole was smart enough not to stop him. Ruby's face was as red as the gem she was named for, and she wouldn't meet his eyes. He had never felt more uncomfortable and unwelcome in the Simms household.

As he washed Charleigh from his hands, he resisted the urge to explain to them that Charleigh was his, had always been his, that he loved her, so it was okay that they'd made love. They didn't need to know shit about them. Consenting adults have sex. So they could all mind their own fucking business and keep their judging looks to themselves.

He dried his hands and went back to Derrick. "You choose one?"

"Yep." Derrick pointed to the one in the center of the pan, the one he would have chosen.

He grabbed a fork and lifted the roll, tore it in two and let Derrick choose his half. They walked outside and sat on the steps, Cole following them, his glare pricking over them the whole way like he thought he was going to steal Derrick.

"What did you and Ruby buy in town?" Josh asked and only half heard Derrick's animated response. His mind was on Charleigh. On what they'd done. It was as good as before. Better. He'd wanted it forever. He thought she had, too, until it was over. The look of disgust she gave him struck deep, shredding the fantasy that they still had a shot with each other.

It was completely inexcusable that he'd broken his own rule about making love to her in that house. Worse that he'd forgotten to use protection. The condom had been burning a hole in his pocket for months. But when the time came to use it, his mind had purged every thought but one—getting inside Charleigh. He prayed his carelessness wouldn't destroy all the trust they'd built between them.

****

Charleigh wiped Josh from between her legs with his handkerchief then washed his scent from her skin, tossed his shirt and handkerchief into the hamper, then pulled on jeans and a T-shirt. Flipping her head over, she gathered her hair into a high messy bun and secured it. On her way out to face the music, she caught a glance of herself in the mirror on the door.

How was it that her face, her body, showed no discernible evidence that reflected the emotions riling on the inside? Her gaze shot to the gold band on her left hand.

When she married Will, she hadn't loved him, but she'd promised to be faithful to him, and she had been, in action if not in thought. Sure, marriage was until death do us part, but knowing that didn't stop the guilt she felt from making love to another man, in her deceased husband's house, with her wedding ring still in place.

Feeling chilled to her core, she realized she could no longer wear the ring. She slid it off her finger and put it in the clay jewelry box Derrick had made her for Christmas. The ring hadn't been heavy on her finger, but its absence made her whole body feel adrift. Anchorless.

Turning away from the guilt in her eyes, she headed into the kitchen, hoping Josh was gone, hoping Ruby and Cole wouldn't look at her with judging eyes or, worse, try to talk to her about what had happened.

The kitchen was empty, but she heard laughter outside. Derrick's laughter, followed by a huskier laugh. Josh's laugh. Her son was laughing, having fun, with his father. Again.

Jealousy, wrapped in anger, plowed through her. This could not happen. She mustn't let this happen. Josh would hurt Derrick, just like he'd hurt her. Pretend to care until he got what he wanted.

She stormed to the door and opened it. Derrick sat on the steps with Josh. She kept the screen door closed, providing a barrier between them.

"Derrick, come on in," she said. "You need to get started on your..." Her sentence halted when she saw the cinnamon roll in his hand. She pushed open the door. "What are you eating?"

"Um..." His gaze left hers and went to the sticky roll, then back to her.

"What's the rule?"

"No sweets until after supper."

"Why?"

"Because if we fill up on sweets, we won't eat the food that's good for us."

"And what's that in your hand?"

"A sweet."

"Do you have an explanation for why you broke the rule?"

His gaze dropped to the roll, which he was pinching with his little fingers. He shook his head. "No, ma'am."

"It was my fault," Josh said. "I asked him to share one with me."

She wanted to lay into Josh, remind him who Derrick belonged to, but she held back. She didn't want to fight in front of Derrick. Besides, she couldn't even look at Josh right now.

"He knows the rule and chose to ignore it. Derrick..." She held the door open wider, signaling for him to come into the house.

In an unusual and heartbreaking bout of defiance, her son scooted closer to his father and wrapped his little arms around his muscular arm.

"I don't wanna go in. I wanna stay with Josh and talk about—"

"I'm not arguing with you. Inside. Now." Shock at his surprising disobedience sharpened her tone.

"No."

"Derrick," Josh said, his response low but quick and firm. "When your mother tells you to do something, it's disrespectful to tell her no."

"I'm sorry."

"Don't tell me. Tell her." He nodded her way but kept his eyes on Derrick.

"Sorry, Mom."

She nodded, but the entire episode was a stake to her heart.

Derrick—her son, her world—had been downright disrespectful to her for the first time in his young life and had apologized not because he was sorry but because Josh told him to. Josh. The man who hadn't wanted them was daring to butt in and discipline his son, like she somehow wasn't capable of doing it herself.

But she was too numb to tell him to fuck off.

And then there was that part of her that begrudgingly appreciated his stepping up. With Will, she'd been on her own in the discipline department, and the burden had sometimes been exhausting.

"Now, what did she ask you to do?" Josh continued.

"To come inside."

"What's the appropriate, respectful response?"

"Yes, ma'am."

Josh nodded and raised his eyes briefly to Charleigh as if saying, tell her.

Her son's gaze rolled up to hers. "Yes, ma'am."

After taking his sweet time rising to his feet, he threw his arms around Josh's neck. "I don't want you to go."

"I'll see you Monday," Josh said, hugging him back.

Tomorrow was Sunday. Josh's day off from them. Thank God. She needed a break from him after this stupid colossal mistake.

The way Derrick was holding on to Josh, she was wondering whether he'd let him go.

"We'll have another shooting lesson," Josh added.

Derrick let him go and grinned up into his face. "Did you buy more bullets?"

It killed her that Josh was the one who had put a smile on her son's face after she'd destroyed it.

"Yep."

"All right!" He held out his sticky hand for a fist pump. Josh accommodated him. It was their thing now. He got hugs and fist bumps. She got defiance and attitude.

Derrick was still smiling when he got to the door. She put her hand on his head, stopping him, and his smile vanished as he looked up into her eyes. She held out her hand for the cinnamon roll.

"Wash up, then go to your room," she said after he gave it to her, keeping her voice low. "I'll be in to talk to you in a minute."

He nodded solemnly, and with an equally solemn "yes, ma'am," went inside.

Charleigh shut both doors and looked toward Josh, but not directly at him, hoping she could keep her voice as low and steady with him. Before she could speak, he did.

"It was half a cinnamon roll," he said and slowly rose to his feet. "And I had the bigger half. Give the kid a break."

She was overreacting. She knew it. It wasn't even about the cinnamon roll or the broken rule. It was about her and her stupidity in trusting Josh again.

"If it was one of your rules he broke, I doubt you'd be as forgiving."

"My rules protect his life."

Even in her anger she didn't miss the little dab of frosting on his lower lip taunting her. She wanted to step in and lick it from his mouth, then feed it to him from the tip of her tongue. That visual didn't make it easy to keep her anger flaring.

"My rules for my son are none of your business. I raised him without your help or advice for nearly six years and still managed to do a pretty good job of it."

"You did a damn good job of it."

His compliment lifted her chin an inch, cooled her anger a degree or two, and the way his eyes danced over hers made her heart pound and her entire body pulse with heat.

"Encouraging him to ignore my rules makes it hard on him, and on me," she said and turned to leave.

He grabbed her hand. "This isn't about the cinnamon roll."

She pulled away from him. "Don't touch me, Josh."

"CC—"

She didn't wait around to find out what he had wanted to say. Rushing into the house, she closed the doors behind her. She pressed her back against the solid wooden one and pulled in some deep breaths, trying to cool the passion his simple touch had stirred. She half expected him to charge after her, but he didn't.

When her legs could function again, she moved on into the kitchen, wrapped Derrick's cinnamon roll in plastic and put it in the refrigerator. Spying the green chile chicken enchilada casserole Ruby had made for their dinner and had asked her to put on—which she hadn't done because she was making mistakes with Josh—she pulled it out, turned on the oven, and slid it in.

Yelling coming from outside had her rushing back outside. Josh and Cole stood near the porch, practically toe to toe, nose to nose, fists at the ready.

"Mind your own fucking business, Ledger."

Cole said something she didn't catch, and Josh punched him in the face. Cole punched him back. The fight was on.

She ran to them. "Stop it, you two! Now!"

Owen had run out from the barn and got between them to break up the fight.

She'd never seen Josh's face so hard and angry. His eyes were narrowed and so was his full mouth.

"I'm the manager of this fucking ranch." The harsh words gritted from his mouth in Cole's direction. "You follow my orders, or I'll fire your ass."

"I can't take orders from someone I don't respect. I quit." Cole spat blood on the ground between them, scooped up his hat that had fallen off in the scuffle, then stormed toward the bunkhouse.

Quit? No! Cole couldn't quit. He knew everything about the ranch. She needed him, would need him even more when Josh left at the end of September after fulfilling his part of the contract. If she and Derrick decided to stay on the ranch, she couldn't make it without Cole.

She ran after him, caught his arm, and made him stop. "Please don't quit. Derrick and I need you, the ranch needs you."

His gaze sliced in Josh's direction before coming back to hers. "I can't work for a dishonorable man."

"Josh isn't dishonorable."

"I know what he did. Earlier." His face went fifty shades of red. The heat in her face said hers had, too.

"He didn't force me or take advantage of me or whatever it is you're thinking. We have history, were once very much in love. We just—"

"I know all about your past. But that doesn't matter. He's the ranch manager now, not your... He can't do things like that now. It's wrong."

"He's a good man, Cole. What we did doesn't change that."

"You still love him?"

Her gaze dropped to the ground, trying to think of the best way not to answer his question. She hadn't had sex for months before Will died a year ago. But the decision to have sex with Josh today was more than needing to scratch a long-time itch. It was about connecting with the man she loved and being with him again in a place where she'd always been deliriously happy and fully complete.

She drew herself up tall to manufacture confidence she didn't possess. "C'mon, Cole. You know that sometimes sex isn't about love."

"But in this case it is." He dropped his hand on her shoulder. "You still love him."

Her gaze met his soft, understanding gaze. "Don't you dare tell anyone, or I'll fire your ass myself," she threatened.

He chuckled softly, telling her he knew she wasn't serious. "Yes, ma'am."

She stepped closer and put her hands on his chest. "Please. Stay."

He slapped his hat against his thigh, back and forth, as if that would help him decide. "I reckon somebody's got to keep him away from you 'til he puts a ring on that pretty little finger of yours."

"Well, that'll be a life-time responsibility you're taking on because Josh Flores isn't interested in putting a ring on my finger. He never was."

"I don't know about that, gal. He looks mighty interested to me."

She shook her head, then leaned in and hugged him. "Thank you."

He hugged her back. "What for?"

"For staying. For caring. For trying to get along with Josh."

Behind her, Josh's pickup spit dirt and gravel as it roared down the road away from her.

Chapter Eighteen

That first morning Charleigh was back, Josh had boasted that he was no longer the gullible boy she had wrapped around her finger. What a load of self-deceptive shit that was.

For months she'd been all over him, making him think that maybe they could try again. But then he'd cooled her fire today, and she blamed him, then rushed to Cole, hugging him.

"That's the last goddamned time, CC," he yelled at the cracked windshield. "I'm done. Fucking. Done. Unwinding myself from you. Forever."

At the turn off to his house, he kept going into town, straight to the Buck Me Bar. Whiskey had dulled his dad's sanity and numbed his pain. Dulled senses and numbed pain was exactly what he needed right now. He wanted to forget about this whole damn day. About her.

It's like the old pickup knew the way by heart, Josh mused as he found himself parked in front of the bar. He pushed open the door and walked in before he could talk himself out of it, pausing inside only to let his eyes adjust to the dim light after the brightness of the sunshine.

"Well, I'll be damned," a smoke- and whiskey-roughened voice called out from the dimness. "I thought my days of seeing a Flores in here were long done."

347

Josh approached the bar where Royal Duran stood wiping down pint glasses. "Royal," he said with a curt nod.

"What can I do you for, Joshua?"

He claimed the barstool his dad had occupied for years. "Whiskey. And keep it coming."

Royal grinned and poured the first shot, sliding it in front of Josh. "You sound so much like your pop I'm getting misty eyed."

"If you're going to insult me, *cabrón*, I'll leave right now." He knocked back the shot and felt the burn from the tip of his tongue to the tips of his toes.

Royal chuckled. "So tell me," he said as he refilled his glass. "What would make the upstanding Joshua Flores come into this shithole, as you so fondly used to call it, and risk his noble reputation to take up his old man's habit? I'm guessing it's the same thing that sent you in here, oh 'bout six years ago."

Royal was right. The last time he'd turned to downing shots like this was when Charleigh left him. That's what she did to him. Made him desperate to do anything to drown out the thought of her. But spilling his guts to the bartender wasn't his style.

Josh knocked back the shot. The burn wasn't as pronounced, but it still felt like his insides were being eaten by acid. He slid the empty back to Royal. "Less talk, more pouring."

Royal filled him up again. And again. And kept filling. Until Josh could barely feel his ass on the barstool. Or his fingers wrapped around the glass. Or the passage of time. But unfortunately, he could still feel the sharp edges of every broken piece of his heart.

The only country song Charleigh had liked, *I Cross*

My Heart, came on the old Wurlitzer in the corner. It had been playing the first time they'd danced and the first time they'd made love and had, from that moment, become their song. They had requested it at every dance, played it on the jukebox in the café where she worked, played it on his phone wherever they were until whenever anyone heard it, they thought Josh and Charleigh. It explained how they felt about each other—*in all the world, you'll never find, a love as true as mine.* At least, that's the way he'd felt. Clearly, he was alone in those feelings.

When the song ended, he fished a bill he thought was a ten from his wallet and held it out toward Royal. "Gimme a roll of quarters, will ya?" He was proud he still had the voice to speak. Royal handed him the roll, which he cracked open and dumped into a nearby empty pint.

He stumbled to the jukebox and leaned heavily on it for support, trying to focus his eyes on the song choices. When he found the one he wanted, he fed in quarters and punched in the numbers. He let the tune, the words, the memories flow over him. When the song ended, he fed in more quarters and played it again. And again.

****

Sunlight streaming in the room through the sheer curtains was like knives thrusting into Josh's skull through his eyes. Raising a hand to his head, he groaned and tried to sit up. He made it half way up before collapsing back against the headboard. His organs flipped and sloshed inside him, cursing him for the effort.

What the hell was wrong with him, drinking like

that? He'd thought that having a front row seat to alcohol ripping his dad's life away had cured him of ever wanting to go overboard with drink. Sometimes matters of the heart trumped good sense.

How many had he downed?

Better question—how had he gotten home? He hoped to God he hadn't driven himself.

The brightness and slant of the rays told him it was a few hours past sunrise. Eyes narrowed to slits, he glanced at the clock on his nightstand. There in its place was a vase of pink flowers. Eyes burning, his gaze loped around the room. Everything he saw filled him with dread until he had to admit the god-awful truth.

This wasn't his bedroom.

It was Beth's.

A glance down confirmed he wasn't wearing a shirt. He lifted the pink sheet. Or anything else.

Shit!

Charleigh would never forgive him.

Beth walked into the room, a mug in one hand, a glass of water in the other, and a smile of satisfaction on her face. Her short, silky pink robe gapped, showing him the curve of her bare breasts.

Ah, fuck! What had he done?

"Morning, cowboy," she said in her silky-smooth voice that today sounded like a thunder clap in his eardrums. She handed him the mug.

Coffee. Thank God. He managed a grunt and sipped. His throat felt like a sand castle had been built in it and left to dry.

She set the glass on the nightstand beside the flowers, pulled a bottle of pain reliever from the drawer, and set it beside it. "Take a couple of these with your coffee."

"How'd I get here?" he asked, forcing his voice to work.

She climbed over him to the empty side of the bed. The jostling make his stomach want to heave out of his mouth.

"Uncle Royal called me, said you were being, in his words, 'a goddamned besotted fool and a stain on the Flores name' and asked me to come get you before you got your ass kicked." She chuckled. "I didn't even know he knew words like besotted."

"What was I doing?"

"You kept playing the same song on the jukebox. Over and over. And over. Wouldn't let anyone near it to play something else."

"What song?"

"What else? *Cross My Heart*." To add insult to injury, she sang the title. "Apparently, you kept shouting to anyone who tried to pull you away, 'It's our fucking song, man. The only one she likes.'"

He'd made a total ass of himself over her. Again. He was likely the laughing stock of the town already. "'Appreciate you getting me out of there."

"Well, you know me...I never miss an opportunity to have you in my bed." She ran her hand up his leg toward his crotch.

He caught her hand, stopping it before it reached its destination.

She pulled it away and shook her head. "Wow. I just don't get it."

"Get what?" He gulped his coffee. It burned his tongue and the roof of his mouth, the pain innocuous compared to the pain in his chest.

Sophia Ryan

"Why you allow her do this to you. You wouldn't let anyone else. Just her. Always her."

"Because she's fire, and I've been cold all my life." He mumbled the line of poetry he'd memorized years ago because it so accurately explained his almost obsessive need to have Charleigh in his life. The line was as true today as it had been the day he'd met her.

"What?" Beth asked.

He didn't have the energy to explain it. So he ignored her question and grabbed the bottle of pain reliever, popped three into his mouth, and swallowed them down with a gulp of water. He didn't speak until he was sure they weren't coming back up.

"Beth, did you and I *do* anything last night?"

"You mean, did we fuck?"

Beth rarely cussed, at least around him, so hearing the rough word come from her cotton-candy lips was surprising but said volumes about her state of mind. He gave a short nod.

"You passed out as soon as I got you to bed. Never even came around as I undressed you." She raised an eyebrow. "Believe me, I tried."

Relief slid over the tense places riding him, and he closed his eyes and released a sigh, feeling his shoulders relax. In this town, Charleigh was bound to hear about what happened at the bar and where he'd spent the night. At least he could tell her, in all honesty, he hadn't had sex with Beth.

"Gotta tell you, Josh. I'm insulted that you're so relieved we didn't have sex. I always thought it was pretty good between us. At least, you never complained."

Her voice was the same easy tone it always was,

but that hurt look in her eyes told a different story. He didn't want to wound her with the truth but was struggling to come up with an answer that didn't.

Spying his clothes sitting neatly folded on the pink flowered chair across the room, he eased back the covers and pulled himself to a seated position at the edge of the bed with the intent to get up, get dressed, and get home. He'd clean up, then go to Charleigh's and try to fix this mess.

"Sorry. Not my intent." Rising slowly, he picked his way to the chair, his head expanding like a balloon with each step, his stomach twisting like a pair of fists wringing out a soaked washrag.

"What happened?" Beth asked from the bed as he grabbed his boxer-briefs and pulled them on, his back to her, followed by his jeans.

"I took a page from my old man's idiot book." He pulled his T-shirt on next, then sat to pull on his boots. Every movement made his body clench to control his nausea and pain. The stench of old booze and cigarette smoke and fresh mistakes branded on every inch of his skin didn't help. "Guess I'm more like him than I thought."

She moved to his side and settled her hand on his head. The light touch felt like a bale of hay had been dropped on him.

"You're nothing like your old man, Joshua. Last night has to do with Charleigh and what happened between you, not just yesterday but six years ago. That's what's at the heart of the pain that won't let you allow someone else into your life."

Boots on, he slowly stood, avoiding her emotion-filled gaze while he buttoned and zipped his jeans and buckled his belt, all while concentrating on not falling on his face or puking on her floor. As he turned and headed toward the front door, Beth reached out and tucked a finger in his belt loop the way Charleigh always had. He grabbed her hand to move it away, and she let him, but she grabbed his hand and held on as she followed behind him down the hall.

He opened the door, hoping no nosy neighbors were out to witness his walk of shame. "Thanks for your help," he said, then turned toward his pickup that was sitting in her drive next to her little red sports car.

She stopped him and tugged him into a hug, her arms tight around his neck. "The one who broke your heart isn't the one who can fix it," she said. "She can only keep breaking it. I can make you forget it was ever broken." Her mouth pressed into his in a deep kiss.

****

It was hard to believe she and Derrick had been without Will for a year. That alone was hard enough, but this break between her and Josh made the pain more acute. But she'd get through it. She'd been through much more difficult things.

At least that's what she told herself as she and Derrick drove into town to buy flowers for Will's grave. After paying for a colorful bouquet of spring wildflowers, she took a shortcut to the cemetery through one of the neighborhoods, keeping to the infuriatingly slow thirty-mile-per-hour posted speed limit.

Josh's bucket of bolts sat in the drive of one of the houses next to a red sports car. She didn't have to wonder too long whose house it was when the front door opened and Josh came out, he in the clothes he'd worn yesterday and Beth in a short little pink robe. They hugged. And kissed.

Oh, God! He'd gone right from her to Beth.

Her heart exploded in her chest. She swore the blast took out a couple of ribs because she was finding it hard to breathe. And her stomach twisted at the shrapnel embedded in it.

She hoped Derrick didn't see Josh. If he did—

"Hey, Josh!" Derrick called out the window and waved.

Josh turned at Derrick's voice. The look on his face when they drove past convinced her that he had done just that…fucked her, then Beth. She wanted to crawl under the seat but instead pressed down hard on the gas to get away as fast as she could, speed limit be damned.

In a matter of minutes, Josh's pickup was behind her, honking and flashing his lights.

"Mom, I think Josh wants us to stop."

Derrick's eyes were big and round and filled with confusion about why she wasn't stopping. In response, she gripped the wheel harder and stomped on the gas.

Josh raced ahead of them and pulled in front of her, forcing a stop. He jumped out, rushed to her door, and yanked it open.

As the old saying went, he looked like he'd been ridden hard and…something, something, goddamned something! She couldn't remember the stupid saying, but she knew hungover when she saw it. His bloodshot eyes, kinked hair, and pale green face said he'd had a wild night. With Beth.

"We need to talk about this," he said, his voice rough.

The smell of cigarettes, booze, and Beth clinging to

him made her sick to her stomach. "No, we don't."

He reached in, turned off the engine, and took her keys. "You're not going anywhere 'til we do."

She unbuckled her seatbelt. "Stay in the pickup," she said to Derrick over her shoulder.

"Yes, ma'am," he said.

When they got home, she'd make a new rule—he never said *yes ma'am, no ma'am* ever again for as long as she lived.

She got out, and Josh closed the door and immediately grabbed her elbow to lead her away from the pickup. She tried to pull away, but his grip was firm.

When they were far enough away that Derrick couldn't overhear them, he let her go and faced her, pure emotion burning in his eyes. "I didn't have sex with her."

She let her gaze crawl over him, head to toe and back up, suggesting he looked like he had. "You can fuck whoever you want. And so can I. And believe me, it won't be you. Ever again." She grabbed the keys from his hand and turned back toward her pickup, but he grabbed them back and her arm to stop her.

"Who will it be? Lance? Cole?"

She flung off his hand. "That's none of your business."

"It *is* my business, by God. *You're* my business."

Again grabbing the keys from his hand, she tried to step past him, but he got in front of her, held her by the shoulders.

"You're going to hear me out."

"Leave me alone." She pushed her hands against his chest.

He pulled her tighter, pressed his chest into hers, his arms around her. "You hurt me deep, Charleigh. *Again*."

"I hurt you?" she scoffed and pushed away. "You're the one who crawled into her bed after we—"

"After you and I made love, you treated me like a piece of shit stuck to the bottom of your boot, and you took Cole's side against me. I went to the bar and drank myself stupid trying to drown the thought of you. Royal called Beth to come get me because he knows we're friends. She drove me in my pickup to her house to sleep it off. And that's *all* I did. Sleep."

She crossed her arms over her chest. "*Where* did you sleep?"

He licked his lips. "Where?" he repeated, obviously stalling.

"The couch?" she asked, hoping against hope.

He said nothing, but his eyes darted away from hers and his hand rose to scratch the back of his neck, which gave her the answer.

"Her bed?" Her voice cracked at the pain of it. At the guilt in his eyes, she covered hers and shook her head at how stupid she'd been. Would she never learn? "You fucking asshat!"

"Charleigh, I passed out the minute my head hit the pillow, and I left the minute I woke up."

"That hug and kiss you gave her this morning on her porch, her in her sexy little robe, said you did more than sleep."

"You hugged Cole yesterday."

"It wasn't a thanks-for-the-fuck hug." She stormed toward her pickup, Josh at her side.

"I didn't fuck her, goddammit!" Tired of chasing

after her, he bolted in front of her and grabbed her. "Baby, I wouldn't do that to you."

"Damn you, Josh." She struggled against him, trying to shove him away, but he wouldn't budge. "I won't let you break my heart again." She pounded his chest with her fists. "I won't."

He caught her wrists and wrapped his arms around her waist. "CC—"

"Leave my mom alone." Derrick's command was the only warning they had before he charged into Josh, shoving him away from her, then pounding him with his little fists.

Josh took his hits, but Charleigh stopped him and pulled him back. "Hey, hey, what are you doing?" she asked, gripping his arms and knelt to face him.

"He hurt you and made you cry."

Surprised to feel tears on her cheeks, she swiped them away. "He didn't hurt me." Not physically anyway. "I promise."

Derrick looked at her like he didn't believe her, then shot a deadly look at Josh as if just daring him to try something again, then back to her. "Then why are you crying?"

"I'm sad…about your dad." It wasn't a lie. She was sad about his dad. Sad that she and Josh were so broken nothing could fix it. Sad that Will was gone. Ah, Will. Her life with him seemed so long ago. She was living the life he'd hated and abandoned. With the man she'd wanted a life with but who'd abandoned her.

What made her think moving here was a good decision?

She stood, and Derrick took her hand.

"Let's go see him." He pulled her toward their

pickup. They got in and continued on to the cemetery.

In the rearview mirror, she saw Josh standing there, watching them go. Saw him bend over, hands on his knees. Probably throwing up. He was hurting. She'd seen it in his eyes and in his defeated stance, heard it in his rough voice.

But he'd hurt her too, dammit. Apparently, it was his pattern to go from her to other women. He'd done it years ago, and he'd done it now. Maybe even other times she didn't know about. Clearly, she wasn't enough for him. And she wasn't interested in being his one of many.

****

A cleaned-up Josh was at her house when she and Derrick got back from the cemetery. So was Cole, standing near him, ever watchful and protective, but the previous look of an urge to do violence was absent. Had they talked it out? Settled their differences?

"Hey, Derrick." Cole said. "I could use your help with the horses." Clearly, he wanted to give her and Josh privacy.

Derrick looked like he didn't want to go. He gave Josh a hard look of warning, then looked at her. "I'm in the barn if you need me."

She nodded and watched him walk away, his no-nonsense stride so like Josh's it was astonishing no one had noticed it.

"Has he always been that protective of you?" Josh asked, watching him, too.

"Yes. Even more so since Will's death."

"A year today?"

She nodded.

"It's a hard day for you and Derrick."

"Yes. It is. So you'll forgive me if I'm not up to dealing with your drama on top of it."

"Don't shut me out, CC. We need to talk about what happened."

"I don't want to talk about you and Beth."

"I mean talk about you and me and what we did yesterday."

"Like you said, it was a mistake. Let's just forget it happened."

His eyebrows furrowed over his puffy, bloodshot eyes. "I never said it was a mistake."

"You apologized for having sex with me."

He eased closer and cupped the back of her head.

He smelled better. Like him. Not like another woman and whiskey and betrayal. But he still looked a little green. "Baby, I apologized for forgetting to use protection, not because I regretted what we did."

Playing back the conversation in her head, she realized it was a plausible explanation. But still she felt the need to guard her still-tender heart. "Are you clean?"

Looking insulted that she'd ask, he dropped his hand. "Of course."

"Good. So am I."

"Are you on the pill?"

"My husband has been dead for a year, and I'm not dating. Why would I need to be on birth control? I'm not sleeping around, if that's what you're suggesting. But even if I were, it's none of your business."

"For God's sake, I wasn't suggesting anything of the sort."

"We're done here."

"No, we're not. We have a hell of a lot to talk

about."

"Like?"

"The reason we made love."

"Let's don't make more of it than it was. Memories got the best of us. That's all." The wounded look in his eyes had her wanting to retract the lie, but she didn't. She was already fragile. Telling him the truth—that she still loved him—would leave her wide open to his lies. And she had too much riding on this contract to have it destroyed by unreciprocated feelings.

He put his hands on her shoulders, holding her in place. "It wasn't nostalgia that had us so out of our minds to be together that we both forgot about protection."

"Then what was it?"

"We still have feelings for each other."

She saw in his soft eyes what she felt inside. The passion was still between them, still driving them to each other. But they'd tried it once. It hadn't worked. Things were even more complicated now than they were back then. And after what he'd done, she wasn't sure she could trust him with her heart. Maybe the hard, painful truth was that they weren't good for each other.

At her continued silence, his gaze dropped to the ground but not before she saw disappointment flicker in his eyes when the answer he wanted didn't come.

"Okay. So you don't have feelings for me." His thumbs tucked into his front pockets. "That's..." He shifted his weight to his other leg. "That's fine." His gaze rose to hers again, and the fire suddenly sparking in them burned out the disappointment from before. "But if what we did yesterday results in a baby, you *will* marry me. Because no way in hell am I letting some other man raise *my* kid. Or Derrick."

A tidal wave of emotion swept over her. His kindness where Derrick was concerned was touching, but she couldn't let that guide her decisions. She had married for her child's sake once. She wouldn't do it again. And she hoped their mistake wouldn't result in a child. It would make their already complex situation even more so.

"Better check your contract. The role of husband and father is way outside your job duties. How about you stick to managing the ranch and let me decide how to run my life."

She rushed inside, firmly closing the doors behind her. He didn't stop her. Or follow her. And this time, she wished he had. Wished he'd been willing to fight for her, for them, and convince her she was the only woman he loved.

Chapter Nineteen

March had roared in like a lion, and across the ranch, a new crop of calves provided a host of new learning experiences. Although most of the pregnant cows and the cows who had calved had already been brought closer to the ranch so the hands could keep an eye on them in case they needed help, Charleigh, Derrick, and Josh took daily rides up to the far north boundary of the ranch on horseback to check for any they'd missed. Today that task was all on Charleigh and Josh because Derrick had awoken with a cold, and with a storm moving in and expected to hit before nightfall, she felt it best for him to stay home with Ruby.

Bundled up so tight in overalls, jackets, gloves, and winter hats they could barely move, Josh and Charleigh worked quickly to fill the water tanks, scatter salt licks, and add protein pellets to the long troughs for the cattle in all the pastures. That done, they unloaded the horses from the trailer and headed into a frigid north wind to make one last sweep of outlying areas, both of them keeping a close eye on the snow clouds banking hard and fast on the horizon. If any cows delivered in the coming storm, the calves could die.

When more than an hour of checking returned no results, they headed back to the pickup at a rapid-as-safe clip through the falling snow. They quickly loaded the horses and climbed into the pickup. Josh started the engine and turned the heater on full blast. It wasn't doing a good job heating, but Charleigh felt warmer just being out of the blowing snow.

Biting the tip of the middle finger of her leather work glove, she pulled it off, then the other one, and grabbed the thermos Ruby had sent with them. She poured coffee into a mug for each of them and handed Josh his after he'd pulled his gloves off.

Hands wrapped around the warm mug, she sipped the hot liquid in silence and stared out into the lacy curtain of white fluttering across the frozen landscape outside the windshield.

In the weeks following their slip into sex, they were careful not to talk about anything but work and extra careful not to touch. He never brought up the husband and dad plan again, but she caught him studying her now and then, as if he was looking for any changes, any swells, that would indicate *baby on board.*

"Today's Will's birthday," he said out of the blue.

She smiled. "I was thinking that this morning."

"Remember his last birthday here?" he said.

Josh and some of their friends had gotten Will drunk and left him naked and passed out on the sheriff's front lawn with the message Pig H8R painted on his chest.

"He got in a lot of trouble over that prank," she gently chastised. "You're lucky he didn't rat you guys out."

"Yeah, well, he deserved it."

"Why?" She always suspected it was more than just a simple desire to prank the rich kid as Will had explained it.

"He was shooting his mouth off, bragging that he

was going to take you away from me." He sipped his coffee and stared into the swirling flakes. "First thing the asshat actually followed through on."

Josh was right. Will had been brilliant at coming up with creative, ambitious ideas, but he lacked follow-through. But that wasn't his point.

"I never gave him reason to think he had a chance with me, Josh. I want you to know that."

"Yet you married him," he said, his eyes gripping hers so firmly she felt her skin vibrate under his stare. She couldn't look away or speak.

"Did you love me, Charleigh?" His voice was tight and guarded like he was armoring up his wounded spots for when she said no.

"You were everything to me," she responded, unwilling to pretend.

He held her gaze for a bit longer before turning away, his disturbing lack of response suggesting he didn't believe her.

"Did you love me?" she asked. "Or was I just someone else to fool around with?"

"Being with you was the only thing that gave my life meaning," he said softly, so softly the roar of the heater almost drowned out the words. But she heard, so focused was she on his face, his lips, his words. "I loved you, CC," he added. "Only you."

"Why didn't you want us to get married or move in together?"

"I had to get through school if we were going to make it out of this place. I thought if we moved in together or got married, I'd fail us both." His gaze captured hers, eyes soft but focused. "But I was always committed to you. To us."

Joy flooded through her at the sincerity in his voice, his face, his eyes, and she swallowed hard to keep it from escaping. "I felt it."

"Then why? Why did you go with him?" His tone wasn't accusatory. It was sad, with a desire to know, not to blame.

She owed him the truth. As much of the truth as she could give. "All I heard that night was that you had a future mapped out that didn't include me. My worst fear was coming true. I was losing you. I panicked and threw out an ultimatum. For as long as I live, I'll never forget the look on your face when I told you to leave and not come back. Like I'd stabbed you in the heart. I knew I'd just made the biggest mistake of my life, but I couldn't take it back. It was already out. And it seemed like both of us were too shocked or stubborn to ask what was happening."

"I came back to ask you that. But you were already gone." He downed the coffee in his mug and set it on the dashboard.

Her heart jammed up into her throat, making breathing difficult, and her hands gripped her mug. "What do you mean, you came back? When?"

"The Saturday you left town with Will."

Saturday. The day her life had changed. "When Saturday? What time?"

"Late morning. I came back to apologize for being such an asshat and to ask you to move in with me that next semester."

"How did you find out I was gone?"

"Molly said you'd gone off with Will for the weekend. I couldn't figure one reason you'd be with him, especially for the whole weekend, but I damn well was going to find out. I called him and texted him, a hundred times it felt like, but he never answered, never called back. I went to his house, but Wyatt chased me off at gunpoint before I got one word out. I went back to the café. Molly said you'd quit, packed up, and left with Will. I called your aunt, who said you'd left town and weren't coming back. If I'd known where you were going, I'd have gone after you. But no one knew where you were going. Or if they did, they weren't telling me."

He stopped talking long enough to pull in a deep, steadying breath as if the sentence that was coming next needed extra help getting out. "Will finally called me that Monday morning." He closed his eyes as if he were seeing that memory play out and feeling every emotion that had accompanied it. "Told me you two were married." He opened his eyes and turned his gaze to her. "I died that day."

The anguish in his fragile, whispered words ripped her soul to shreds, and the ugly, unbelievable truth shook her. Will had known Josh was in town looking for her and hadn't told her. All these years she could have been with Josh. Derrick could have had his father. Josh his son.

Damn you, Will. You betrayed me…and Josh…and Derrick, just because you wanted me.

She set her mug beside his. "I didn't know, Josh. I swear."

"I know you were mad because I said I wasn't ready to get married. But how could you just leave me after all we'd meant to each other? I thought we—" He swallowed tightly instead of finishing his sentence, and he wouldn't look at her.

"I was with Will that Saturday because I'd asked him to take me to the university to see you. I wanted to tell you I didn't want to break up. When we got there, I went to your room. You were in bed, fucking some redhead. That's the moment *I* died."

His gaze swung to hers, his eyebrows furrowed. "That wasn't me. It was my buddy, Travis, and his girlfriend. They needed to use my room for the weekend."

"You in the habit of allowing people to fuck in your bed?"

"My price for letting them use my room was to borrow his pickup so I could get home to you and fix our relationship."

The room was dark, and she'd gone no farther in than the doorway, but she would've bet her life the guy was him. In fact, she *had* bet her life on it. And lost. Her hand rose to her mouth, and she swallowed back the bile but not the groan that rose in her throat at the horrible, preventable, mistake she'd made.

"I thought you knew me well enough to know I'd never cheat on you," he continued when she didn't respond.

"I never thought you would. But the things you said to me that night, the way you left me, the girl in your bed, the fact that you never came back or even called me to try to resolve things…it added up to you not wanting a future with me. I thought you were done with me."

"I know you. If you thought that was me with that girl, you'd have yanked me out of bed by my dick. Yet all you did was run away and marry Will. It doesn't add up."

"The night you left me, my world shattered. Seeing you with that girl broke what was left of it into a million pieces. Without you, I had nothing. When Will asked me to go to California with him and start a new life, I said yes because I had no life here without you."

"Would you still have gone with him if I'd gotten home in time?"

"No." She shook her head to emphasize the word. "If I'd had any idea you were in town looking for me, I wouldn't have gone with him. I never wanted to be with anyone but you."

"I'm guessing that's why he didn't answer my calls or tell you I'd called. He always was in love with you."

She knew it, too. And Will's betrayal made her sick to her stomach. He knew how she felt about Josh, and he purposely kept them apart so he could have what he wanted. Anger singed the edges of the fondness she'd developed for him over the years.

"He was your husband and Derrick's dad, and at one time my best friend, and I'm sorry he got cancer and died so young, but I'll never forgive him for what he did to us."

She wasn't sure she could forgive Will either. But the bigger question now was whether she and Josh could forgive each other. Forgiveness was the first step, the step that would pave the way for her to tell him the rest of the story.

"I understand your anger, Josh. I feel it, too. And the sense of betrayal is… God, it's massive. But now that we know the truth, I feel lighter than I've felt in a long time. Maybe we're not ready to forgive Will, but let's forgive each other."

"You ripped my heart out when you left, CC. And

every day that I see Will's son—the son that should have been ours—it reminds me all over again." He lowered his head and shook it softly, then raised it and looked at her. "But despite everything…" He took her hand in his, linked their fingers, kissed the back of her hand. "I still love you. And I need to know, right now, whether you still have feelings for me. If you don't, least I know and I can stop thinking that maybe we can try again."

She lunged across the seat to him, cupping his face in her hands, and kissed him hard, her mouth devouring his. He wrapped his arms around her, and she knocked off his hat and dug her fingers in his hair to hold his mouth closer to hers. As one, they lay back on the seat, his body stretched out over hers.

Easing back from the deep kiss, she met his eyes. "You asked me why I kept your T-shirt and wore it all those years. It was because it kept me connected to you. I kept everything you gave me for the same reason. I never stopped loving you."

"I never stopped loving you either." He groaned and kissed her again.

"Baby, there's…something else I…need to—" she said between kisses. She was about to tell him about his son when twin beams of light stabbed into the darkened cab. At the rumble of a pickup up ahead of theirs, he rose up and squinted out the windshield.

"Hold that thought," he said. "We've got company." He kissed her again, with promises for more to come.

They rose up in time to see Cole exit the other pickup. Head bent against the storm, he rushed to her side. She rolled down the window when he appeared there.

"Everything okay?" he asked, eyeing both of them.

"Everything's great," Josh said, grinning.

"Well, Derrick was getting mighty worried about his momma, with the storm and all, and insisted I come look for you when you didn't answer your phone."

"We didn't get any calls," she said and looked at Josh.

Josh fished his phone from his pocket and checked it. "The storm must've blocked the signal."

"You should ride back with me," Cole said to her. "It'd be faster. Safer."

"Thanks, but I'll ride with Josh."

Cole's eyes darted to Josh, then back to her. "All right. See you at home."

He rushed back to the pickup and climbed in. But instead of turning it around and heading back to the ranch, he got out again and came back. She rolled down the window again.

"Derrick insists on riding with you and Josh," Cole said.

"He's here? You brought him?" she said.

"He's as stubborn as his mother."

She looked at Josh to get his opinion.

"It's warmer in Cole's pickup," he admitted. "This old heater's almost dead. It's bound to get pretty cold before we make it home. And with him sick…"

She reached across the seat and squeezed his hand. "We'll be all right."

At his answering grin and nod, she turned back to Cole. "I'll come get him."

"Naw, stay put. I'll bring him."

She rolled up the window, and minutes later, Cole

and Derrick emerged from the vehicle, Derrick bundled up tight and grinning from ear to ear, Cole carrying a folded blanket.

Josh leaned over to open her door, stealing a quick kiss in the process. "We'll continue this conversation later."

"Count on it," she said and kissed him again.

"I was worried about you guys," Derrick said as he crawled in, grinning, his blue eyes shining like this was some grand adventure.

She sandwiched him between her and Josh to take advantage of their body heat.

"Scoot on over here, bud," Josh said, holding out his arm to him, and he did.

Cole handed her the wool blanket. "You might need this before you get home."

"Thanks, Cole."

With a look that said he thought she was making a mistake, he shut the door and left.

She scooted closer to Derrick and spread the blanket over the three of them, uniting them.

"How come you didn't answer when I called you?" Derrick said to Josh.

"The storm's blocking the signal."

"How come you took so long?"

"When you're pulling a horse trailer, you have to take it slow, and with the weather, we knew we'd have to take it extra slow."

"Do you think we'll go riding tomorrow?"

"The way it's coming down, I doubt it."

They talked. And talked. And talked some more. Derrick hung on Josh's every word, wanting his opinion about everything, then often forming his opinion around Josh's. She just listened, smiling at the joy of being with the two people she loved most in the world.

Father and son seemed to have rebuilt the trust between them to an even higher level. A level where Derrick felt free to ask him any question, make any statement, without hesitation. Josh answered his questions freely, taking every one as an opportunity to teach him something or just to get to know him.

However, the colder it got, the quieter Derrick got. And soon he was shivering. Her toes and fingers were cold, and so was her face, so she knew his were. Their breath hung in the air, and Derrick was coughing, his cheeks flushed, his nose red and runny. She should have made him ride back with Cole.

She pulled the blanket off them and lifted him into her lap. She scooted over right next to Josh, as close to him as she could get without being in his lap, then spread the blanket over them again, tucking her part around Derrick.

Josh put his arm around her and held her close, giving her more of his heat, and she wrapped her arms around Derrick, holding him close. Derrick tucked himself into a ball, facing Josh.

She had never been so glad to see the lights of home. Josh pulled the pickup around by the barn. Leaving Derrick inside, wrapped in the blanket, she and Josh unloaded the horses and fed them.

"That'll hold 'em for tonight," Josh said. "If I can't get back in the morning, do a normal feeding, and check their water because it's likely to—"

"No, you're staying here tonight."

He shook his head. "I need to check on my place."

"In case you haven't noticed, it's a blizzard out there, your right windshield wiper is barely wiping, and the heater isn't heating. It's foolish to drive in these conditions. You could miss the turnoff or slide off into the ditch. And what if the pickup dies between here and there? You'd freeze trying to get to shelter. Have you thought about any of that?"

He grinned at the panic in her voice. "I like it when you worry about me."

"Don't tease me, Josh. Not about your safety."

"Baby, I'll be all right."

His consoling tone didn't ease her worries. "You will be if you stay here," she said, sliding her arms around his waist and pressing against him through their layers. "Stay. Share my bed tonight."

His arms went around her, too. "As tempting as that sounds, I have responsibilities."

When they'd been together before, school came first and she came second. Now, the ranch came first and… "And what I want comes last." She pushed out of his arms and headed to the door, but he caught her, drew her in to his body, and pressed her against the wall. Kissed her. Hard. Thoroughly. Then he met her eyes.

"Let me be real clear. There's nothing I'd like more than to climb into bed with you and stay there 'til the storm clears. And beyond that. But I have responsibilities I *have* to see to. Now you have to decide what kind of man you want. One who shirks his responsibilities, drops everything to pursue his own pleasures. Or one who does whatever is necessary to take care of his family and the people and animals that count on him."

She dropped her head on his chest for a second, trying not to cry but close. So close. She'd been so damn weepy lately. It was annoying.

Gaining control of her emotions, she looked up into his loving eyes. "I want you, Josh. Just as you are. So be careful. I just got you back."

He gave her that sexy half smile that always flipped her heart. "Careful's my middle name, darlin'."

"Amado is your middle name." Like Derrick's. "Beloved," she whispered and pressed another soft kiss to his mouth.

"Let's get Derrick inside," he said after she eased back.

Back at the pickup, Josh unhooked the trailer, then drove them close to the house. He carried Derrick into the mudroom, set him on top of the dryer, then helped him off with his coat, hat, gloves, and boots, then set him on the floor.

"Go take a hot shower to warm up, then put on your pjs," he told him with a gentle swat.

Teeth chattering, coughing, Derrick headed toward the bathroom, and she and Josh pulled off their outerwear and boots.

Ruby's warm voice welcomed them from the kitchen. "You two come thaw out by the stove while I pour you a nice cup of hot coffee."

They moved to the propane heater set along the kitchen wall and warmed their backsides.

"'Preciate it, Ruby, but I need to be getting on home," Josh said. "I haven't been able to reach Quino, and I know he needs help locking things down before the storm gets worse."

Ruby didn't look any happier at his response than

she'd been, but she hid it better. "How about a thermos to go?"

"Be glad to have it. Thank you."

"Least we can do." She grabbed a thermos from the cabinet and filled it with coffee.

Josh's gaze cut to Cole, who sat at the table in his stockinged feet, one hand around a mug of coffee, then back to her. "The bunkhouse isn't built for this kind of cold. All right if Cole and the others stay in here tonight?"

"Of course," she said.

Ruby capped the thermos and set it on the counter. "I'll go change the sheets on the guest bed and make up the couch."

"Don't go to no trouble, Ruby," Cole said.

"No trouble at all," she said and left to take care of it.

Josh addressed Cole. "Charleigh and I took care of the horses tonight, but—"

"She and the boys and I'll handle the morning feeding."

Josh nodded. "I put snow chains on the tractor couple days ago when the storm was forecast. You'll need to drop hay—"

"We'll handle that, too, Josh. I know you got your hands full with your own, and this ain't my first rodeo."

Charleigh noticed that Josh's jaw was gripping like he wasn't happy with Cole's comments about them handling things fine without him.

"Good. I'll go then." His eyes met hers. "Walk me out?"

She grabbed the thermos on their way to the mudroom and watched in silence as he pulled back on his cold boots, coat, and gloves.

Their eyes met and held tight, then he eased her over to the door, where no one in the kitchen could see them. She went eagerly into his arms. They didn't say any last words of goodbye, didn't kiss. Just held each other. After a too-short moment, he pulled back, grabbed his hat and anchored it on his head, brim low to his eyes. He kissed her, hard and quick, then grabbed the thermos and headed out the door.

From the door she watched him go. All she wanted to do was run after him, pull him back inside, take him to bed and never let him go. But she didn't. A man like Josh had to do what he thought was right, with no interference, no matter how good intentioned.

Her heart sitting heavy in her queasy stomach, she closed the door, went back to the kitchen, and just stood there, for some reason unable to do anything else.

"He'll be all right," Cole said, his consoling tone saying he'd seen her worry playing across her face, in her eyes.

"He shouldn't be going out in that," she said. "It's ridiculous."

"A rancher's life depends on his stock, and his stock's life depends on him. Rain, snow, mud, flood, bitter cold, scorching heat, sickness, death, celebration—the stock comes first. The crop comes first. Or it all could be lost. If it's all lost, the rancher, and everyone he or she cares about, loses. It's why he's going out there when he'd rather stay here with you. It's why he'll risk his life to get back here tomorrow to check on you and this ranch. This is what you'll be signing up for if you stay, Charleigh. It's a hard life. It takes no prisoners."

It's the most she'd heard Cole say at one time since she met him. It touched her that he did to help her understand. "I'm beginning to realize that."

Ruby came back in, arms full of bedding. "The bed's ready, Cole, and this should keep one of you warm enough on the couch, but I'll leave the heat up, just in case. We're in for a bitter cold night. Thank goodness Josh saw fit to have the propane tank serviced and refilled early." She continued on into the living room and made up the couch.

Owen and Emmett came in, and the six of them ate a quiet supper. Charleigh helped Ruby clean up, then got Derrick into bed. He fell asleep part way through the book he'd asked her to read. She lay next to him, rubbing his back, replaying in her head the day's conversation with Josh. Thinking about him out there now, alone and cold. Wishing he was in her arms.

Despite the howling wind and swirling snow battering the house outside, inside it was warm. But Josh was in the cold pickup, the heater probably shooting out ice cubes instead of heat. She'd left the blanket for him, he had hot coffee, and she'd kept the porch light on in case he needed a beacon back to the house.

Leaving Derrick, she showered, pulled on her T-shirt and socks, and climbed into her bed. Josh was tough and smart and experienced in the ways of a rancher. He'd be okay. She had to believe that, because she couldn't even call him to make sure he'd gotten home okay. She would not sleep a wink tonight.

The storm grew louder, the wind howling and snow pelting the window, furiously pounding as though demanding to be let inside. It had been bad the day she'd buried Will, but not this bad.

As loud as the wind was, she wasn't sure, but she thought she heard the rumble of an engine. Then she saw a weak flash of headlights and knew it was Josh. Bolting out of bed, she ran to the door and looked out the small window pane. His pickup sat in her drive, buried in at least half a foot of snow.

He cut the lights, turned off the engine, climbed out, and hurried to the door. She opened it and pulled him inside then shut the doors. He felt like a snowman. She pulled off his hat, his gloves, and set them on the dryer. Pulled off his coat and laid it over the washer to dry. Pulled off his boots. Pulled him by the hand into the kitchen, down the hall, and into her room.

He stood before her, shivering, as she removed his stiff, cold clothes and pulled him into bed with her, blankets and comforter up around them. She wrapped him in her arms, in her legs, and held him tight against her body.

"How bad was it?" she whispered into his hair.

"I couldn't see a foot in front of me," he said, his voice trembling from the bone-penetrating cold. "Drifts had narrowed the road to my place. Snow was coming down harder the farther away from here I got. The heater was sleeting instead of heating. That right wiper froze. I realized I wasn't going to make it home. I headed back, hoping the pickup would get me here."

She squeezed him tighter. "I'm so glad you came back."

"I saw your light in the distance. It kept me on track."

"I kept it on for you. Just in case."

"You sure you want me here?" he asked. "In your

bed? They'll know."

It's where she'd always wanted him. "I don't care who knows. I want you here. Are you sure you want to be here?"

"I shouldn't be here, but right now, there's no other place I want to be."

His head on her chest, his arm around her, she combed her fingers through his hair. He closed his eyes, and her name whispered from his lips in a sigh.

Contentment filling her, she closed her eyes, too, and committed to memory this feeling of him in her arms. If she lost him again, this moment would have to carry her through.

Minutes later, she heard his deep even breathing and realized he slept. Other than making love with Josh, the best feeling of all had been sleeping with him, next to him, around him.

****

Josh awoke wrapped in Charleigh's arms, the frigid gray predawn light casting shadows on her face. It was going to be a miserable, shitty day to be outside working, but it was the best morning he'd had in a long time. It was how it was supposed to be with them...waking up together. That she was with him like this filled his heart with peace. So did her confession that she still loved him. Had never stopped loving him. Never would have left him had Will not betrayed them.

He nuzzled his face in her hair and breathed her into his soul, and in that instance, he knew that if there was such a thing as heaven, this was it. He was tempted to wake her with kisses and caresses, like he used to those mornings in her apartment, but she looked so peaceful. And he knew where kisses and caresses would lead. The weather had forced him to sleep in Charleigh's bed, but he wasn't going to make love to her in Will's house. Well, not again.

Kissing her forehead, he eased from bed. She'd want to go with him today to check on the ranch. But with Derrick still sick, it would be best for her to stay home. Besides, he didn't want her out in that mess.

Deciding to let her sleep, he gathered his clothes from the floor and went into the bathroom. He washed up and brushed his teeth with a new toothbrush he'd found in her cabinet. After getting dressed, he tiptoed to the kitchen so as to not wake anyone in the house. It wouldn't be good for anyone to know he'd slept in her bed.

Unfortunately, Ruby was already at the stove, putting on a pot of coffee and shoving a pan of biscuits into the oven.

She grinned when she saw him, her whispered good morning filled with knowing but not judging. "Have a seat. You'll need a hearty breakfast before heading out this morning."

"Yes, ma'am." He took a seat at the head of the table that had at some point become *his* place.

The smell of breakfast cooking awakened Cole, Owen, and Emmett, and the four of them wolfed it down then headed to the mudroom to don their heavy outer gear.

"What about Charleigh?" Cole asked Josh.

"We got this. Let her sleep."

"She ain't gonna like us leaving her behind."

No. She wouldn't. "Derrick's sick, and he'll need her today."

"It's your neck," Cole said, and the four headed out

into the falling snow.

****

Charleigh jerked upright in bed, eyes searching the room for Josh. He was gone. So were his clothes. The aroma of bacon and coffee permeating the air told her that maybe he and the others were still here.

She jumped out of bed to dress. The sky outside her window was dull gray, and it was still snowing, but not as hard as before. The wind had calmed, blanketing the house in an eerie quiet like the inside of a drift.

One leg into her jeans and nausea hit her like a brick, turning her stomach inside out. She ran to the bathroom and vomited. God! She couldn't be sick now! Josh needed her. Derrick needed her. Her ranch needed her.

Fighting back the lingering nausea, she rinsed her mouth and face, brushed her teeth, hurriedly finished dressing, and rushed into the kitchen. It was empty. A glance into the living room showed an empty couch, the bedding folded neatly at the end of it. Cole was gone, which likely meant so too were Owen and Emmett.

"Morning," Ruby said as chipper as a robin as she came out of the mudroom with quart bags of green chile from the freezer. "How about a nice cup of hot coffee to light your fire."

"Did he leave?"

"The four of them were getting ready to head out when I started the coffee. I convinced them to stay for a bite to eat. They wolfed it down, then headed out in the tractor to check on the stock. They left not more than twenty minutes ago."

"He should have woken me up."

"He wanted to let you sleep. Said Derrick would

need you today."

"I should be out there with him."

Ruby chuckled. "Don't you worry about that. They'll need to repeat this tonight, then tomorrow morning, and so on, 'til the storm passes. You'll get your turn."

"Thank you for making breakfast. I should have been up to help you with that. I'm sorry. I…" Feeling fully drained, she collapsed into the dining chair and dropped her head in her hands.

Ruby put a comforting arm around her. "There now, it'll be all right. I'll get you some breakfast, and it'll give you a whole new outlook. Then maybe you can crawl back in bed for a spell. You're looking a might peaked. One egg or two?"

The thought of food sent Charleigh scrambling back to the bathroom.

Chapter Twenty

The storm soon passed, but it was a couple of frigid and exhausting days for everyone, especially for Charleigh, who despite battling the lingering effects of the flu every morning upon rising was right beside Josh and her crew, pre-sunrise to post-sunset, day in, day out. Derrick's cold got worse before it got better, and she made him stay home with Ruby.

After a particularly long and exhausting day, well past lunch time, Josh finally called a halt, declaring he'd starve if he didn't eat. They were closer to his place than hers, so they went there for a quick bite. She'd found that after she moved around, the nausea passed, so by lunchtime she was ready to eat an entire steer.

First stop for her was Josh's bedroom and to the only working bathroom. She seemed to have to pee every five minutes these days.

Josh was sitting on the edge of his bed when she came out. "What are you hungry for?" he asked.

Her eyes met his, reading a hunger there that had little to do with food. In a response more powerful than words, she knocked him back onto the bed and lay on him, a tangle of arms, legs, hands and kissed him.

He rolled them over and left a trail of kisses across her face, down her neck. He palmed her breasts as he took her mouth again, and she wrapped her legs around him, arching up and hard against his bulge.

They didn't hear the front door open or close, but they did hear, from the living room, Quino let loose with a string of Spanish. The increasing volume of his voice told them he was headed toward the bedroom.

They separated quickly but not before he'd entered the bedroom.

"*Aye, mierda*," he said and quickly turned around and left the room. "Sorry, Josh. Miz Simms."

"What it is, Quino," Josh called out as he and Charleigh got off the bed.

"The *vaca* we brought in to watch?" he responded from just outside the door. "She's struggling, and it's been about an hour."

"We'll be right there."

They heard Quino's retreating footsteps and the front door opening and closing.

"Sorry," he said, pulling her into his arms. As if seeing the disappointment in her eyes, he added, "We'll get our chance."

She grinned. "You promise?"

"I promise." He kissed her, letting his lips cling to hers for a hungry moment. "You ready to birth a calf?"

"You bet."

"Derrick should see this. You think he's well enough to come over?"

"He'd never forgive us if we didn't let him see it."

He called Ruby on the way to the barn and asked her to bring Derrick over to watch.

In the pen, the cow was bellowing, kicking at her stomach.

"She's hurting," Charleigh said after several minutes had passed with no progress. "Can we do anything to help her?"

Josh nodded. "Wash up with me." Pulling off his long-sleeved shirt, Charleigh doing the same, they washed up at the sink. When they went back to the pen, Derrick stood with Ruby nearby, his eyes as big as saucers.

Josh went into the pen and took a moment to rub the nervous heifer's head and speak low to her, then he got into position behind the cow, Charleigh beside him.

"Hold her tail up," he told her.

She did as he asked, and he gently stuck a hand up inside the cow and felt around. He pulled out then wiped his hands on a cloth Quino tossed him.

"This is the cow's first delivery," he explained to Charleigh, "and the calf is too big. If we don't get it out, both of them could die."

"What do we do?"

"We pull."

Quino handed him ropes, and Josh reached back inside the cow, taking a rope inside the womb. "I'm putting a half-hitch on the fetlock joint of both feet and a second just below the knee. It minimizes injury and prevents the rope from cutting into the calf's legs," he said. "Spreads out the pressure."

He held on to the ropes while she scooted in front of him, and took hold of the ropes near his hands.

"Pull in an out-and-down motion," he explained. "We need to work with the cow's pelvis and gravity to force the calf out."

Charleigh got a good grip on the rope and together they pulled. She was pulling so hard she was nearly horizontal with each tug. Again and again, they pulled and were finally rewarded with the emergence of the calf's two front legs.

"I see it," she said, excited by the first sign that their efforts were working.

"Keep it up."

The cow was bellowing, but they were unrelenting as they pulled. The calf's nose finally peeked through, its long, thick tongue hanging from its mouth.

"That's it, *mamita*," Josh murmured to the cow, his voice calm and soothing. "You're doing fine."

Mamita pushed, Charleigh and Josh pulled. Again and again. Soon the calf's entire head appeared. Shortly thereafter, its shoulders pushed through. Another few pushes and pulls and the entire body slid out, plopping with a wet smack onto the layer of hay between Charleigh's legs, bloody and slimy amniotic fluid covering its matted hide.

Josh quickly pulled the calf away from behind the mother and cleared the goop from its nose and mouth.

"He's not moving," Charleigh said.

"Or breathing." Josh straddled the calf, grabbed a straw of hay, and tickled the calf's nose. "CC, rub the calf, vigorously."

She knelt beside him and rubbed the calf's side, up and down, with both hands, jiggling it, trying to force its lungs to take that first breathe. In seconds, it began to make wheezing sounds and drew its first breaths of life. At the sight of the little thing opening its big brown eyes, Josh sighed in relief, then untied the ropes and motioned for Charleigh to stand back.

"Untie her, so she can meet her son," he said to Quino, who had remained by the cow's head to control her movements.

Quino loosened the halter ropes, and the cow

turned to her calf, licking it, bonding with it, imprinting her scent on it.

"Should we help him up?" Charleigh asked Josh.

"He'll figure it out."

Soon the newborn started thrashing, trying to get up. Finally finding its feet, on wobbly legs it wandered to its mother. Josh guided its head to her ready udder. At the first taste of mama's milk, the calf began sucking eagerly.

Seeing the new life, seeing the pride on Josh's face filled her with indescribable joy. He had brought this living thing into the world. He had saved it and the mother. If he hadn't intervened, they both might have died. A good rancher knew these things and acted accordingly, taking care of business, not when it was convenient, but when it was required. That's the kind of man he was. The kind of man she wanted. Without contemplating the action, she wrapped her arms around his waist. Despite onlookers, he put his arm around her, too.

"You did good, CC," he whispered against her forehead then pressed a kiss to that spot.

After a few minutes watching the calf nurse hungrily, Josh left Charleigh's side and gathered up the equipment they'd used. "Let's give them some time alone. Help me clean up?"

With a nod, she followed him out of the pen and back to the sink at the far end of the barn. Together, they cleaned up, and he showed her how to clean and sanitize the equipment before putting it away.

When they had stopped back at the pen for a last check on mama and baby, she noticed the barn had cleared out, the hands moving on to other duties. She didn't see Derrick or Ruby, either, so she figured they'd gone home.

The job done, she and Josh headed to his house. They pulled off their dirty clothes in the mudroom where the washer-dryer was and got their clothes washing so she'd have something clean to wear home. Then she grabbed his hand to pull him toward his bedroom. In a surprise move, he picked her up in his arms and carried her there.

They were going to get their chance, and they were getting it now.

****

Hot water beat down over their intertwined bodies, allowing Josh's palms to glide easily over the soft swells of Charleigh's slick, soapy flesh as easily as her hands were over his hard, ready body. He kissed her, bit her lips, sucked her tongue into his mouth before kissing down her neck, her chest, and lower, relishing every taste and not moving on until he'd committed each to memory.

A quiver raced through his body when she slid her hands down along his stomach to the hardness jutting from between his legs, stoking the desire between them.

"Take me to bed," she breathed the plea against his mouth after they'd washed and rinsed, then leaned in and nipped his bottom lip.

Without further discussion or contemplation, he turned off the water, flung open the curtain, and grabbed the towel hanging on the rack. He hurriedly dried her, then himself, and she grabbed his hand, leading the way to his bed and jumping in. Before climbing in beside her, he pulled a string of condoms from the bedside table, tore one off, and dropped the string onto the table.

"I see you're prepared this time," she teased.

He chuckled. "Mistakes, lessons." He then broke the speed record for rolling on a condom and joined her on the bed.

Laughing, she fit her body to his, arms and legs wrapped around him, and he pulled her close, letting the scent and feel of her draw him the rest of the way in. His hands roamed the curves of her ass, the smoothness of her back, the lean muscles of her thigh draped over his. Her hands roamed his shoulders, and her fingers curled into his hair to hold his mouth against her as his lips traced the line of her jaw.

"Josh," she breathed, arching into him. "I want you. Don't make me wait any longer."

Her words thrumming in his ears alongside his pulse, he eased over her. Keeping his eyes on hers, he entered her slowly, fully, filling her, his entire body clenching at the feel of her sweet heat surrounding him again.

At the moment of connection, her breath suspended and her eyes fluttered closed. Her head fell back, a broken sigh easing from her lips. And she smiled. She smiled at the joy of being connected with him again.

He didn't move. He just stared into her face. Her beautiful face. The face he saw in his dreams. He still couldn't believe he was with her, where he'd always wanted to be, their bodies connected in love.

Her eyes opened half way open to meet his. "What's wrong?" she whispered.

He shook his head, his eyes dancing over hers. "Absolutely nothing." Everything was perfect.

"You're not moving," she said, arching her hips up

into him.

"I want to live in this moment with you forever," he said.

Her fingers slid up into his hair, caressing him, and she leaned up and kissed his mouth. "I love you, Josh Flores."

"I love you, Charleigh…" He didn't know what name to call her. She was no longer Cooper or Simms.

"Flores," she whispered. "Can we pretend it's Flores? Pretend that we got married all those years ago?"

"Charleigh Flores. I love you."

He kissed her deeply, feeding the blaze flaring between them, and started to move in a slow, patient rhythm meant to tease out her climax breath by breath, kiss by kiss, touch by touch until it ripped her soul from her body.

However, her thighs locking around his hips, her core gripping him tight and deep, changed the game, and he accelerated the pace, knowing she was as desperate for release as he was. Every brisk but deep stroke had him fighting hard to hold on to the thin rope tethering him to this world, wanting her to find her pleasure first and lead the way to heaven.

But then she gasped, grunted, every muscle in her body tensing, and she unraveled completely in his arms, his mouth capturing hers to swallow her familiar cries of pleasure. Her every groan, every shattered breath, every trembling shudder combined into one force that sent him roaring after her, a tsunami of pleasure taking him.

The world fell away under them, stranding them in this moment, on this slim slice of paradise where he and

Charleigh lived and loved and breathed each other. It was all that existed, but it was fading fast, dissolving like the fiery sunset dissolving into the frigid darkness of the late March day.

He came back to himself still connected to her, their chests heaving in sync, passion-slicked bodies tied together in a knot of love and satisfaction. He met her hazy gaze and saw pleasure still flickering through her like a firefly through a dark summer night.

He could do this all day, every night—put that look on her face—and it would never be enough to say *enough*. He had to find a way to make sure he got the chance.

Touching his lips to hers in a loving caress, again and again, he drank in her essence, her taste, her sighs, wanting to fill up on her while he could, knowing the end could be closer than he thought. But he wouldn't think about that now.

Easing back, he smiled and caressed her face. "I'll be right back." Kissing her once more, he left her arms and went to the bathroom.

Disposing of the condom after sex was a simple act, something he'd done hundreds of times. But this time, it meant something more than just sexual satiation. This time it was marking the significant act that had just occurred between him and Charleigh.

They'd acknowledged their love, shared their love, and showed their love in the most awe-inspiring way humans could. Now that he'd experienced the joy of her again, he wouldn't give it up. No matter how complicated things got between them, he would fight to keep her this time.

Hurrying back to bed, he climbed in and wrapped

around her, ready to love away any barriers that could thwart that plan.

****

Charleigh couldn't stop smiling. But it wasn't just on the outside, on her mouth. She was smiling on the inside, more content than she'd been in a long time— since the last time she'd made love with Josh. In his arms was where she'd always found peace.

Unfortunately, things were complicated between them and would remain that way until she knew how he'd react to her secret. But no matter how complicated it got, she wanted him, wanted to be with him, and she'd do everything in her power to have him.

His calling her Charleigh Flores as they made love had been a dream come true. Something she'd wanted forever. Something she'd dreamed about. Her heart was so full in her chest, her lungs barely had room to breathe. The sound of him saying it would stay with her forever, even if he didn't.

Josh's phone rang, pricking her bubble of bliss and allowing the world to seep in. "Don't answer it," she said, draping her leg around him, hoping he'd ignore the interruption and let them stay in this fairy tale a little longer.

"It's Ruby," he said, holding out the phone.

Worried it might be about Derrick, she took it. "Hi, Ruby. Everything okay?"

"Oh, everything's just fine. I was just wondering whether to expect y'all for supper."

"Josh and I'll be there in about an hour." She smiled when he held up two fingers. "How's Derrick? What did he think about the birth?"

Ruby didn't respond immediately, but when she

did, her voice trembled with worry. "Charleigh, he told me you said he could stay, so after the birth I left him in the barn and came on home."

The panic in Ruby's voice squeezed her heart and echoed in her response. "I'll call you back," she said, then hung up and jumped out of bed.

"Oh, God. I've got to find him," she said after explaining to Josh what Ruby said.

"Let's start with the barn," he said as he buttoned and zipped his jeans. She pulled on the T-shirt he handed her, and they rushed out of the bedroom.

Josh caught her arm as they passed the living room and pointed to the couch. Derrick was curled up under the afghan Charleigh had made for Josh for Christmas, sleeping. She took a step toward him, but Josh caught her arm.

"Let him sleep," he whispered. "I'll get supper going in a bit, and we'll wake him up to eat. In the meantime…" He took her hand and pulled her back to bed.

After calling Ruby and letting her know they'd found Derrick and that they were staying for supper at Josh's, she and Josh crawled back into bed, and they took the long, slow route to round two in paradise.

****

From the warmth and comfort of Charleigh's arms, Josh stared out the bedroom window. The elements that made up his ranch stood ebony in the ivory moonlight. In his mind, he pictured each building, each piece of equipment, each stretch of fence, each corral, each pasture of cattle and field of alfalfa, each windmill and water tank. It was all his. At one time, he could have left this place. Easily.

But not now.

His sweat and blood were in this ranch. It's all he knew. And he liked it. Hell, he loved it. He hadn't always because of his dad, because of the painful memories of the people he'd loved leaving him. But with his dad's death, he'd made peace with the ghosts of the past and had made this place home.

He thought about today. Charleigh in the barn with him, them working as a team. Her in his house. In his bed. Her making love to him so eagerly and lovingly. It was even better than before, when she was his whole world and nothing else mattered. She belonged here, with him. And he hoped she'd stay. Because of him. Because of them. Because of the love between them.

But he wasn't a hundred percent certain she would.

They'd said their I love you's and made love, but they hadn't labeled their relationship. Were they together or not? Dating or just having sex? To him, it wasn't just nostalgia, scratching an itch, a convenient distraction that would last as long as she was here and fade the second she sold the ranch. To him, the thing between them was—and always had been—love. But what was it to her? The gut-wrenching feeling that this was all temporary lodged in his heart.

They would have that discussion, but one thing he knew for sure was that it had to be her choice to stay. He wouldn't try to manipulate that choice. If she wouldn't stay, he'd have to let her go. He'd learned that lesson when his mom had left. The memory was strong of his trying to get his granddad to drive him around to look for her and beg her to come back. His granddad had comforted him, dried his tears, but told him that when someone decides they want to leave, don't beg them to stay. Love has to be a gift, not a cage, he'd said.

The meaning in those wise words, in that gentle hug, being that if his mother had loved him enough, she would have stayed. By the same token, if Charleigh loved him enough, she'd stay. End of story.

Yeah, end of story, but it didn't ease the bitter uncertainty balled up in his chest. He swallowed it down, deep, before it broke open and had him forgetting his granddad's lesson.

At least he had her in this moment, and in an instinctive move of pure possession, he drew her body tighter against his.

She turned to face him and snuggled against him, finding his lips with hers and sliding her hand between them, caressing and stroking him awake. "Are you ready to go again?"

He didn't say anything.

"Are you okay?" she whispered, her tone telling him she sensed something was wrong.

He wouldn't beg, but he would tell her what he needed. "If you're going to leave me again, tell me. I deserve to hear you say goodbye."

Her eyebrows furrowed briefly before smoothing out. She cupped his face and kissed his lips. "I will, baby. I promise. But right now, I'm here with you, and I'm not going anywhere."

She kissed him again and rose up over him to join her body with his, rocking against him in a rhythm their bodies had perfected years ago. And for a few sweet moments, only pleasure consumed his mind, body, and soul, pushing aside every ambiguous thought, every feeling but the love for her that was racing through his veins, keeping him alive.

****

"How about I make us something to eat?" Charleigh offered with an amused chuckle half an hour later when Josh's stomach growled.

"How about I do it?" he said.

"You can cook?"

"Bacon and eggs."

She grinned. "My favorite."

"I wouldn't turn down your help, though. We make a good team."

She kissed him. "We do." She got up. "But I need a shower first."

While she jumped into the shower, he washed his hands and face and rinsed his mouth. Before leaving the bathroom to her, he laid one of his T-shirts and a pair of boxers on the toilet seat for her to wear, then pulled on his jeans and T-shirt. He headed to the mudroom to put her clothes in the dryer so she'd have something to wear when she went home. After starting the dryer, he headed to the kitchen.

Derrick was standing at the fridge, door open, looking in.

Josh stood beside him, reached out his hand and tussled his hair, and gave him a look that said, *boy, you're in trouble.*

As if Derrick could read it, he gave him a sheepish little grin. "I just wanted to stay here with you and Mom."

"You should have let us know."

"I know. I'm sorry. But you guys were kinda busy."

Yes, they were. "You hungry?"

397

Sophia Ryan

"Starving."

Josh pulled eggs, bacon, butter, and milk from the fridge.

"Are we having breakfast?" Derrick asked.

"We're having breakfast for supper because it's quick and I'm starving, too. Wash up. You can help me."

He got the bacon to frying as Derrick dragged the little step stool from the corner of the room to the sink and washed up. He then scooted it to where Josh stood at the counter.

Josh cracked an egg into a bowl to show him how it was done. Derrick picked up an egg and tried it. The yoke broke.

"Oops!" Derrick looked worried.

"Scrambled eggs it is," Josh said.

Derrick grinned. "My favorite."

"Mine, too." Josh cracked another four eggs into the bowl, splashed a little milk in it, and handed Derrick a fork. "Stir that up."

"You and Mom slept together again," Derrick said, stirring.

Josh added salt and pepper to the mix. "Um..."

"Do you love each other again?"

His eyes met Derrick's, and he nodded. "Yeah."

"You guys getting married?"

The memory of his calling her Charleigh Flores as they'd made love triggered a soft grin. "We haven't talked about it yet," he said. But they damn sure *would* talk about it.

"Well, if you want to, get married, I mean, I'm okay with it."

"Good to know."

When the bacon was ready, Josh cooked the eggs while Derrick put slices of bread in the toaster.

"I like Ruby's biscuits better than toast," Derrick said.

"Me, too, but I don't bake."

"You should eat at our house every day, then you can have biscuits all the time."

"I'll keep it in mind."

Josh dished up the food into three plates and set two of them on the table, leaving the third covered on the stove to keep warm. He had walked back to the counter to pour himself a cup of coffee when Derrick said, "Hey, Mom."

Charleigh stood in the doorway in his T-shirt and boxers, her wet hair pulled up into a messy bun secured with a pen she'd found. It did something to his heart, turned it to mush, seeing her there. In his shirt. In his house. His touch and kisses and scent and love marking her body.

"Hey, yourself," she said. She moved to the table and kissed Derrick on the top of his head. Then she went to Josh, leaned in, and kissed him on the mouth.

Happy but surprised she didn't hold back just because they were in front of Derrick, he slid an arm around her waist and eased her closer to deepen the kiss.

When she pulled back and met his eyes, the love sparkling in their depths assured him she was on board with their relationship.

"Hi," she whispered.

"Hi. Hungry?"

"Starving." She grinned and pressed into him, only slightly but enough that he knew exactly what she was

Sophia Ryan

hungry for. Vivid images of what he'd do to her if they were alone in the kitchen pushed him to kiss her again. "Have a seat. I'll bring you a plate."

"Thank you."

She sat in the chair facing Derrick. "You know we need to talk about earlier."

"About you and Josh sleeping together?"

Her gaze darted to Josh as he set the plate in front of her. "About you lying to Ruby and not telling Josh and me that you were here," she clarified as Josh took his seat.

"Ruby said I shouldn't say a word while we were watching 'cause it would upset the momma cow." He shoveled more egg into his mouth. "You make the best eggs, Josh."

"You were right to do what Ruby told you," Charleigh said to refocus them, "but after it was over, you should have told us you were still here."

"Well, I was going to, but then you guys were taking your clothes off. So I just sat on the couch waiting, and when you guys didn't come back, I fell asleep."

"Do you need to talk about what you saw?" she asked. "With Josh and me?"

"Nope. Josh said you guys love each other again."

Her face warmed, and a soft grin lifted her lips. "Yes, but back to the lying. You told Ruby I said it was okay for you to stay. You never asked me if you could stay."

He set his fork down. "I just really wanted to stay with you and Josh."

"Derrick, you and I have talked a lot about how important it is to be a man of your word," Josh said.

400

"But I never promised anything to Ruby, I just—"

"Lying is just as bad as going back on a promise. And not telling somebody something or hiding it on purpose is the same as lying."

Derrick's eyes darted to Charleigh, then back to Josh. "What if you have to lie for a good reason?"

He shook his head. "There's never a good reason to lie."

"Well," Charleigh interjected, "there's those lies you tell because you don't want to hurt someone's feelings."

"But it's best to tell the truth," Josh jumped back in. "If people know you're a liar, they won't trust anything you tell them, and if they don't trust you, they aren't going to want to have anything to do with you. Honesty and trust go hand-in-hand. They're everything, Derrick. Without them, you can't build or keep good relationships. And without good relationships…well, that's a sad and lonely way to live."

Derrick's gaze dropped to his plate. "I'm sorry I lied. I won't do it again." Then the boy's crystal blue eyes caught Josh's, and the strength in that connection made the hairs on the back of his neck stand up. "Do you still love me?"

Josh had to blink his eyes a couple of times to push back the twinge in his jaw. The "of course" rolled off his tongue before he realized he was going to say it. The second it was out, he realized it was absolutely true. He loved this kid. Will's kid. No. Charleigh's kid. And, if he had anything to say about it, his kid.

Derrick jumped up and launched himself at Josh, hugged him, and Josh hugged him back, amazed again at the kid's outpouring of love that included him.

"I love you, too, Josh. So much."

When Derrick left his arms and went to Charleigh to hug her, Josh took to his feet and refilled his coffee cup to get his emotions under control. He looked back at the two of them, in that moment realizing they were the best part of his life, and that he couldn't give it up.

****

Charleigh smoothed back Derrick's hair and kissed his forehead. "You'll need to apologize to Ruby for lying and for worrying her and ask her to forgive you. I know she will because she loves you. And when you love someone, you forgive them."

She felt like a hypocrite, chastising Derrick for lying while she was asking him to keep their secrets, like his birthdate and the state of their finances before they'd come here. Of course, technically, in her mind, secrets weren't lies, but it still felt sickening, made worse by the look Derrick had given her when he asked Josh whether it was sometimes okay to lie and he'd said no.

When they got home, Derrick apologized to Ruby for lying. They hugged and, as she predicted, all was forgiven. She hoped Josh and Derrick would be as forgiving when she told them her lie, er, secret.

Or maybe even two.

Charleigh's assumption was that what had gripped her since the snow storm was a lingering case of the flu. But while vomiting and exhaustion easily could be attributed to the flu, a missed period could not. Her suspicion about what was really going on prompted a trip into Wilton a week later. She did not want the busybodies in Chismes Point to see the item she bought.

She stopped at a fast food place on her way out of

402

town and rushed into the restroom. Locked behind a stall door, she took the small box she'd bought at the drug store from her purse and opened it. At the results moments later, her cheeks flushed and her heart swelled like a balloon in her chest.

This time she'd do this the right way. She'd tell Josh about this baby, and together they'd decide what was next. While she was at it, she'd tell him about his other child, too, and pray he didn't hate her for not telling him sooner. After all, it was a secret, not a lie. And she'd had a good reason for keeping it.

Telling Josh might risk everything she'd worked so hard for, might make him so angry that he cancelled the contract and refused to have anything to do with her or his kids. But telling him was the right thing to do. Always had been.

He loved her, but did he love her enough? She'd find out tonight.

The sense of déjà vu sent a chill up her spine.

Josh and Derrick were home from their shooting lesson by the time she got home, and Derrick was full of excitement about the bullseyes he'd gotten. He was practically glued to Josh's side, and Ruby was in the kitchen, making supper, and then Cole came in, drawing him into a conversation about tonight's cattlemen's meeting, which she'd forgotten about.

Her news would have to wait. It wasn't something to be rushed through. After they got home from the meeting and put Derrick to bed, she'd pull Josh to her bed, make love to him, and then tell him he was going to be a father. For the second time.

****

The meeting droned on and on, much longer than

403

she'd thought it would. Everyone and their dog seemed to want their fifteen minutes of mic fame. Derrick had fallen asleep on Josh's shoulder an hour into the meeting.

"I should get him home," she whispered to Josh.

He glanced at Derrick, then checked his watch.

"I can drive us home," she said. "I know you need to stay."

"You sure?"

"I'm sure." She leaned in to whisper in his ear. "But I'll wait up for you."

He leaned in, too. "It might be pretty late."

"I'll wait up."

He grinned then turned to Quino and Cole, who sat on her other side. "Charleigh's going to get Derrick home. I'll carry him out and be right back. Can you two listen for any substantial information if it comes?"

"Sure thing, Josh," Cole said. Quino nodded.

Josh picked up Derrick and started down the bleachers, Charleigh behind him, her finger hooked in his belt loop.

"Well, now, ain't that a familiar sight," said the chairman of the local association, Harlan Schmidt, as they headed to the door. "Josh and Charleigh rushing off to his pickup."

They turned to face him.

"Y'all ever figure out what it is they're doing in there?" he snickered.

At the chuckling crowd, Josh's jaw working showed his annoyance, but his response was calm. "Chairman, maybe you should focus your attention on doing the job the good people of this community voted you into office to do—keeping our subsidies—and stop spreading gossip."

At the crowd's applause, Josh settled his hand at her back and guided her toward the door.

He got Derrick into the SUV, clicked the seatbelt around him, and closed the door. He wrapped his arms around her, drew her close, and kissed her. "See you in a bit. Love you."

She smiled. Hearing him say he loved her never got old. "Love you," she said, leaving his arms and climbing into the SUV. He shut the door, and she started the engine and headed home. In the rearview mirror, she saw him watching her go, hand raised in farewell.

She couldn't lose him. God, please let tonight work out.

****

Cole's pickup arrived nearly two hours later. Josh got out and headed to the house door. She had been waiting for him and was able to open it before he knocked and woke Ruby and Derrick. She went into his arms and kissed him, then took his hand and tried to lead him into the house. He dug his heels in, nodded toward his SUV.

"I want you in my bed tonight," she whispered.

"Not a good idea."

"Why not?"

"You heard Harlan. That's how the whole town thinks, and that's without proof. You want it spread all over town that your ranch manager sleeps in your bed—with your son and your ranch hands just feet away?"

"No one here will say anything."

"Not on purpose, but all it would take is one slip—

Derrick telling Nikki I spent the night, Nikki telling her mom, her mom telling everybody she knows, and soon the whole town knows."

"So what if they do? It's none of anyone's business but mine who I invite into my bed."

"You know that's not how it works in this town."

"I'm so damn tired of that argument," she said and pulled away from him. "I can't believe you're asking me to stay and raise Derrick in this kind of ridiculousness."

"I haven't asked you to stay. That's up to you."

"Don't do that."

"Do what? Be honest?"

"Pretend you don't give a damn whether I stay or go."

"I've made it perfectly clear I want you to stay. But whether you do is your call, not mine. That's all I'm saying."

"We don't have to stay here, Josh—you, me, Derrick. We'll have enough money from the sale of this place to go anywhere and do anything we want. You could finish your vet degree, practice anywhere you want. We could start over in a place where no one cares what we do or don't do."

"Listen to me, Charleigh." He grabbed her arms. "I love you, and I love Derrick, but I'm not leaving here. My blood, sweat, and tears are in this land now. I won't give it up. Especially to live off goddamn Simms money. If you want to be with me, it has to be here. In this community. At *my* ranch."

She shrugged off his grip and stepped back. "Six years ago, school was your priority, and what I needed came last. Now, your ranch is your priority, and again,

I'm last. But now I have Derrick's welfare to consider, and I want more for him than growing up in this judging, tight-ass community with a father who puts him last."

His face blanked stone-cold at her words, only his eyes showing emotion, like an ice storm come unleashed. "Is this your warning that you're leaving me?"

"Why should I stay?"

Pain flashed in those eyes before transforming to anger. "You're the only one who can answer that, sweetheart," he growled, his voice hard and bitter, his lips and eyes narrow with fury. In a furious stride he marched to the SUV.

Instead of heeding the advice of the voice inside her screaming for her to run after him, pull him into her arms, and fix this before it was too late, she watched him climb in and tear off down the road. Her heart sliced open and aching, dripping emotion like blood, she went inside.

Ruby stood in the kitchen in her fuzzy robe and pin curls. "Everything all right?" she asked, although she had to have heard their argument and known that everything was anything but all right.

Charleigh tried to keep her composure, but the tears were coming. She shook her head and broke down. "No. Everything sucks."

Ruby hugged her, then led her to the kitchen table and sat her down in one of the chairs, taking the one next to it. "What's the problem?" she asked, patting her arm in a motherly fashion.

"It's complicated," Charleigh said, wiping her eyes with her fingertips.

"Matters of the heart usually are." She handed her a tissue from the box on the kitchen counter. "Let's you and me put our heads together and see if we can't uncomplicate it a bit."

Charleigh nodded and dabbed her tears but didn't comment. It was times like these that she missed her mother most, so she was glad to have Ruby, who had become somewhat of a surrogate mom in the seven months she'd been here.

"You love Josh. Josh loves you. Do I have everything right so far?" Ruby asked.

"Yes." Charleigh said with a sniffle.

"You love each other, but you're fighting. What about?"

"Everything."

"Name one."

"He wants us to stay here, but I don't know if I can."

"Why?"

"Because everyone is so judgmental and I don't want Derrick growing up in that atmosphere."

"Who's judging you and Derrick?"

"Everyone."

"Name one."

"Oh, c'mon, Ruby, you know as well as I do that everyone in this community is talking about us, about Josh and me, and Josh is letting it determine his behavior."

"So, there's something you want him to do and he won't do it because of what people might think. Is that right?"

"Yes."

"What do you want him to do that he won't?"

Heat flared in Charleigh's cheeks. "I wanted him to stay the night with me, here, in my house. He said that if people found out, it would affect how they treat us. I say it's none of anybody's business."

"Josh is right. It's the way it is in small towns."

"It never bothered him before."

"He's a different man now. Your running off with Will Simms changed him."

This was the first time Ruby indicated she knew what happened between her and Josh.

"Do you have any idea what happened to him after you left?" Ruby asked.

After living here again, she had a pretty good idea. "Not really."

"Most people pitied him. Some laughed at him behind his back. A few were hateful enough to laugh in his face. He didn't come back here for a long time, 'til his daddy, Sam, got sick. It wasn't easy for him to come back, face down his humiliation. Your leaving him the way you did connected him more with his dad in the town's eyes. Like father, like son, they said. You know his momma, Angela, ran off with the sheriff when Josh was a little boy. Left a note. Didn't even have the decency of telling him to his face."

Charleigh knew. What's more, she knew that every female Josh had ever loved had left him—his sister and grandmother died, his mother abandoned him, and then she did. He already felt unwanted because of everyone he'd lost and because of how his dad treated him afterward, but her leaving had been the nail in his ego's coffin. Looking back didn't do any good, but every day she wished they could go back and change that night their lives fell apart.

"Sam had pretty much run the ranch into the ground. He spent more time keeping that barstool warm than working his ranch, and businesses refused to lend him credit, saying he was unreliable. All his hands left because they weren't getting paid. Only Quino stayed out of loyalty to the family. That's what Josh came home to. Not only did he have to get the ranch back on track, he also had to overcome the stain on his family name and rebuild his own reputation."

Charleigh sat in stunned silence. The realization that he'd had to overcome so much and do it all on his own broke her heart. She wished she'd been by his side, helping him, making his burden lighter instead of adding to it.

"He worked hard to get past it, to get people to see him as a good, honorable, trustworthy man," Ruby continued. "That ranch of his has never been more successful, and his reputation has never been better. And now, here you are, back in town. If he's going back to the woman who cheated on him, it calls into question his good sense. Once a fool, always a fool, they say. Being wrapped around a lying woman's finger ain't a good position for a strong, proud man to be in."

"I never lied to him or cheated on him."

"You ran off with Will after being head over boots in love with Josh. Now you're back, claiming the Simms fortune and trying to reclaim Josh now that your husband is in the grave. Can you see why people would find that tasty cud to chaw on?"

"I guess."

"Josh cares about his reputation, but he also cares about yours and Derrick's. He knows that how people see you affects your standing in the community, affects your ability to do business the way you need to, affects Derrick's ability to get along and find his place here."

Ruby's opinion mattered, but that didn't mean the community was right in negatively judging her for actions she couldn't defend herself against. "No one knows why I did what I did. Why can't they mind their own business?"

Ruby's resolve remained firm. "Because this is how the small-town game is played. You play according to the rules or you pay."

"I had no choice. I did what I did for Derrick."

"You up and leave the love of your life without even the courtesy of a goodbye…for your son's sake?" Ruby shook her head. "I'll be the first to admit I'm a few sandwiches short of a picnic, but that just don't make sense to this old brain of mine."

She loved Ruby, but the woman was a master gossiper. If she told her the story, it would be all over town in a matter of days, hours maybe. Which might not be a bad thing except for the possibility that Josh would hear it from someone else before she'd had a chance to tell him herself.

"Isn't it time you unpacked that weighty burden you been carrying all these years?" Ruby asked.

Charleigh had wanted Josh to be the first to know everything, but Ruby was right. She needed to tell someone. Steeling herself with a deep breath, she spilled the truth, the whole truth. Through it all, Ruby didn't blink, didn't balk, didn't react. It was almost like she already knew.

"I love Josh," Charleigh continued. "He's the only man I've ever wanted to be with. But I don't think that'll matter to him when he learns the truth."

"Maybe not, but he needs to know. And so does Derrick," Ruby said.

"I was going to tell Josh tonight. But we fought. Again."

"You fight because the secrets act like a wall between you. You and Josh belong together. What I don't understand is why you're holding back."

"He has the ability to destroy the contract. And if he's that mad that I didn't tell him about Derrick, he might do it, and then Derrick and I will have nothing, nowhere to go."

"Do you really think Josh would do that to his own son?"

She shrugged. "I don't know."

"Yes, you do. You know he wouldn't. Not just because Derrick's his son, but because that's not the kind of man he is. He had refused Wyatt's contract to work with you until Wyatt threatened to disinherit Derrick. Despite how hard it would be for him to see you again, he agreed to the contract so Derrick wouldn't lose everything."

"Okay. You're right. He wouldn't do that to Derrick, but I won't get off so lucky. Trust is a huge issue with Josh. This news could destroy every bit of trust and love he has for me."

"The reality is that he's Derrick's father. And that baby's father." Ruby's eyes cut to Charleigh's stomach then back to her shocked face. "I've never been fortunate enough to have my own children, but I've been around enough pregnant women to spot the signs."

Charleigh nodded. "From February, when he and I…"

"Yeah, I remember." She chuckled. "It was written

all over your face and his."

She shook her head. "I was so embarrassed you guys caught us."

"I'm surprised we didn't catch you more often. There's so much love and passion between you two, it sizzles in the air when you're within fifty feet of each other."

"I love him, Ruby. With all my heart."

"And he loves you. But whether you and Josh end up together is less important than Derrick and that baby knowing their father."

She nodded. If Josh were a bad man, a terrible father, then that would be a reason to keep them apart. But he wasn't. He was a wonderful man and a loving father figure to Derrick. He loved him. He deserved to know his son, and Derrick deserved to know his father.

"You said you went with Will so Derrick would have a mother and father who loved him. Well, you have that now, here, with Josh. You always did. If your kids are your priority, then do what's best for them. That means letting Josh have a place in their life as their father, whether or not he has a place in your life as your husband."

Chapter Twenty-One

Josh showed up Saturday morning as usual for their ride and for Derrick's shooting lesson, but he didn't hang around afterward like he usually did.

He didn't come by Sunday while Ruby and Cole were at church.

He didn't come by early for breakfast or stay for supper on weekdays.

And when he was there, he barely spoke to Charleigh and even was a bit distant with Derrick, just going through the motions. Derrick noticed it, too, and seemed intent on punishing her for it by becoming sulky and determined to challenge her on nearly every issue. They were all miserable. And it wouldn't get any better when she told Josh her secrets.

Her heart-to-heart with Ruby had made her realize that whatever role Josh ended up playing in their lives, she had to make a place for her and Derrick in this community. She wouldn't take him from Josh again, unless that's what Josh ultimately wanted. A first step to making her place would be to get to know people and get involved.

She had already been helping Ruby behind the scenes with her various fundraising projects, so when she asked her to come to the planning meeting for the spring fundraiser for the elementary school, which needed new playground equipment, she agreed to go.

She took Derrick with her to play with the kids who would be there. With him not in school, she wanted to give him every opportunity to be around kids his age.

"I recommend we do what we did last year," Beth said as soon as the meeting was called to order. "A dance, with food and drinks, and an auction."

"We do that every year," Mary Rogers said with a groan, which elicited several murmurs of agreement among the dozen women at the table.

"Because it works," added the pastor's wife, Agatha Beaumont.

"I, for one, am tired of the same old thing," Ruby joined in, "and I'm sure members of our community are, too."

"So come up with an idea," Beth challenged her.

"Charleigh had an idea that'll knock your socks off clear to Texas."

The room went silent and all eyes turned to Charleigh. She'd mentioned the idea to Ruby earlier, but she thought Ruby would be the one passing it along.

"Go on and tell them your idea," Ruby prodded.

"Oh, well, it was just…" Charleigh cleared her throat and straightened in her chair, trying to turn the heat down in her cheeks. "When Derrick and I lived in California, one of the school's fundraisers had a games night theme, and it was very successful."

"You want a bunch of adults, most of them elderly, to run around playing games?" Beth snarked. "Clearly, you don't know this community."

"And we don't hold to gambling around here," Agatha added in a lecturing tone.

"I'd like to hear more about your idea, Charleigh," said Teri Barnes, Derrick's teacher and Cole's girlfriend. "What kind of games did they have?"

"It was a mixed bag. Board games set up on different tables, activity games like mini bowling and mini golf, a poker tournament. I know dominoes is big around here. We could do that in addition to or instead of card games. Plus there were food and drink booths and service booths, like hand massages, nail art, face painting, hair braiding, temporary tattoos. Will did the tattooing with markers and people really loved it."

"People here aren't interested in tattoos," Agatha said, shaking her head. "This isn't California, thank the Lord."

"I think it's a great idea," Teri said, smiling. "All of us have board games just sitting in our closets at home, and my parents still have my indoor bowling set somewhere in the garage. I'm sure we could scrounge for everything we need without having to buy much."

"How did they charge?" asked the school principal, Colleena Green. "Entry fees? Per game fees?"

"There was an entry fee, and then people bought tickets so they could visit the booths that interested them. Part of the draw, too, was that each person would get a card listing all the booths. They got a stamp from each one they visited. Those who visited every booth were entered into a drawing for a grand prize that was donated by a local merchant…a trip, movie tickets, a piece of art, dinner for two…that kind of stuff."

"We could get all the stores in town to donate something, and we'd put them all in a basket as the grand prize," Inez Garcia, Ruby's best friend, said.

"And we could all bring food for the booths," Ruby said.

"George and I'll be happy to donate soft drinks,

bottled water, and ice," Mary said.

"Everyone will be expecting us to do what we've always done, and doing something different like this is bound to pull more interest," said Kelly Iverson, the woman Will had dated through high school, who was expecting baby number three with her husband, Trey.

"We'll regret this." Beth said. "People around here like the tried and true."

"Let's put it to a vote. I say we go with Charleigh's games night idea." Ruby raised her hand, and soon every member did, too, except Beth and Agatha.

The ayes carried it, so the committee spent the next hour talking through the plan, writing it down, and assigning tasks. Will had taught her some tattooing techniques, so she volunteered to run that booth, and she and Ruby would bring appetizers and desserts for the food booth.

At the end of the meeting, Charleigh gathered up Derrick and got him buckled into the pickup. She had closed the door and walked around to the driver's side, preparing to get in, when Beth stopped her.

"I'm surprised at you, Charleigh. Getting involved in community business when you're not part of the community."

"I don't know, I felt pretty included tonight."

"A piece of friendly advice…don't let any roots get started in this soil. It'll just make it harder on your boy when you two pull up and leave."

"Who said we're leaving?"

Beth blinked a few times. "Josh said you were leaving when the contract was up. After you'd sold the ranch."

"I changed my mind. We're staying."

Beth's face turned as red as her little sports car. "Don't think you're getting Josh. He belongs with someone who understands what he needs and can help him live the life he's chosen. You've never belonged here, and you never will. You're not good for him."

Charleigh took a step closer to Beth and saw fear flash in the woman's eyes. Nice to know her badass reputation was still intact. "Look, Beth. I don't know what's going to happen between Josh and me. But just so you know, I love him, and I'm going to do everything possible to make sure we're together. I know you love him, too. My friendly advice to you is to bring your A game, because right now, I have the advantage. And I plan on keeping it."

Beth scrunched her mouth like the words she was chewing were as hard as rocks, but in the end, she said nothing, just stormed away, got into her car, and zoomed off down the road.

Ruby joined her at the pickup. "Beth congratulating you on your innovative idea?"

Charleigh grinned. "We were swapping little pieces of friendly advice."

"Sorry I missed that." Ruby chuckled as they climbed in and headed home.

****

The event plan came together quickly, and two weeks later, Charleigh and Derrick rode into town with Ruby to set up the booths and decorate for the fundraiser. People would start arriving around seven. Hopefully. If the fundraiser was a bust, she might as well pack up and leave town the minute it ended.

The second Josh entered the community center, she knew it, like her radar was on high and tuned only to him. After buying a long rope of tickets, which he methodically folded then separated and slid into his pocket, he headed into a group of men who looked to be about his age. Cole was there, as well as Lance and Randy, and a few other guys she recognized but didn't know well. They welcomed him heartily, with handshakes and back pats.

Despite his differences with some of them, he was one of them. Had been his whole life. He belonged, like they did. She was a newcomer, and always would be. Even if she lived a hundred years and died there. That knowledge brought back her conversation with Beth.

Beth and Josh had known each other their entire lives, too. They'd been born here, gone to school together, attended various activities together—from 4H and FFA to vacation bible school—knew the same people, shared similar stories, led a similar life. The daughter of a farmer, Beth understood the lifestyle Josh had chosen and would understand what he needed in a wife, a partner, the mother of his kids.

Speaking of the devil always makes her appear. Least that's what Charleigh had heard Ruby say a dozen times or more. She realized how very right she was when Beth inserted herself into the group of men and pulled Josh aside.

As they chatted, she touched him—his arm, his hand, his chest. He didn't touch her once. She looked happy, smiling and laughing. And dammit, he did, too. She took his hand and led him to the desserts booth she was running. He shook his head, refusing her offer and keeping pocketed the tickets he'd bought. For some reason, that made Charleigh happy, and she couldn't keep from smiling.

After making the rounds at most of the other booths, Josh finally came to hers.

"What do you recommend?" he asked her when he'd made it to the front of the line of mostly teens, mostly males, and sat in the chair.

She'd drawn out examples of tattoos she could do and set them on the table for people to browse through. "Do you want to look through the samples?"

"Choose something for me." He handed her a ticket.

She grinned. "Hearts and flowers it is."

He grinned, too, knowing she was kidding.

"Where on your body would you like me to put it?" she asked.

"Where do you usually put it?" he asked.

"This is a family-friendly event, so we're limited to certain body parts—wrists, hands, arms…"

"Wrist it is."

"May I help you roll up your sleeve?"

That he chose to do it himself said either he was still upset with her and didn't want her to touch him, or that he was just being careful in public. Whichever it was, watching him unsnap his cuff and roll up his sleeve conjured up anything but family-friendly thoughts in her mind. His bare arm, skin tanned to burnished gold, brought back memories of the hours she'd spent in those arms, in his bed, weeks ago. The warmth of his skin against hers when she took his hand in hers to clean and dry his wrist was a pleasure she'd missed.

Her hands trembled slightly when she picked up her fine-tipped black marker, but she gripped it firmly, focused her mind, and started drawing the symbol she knew by heart. The look in his eyes when he recognized the Flores brand appearing on his wrist was something she'd never forget. Whether the awe was for what his brand meant to him, or that she'd thought to choose it for him, she didn't know. But her choice seemed to have made him happy, and that's all that mattered.

The symbol finished, she sprinkled baby powder on it to set it, then brushed off the excess with a fluffy makeup brush and sprayed the tattoo with hairspray.

He admired her work then lifted his gaze to hers. "I'm surprised you remembered it."

"I never forgot it," she said, her gaze dancing over his. The sights and sounds and smells of the community center faded, and she allowed herself an indulgent moment to get lost in Josh's bottomless blue gaze.

"Hurry up, Josh," grumbled one of the teens in line. "The rest of us want a turn."

"Some things are worth waiting for, Chase," Josh said, maintaining eye contact with her.

"Do you want your card stamped?" she asked.

He handed it to her. She stamped it next to the tattoo booth entry and handed it back.

"Thanks," he said and started to stand.

She put her hand on his arm, the one without the tattoo, stopping him. "I'm sorry, I can't let you leave looking like that."

The guys behind him in line groaned.

"Like what?" Josh asked.

"One sleeve up, one down." She unsnapped his cuff then rolled up his sleeve to match the other one. "What would people think? Your reputation would be ruined."

She lifted her flirty gaze to his. Disappointment

421

filled his eyes instead of the humor she thought she'd see at her teasing. He stood and, without a word, walked away.

Before she could analyze what had gone wrong in that exchange, Chase, aka toe-stomper, slid into the chair. "Can you do a tattoo of you naked?"

"Sure."

Surprise and joy widened his eyes and his smile. "Really?"

"Yeah. Just bring your mommy over here to tell me she's okay with it."

At his friends' laughter, he turned red but laughed good-naturedly. "Just do what you did last time."

"A pink unicorn?"

His friends laughed again, punching his arm.

"A red and black skull."

She grinned. "You got it, dude."

****

By ten, everyone had gone home except the organizing committee, who was cleaning up. After hours of working, talking, smiling, controlling flirty boys, and trying to keep a jealous eye on Josh, Charleigh was exhausted. All she wanted was to get home and have a long, hot bath.

Ruby found her taking down and putting away the decorations so her booth could be dismantled.

"Well, gal, we did it," she said and hugged Charleigh. "People have been telling me all night how much fun they had, and that they'd enjoyed it not being the same old thing. We raised more money tonight than any other fundraiser. Thanks to you."

"I only provided the idea. Everyone made it happen," she said, smiling, pleased she had made a contribution that actually succeeded.

"It takes a community, that's for sure. The committee is so impressed with you, they want you on all the fundraising events."

"Oh. Well, I'd like that. Depending on the work load at the ranch, of course."

"Did you have fun?"

"I did. People were friendlier than I thought they'd be. When I was here before… Well, let's just say, I didn't make many friends."

"You're trying to fit in now. And they see it."

Charleigh smiled wryly. "We both know you're the reason they're willing to give me a try. So thanks."

"You know you're going to have to top this with the next event."

"Guess I better put on my thinking cap now."

Ruby laughed. "Tomorrow is soon enough. Tonight, just enjoy the thrill of success."

"I'll do that. Right after I get this booth taken down."

"No, right now, I want you to get on home, get your youngin' to bed, and get off your feet."

"I will. I'm almost finished."

Ruby leaned in a bit to whisper, "Expectant moms need lots of rest. So, as the committee chairwoman, I'm ordering you to shoo."

Charleigh glanced around to make sure no one was around to hear Ruby's words. "We can't. We rode in with you," she said in a final protest.

"That's why I asked Josh to take you home."

"Oh, Ruby, I wish you hadn't done that. You know he's—"

"Ready to go, Mom?" Derrick said behind her, and

she spun to face him.

Josh was at his side.

"Josh is giving us a ride home tonight. Isn't that great?"

There was no fighting it.

"I'll get my things." Giving Ruby the stink-eye, she grabbed her purse along with the box of tattoo supplies and emergency just-in-case office and decorating supplies she'd brought from home. Josh took the box from her hands. She was ready to argue that she could carry it but decided that she didn't want to argue at all.

"Goodnight," she said to Ruby, who was hugging Derrick.

"Night, folks. I'll be awhile, so don't wait up." She left them to join some of the others tearing down the booths.

On the drive home, Derrick chatted on like normal, thrilled to have Josh's attention again, but she and Josh said little to each other.

At the house, he surprised her by getting out, too. It was on the tip of her tongue to ask him why he was coming in but then remembered he was carrying in her box of supplies.

"Derrick, it's late, so wash up, brush your teeth, and get to bed," she said once they were in the house. "I'll be in to tell you goodnight in a bit. Josh, thanks for the ride home. I'll walk you out."

"Mom, Josh said he'd tuck me in and read me a book, remember?"

"Oh. I must have missed that."

"If it's all right," Josh asked.

"Of course."

"I'll tuck him in then head home. No need to walk me out."

"Okay. Well, goodnight then. I'm going to soak in the tub for at least an hour."

She headed to her room. Closing the door, she stood with her back against the solid surface for a few seconds and exhaled a deep sigh, numb and buzzing by the success of the night, but also by the fact that Josh was here doing daddy duty because he wanted to. He wouldn't desert Derrick. She knew it.

She kicked off her heels and undressed, tossing her clothes into the hamper. She did a few stretches to ease the kinks in her back and legs. She pulled her hair up into a high topknot and slipped into her robe. Then she sat on her bed rubbing her tired, aching feet. She wasn't used to high heels, but they'd been appropriate for the event.

Every action was performed slowly and methodically, meant to give Josh time to oversee Derrick's teeth brushing and washing up, get through a book, tuck him in, and leave the house before she came out. She was too tired to face him tonight. She'd end up saying something stupid like *take me somewhere, anywhere, and make love to me.*

After a sufficient amount of time, she headed to Derrick's room to kiss him goodnight. Through the ajar bathroom door, she heard voices. She eased it all the way open. Derrick and Josh stood side by side, facing the tub. The water was running, and Derrick had one of her bath bombs in his hand.

"She likes the green one better than the pink one," Derrick said.

Josh took it from his hand, smelled it. "'Cause

green's her favorite color?"

"Yep. And 'cause it smells like spring. Spring's her favorite season 'cause she says it brings new chances."

Josh tossed it into the tub in the stream. The scent of new plants and flowers bloomed.

"What's going on in here?" she said.

Her two guys turned toward her.

Derrick was grinning ear to ear. "Me and Josh are making your bath for you."

"I see. What did I do to deserve the princess treatment?"

Her son hugged her. "'Cause you're the best mom in the world. And Josh said you worked really hard tonight."

Her eyes darted to Josh then back. "That's really nice of you guys. Thanks."

Josh put his hand at Derrick's back. "Let's get you on to bed. We have an early day tomorrow with our ride and our shooting lesson."

"That reminds me," she said, "I'll have to pass on the shooting lesson tomorrow."

"Again?" Derrick said.

"Yeah, sorry. Ruby and I need to count the proceeds of tonight's event and write a final report, and we'll need most of the day to get it done."

"But you're still coming on the ride?" Derrick asked.

"You bet. Now tell me…did you brush good?"

"Yep. See?" He opened his mouth wide to show her his clean teeth. "I flossed, too."

"Good. Now give me a hug in case you fall asleep before I finish my bath."

He did, then turned to Josh, took his hand, and led

him to the door. "It's pretty late. How about you stay the night? You can sleep in my room. Or in the guest room. Or on the couch."

They left, closing the door behind them, so she didn't hear Josh's response. Not that she needed to. The answer would be no.

She pulled off her robe and hung it on the door hook, stepped into the tub, and lay back with a sigh, eyes closed, the hot water already doing its job easing the aches in her body. That Josh had done this for her, had been thinking about her, eased the aches in her heart.

The water hadn't had a chance to cool before Josh came in and shut the door behind him.

"That didn't take long." At his confused look, she added, "The book."

"He fell asleep halfway through. Do you mind me being in here?"

"Not at all."

He sat on the closed toilet seat and leaned forward, arms propped on his knees. Their eyes fused, and the want riding that gaze sizzled between them, heating the already steamy air. He might be upset with her, but he wanted her as much as she wanted him. That much was obvious.

Just days ago, she would have felt comfortable expressing that want, exercising that want. With no hesitation, she would have taken his hand and pulled him into the tub with her. She would have caressed and stroked his body with love and eagerness, and he would have done the same to hers. They would have joined as only they could, with soul-binding passion. But now?

"If you keep looking at me that way I'm going to

Sophia Ryan

think you want to join me in my bath," she teased and studied his expression for the answer. The light sparking in his eyes said those desires were alive, but his clenched body, his distance, said he had a tight rein on them.

"I don't take baths. Especially ones that smell like a flower garden exploded in it."

"Don't knock it until you've tried it. It's amazing," she sighed. "Thank you for this. It's just what I needed. My whole body aches, especially my feet. I'm not used to high heels."

Slow and easy, he shifted onto the edge of the tub and reached into the water, lifted her leg, setting her foot in his lap, and massaging it.

"What are you doing?"

"What does it look like?"

"It looks like you're being nice to me. It's scaring me," she said with a grin. He didn't return her grin, and her heart sank a little deeper in her chest.

"What was tonight about?" he asked.

"Um, well, it was a fundraiser..." she murmured, his hands on her skin making her entire body tingle.

"I mean, why were you involved?"

"Why wouldn't I? I live in this community. It's my home."

"For how long?"

"Seventy, eighty years hopefully." Joy spread a full smile on her lips. "I'm staying, Josh. Derrick and I are staying."

His hands stilled on her feet. "Why?"

"Several reasons."

"Like?"

"Staying is what's best for Derrick."

"Is it what's best for you?"

"Yes."

"Why?"

"Because here is where you are. Because I love you. Because I want a life with you."

****

Charleigh. His woman. His world. His life. Was staying.

His breath caught in his throat at the words he had, for months, hoped to hear her say. But now that she had, instead of it bringing the joy and relief that it would save him, it stirred up the anxiety that it would again destroy him.

He couldn't speak, couldn't move, could only stare at her. As if knowing it could be the last time he'd have the right to see her this way, his gaze slowly caressed every inch of her flushed, wet, delicious body. All he wanted was to climb into that spring-scented tub and make love to her until the water boiled from their passion. But he wouldn't. Not even for the pleasure that could heal him, at least temporarily, and let him pretend their love stood a chance this time.

"I thought you'd be happy," she said, her voice quiet. "You said it's what you wanted. Have you changed your mind about us?"

It was what he'd wanted. But now he knew it wasn't enough.

Severing his gaze from hers, he released her foot and stood, moved away from her, from the tub, from temptation. Resuming his spot on the toilet seat, he propped his arms on his knees.

"Do you know what chaff is?" he asked, staring down at the tile floor.

"Yeah," she said. "The hard outer layer of wheat that has to be removed for the grain to be usable."

He smiled inwardly at the pride lifting his heart that she'd been reading about another side of this life because she wanted to understand the full scope of the job.

"My granddad used to say that relationships were no good either unless the chaff was removed from them," he continued. "Chaff being the lies, secrets, disrespect, abuse, and anything else that blocks access to the heart of love."

"What does that have to do with us?"

"Everything," he said. "I need absolute honesty and commitment from all the people in my life, but especially from the woman I love. I need to be able to trust her with my heart, my mind, my soul, my body, my life, my reputation. I need to trust that she's willing and able to protect the vulnerable, life-sustaining grain that is our love, no matter the storms we might face."

"You have that with me."

He shook his head. "The night of the cattlemen's meeting, you threatened to leave me because I wouldn't make love to you in your bed. You asked me why you should stay, even though the reason should have been obvious—because you love me and don't want to lose me again. But you didn't say that. I realized that's how it might always be with us. I love you, Charleigh, but I can't live with constant worry that any argument we have will end up with you leaving me."

"I'm not leaving you, Josh. Ever again. I left you before, and it was the wrong decision. I should have stayed and fought for you. For us. I won't make that mistake again."

"Then fight for us now by being honest with me."

"I'm doing everything I can to show you I love you, that I want a life with you, that I want to stay here with you. If that's not fighting for us, being honest, I don't know what is."

"Tell me the secrets you're keeping from me. Secrets about you and Will, your marriage, why you left me and went with him. I don't know why you won't tell me, but until you do, until we remove that chaff, we don't stand a chance."

"First of all, I already told you why I went with him. And second, yes, there are things about my marriage I haven't shared with you. But it was *my* marriage. I get to decide what I share and what I don't. Not you."

He hung his head and glared holes in the floor trying to cool his frustration. This had been an opening for her to tell him the truth, the whole truth, to save their relationship. He had given her a chance to walk through and spill her secrets at his feet so they could sweep them up, throw them away, and move forward together.

But she didn't. Instead, she went on the defensive, like a woman who was hiding a monster that was too hideous for the light of day.

"You can have your secrets or you can have me, but not both," he said.

"I have scars and broken pieces and permanent bruises inside me from the last time I trusted you with my heart and soul," she said.

"Same here."

"And if I bare my soul and you don't like what you see? Will you even try to forgive me or just judge me?"

431

"If your secrets hurt as much as your leaving did, I may not have enough heart left to forgive you."

She didn't say anything else, and he could see in her glassy stare that she'd shut down. So there was nothing left to do but leave this room before his love for her severed his remaining threads of control, and he pulled her up out of that tub, carried her down the hall to her bed, and made love to her. All night long. Like she wanted. Like he needed. Giving her the rest of his soul, his pride, his ego, his heart.

He stood and moved to the door.

"Josh," she called out, and he turned back to face her. "You'll never find a love as true and right as mine, but I won't wait forever for you to see it. So while you're thinking about whether you can forgive me my secrets, I hope you're also thinking about how you're going to feel seeing me end up with another man because you let your stubborn pride win out over my love for you."

A sardonic little grin worked its way onto his mouth. "I've had to imagine you with another man for the past six and a half years, CC. It fucking destroyed me. But I can do it again. 'Cause it'll hurt less than a lifetime of waiting for your secrets to explode in my face."

He watched her swallow the pain of his words and absorb them deep into her breaking heart. Watched the tip of her nose redden and her lips pinch to stop their tremble. Watched her wipe away tears—tears he'd caused by his callousness.

"I love you," she choked out.

"I love you, too."

"Then tell me you can let go of the past."

Ignoring the pleading in her eyes and her voice, he grabbed the knob and forced himself to turn it. Forced himself to open the door and walk through. Forced himself to close it solidly behind him.

****

At the soft click of the closing door, the steamy air in the room from their heated exchange chilled. Nothing sounded in the room but the slow drip of the faucet and the heartbreaking sizzle of their second chance being snuffed.

He loved her, but as soon as she revealed her secrets, that love would die. He'd be done with her, unable to forgive her. Like he predicted, the chaff will have destroyed them.

After giving herself a few self-indulgent minutes to cry, she pulled the plug, climbed out, dried off, and put on her robe. She padded into Derrick's room, kissed him on the forehead, then went to her room.

Out of habit, she reached into the drawer for Josh's T-shirt. Instead of putting it on, she hugged it to her body. It had kept her tied to him through the long years without him. But it was time for her to face reality. She had lost him. Or soon would.

Putting the shirt back into the drawer, she climbed into bed naked and ran her hands across the places on her body she had wanted him to touch tonight and imagined it was him doing it. She would wear only his imagined touches to bed tonight, let them caress her into beautiful dreams of him, of them, of how they could be.

Despite the exhaustion and emotional roller coaster ride of the previous night, she awoke early after a hard sleep. After washing up and dressing, she headed to the kitchen to help Ruby with breakfast. At her invitation, the hands had started joining them for breakfast. It meant more work and cost, but she liked having them there. She'd always wanted a big family.

Derrick was already at the table, sitting beside Josh, who was in his usual spot.

"Morning, Mom," Derrick said when he saw her.

"Good morning," she said and kissed the top of his head. "You're up early."

"I heard Josh talking to Ruby, and I got up. Did you know he stayed the night on our couch?"

Her heart bloomed in her chest. "No, I didn't."

"Hope you don't mind," Josh interjected. "It was pretty late, and I was too tired to think straight, much less drive."

Was that a hint that he hadn't been in his right mind last night when they'd argued? She could hope, even though she knew that wasn't what he'd meant. "You're always welcome here."

Cole, Owen, and Emmett shuffled in and took their places at the table, each of them pinning Josh to the chair with a suspicious glare.

"Josh. You're here mighty early," Cole said, voicing what each of them was thinking.

"He stayed the night here," Derrick volunteered cheerfully.

"You don't say." Cole's disapproval was evident in his tight tone and the disapproving glare he directed at Josh.

Josh glared right back, daring him to say something.

She set her hand lightly on Josh's shoulder. "I hope the couch was comfortable enough. Next time you're welcome to take the guest bedroom." She said it to Josh, but then slid her gaze to each of her hands', a silent warning to knock off the pissing contest.

"I'll do that," Josh said. "Thanks."

She turned to help Ruby get the meal on the table.

Unfortunately, her words didn't seem to calm the tension at the table. The men were protective of her, and she appreciated it, but she wouldn't have them making Josh feel uncomfortable in her home. He had as much a right to be there as they did...more even.

Breakfast over, the hands headed out in the pickup to fix some breaks in the fences she and Josh had located days ago. She, Josh, and Derrick saddled up for their ride.

Derrick loped in a circle in the pasture, practicing the skills routine Josh had given him, as Charleigh and Josh watched. They hadn't spoken two words to each other since the ride began, so it surprised her when he spoke up.

"You didn't need to explain to them where I spent the night."

"You know how people talk."

"Don't tell me you're finally worried about your reputation?"

"No. Yours."

"Since when."

"Since I discovered how important it is to you and how hard you worked to get it."

His lips pinched tight. "Ruby been talking again?"

"She means well. Plus, I heard what you said a few weeks ago. I mean, I get what you were saying about a person's reputation being important. Despite my teasing at the fundraiser last night."

"Yeah, well, your protectors didn't believe you anyway."

"It's funny." She met his eyes and held them tight. "Even when you tell the truth, people still only believe what they want to believe. The sad thing is, it's usually a belief that doesn't make them happy."

She urged her horse forward to where Derrick was and raced him across the pasture, smiling at the pure joy of it. Spring was in full bloom across the land, the hope of renewal alive in every tasty breath, every scent, every sight, every sound singing around them. It was her favorite time of year, and it was glorious to be out in the middle of it.

This was the good life she'd dreamed of giving Derrick, even before he was born. A place where they were safe, had enough to eat, could pay their bills, enjoy some pleasure in life, and have family and friends who cared about them.

Ironic how that good life had been here all along. Not so much this ranch, but Josh. She never should have left him. She should have had more faith not just in him but in them, their love. If she had, she wouldn't have the Simms ranch, but she'd have Josh. He was the good life. For her and their kids. And she and their kids were the good life for him. If only she could get him to see it. She had one chance to get it right.

After they'd put away the horses, Derrick grabbed his gun and the box of ammo from the house and jumped into Josh's pickup so he and Josh could head out for their shooting lesson. Before Josh could climb in, Charleigh pulled him aside. Taking his hands in hers and linking their fingers, she held his gaze tight in hers.

"Let's go for a drive when you get back. Just the

two of us. I've got some chaff I want to get rid of."

As a grin lifted his lips, she leaned in and stole what might be her last kiss from the man she'd never stop loving.

Chapter Twenty-Two

All through the lesson, Josh pondered Charleigh's comment. Was this it? Were they finally going to get past the secrets keeping them from being fully together? Whatever the secrets turned out to be, he was ready to hear them. He couldn't imagine anything so bad that it would destroy their second and maybe last chance at love. Except maybe if she had cheated on him with Will while they were together.

"You've really improved," Josh said to Derrick as they walked back to the pickup. The boy had hit mostly bullseyes today. "I think you're ready to try the pistol next week."

"Really?"

He patted his back. "Yep."

"All right!" Derrick said with a fist bump.

The kid was awesome, brought a great attitude into every situation, was eager to learn and work hard. He was the kind of kid he'd hoped he and Charleigh would have. The thought that he'd lose Derrick if he and Charleigh couldn't work out their issues was a punch to his gut.

During the wee hours of the morning, lying on Charleigh's couch mere feet from her bed where he wanted to be, he'd decided he was ready to let the past stay in the past, call a do-over, fight a fucking war to keep her and Derrick in his life. His coming discussion with her would determine whether he could follow through on that decision. He knew this might be his last chance at true happiness, true love, so he'd give it everything he had.

"I have to miss my shooting lesson next weekend," Derrick said on the way home.

"Oh? Why's that?" Derrick never missed his shooting lesson. It had to be something pretty important.

"Tommy Collier's birthday party. We're going roller skating."

Josh grinned, giving him a side eye glance. "Can you roller skate?"

Derrick laughed. "No. But Nikki said she'd help me."

"So, you and Nikki still friends?"

"Yeah. Last night she said she still wants to be my girlfriend even though I'm not in her class anymore. I told her yes."

"What changed your mind?"

"Tommy likes her, too, and I don't want another guy to be her boyfriend."

"Not sure that's a good enough reason."

"Well, she likes me and I like her, so that's three good reasons."

Maybe the five-year-old was on to something. Josh loved Charleigh and didn't want to see her with another man. She loved him and wanted to be with him. It really was a no-brainer.

He pressed harder on the gas pedal, suddenly eager to get home to Charleigh and tell her he didn't want to lose her and was willing to do anything to keep her and Derrick in his life. Even a do-over that kept her secrets secret if that's what she needed.

A grin on his face, he tussled Derrick's hair. "So, what are you going to do on *your* birthday?"

"Well, I never had a real birthday party, with friends and all that, so I want to have one. But I'd want everybody to come out here and ride horses. Would you come if I do?"

"You bet. When is your birthday, by the way?"

"May 22, but that's on a weekday, so I'd wait 'til the weekend for the party."

May 22. May. May? Josh's eyebrows furrowed in confusion. No. That couldn't be right. Derrick's voice faded away as Josh did the math in his head. If he was born in May, then he was conceived in August. He and Charleigh had been very much together that August.

Either she had been cheating on him with Will. Or…

He turned toward Derrick to ask him to clarify what he'd heard but instead just looked at him. Saw him as if for the first time. His hair—thick, straight, and the color of ripe wheat like his, not curly and golden like Charleigh's or dark brown like Will's. His eyes— clear blue and fringed with spiky black lashes, like his, not the color of pure honey like Charleigh's or brown like Will's. His mouth—full, wide, with that crooked grin. Like his. The dimple on his right cheek. Like his. His sunkissed complexion, like his, courtesy of his Spanish heritage.

Oh. Goddamn.

Chills stampeded across his body, head to toe.

Derrick wasn't Will's son.

He was *his* son.

The truth squeezed the air from his lungs, and he

couldn't breathe, couldn't tear his eyes from...*his son.* He braked before he drove off the road. Downshifting, he shut off the engine.

"How come we stopped?" Derrick asked, looking out the windshield down the road to see what might have made them stop.

Josh's tongue was thick in his throat as he asked his question. "Your birthday is in May?"

Anxiety rounded Derrick's eyes. "Oh, um, I mean August," he said in a weak little voice and whipped his head around to look out the side window. "I get confused sometimes."

"Derrick, look at me." He kept his voice low and nonthreatening but insistent.

Derrick finally turned toward him and met his eyes. And he knew the truth.

"Don't lie to me, son." He'd referred to Derrick as *son* before in the past, but in light of their new reality, hearing the word come from his mouth sent a warm shiver up his spine where it exploded in his skull.

The boy's face scrunched up, worry filling his wide blue eyes. "Don't tell my mom I forgot. She'll be disappointed in me."

"Did she tell you to lie?"

"She said it's not lying. It's just keeping an important secret."

"The secret being that your birthday is in May, not August."

He nodded.

"Why?"

He shrugged. "I don't know." His chin trembled. "Are you mad at me?"

The lies weren't Derrick's doing. They were

Charleigh's. "No. Come here."

Derrick lunged at him, hugging him.

He'd hugged Derrick before, but this time he was hugging his son. This time he felt his son's little heart beating against his. His blood pumping in his veins. His breaths inflating his lungs. A full-body rush of love roared over him and through him, the likes of which he'd never felt before.

His son. God! He had a son.

A son created from his and Charleigh's love. A son taken from him in her deception.

"From now on, your birthday is May 22, you hear. No more secrets."

He shifted back. "Yes, sir."

"Tell me again…when is your birthday?"

Derrick smiled. "May 22."

"Damn straight." He hit the starter, shifted into gear, and headed on back to the house at a faster pace. He would get the entire story from Charleigh, but as far as he was concerned, the matter was settled. Derrick was born in May, making him *his* son. And Charleigh had kept him from *his* son for six years. Six goddamn years! Half the boy's childhood.

Father and son were quiet for the rest of the ride home, Josh lost in thought about what he was going to say to Charleigh. Derrick probably worried about Charleigh's reaction to his spilling the beans on the secret she'd insisted he keep.

As they pulled into the yard, Charleigh came out of the house, a welcoming smile on her delicious pink lips. She had showered, her damp hair already springing up in thick, loose curls over her shoulders and down her back. A little green sundress and sandals had replaced her jeans, denim shirt, and boots. Around her neck was the silver heart necklace he'd given her, a symbol of their love.

He turned off the pickup. "Take your gun and go on into the house," he told Derrick as he leaned over to open his door for him.

"Can I say hi to Mom first?"

"Tell her hi, then get inside. I need to talk to her."

"You going to tell her I messed up?"

"I need to talk to her about it, but I promise she won't be mad at you for it."

Derrick grabbed his gun and the box of ammo, climbed out, and headed toward her. "Hi, Mom. You look beautiful." He hugged her, then headed to the house as Josh joined them.

"No kiss?" Charleigh said to Derrick's retreating back.

"I have to put my gun away."

She greeted Josh with a radiant, loving smile. Damn, she did look beautiful. A beautiful little liar.

"Hi," she said, putting her hands on his stomach and leaning in, begging a kiss.

And she smelled good. Like spring. Or maybe that was what deceit and lies smelled like.

He jerked back. "At any time while you and I were together, did you have sex with Will?"

She dropped her hands from him and stepped back, a furrowed frown replacing her smile. "No. Of course not."

"Then how do you explain that Derrick was born in May?"

****

Josh's harsh, accusatory words sent Charleigh's

heart plunging into her stomach.

He knew! Derrick must have let the truth slip.

This was so not how she'd wanted him to find out. While she'd worked with Ruby today, she'd planned out how to tell him. Now that plan was out the window, and she was forced to fly by the skinny straps of her sundress.

She opened her mouth to speak, but nothing came out. Her tongue darted out to wet her suddenly dry lips, but it didn't help her speak the truth or the lie.

"Don't even think about lying to me, Charleigh. I know Derrick was born in May, which means you got pregnant with him in August. We were still together then."

She stared at him, begging him with her eyes to understand, even before she'd spoken a word.

"Is he my son?"

She heard Brutus barking but couldn't turn her attention from the drama playing out right before her eyes.

Josh gripped her arms. "Answer me."

The barking continued, along with an unfamiliar sound. But her brain couldn't focus on anything but Josh—his anger, his rigid stance, his fingers digging into her flesh, the moment of truth she'd hidden for so long. It pummeled her from all directions.

"This is what I wanted to talk to you about today," she managed in a pleading tone, hoping he'd give her a chance to explain.

His eyes narrowed in fury, and his lips thinned. "Say it."

"Derrick is your son."

The sudden release of the truth ripped a hole in the

bubble surrounding them, filling the air with the distinct roar of a cougar and Derrick's scream and jerking her attention from Josh. Over by the trash bins, a cougar had Derrick pinned to the ground. Brutus, barking ferociously, circled the animal, nipping and snapping, drawing the powerful swipe of its paw.

"Oh, God!" She charged toward them, shouting, waving her arms. Derrick's gun was on the ground, near him. She grabbed it and checked it. A single bullet lay in the chamber. She aimed and shot, hitting the cat in the head. It collapsed on top of Derrick. She hadn't realized Josh was there until he was lifting the cougar off their son.

She knelt beside Derrick. So much blood. Derrick's. The animal's. On him. The ground.

"Derrick!" She gently lifted him in her arms.

"Mom," he mumbled, then closed his eyes, drawing a moan of agony from Charleigh that originated from deep in her core. She felt Josh trying to take him from her but she held tight.

"Charleigh, we have to get him to the hospital," he said.

She heard his rough voice but was paralyzed, unable to let her baby go. He pulled Derrick from her arms and laid him on a blanket he had unfolded beside her.

"Get in the pickup," he demanded as he wrapped the blanket around Derrick. "Now," he yelled when she stayed put.

She jumped up, ran to the pickup, and climbed in. Josh was right behind her, Derrick in his arms wrapped in the blanket. He handed him to her, slammed the door, and rushed to the driver's side.

He raced toward town, not even slowing for the bumps. She heard him on the phone but couldn't seem to grasp the meaning of his words. But she understood the fear in his voice. He'd just found out he had a son, and now he might lose him.

Medical personnel were waiting for them at the hospital entrance with a gurney. Josh took Derrick from her arms, laid him on the gurney, and the personnel took over, whisking him away. She tried to follow, but a person with a clipboard rushed in, blocking her.

"Ma'am, is that your son?"

She heard the words but couldn't seem to respond.

Josh's arm went around her. "This is Charleigh Simms. That's her son, Derrick."

"Charleigh, I need to get some information from you to help us give Derrick the best care we can. Please come this way."

Josh guided her after the woman to a small room.

"Charleigh, how old is Derrick?"

"He's five."

"Six next month. May 22," Josh added, the only official information he was likely to know about his son.

"Is he allergic to any medications?"

"Not that I know of," she said. "He's never been sick, other than a cold."

"Is he up to date on his immunizations?"

"Yes."

"Josh, you said on the phone it was a cougar attack?"

"Yes."

"Any signs it was rabid?"

"No, but one of my men is taking it to the vet for

testing now."

God, he'd thought of everything.

"Charleigh, do you know Derrick's blood type?"

"He's AB," she said.

"Are you a match?"

"No, but…" Her gaze rose to Josh.

"I am," Josh said.

"Are you a relative?"

"I'm…his father."

"Oh." The woman quickly hid her surprise. "Well, come with me, please." She scurried Josh away, and some nameless, faceless man led her to a small, empty waiting room with instructions to wait for a Doctor Glass, who would come in to update her about Derrick's condition as soon as he could.

Josh soon came back, his face pale, Derrick's blood covering his shirt and pants. Her legs were clay, but she stumbled over to him and threw her arms around his waist. She needed him, his comfort, more than she'd ever needed it before. His arms stayed at his sides, and his body stiffened against hers.

She looked up at him. "I know you're angry, and you have a right to be, but right now we need each other. Because our son is fighting for his life. Let's deal with everything else after we know whether he'll...whether he'll…"

She broke down, letting it all go, her tears wetting his shirt. When he showed no signs of comforting her, she turned away, but he stepped forward and grabbed her, pulling her back to him. He hugged her tight, like she needed, and clung to her, like he needed, and they absorbed each other's fear and comforting touches.

"He'll be okay," Josh murmured in her ear.

"You promise?"

He didn't answer.

"I need to hear you say it. Derrick says you always keep your promises."

"I promise."

****

Josh led her to the row of chairs. They sat. Waited. While his thoughts went wild.

Derrick was his son. And Charleigh hadn't told him. And now Derrick was fighting for his life and might never know he was his father. She was right. Now wasn't the time to have it out about what she'd done. But he couldn't help himself.

"How could you do it, Charleigh? How could you keep my son from me? Not tell me?"

"That night you left, you said you didn't want marriage or kids with me. I didn't tell you about the baby because you might have insisted we get married."

"Isn't that what you wanted?"

"I wanted you to marry me because you loved me and wanted to marry me, because you wanted me in your life, not because your conscience told you it was the right thing to do. I didn't want you like that, have you end up resenting us."

"You should have been thinking about what was best for our baby, not yourself."

"Every single decision I made was about what was best for him."

"Will-fucking-Simms was best for him? Not me? His father?"

"Will was the only person I had to help me."

"Bullshit! You had me."

"No, I didn't. You didn't want me or a baby. You

made that real clear."

"I did want you, and I would have wanted our baby, but regardless whether I did or not, you should have told me."

"That's why I had Will take me to your school. To tell you. But when I saw that girl in your bed, I knew I wasn't getting help from you, so it didn't matter whether you knew. I knew you wouldn't care."

"But you knew Will would."

"I told him I was pregnant and that you didn't want us. With no hesitation, he asked me to marry him. He said he loved me and would love my child as his own. Said he'd take care of us."

"I saw the pictures, Charleigh. I know how good he took care of you and my son. That hovel you lived in. No money. No food half the time. Fuck." He dragged his fingers across his skull in anguish that they'd lived like that because of him, because he hadn't been there for them.

Her face reddened. "Our money trouble didn't get that bad until Will's illness progressed. He couldn't work, and the medical bills piled up. He did the best he could. So did I."

"He lied to you, betrayed us both, stole you and my child from me, put you on the brink of financial ruin, and you're still defending him."

"At least he stepped up."

"If I didn't step up, it's because you didn't fucking tell me."

"Okay, fine." She jumped out of her chair and glared at him. "It's all my fault...for being stupid enough to get pregnant with your child, for being scared shitless about how I was going to take care of our baby, for feeling completely helpless and alone after you abandoned me, for not knowing what the hell to do, for marrying a man I didn't love just to make sure your child had a better life than I could give him alone. And you? You're completely blameless. Happy now?"

****

Charleigh spun away from Josh and stormed to the door, stared through the window, hoping the doctor would come in and give them some word about Derrick and save her from this damning conversation.

The shuffle of boots on carpet sounded behind her, and she felt the heat of Josh's body all along her backside. Despite their hateful words, she hoped he'd wrap his arms around her to comfort her, tell her he accepted his share of the blame for what happened, but as angry as he was, she knew it was a wasted wish.

"From now on, things are going to be different," he said.

Her body went cold as she spun to face him. "What does that mean?"

"It means I'm claiming what's mine." He stared down at her, eyes like ice.

This was the moment she had been dreading. Why she had been so hesitant about coming here. And here it was. Poised to destroy everything.

"I won't let you take him from me, Josh."

"I wouldn't take him from his mother. But I won't let you take him from me either. Ever again."

He'd given her an inch, so she'd try for the mile. "I want to be the one who tells him."

"When?"

"After he's home and recovered from this."

"Fine. But I want to be there when you do. I don't

want you telling him I didn't want him."

"I'd tell him the truth about what happened," she said, frustrated that he automatically thought she'd lie to her son.

"Sure you would."

"I don't lie to my son," she said, her words clipped.

"Only about important things, like who his father is."

"Asshat." She threw the insult at him and stormed toward the chairs. A wave of vertigo plowed into her halfway there, leaving her body weak, drained, and beat up internally. She slowed, teetered, and her knees buckled. Josh caught her as she collapsed. He carried her to a chair and set her on the hard plastic.

She slumped over, letting her head hang between her knees, and willed the wave to pass, hoping she wouldn't vomit in front of him.

"Any other secrets you're hiding from me?" His voice was strained with suspicion as if he already knew the truth.

The vertigo receding, she eased into a semi-upright position, swallowed back the nausea, and looked him straight in the eye. "I'm pregnant."

****

Pregnant.

Knees weak, Josh crossed the room and barely made it into the chair beside Charleigh. Leaning forward, arms on his knees, he stared down at the floor.

Pregnant.

Of course. He had noticed her tired eyes and pale face, her lingering bout of queasiness she'd brushed off as the flu, her frequent bathroom trips, her full breasts like ripe melons in the tub the night before. Then there were the mood swings and the tears. He didn't have much experience with pregnant woman, but he was familiar with the list of symptoms.

"Mine?" The stupid word tumbled out before he could stop it.

"Of course it's yours." She didn't say asshat, but her tone screamed it.

"How do you know?"

"How do I know it's yours?"

"How do you know you're pregnant?"

"I did a pregnancy test that day I went shopping in Wilton."

His head jerked toward her. "That was weeks ago. Were you planning on hiding this baby from me, too?"

"I was going to tell you the day I found out, but we had the cattlemen's meeting."

"You telling me you're pregnant with my kid was a hell of lot more important than any meeting."

"I was going to tell you afterward, but we got into another argument."

"You had plenty of other days after that to tell me."

"Oh, like when you barely said two words to me on the horse rides, or the second before you rushed off after Derrick's shooting lesson, or on Sundays when you couldn't be bothered to come around, or when you were too busy to stay for supper, or when you and the hands ran off without Derrick and me to string line, or last night when you pretty much said we're over? When, Josh. When was I supposed to announce the happy news?"

"You should have told me when you first suspected it."

"Well, I'm telling you now."

The silence enveloping them was almost as painful as the shameful memory of his aloofness the past few weeks. She was right. He hadn't been available to her or to Derrick much. He had let his frustrations with Charleigh send him into autopilot, where he was just going through the motions of his duty to them. He *was* an asshat.

"So…you're sure?" he said.

"I need to see a doctor to be a hundred percent sure. But yeah."

"While we're here, you're seeing a doctor."

"I'll see a doctor after I know Derrick is okay."

They sat in silence again, his mind loud with the thunder of thoughts stampeding through it, questions demanding answers.

"From February? When we didn't use protection?" he asked her.

"Yep."

"And Derrick…that Sunday morning before I left for school and we were out of condoms?"

"Yep."

"The only two times we didn't use a condom we got pregnant. What are the odds?"

"Obviously really good."

He leaned back, his head against the wall. In the span of an hour, he'd discovered he was a father with two kids.

"I have two kids," he said, needing to hear it out loud to cement it in reality.

"You don't have to," she said.

"What does that mean?"

"I know you never wanted kids. Now's the time to decide whether you do, before the truth comes out. If you don't, then—"

"I'm not abandoning my kids."

Doctor Toby Glass came through the door, interrupting the conversation.

They stood as he approached, and Josh held out his hand. "Toby, how is he?"

"Josh," he said, shaking his hand, then taking Charleigh's hand. "Mrs. Simms, I'm Toby Glass, Derrick's doctor."

"Can I…can we see him?"

Toby clasped his hands together in front of him. "Soon, we're still working on him."

"What do you know so far?" Josh asked, cutting to the heart of it.

"The cervical spine, head, and chest radiographs were normal, meaning there were no fractures or pneumothorax. But he has several puncture wounds and lacerations, which are being irrigated and explored."

"I'm guessing you won't be suturing the puncture wounds?" Josh said.

"No, we won't. As you know, in general, it's unadvisable to suture them because they're at high risk for infection. But the slashes I'll suture. I won't know the extent of any possible muscle damage until I get in there. He's received blood, as well as antibiotics and a dose of rabies immune globulin."

"A rabies shot?" she asked, her tone saying she was horrified at the thought.

"Lance is inspecting the animal to determine whether it was diseased. We'll hold off on further RPEP until I receive his report." His gaze cut to Josh. "Smart thinking having Cole take it to Lance immediately. How big was it?"

"Young. Certainly not full grown."

"I thought so. Had it been full grown, this would have been a much different conversation." His gaze darted between them. "Any more questions?" At their silence, he continued. "I'll keep you updated on your son's condition." He patted her arm, shook Josh's hand again, then left.

Josh and Charleigh stood in silence, absorbing the news. It wasn't as bad as he'd feared. He'd read about much worse injuries while he was in college—kids who had been killed or left paralyzed from cougar attacks. Charleigh had probably saved the boy's life by attacking it the way she had, then shooting it without hesitation. Thank God Derrick had had the time, forethought, and skill to load his gun.

"It sounds like he's going to be okay," she said, pulling him out of his thoughts.

"That's the way I heard it."

They stared at each other.

"Derrick's right," she said. "You keep your promises."

"A man's word is his bond."

"He says that all the time. Like father like son, I guess."

"Now you need to keep your promise." At her confused look, he clarified. "I want you to see a doctor. Now."

"I'll schedule an appointment, but there's no way they'll see me today."

"We're getting you an appointment for today."

Josh talked to one of the nurses, who was able to get Charleigh in right away for a quick exam and pregnancy test, which determined she was about eight weeks along.

The nurse then took them to a room to let them clean up and change into scrubs so they didn't have to sit in their bloody clothes. Josh took her back to the waiting room, then went to fill her prescription for prenatal vitamins at the hospital pharmacy. When he returned, Toby was there, telling Charleigh the cougar was negative for rabies.

Josh had only one question. "Can we see him?"

****

Derrick was weak, but he smiled at them when they entered the room. Josh stood next to Charleigh, his hand at her back, his other hand on Derrick's leg, looking at him through new eyes. Derrick was his son. He could see it now. The similarities. How had he not seen them before? The boy was his, through and through.

And he'd almost lost him.

Well, no way in hell was he losing him now. Or the child growing inside Charleigh.

But Charleigh?

How could he ever trust her again? He thought he could handle whatever secret she had been hiding. But this? Keeping his child from him? That was unforgivable. No way could he build a strong, loving relationship with a woman who lied about the most important thing to happen in their life.

The nurse soon came in and asked them to leave, saying Derrick needed his rest.

Outside the room, Charleigh nearly fainted again. He caught her. "I'm taking you home."

"I'm staying here."

"You heard Toby. Derrick's going to be fine."

"He's never been away from me. If he gets scared, I want to be here."

"You're no good to either of our children if you're falling on your face."

"Must you argue with me about everything?" she snapped. "I know what's best for me and my son, so just stay out of it."

The fury in her voice, her face, her stance told him everything he needed to know. She didn't want him or his interference.

"Fine, Charleigh. You win. Do whatever the hell you want." He spun on his heel and stormed down the hallway to the exit. He shoved it open with a loud bang and kept going, even when she called out his name.

****

What the hell was the matter with her? She leaned against the wall and slid down it to the tiled floor. She'd done it again. Pushed Josh away. All he'd wanted to do was help her, and she had pushed him away.

She loved him. She wanted him in her life, in their kids' lives. She couldn't make the same mistake again.

Fear of losing him rose up in her like a firestorm and yanked her up off the floor.

"Josh," she called out his name, but he ignored her and kept going. She raced down the hall after him and pushed out the door in time to see his pickup leaving the parking lot.

The universe had given her a second chance with the man she loved, and she'd squandered it.

****

Josh went home to shower and change, then headed to the Simms ranch to check in with Cole on the work in progress. Ruby ran out the second he pulled up in front of the house.

"How is he?" she asked, worry in her eyes and voice.

"He'll need a few days in the hospital, but the doctor said he'll be all right."

"Thank the Lord."

"Cole back from town?"

"Yes, he's with Owen and Emmett in the Nelson pasture."

"Good. I'm headed there myself." He turned back to his pickup.

Ruby touched his arm to halt him. "Maybe it's not my place to say, Josh, but Charleigh needs you. So does Derrick. Your place is with them, not out working on fences."

"You're right. It's not your place."

He turned from her shocked look, got into the pickup, and headed toward the pasture.

Work. That's what the contract was about. That's why he was here. Not to be Charleigh's lover or even father figure to Derrick or the baby. Although, he *was* their father.

He'd stick to doing his job, take care of his parental responsibilities, and dump everything that had to do with her. Then everything would be as it should be.

Chapter Twenty-Three

After two days of working himself to near exhaustion so he wouldn't be tempted to go to the hospital, he couldn't stand it anymore. He needed to see his son. Even if it meant seeing his son's mother. Even if she didn't want him there. Even if seeing her broke off more of his heart.

A glance in Derrick's room showed that Charleigh wasn't there and Derrick was asleep. He went in and stood beside him, staring down at the little form in the big bed.

His son.

His gaze slowly took him in, touching on every feature, marveling at the truth that he had a son that looked just like him. The school pictures he'd dug up his first night of fatherhood reconfirmed the resemblance and made him feel stupid for not seeing it the first day he'd met Derrick.

Swallowing around the lump lodged in his throat, he reached out and set his hand on his son's, loosely wrapping his fingers around the small hand.

"Hello, Josh."

At Charleigh's whispered voice behind him, his body tensed. He released Derrick's hand and stuck his hands in his pockets.

"How's he doing?" he asked, keeping his gaze glued to Derrick.

"He's been asking for you."

Guilt didn't let him respond. Fortunately, Charleigh didn't belabor the point.

"Toby said he's healing remarkably well. He might be able to go home tomorrow."

Toby. Not Dr. Glass. Not the doctor. *None of your business, Flores. She's none of your business now.* He nodded. "Good." He placed his hand on Derrick's chest, felt the strong, reassuring heartbeat beneath his palm. "Good," he whispered again, then turned to leave.

She caught his arm. "You don't have to go."

He pulled away and headed toward the door. "Tell him I came by."

"Josh," she said, a tremor in her quiet voice that drew his gaze to her face. She came to him where he stood at the door. "In the middle of all this, I'm not sure I said it, but I'm sorry."

"About what? All your lies? Your betrayal? Keeping my son from me?"

"That I didn't tell you everything sooner. But also how I acted the other day when you were trying to help me. I was frantic about Derrick, and I'm used to making decisions about him on my own. I'm calling a do-over. I want your help. I *need* your help. I need you, Josh."

He shook his head. "All the do-overs in the universe won't fix what's broken between us. We're not right for each other."

"We're perfect for each other. From the second we met. Remember what you said to me that night at the 4-H dance, the first time we danced to our song?"

The words branded on his heart and soul the moment he'd said them. "Stupid words from a stupid kid."

"You kissed me for the first time, then looked into my eyes and said, 'I feel like I've been born tonight, that I didn't exist before you.' I said I felt the same way, and after another kiss, you said, 'We belong to each other now. Forever.' And I agreed. We still belong to each other, Josh. We branded each other that night, and we'll belong to each other forever."

He shook his head and had turned to get the hell out of there when Derrick called out his name.

He drew a deep breath to clear the anger from his voice, then made his way back to the bed, a smile in place for Derrick's sake.

"Hey, bud," he said.

"I was hoping you'd come see me," Derrick said, a weak smile on his face.

"Sorry I didn't come sooner."

"It's all right. Mom said that because we're here, you're doing all the chores, but that you'd come as soon as you could. I know work comes first."

His already battered heart took another hit. No. No, that wasn't right.

Family first, work next, because there's no replacement for family lost.

That was what his granddad had always said. He'd lost that lesson somewhere through the years when one by one he lost his family. And then Charleigh. But he had a family again—Derrick and the baby—and he'd put them first. Always. From now on.

He swallowed the lump in his throat. "How're you feeling?"

"Pretty good. Doctor Toby said I might get to go home tomorrow."

"Hey, that's great news."

461

"Would you come get me and take me and Mom home tomorrow?"

"You bet. What time?"

"What time, Mom?"

"After Toby makes a last check on your wounds, he'll decide whether you can go home. Probably around ten."

"Around ten," Derrick repeated and yawned.

"I'll be here. I better go now so you can rest."

"Can you stay a little longer?" Derrick reached out his hand for his.

"You bet." Josh sat on the edge of the chair that was pushed up close to the bed, a blanket draped over it—probably where Charleigh had camped out for the past couple of days—and took his son's hand in his.

Charleigh brushed her hand across his back. "Thank you."

Her touch was like lightning arcing through him. His entire body came alive at her touch. Always had. Probably always would. Because she was fire, and he'd been cold all his life…except when he had been with her.

She walked around to the other side of the bed and sat in the chair there, tucking her legs under her, and he worked to keep his eyes on Derrick and away from her.

Toby came into the room. "Hey, Josh."

Josh released Derrick's hand long enough to stand and shake the doctor's hand. "Toby," he nodded. "Thanks for taking good care of him."

"He comes from hardy stock." He patted his back, then smiled and winked. Then he addressed Charleigh. "Can I talk to you outside?" He nodded his head toward the hallway.

"Of course." She rose, and they stepped outside together.

Well, son of a bitch. It hadn't taken her long to get another guy on the hook. And a doctor, no less, not a poor rancher. He had to face it. He'd never have Charleigh. But he'd have his son. And another child in about seven months. That would be enough. It would have to be.

It would be hard seeing her with another man, but for his kids' sake, he'd try to get along with them…as long as they didn't try to take his kids from him.

"I miss you, Josh," Derrick said.

He pushed his anger and jealousy down to deal with later. Derrick didn't need to see it. He resumed his seat and took his son's hand again. "I miss you, too. So does Brutus."

"Is he okay? The cougar scratched him bad. I think he was bleeding a lot."

"Lance fixed him up. Ruby said he's not happy about the neck cone he has to wear, though. And he's been pretty miserable without you running around with him."

Derrick grinned. "I can't wait to get home and play with him. Do you think he'll remember me?"

"Of course."

"Josh."

"Yeah, bud?"

"I couldn't shoot the cougar. I mean, I had him in my sights, but I couldn't… I never shot an animal before. Are you disappointed at me?" A tear rolled from the corner of his eye that ripped open Josh's heart.

"No, I'm not disappointed in you. The decision to kill something should never be easy."

"But what if I need to protect Mom or Ruby or you, but I can't because I can't shoot, and then because of me you guys die?"

"You'll be able to do the right thing at the right time. When it comes to protecting the people you love, something just kicks in, inside here." He tapped the boy's chest at his heart. "Kinda takes over, and you suddenly become able to do anything you have to to keep them safe. Even lay down your own life."

It's what he'd do for Derrick and his unborn child…even for Charleigh. "It's what your mom did for you when she saw that cougar on you. She risked her life to save yours."

"My mom rocks."

"Yeah. She does."

"I'm glad you taught her to shoot."

"Me, too."

"You rock, too, Josh."

Derrick raised his hand for a fist pump, and Josh obliged just as Charleigh came back into the room.

"The doctor didn't change his mind about maybe letting me go home tomorrow, did he?" Derrick asked as she sat in her chair.

"No," she said. "But he did say you need to rest."

"Okay." He turned back to Josh. "My head kinda hurts, so I'm going to go to sleep. But can you stay 'til I do?"

"I'll wait 'til I hear you snoring."

He grinned. "I don't snore. But Mom does."

"I most certainly do not," she said with a mock scoffing tone.

Derrick chuckled, then closed his eyes.

Josh stayed beside him, holding his hand. He could

feel Charleigh watching him, and he finally gave in and met her eyes. His heart pounded at the wild emotion riding her gaze.

They remained that way until he heard Derrick's steady, even breathing, and knew he slept. He'd kept his promise to stay until he fell asleep, so he could leave now. But still he didn't. This was where he wanted to be. Not in the hospital, of course, but with Derrick. His son. And Charleigh. The woman he loved. Even if he couldn't have her.

"Thank you," she whispered.

"You already thanked me."

"That was for coming to visit him."

"Then for what?"

"For getting him here in time to save his life. For giving him the blood that helped save his life. For being here for him now. For being his father."

He nodded to acknowledge her appreciation.

"He misses you," she said. "So do I."

"You seem to be fine. Toby has a good bedside manner."

Her eyes widened in surprise at his thinly veiled accusation. "Toby is Derrick's doctor. If you're suggesting anything else, you're wrong. And if you want to know what he talked to me about in the hallway, then just ask me."

"Derrick is my business. That baby you're carrying is my business. The Simms ranch is my business for another five months. That's it. If your discussion with Toby was about any of those three things, then tell me. Otherwise, it's none of my business."

"Am I not your business anymore?"

Not wanting to have this conversation, he eased his

465

hand from Derrick's, stood, and rushed out the door.

She caught up with him in the hall and grabbed his arm, stopping him. "You like honesty so damn much. Here it is. There's only one man on earth I want to be with, and it's not Toby Glass. It's not Lance Barton. It's not Cole Ledger. It's you. Only you. I want to be your business. I want to be your lover, your wife, your best friend, your partner, the keeper of your heart, the mother of your children. And I'm standing here in front of you, as vulnerable and exposed as a grain of wheat without its protective chaff, my heart and soul open, telling you I love you and want you in my life. Forever. I know you love me, too. We can have the life together we always wanted, but we have to fight for us. And we do that by forgiving each other."

The emotion flowing from her was palpable. He felt it all the way to his bones. It thundered inside him, energizing all the pieces of his heart she'd ever broken. He felt them shifting inside his chest, the burning edges fusing together like puzzle pieces. But he'd heard pretty words of love from her before, and she'd left him. Broken him. Lied to him. Kept his kid from him. Their trust had been destroyed beyond repair. Without trust, love couldn't survive.

"I'll be in your life, Charleigh, but only as far as it relates to raising our kids. I can't do more than that because I don't trust you."

As the first teardrops formed in her eyes, he hardened his heart and eased his hand from hers. "See you tomorrow at ten."

He headed down the hallway toward the exit, anger and regret fueling his every step. Anger at her, at himself, at the situation. Regret that his last chance at the life he wanted with the woman he loved was shattered beyond repair.

Against his better judgment, he glanced back over his shoulder. She was still at the door, watching him leave her again, the tears flooding her eyes and rolling down her cheeks, her misery and love on full display. Just like it had been the first time he left her.

And just like that night, he wanted to rush back to her, hold her, kiss her, tell her she was his life, his soul, his reason for breathing. But it would be a mistake that would lead only to more misery. Ignoring the tears flooding his heart, blurring his vision, he kept going and pushed out the exit.

****

Josh sat on his porch swing, rocked it slow with the heel of one boot in the velvet night, tilted the lip of the longneck bottle to his mouth, drinking deeply as he thought about his son.

He was glad he'd gone to see him. He should have gone long before today, but he hadn't been ready to face Charleigh. He'd make it up to Derrick in the days and weeks and months to come, show his son that he was a good father. Hopefully he could figure out what that looked like.

Quino approached him out of the darkness. "The boy all right?"

He nodded. "Good enough that he's coming home tomorrow."

"How's his mama holding up?" He sat at the other end of the swing.

"'Bout like you'd expect."

The gentle breeze that tussled the tree at the side of the house carried on it the scent of the fertile ground in the south section that he'd soon need to plow and plant in wheat and hay. Somewhere near the barn, the call of a hoot-owl stirred the quiet night.

It was quiet here, peaceful. Odd how there was a time he couldn't wait to get away from this place for the very same reasons he now wanted to stay. Peace and quiet. Only, not so much peace filling him tonight, and his thoughts were anything but quiet.

"*Joven*, I've known you your whole life," Quino said. "I was here the day your mama brought you home from the hospital. I taught you to ride, rope, and punch cattle. I promised your daddy on his deathbed I'd be here for you, watch over you. And I've done that, without meddling in your business."

"Spare me the lecture, *viejo*, and just get to the point."

"You should be at the hospital *con tu hijo*."

"My son?" Josh's head spun toward the man who had been in his life forever.

Quino scoffed as if he'd seen the surprised look in Josh's eyes. He doffed his hat. "That boy is the spittin' image of you at that age. I'm surprised you didn't see it right off."

"Yeah, well, I didn't know I had a kid, so I guess I wasn't looking for it."

"Why didn't you know?"

"She didn't tell me she was pregnant. She just left."

"That why you're not there with your boy now? 'Cause you want to punish his mother, the woman you love?"

"She didn't tell me about Derrick, and she's known for weeks that she's pregnant with our second child, but she didn't tell me until the day Derrick got hurt."

Quino laughed. "*Dos hijos*. Good for you, *joven*. Well done." He patted him on the back. "Least you know the equipment works."

Josh gritted his teeth. "That the best you got? Good job knocking up your woman, twice?"

"So you admit she's your woman."

He slowly shook his head. "I can't be with someone who lies about something as important as our kids. Who up and leaves me without explanation. I can't trust her."

"The reason she left you for Will Simms…you do anything that could have caused it?"

Instead of responding, Josh finished off his beer, set the empty down bedside the other two, and considered having another to help numb the memories rushing forward of all the justifiable reasons she'd left him for Will.

"I remember that night," Quino said, staring off into the distance as if viewing the conjured memory. "You drove your daddy home from the bar in his pickup. I remember it because it was out of the ordinary. You usually stayed with her all weekend, but you were home on a Friday night, wearing a thundercloud for a hat. A week later, she was gone, and you were never the same. It was like a part of you died."

Quino didn't ask *What happened that night?* out loud, but the question hung between them, demanding to be answered.

Josh leaned over, lodging his arms on his knees, his hazy stare on the cracked bricks of the porch he needed to replace. Someday. Along with a million other things that needed replacing or fixing on this damn ranch.

"She started talking marriage and babies. I loved her, more than anything, but I was in no position to take on that kind of responsibility, and I told her so. I had to get through school if I was going to get off this ranch and away from my dad. We fought about it."

"Had she ever talked about marriage and babies before that night?"

"No. Never. It was just out of the blue."

"Sounds like she had a particular reason for talking about them particular subjects."

"Well, yeah, I know that now. Only because she just told me. Nearly seven years later."

"What was her reaction to you telling her you weren't interested in putting your ring on her finger and your babies in her belly?"

"She kicked me out and told me not come back."

"She thought you'd left her for good, she had a baby coming, and she was all alone." He spat a stream of tobacco juice into the nearby shrub. "She musta been plumb scared to death."

Prickles of shame flushed over Josh's skin as he remembered her saying that she'd been scared shitless about taking care of their baby on her own.

"Gotta admire the little gal's courage," Quino continued. "A lot of women in her situation would've gotten rid of the baby or given it up. Can't imagine how hard it musta been for her to marry a man she didn't love just so that baby could have a half-decent life." He crossed his arms over his chest. "*Esa mujer tiene cojones de acero.*"

Josh sat upright and leaned back against the swing back, a little irritated by his mentor's singing of her praises. "Look, I know I fucked up, but she did, too.

She should have told me. I'd have been there for her if she had. But she didn't. She kept it from me, then and when she came back. And she kept this pregnancy secret, too, even though we were getting...closer. It makes me sick to my soul to know that if Will hadn't died and Wyatt hadn't created the contract, I *never* would have known I had a son. So, yeah, I agree that she has balls of steel, but unlike you, I don't consider it admirable."

"Sounds to me like she don't trust you with the truth. Can you think why that might be?"

Unfortunately, he could think of several reasons. He'd said several times he didn't want kids. He hadn't been there for her for Derrick. She probably figured he wouldn't want the second child any more than he'd wanted the first. He'd said other things, too, that would make her think he didn't want her. Then there was the big one: He had the power to dissolve the contract that provided her only means of support and had even threatened her with it to get his way.

She was right. He was an asshat.

"Do you love her?" Quino asked.

Despite everything, he did. But it didn't matter. "Love without trust is a pickup without gas. It ain't going nowhere."

"Quit quoting your *abuelo* and just think for yourself. You love that gal. It broke your heart clean in two when she left you. She's back, still in love with you, still wanting to be in your life. And you created *dos hijos* from that love. If all that's keeping you apart is no gas in the pickup, then put some in. Fast. It's long past time you gave her and that boy the Flores name."

"It's not that easy."

"It is that easy, *mijo*. The good Lord has given you a second chance with the only woman you've ever loved. The only woman you've ever wanted to love. You won't get a third chance. You're gonna lose her for good this time if you don't do the right thing. I've seen how men look at her."

Like they couldn't wait to put their ring on her finger and their babies in her belly. Yeah, he'd seen it, too.

"Your *abuelo* once told me that the cost of not following your heart is spending the rest of your life wishing you had." Quino anchored his hat on his head. "You'll regret letting her go." He stood and walked away into the dark.

****

All night, Charleigh had thought about the situation with Josh, and as morning dawned, so too did the conclusion that letting him go might be her only option if she couldn't get him to see that they could get past the storm they were in.

Living without him would be difficult. But she'd done it before. Like she'd told him when she first arrived, she was tougher now than she'd been when he'd known her before. Her toughness had grown exponentially in the seven months she'd been here. Thanks in part to him. She was a survivor. She had to be. For her kids' sakes.

Even if she couldn't have Josh, there was comfort in knowing her kids would. That he wouldn't abandon them. She knew that now. With a hundred percent certainty.

She already had Derrick checked out from the hospital when Josh arrived. They headed home in relative silence. When they hit the dirt road leading to the ranch, she asked Josh to pull over. Once they were stopped, she unbuckled her seatbelt and turned to face her son, who also had unbuckled his seatbelt. Josh did, too.

"Derrick, Josh and I have something to talk to you about," she said.

"I know. I shouldn't have tried to shoot the cougar myself. I won't do it again."

"Yeah, that. But, no, this is something else. You know that I used to live in Chismes Point, after my parents died."

"Yeah."

"And you know that Josh was my boyfriend."

"Yeah."

"We loved each other back then. A lot."

"I know. Josh told me."

"You're probably wondering why, if we loved each other, we didn't end up together."

"Yeah, I wondered that."

"Josh and I had an argument one night, and we broke up. I was really sad because I still loved him so much. But I thought he didn't love me anymore."

"But you did love her, huh Josh."

Josh nodded. "I thought she didn't love me anymore."

"How come you guys didn't just tell each other that?"

"We both decided to do that at about the same time," Charleigh said. "He was in Chismes Point trying to find me while I was at his university trying to find him, but—"

"But it was too late," Josh said.

Sophia Ryan

"Why was it too late?" Derrick asked.

Josh looked at her to respond.

"Will saw how sad I was, about losing Josh. He asked me to go to California with him so I wouldn't have to be alone."

"Why did you say yes if you loved Josh?"

"For a couple of reasons. When I asked Will to take me to Josh's school so I could tell him I still loved him, I thought I saw Josh in bed with another girl, and it was then that I knew for sure he didn't love me anymore and that we weren't getting back together."

"You were with another girl?" he asked Josh.

"No. It wasn't me. I was in Chismes Point at the time, looking for your mom. I didn't know she was looking for me."

"When I lost Josh, I realized I couldn't stay in this town without him, so I agreed to go with Will. But another reason I went with him was because I was going to have a baby. If Josh didn't want me, I knew he wouldn't want the baby. Will told me he loved me and my baby and would take care of us. The main reason I went with him was because I wanted to make sure my child had a mom and a dad who wanted and loved him. Do you understand what I'm saying?"

"I'm the baby?" At her nod, his gaze cut from hers to Josh's and back. "And Josh is my real dad?"

"He's your biological father."

"You didn't want me?" he asked Josh, his voice small and quiet and confused.

Pain flashed in Josh's eyes before he blinked it away to answer the question. "Derrick, if I'd known about you, I would have wanted you. I would have loved you. I damn sure wouldn't have let you and your mom leave town with Will."

Derrick leaned into Josh, who pulled him into a gentle hug to not risk popping his stitches.

"I love you, Dad," he whispered.

"I love you, too, son," Josh whispered back.

After a long moment, Derrick shifted back, a little grin on his face. "I asked Santa for you to be my dad, and he made it come true. This Christmas I'm going to ask for a baby brother or sister so they can help me with the chores. Or maybe a puppy."

Charleigh's eyes met Josh's across the seat. Derrick would get one of his wishes. But a month early.

"Do you have any questions?" she asked him.

"Why didn't you tell me Josh was my dad?"

"I thought you were too young to understand. You'd have wanted to see him, and based on how we'd ended things, I didn't think he'd want that, and I didn't want you to get hurt. I had planned to tell you when you got older and let you decide what you wanted to do."

"Dad—Will—loved me even though I wasn't his, didn't he?"

"To him, you were his son and he was your dad. He loved you so much."

"I loved him, too."

"He knew that. You were his whole life."

"He loved you, too, Mom. He told me so, all the time, saying you were the best wife in the whole world."

She nodded, the catch of tears in her throat making speaking difficult. Will had loved them. Despite his lies, that much was true. When Derrick sat quiet, too, she prompted him. "Any more questions?"

"When are you and Josh—Dad—getting married?"

Neither of them responded.

Derrick looked back and forth between them. "You gotta. I want my parents married."

She loved Josh, wanted to marry him. But he'd been pretty clear last night it wasn't going to happen.

"You said you love each other," Derrick continued when they didn't respond. "Once you have love, it doesn't go away. It's always there, even if you're not using it. You just gotta decide to use it again, and it'll get stronger. Like doctor Toby said I have to use my arm muscle to make it strong again."

The only sound in the pickup was the ringing of the boy's simple but profound statement. She would take one final stab, pour out her heart, and if Josh still didn't want her, then she would let it go, knowing she'd tried everything in her power to keep him.

"Josh…" She licked her lips, wishing she had a bottle of water with her to soothe her parched throat. "Maybe this isn't the right time or fair of me to do this in front of Derrick, but I love you, and I want to marry you."

As Josh's eyes fused with hers, she was surprised to see a light there, a spark, flickering warm instead of icy indifferent. Then he smiled, that sexy half-grin she loved.

"If that's a proposal of marriage, Cooper, it's a pretty lame one."

Her heart flipped up into her throat at his words, and she couldn't breathe for few seconds at the realization that maybe she hadn't lost him yet.

"Lame?" she exclaimed. She looked at Derrick. "Lame?"

He laughed.

She got out of the pickup and went around to Josh's side. Opening his door, she motioned with her hand for him to get out. "Out of the pickup, Flores."

He climbed out, then helped Derrick out.

Taking Josh's hand in hers, Charleigh dropped to one knee in front of him. "Joshua Amado Flores, I—"

"Hey, Amado's my middle name, too, Dad," Derrick said.

Josh's smile grew. "You gave him my name?"

"Yes. Now do you guys mind? I'm in the middle of a proposal here."

They laughed, and Josh gestured for her to continue.

"Josh, I love you with all my heart, my soul, my body. I always have, and I always will. We should have married each other years ago," she continued. "We can't get those years back, but we can make things right for today and tomorrow…for you and me, and our kids. Let's spend the rest of our life together like we were meant to. Marry me."

"Where's my big-ass ring?" he teased.

She laughed. "Just say yes, and I'll get you one."

He scoffed. "Everybody knows the proposal isn't official without a ring. But, uh…fortunately"—he dug into his pocket—"I've come prepared." He pulled out a white gold twisted eternity band with rubies, their birthstone.

She covered her mouth with her hands, eyes wide in shock, and dropped to both knees, astounded by this turn of events.

He dropped to his knees in front of her, then sat back on his heels and held up the ring. "I wiped out my bank account that Saturday to buy you this. It was the token of commitment you'd asked me for. And deserved. More than that, it was my promise to love you forever, be with you forever, and do everything in my power to make you happy if you chose me. I didn't know what the future would bring us. But I knew I wanted you with me for the ride."

Tears clogged her throat, leaving her speechless. She couldn't believe this was happening, truly hadn't believed she still had a chance with him.

"After you left with Will, I carried it around in my pocket as a reminder not to fall in love again. In a way it worked because all it did was keep alive the love I had for you. It was because I stopped to get this ring that I didn't get home in time to stop you from choosing another man. I won't let that happen again."

He stared at her as if he were drowning and she was his only chance at survival.

"I'm here, CC. On both knees. My heart open and beating outside my chest, begging you to choose me this time. Begging you to marry me and be my wife, my lover, my partner, my best friend, the keeper of my heart, the mother of my kids."

The words she'd said to him, said in his deep, loving, low voice, were a hallelujah chorus to her ears. She cupped his face in her hands and stared deep into his eyes, holding tight as if she were the one drowning. "Baby, I chose you the day I met you. I fell in love with you the night I kissed you. I haven't stopped loving you for even a day since. All I ever wanted and needed from you was your love. But since that ring is your promise to love me forever, I'll wear it for the rest of my life as my promise to love you forever."

He grinned. "Is that a yes to my marriage proposal?

I need to hear the word."

She wrapped her arms around him, her hand in his hair. "I asked you first."

He drew her closer. "Oh, baby, it's a hell yeah from me."

"Good, 'cause it's a hell yeah from me, too." The second her yes was out, he kissed her deep to seal their forever promise to each other.

"Dad, it's not 'ficial 'til you put the ring on Mom's finger," Derrick said.

They kept kissing.

"Guys! Come on!"

Josh eased back, took her left hand in his, and slid the ring in place. "This is an eternity ring, you know. It means forever."

"Forever's good," she said. "It's exactly what I had in mind, back then and now."

He kissed her hand, right above where his ring sat. "Back then, I couldn't imagine a life with a wife and kids, but now I can't imagine a life without you and our kids. I love you, Charleigh Flores."

"I love you, Josh Flores," she whispered against his mouth, then pulled him in for another kiss to seal his promise.

"Wait a minute," Derrick said. "Kids? What kids?"

Epilogue

Josh pulled the SUV to a stop in front of the house and released a tired sigh. Man, it was good to be home. Not that he hadn't enjoyed the honeymoon. He'd just missed…home.

Charleigh, in the seat beside him, grabbed his hand and linked their fingers. "It's great to be home, isn't it?" Happiness curved that sweet mouth into a soft smile.

"You bet." He leaned in and kissed his wife.

His wife. Nothing had ever made him as happy as being husband to the woman he'd loved since he was sixteen years old. His life was complete. He knew what he wanted, where he was going, his purpose, why he was put on this earth. The top reason was to love her and make her happy. Coming in a close second was to be a good father to his son, his yet-to-be-born daughter, and the other kids he hoped he could talk Charleigh into having. He was the luckiest, richest man on the planet.

"Let's go in," she said. "I have to pee."

"You sound like our son," he teased.

"It's our daughter's fault," she said, patting her five-month-big belly.

He opened his door and went around to her side, where she had already climbed out. He bent and swooped her up in his arms.

"What are you doing?" she asked with a chuckle.

"Carrying my wife over the threshold."

She kissed him. "I don't think I'll ever grow tired of hearing you call me your wife."

At the front door, she opened it and he pushed it open with his foot. That first step over the threshold into married life felt all new, even though they'd been married for two weeks.

He had planned to carry her straight to their bedroom and make love to her for the first time in their new home as husband and wife. But a few steps into the house, he stopped, surprised to see a big box wrapped in wedding gift wrap near the couch.

"A gift," Charleigh said, as surprised as he. She kicked off her shoes. "Who could it be from?"

Before their wedding they had specifically said no gifts. Charleigh had planned their July Fourth wedding around a fundraiser she and her committee were holding. She asked that guests, in lieu of giving gifts, which they didn't need, attend the fundraiser and give generously to the cause, which this time was to buy new computers, printers, and tablets for the local middle school.

"Only one way to find out." He set her on her feet.

As she gingerly lowered herself onto the floor near the gift, he pulled off his boots, then joined her. Together, they ripped the paper off and opened the box. Inside, on top of what looked like photo albums, was a sheet of paper. Charleigh unfolded it, skimmed to the bottom, and smiled.

"Who's it from?" he asked.

"Ruby."

"What's it say?"

"My dear Charleigh and Josh," she read aloud. "I know you said no gifts, but the people who gave you this one—Will and Wyatt—couldn't be here.

"During his last days, Will called Wyatt, told him what happened the day he left with you. At the end of that call, he secured his daddy's promise to take care of you and Derrick in his will. Wyatt agreed to Will's request so he could right the wrongs he'd done to his son but also to help Will right the wrongs he'd done to you two. I know this because Wyatt confided in me. Yes, I knew your story before you got here, Charleigh. But I know you'll forgive an old woman her secrets, because that's what families do.

"Inside the box are three photo albums and Will's phone. Charleigh, you may recall that Will took pictures on his phone of Derrick growing up. He asked Wyatt to have them printed and to get them to you and Josh. Wyatt and I had a kick of a time going through them and making the albums. He said he'd never seen Will so happy. Wyatt asked me not to give them to you until the year mark was up or if you and Josh were getting married. He knew it would take time for you two to heal the deep wound between you and didn't want this to force the issue before you had faced it and resolved it.

"Will's dying wish was that you and Josh live the life with your son that you would have if he hadn't taken you away. His talking to his daddy and putting in place the idea for the contract that would bring you two together again was him trying to make up for what he did. The video on his phone will explain it better than I can.

"Anyway, you and Josh now have each other for the rest of your lives. Be happy about that, and let everything else go is my advice. Keep each other close in your hearts and do everything in your power to stay that way. And never forgot that love isn't just what you say, it's what you do.

"Wishing you all the best of this world and giving you all my love. Ruby"

Charleigh folded the letter and set it aside.

Josh thought back to his last meeting with Wyatt. A lot of things made more sense now. Particularly that idea of his wanting Josh to marry Charleigh. If he'd told him the truth in that moment, would it have changed anything between him and Charleigh? Or would he have let his fresh anger for her for keeping Derrick from him pile on his old anger of her leaving him and let it get in the way of his getting to know her again?

It didn't really matter. Like Ruby said, they were together now. That's all that mattered, not the path they'd taken to get there.

"Did you have any idea Will had talked to his dad?" Josh asked.

She shook her head. "No."

He picked up Will's phone. "Are you ready to hear this?"

She released a slow breath. "Yes. Are you?"

"I've been ready to hear his explanation for nearly seven years."

Charleigh snuggled into his side, her arms around his waist. "Play it."

His arm around her, he tugged her closer, then turned on the phone and found the video.

It was a shock to Josh when Will's face filled the small screen. It was clear his illness had taken a toll on him. Thin and frail, his face was pale and sallow, his eyes heavy and flat, like his stores of energy were nearly depleted. Despite the nasal cannula in place for oxygen, he managed a grin.

Seeing him opened up the floodgates of Josh's childhood memories. That had been his best friend, confidant, teammate, classmate. He'd been healthy and full of life the last time he'd seen him. The face in the screen wasn't him, wasn't the man he'd cursed to hell for stealing Charleigh, for stealing his life.

"Hey, dude. You been waiting for this explanation for years, so I'll get to it. LeeLee, if you're listening…I love you. You and I had our goodbye talk last night, but you'll want to hear this message, too." He took a few ragged breaths and continued.

"Josh, I knew that Travis was the one with that girl in your room that Saturday and that you'd come back to town to make up with LeeLee. I didn't tell her because I wanted her. I loved her. Loved her for as long as you had. I was finally getting a chance to be with her, and, dude, I just couldn't give her up. If I'd told her the truth about you, she never would have gone with me. So I kept quiet and let her think the worst about you. I'm sorry for that. I know that losing LeeLee was the worst thing that ever happened to you because saying goodbye to her, and Derrick, is the worst thing that's ever happened to me. Those years with them were…" His voice cracked, and he spent a few seconds trying to catch his breath.

"They were the best years of my life. But if I had to do over it again, I'm not sure I would. Don't get me wrong. We had some really great times. But she was never really happy with me, not like she was with you. She never made me feel unloved, and to spare my feelings, she never talked about you, but it was clear where her heart was. She never stopped loving you."

His voice faltered, but he smiled and kept going. "And Derrick…oh, man, that kid is my world. He brings so much joy to my life. I'm sorry I took from you the chance to be a father to your son. It's one of life's most precious gifts. One I hope you're getting to experience."

He took another few, slow, deep breaths as if trying to recharge his strength. But he was fading. It was evident in his voice, in his face. This confession was taking it out of him, his body and his emotions. Hell, it was damned painful to watch.

"I took care of them, Josh, the best I could, and I loved them with all my heart. I hope you'll love them, too. With you is where they belong. So try. Try to get past what happened. LeeLee didn't know you came back for her. It's not her fault. It's mine. With this message, the photos, me talking to my dad about willing the ranch to them, giving you back Antelope Spring, I'm trying to right my wrongs. All of them. But what happens now is up to you." He grabbed the bottle of water on the table near him and drank, then set it down before continuing.

"Welcome them into your life, fully. You'll be the richest, luckiest man on the planet if you do. I hope you do the right thing and marry her like you should have years ago. If you don't, well, then, you're a fucking asshat."

He tried to chuckle, but it sounded more like an expulsion of a cache of air, like his body had no energy to conjure up a genuine laugh, but he held the smile.

"Seriously, dude, do whatever you have to do to

keep Charleigh and Derrick in your life. I promise, you won't be sorry."

Another long pause filled the room as they listened to him fight for breath.

Josh glanced at Charleigh. The tip of her nose was red. Tears clung to her lashes and rolled down her cheeks. He kissed her eyes, tasting her grief and appreciation for the man who had been her partner for five years.

He pulled her closer. "Baby, I'll do everything in my power to keep my family happy. I promise."

"I know." She kissed him. "So will I."

Will's voice pulled their attention back to the screen. "I'm totally spent, dude, but I have a couple more things to say, and I'll use my last breath to say them." He licked his lips. "First of all, I'm asking you to forgive—me, yourself, Charleigh. Forgiveness is the highest, most beautiful, most powerful form of love there is because it heals wounds, brings peace, and opens the way to happiness and lasting love." His breathing was shallow now, but he kept going. "Second, I'm not happy to die. But I am happy that I can go saying I've known true happiness. And it was because of LeeLee and Derrick. I love you, Charleigh Renee Simms, with all my heart. Thank you for the best years of my life." Tears rolled down his cheeks, but he didn't wipe them away. "Take care of her, Josh. Take care of our boy."

The video stopped, and Josh set the phone on the coffee table. He and Charleigh sat together, arms around each other, letting the cleansing waves of truth wash over them.

Will knew exactly what he was doing when he'd

created that video. Seeing it, hearing it had cracked open the last little closed-off section of Josh's heart where he'd kept his anger for Will fed and alive. As the pain melted, dissolved into nothing but a tender spot, he realized he was forgiving not just Will for stealing Charleigh, but himself for acting like an asshat all those years ago and not doing everything in his power to keep Charleigh, the love of his life, from feeling like she had no choice but to go with Will. The lightness and warmth in his chest filled him with hope and the knowledge that he'd remember this lesson for the rest of his life. If he didn't take care of the people who meant the world to him, somebody else would get that honor.

"Man," Josh said.

"Yeah," Charleigh said, her voice trembling.

"I think I can move past this now. Forgive him."

She swiped her tears with her fingertips. "Me, too."

He fished his handkerchief from his pocket and handed to her. "I hope you'll forgive me, too."

"For?" she said, drying her tears.

"For not being the kind of man you needed and deserved back then."

"Baby, you've always been the man I've wanted and needed. But if you think you need forgiveness, you've got it. Do you forgive me?"

"For?"

"For not trusting you and giving you the chance to be the man I knew you were."

"Forgiven."

Josh cupped her cheek and kissed her mouth, long and sweet, showing her how glad he was she was his. How glad he was she was in his life. "Are you ready to look at the pictures?"

"Yeah."

"Did you know about them?" he asked as she pulled out the first album labeled Charleigh.

"I knew he took them," she said. "We never could afford to print them. I searched for his phone after he died, but I never found it. I was convinced that someone from the hospital had taken it. I had no idea he'd sent it to Wyatt. I had no idea he'd even talked to him."

"If he hadn't, we wouldn't be together now."

"I know. And he knew. Which is why he did it."

Picture after picture in the first album was of Charleigh, her stomach in various stages of roundness from her pregnancy, her alone and with Will at her side. Later pictures of her holding the newborn Derrick. The next album was all Derrick, him growing up, capturing his milestones—sitting up, crawling, walking, feeding himself, first tooth, birthdays. The third album, titled family, showed pictures of the three of them, of husband and wife alone, of mother and son alone, of father and son alone, at home and outside, having fun.

The pictures showed that they'd been a family. A happy family. It hurt, seeing his family without him. But it was through these pictures that he could see that Will had tried to take care of her and Derrick, not so much with money and things, but with love.

He could see in Charleigh's face, her eyes, when her affection had started to grow for Will. Her sadness faded a little as time passed and as she became wrapped up in Derrick. He saw Will's illness take its toll on all of them in the later pictures. He saw the sadness return to her eyes, along with worry. Saw the enthusiasm leave Derrick's eyes. There were no pictures after

Will's death.

As he placed the albums back into the box, Josh looked at the wedding band on his left hand. He smiled thinking about his wife, his son, and his daughter who would join them in a few months. His heart was so filled with happiness, his life so filled with love, that there was no room for any negative emotions where Will was concerned.

He'd love to get back the lost years, but things were so good now, he had nothing to complain about. He had them now. And he'd hold them forever. In his heart, and in his arms.

"I'm grateful to him for these pictures," Josh said. "Especially the ones of Derrick. I hate that I missed most of his childhood."

She climbed into his lap, straddling him, cupped his face. "I'm sorry. You know that."

"I know. And I'm sorry I wasn't there for you and Derrick."

She kissed him. "I know."

He put his hand on her stomach, where their daughter was growing bigger every day. "I'm not going to miss a second of her life."

"Does that include dirty diaper patrol and two a.m. feedings?"

He chuckled. "I'll gladly share it all with you."

"Your generosity… That's why I married you."

"Just my generosity?"

"That and a million other things."

"Name one."

Smiling, she leaned in and nipped his ear lobe. "Take me to our bed, Flores, and I'll show you."

He was carrying her to their bedroom when the

front door flew open.

"Mom, Dad! You're home!" Derrick rushed to them, giving Josh mere seconds to set Charleigh on her feet before their son tackled them in a bear hug. Then he rubbed his mother's stomach and leaned down to whisper to his sister. "Hi, Katie, girl. I missed you."

Obviously feeling the same way, Katie kicked against his hand, making him laugh.

"I thought you guys weren't coming home 'til tomorrow." he said.

The plan had been to come back a day early to have the house all to themselves, but this was good, too. "We missed you too much," Josh said, holding out his fist, which Derrick bumped with his.

"I missed you guys, too. Did you bring me something?" He glanced around the room and saw the box on the floor. "Wow! Is that my present?" As he ran to it, Ruby walked in.

"You're back," she said. "We didn't expect you 'til tomorrow."

"We were ready to get home to our family," Charleigh said as Ruby hugged her, then Josh.

Quino came in behind Ruby, carrying bags. "*Hola, mijos,*" he said with a smile and a nod. He set the bags in the kitchen and came back, shook Josh's hand, and then lifted Charleigh's hand to his mouth and kissed it.

"We came over to stock the fridge so when you got home you—" Ruby halted when she saw Derrick digging into the unwrapped box. "I see you found the present."

Charleigh took her hand. "Thank you, Ruby."

"It answered a lot of questions." Josh kissed her cheek. "Thanks."

"Guys, come look at the pictures with me," Derrick called out. He had plucked an album from the box and was sitting on the couch with it open on his lap.

Ruby and Quino sat on the couch with him, and together they leafed through the albums, ooing and ahhing like any good grandparents would as Derrick captioned each photo.

Josh and Charleigh hung back, arms around each other, watching their family in action.

"Is this what you imagined?" he whispered.

"Better than what I imagined."

"So, I guess you could say I made your dreams come true," he said, grinning proudly.

"Absolutely, as long as you agree I'm the miracle that made your life complete."

"Absolutely."

They'd both gotten what they wanted and so much more. He drew his wife closer against his heart and kissed her until their son's voice interrupted.

"Dad, come see my baby pictures," Derrick said, then chuckled. "I was so cute."

As Josh and Charleigh joined their family, he knew their lives would be this way from here on out, filled with love, laughter, and happiness. He'd make sure of it.

As his granddad always said, *what you do for yourself is gone when you're gone, but what you do for others is your legacy.* He couldn't think of a better legacy than love.

Sophia Ryan

About the Author

I write the kind of books I like to read: stories where heat sizzles off the page and the characters always get their happy ending. When I'm not writing about passion, I'm indulging in it—yoga, hiking, laughing with friends over hot chile and cold beer, being lazy and crazy with family, and, of course, writing.

~*~

Visit Sophia at
http://sophiaryan.webs.com
sophiaryan@live.com

~*~

To chat with Sophia Ryan and other Wild Rose Press authors, join us at
www.groups.yahoo.com/group/TheWildRosePress.